By the same author

Dark Lantern
A Very Civil War
Out of the Shadows
The House on the Hill
Three Sisters

The Widow

CAROLINE ELKINGTON

Copyright © 2020 Caroline Elkington
All rights reserved
www.carolineelkington.net

For Groucho, Pigpen, Coop, Shake and Thumper with much love and thanks for all the boundless enthusiasm and support.

Decorating fairy-castle birthday cakes with buttercream icing — in steamy July heatwaves — fades into insignificance in comparison with your Trojan efforts.

One

Nathaniel Heywood caught a tantalising glimpse of gilded stone between the ranks of obsessively trimmed topiary; the afternoon sun glittered wickedly on diamond-leaded windows, momentarily blinding him, as he approached Winterborne Place from the south side. Both he and his horse were tired and more coated with dust than he would have liked for this first visit, but he had made the rash decision to ride the whole way instead of travelling by carriage as the weather seemed conducive to being outside in the fresh air and he was more than glad to be out of London. What he hadn't reckoned on was how hard and dry the roads were already, despite it still only being early June. The journey had taken far longer than he'd planned, and he was saddle-sore, thirsty and rather wishing he hadn't agreed to the venture in the first place.

God, he didn't even really like the man! Although, he knew him quite well now, having been introduced by his dearest friend Emery Talmarch, one roisterous night at Boodle's. Emery was, as usual, three sheets to the wind and brimming with unquenchable affability and had taken it upon himself to, as he later explained it, put two friends together, hoping that they might find some mutual benefit in furthering their acquaintance. Emery was very inclined to think that a good introduction could solve any problem, and they certainly had problems.

Nathaniel had been stone cold sober and wary as hell of this new friend of Emery's. Not because he'd heard anything new and untoward about him but because he wouldn't even have allowed Emery to choose a flower for his buttonhole, let alone a potential business partner. Emery was a martyr to his emotions and drank to forget, which made him inclined to be erratic and prone to acting upon strange whims. The problem was that whilst under the pernicious influence of brandy he was inclined to forget the more important things in life, like where he lived, whom he owed money to, how to recognise who was likely to be trustworthy or where he'd left his horse. He was turning into a regular loose screw. Nathaniel had all but given up on thoughts of rescuing him as he found he was barely able to make a dent in Emery's reckless dive towards oblivion. The best he could do was to try to make sure he didn't hurt himself or anyone else in the process, but other than that it was just a case of standing by and watching his dear friend succumb to drink's lethal charms. Agreeing to this latest proposition was the least he could do for him; his acquiescence had immediately given Emery a glimmer of hope. He knew that Emery was floundering in a mire of debt and although Nathaniel had frequently offered to help him, he'd been jauntily rebuffed, and Emery was now hanging his rather rose-tinted hopes on the results of this meeting. It appeared that Emery, as the official go-between, would be paid a substantial amount for a satisfactory outcome. He wouldn't say more; he just tapped the side of his nose as if he was in possession of some exceedingly significant facts. Nathaniel had no choice but to trust that this time his friend wasn't leading him on yet another path to nowhere. There had been plenty of ill-advised incidents in the past and he didn't care to dwell upon how easily he had been enticed into them. Emery had exceedingly endearing ways and was hard to refuse.

He reined in his horse to a gentle amble as he crested the gently rolling hill above the house and took a moment to enjoy his first sight of the beautifully landscaped park. The prospect was artificially stage-managed but so cleverly constructed that it looked as though Nature had fashioned it, not the meddling hand of Man. An impressive, grassed avenue had been created by cutting a swathe through the dense beech woods, so that as one approached the house it provided an unimpeded view of the owner's wealth and social standing. In the distance Nathaniel could see what looked like a well-established maze, orchards, meadows, some outlandish topiary, a good-sized lake and part of a meandering river, and a large formal parterre in front of the magnificent Elizabethan manor house.

Casting another admiring glance over the garden he was startled out of his reverie, when out of the corner of his eye, he caught sight of a flash of scarlet, shockingly incongruous and brilliant in the hard sunlight, moving swiftly between the dark hedges.

Pulling his horse to a standstill, halfway down the hillside, he tried to see what was flying like some exotic bird across the garden.

Nathaniel anticipated where he might next see it and waited. And there, in the bright gap, a billowing red gown, a tangle of long dark hair, petticoats lifted and barefoot, followed by two madly capering hounds of some description and then a small girl, in white, gamely trying to keep up. He stood up in his stirrups to try to get a better view in the next gap and watched as they raced helter-skelter down the grass path. He thought the girl must have called out because the scarlet gown slowed, grabbed the child's hand and together they raced on through the parterre, around the side of the house and disappeared, dogs barking and child laughing.

He smiled to himself, remembering Emery telling him that there was a daughter; he couldn't remember her name. He had forgotten to mention a granddaughter. Well, whoever they were, they were obviously late for something.

He continued down the slope and joined the tree-lined drive which wound around the garden to the right of the house.

He dismounted and led his horse the rest of the way, skirting the house looking for the stables. He was greeted by some surprised grooms and a stable lad, who happily took his horse and nodded knowledgeably when Nathaniel gave him very specific instructions on how to care for the animal.

After making a forlorn attempt to brush the dust from his clothes, he wearily climbed the shallow steps to the elegant terrace in front of the house. He didn't have to knock, as a liveried footman was already standing in the open door, waiting to welcome him. The silent servant took his coat and tricorne, his crop, gloves and his saddle bag and then a bustling maid appeared and showed him through the elegantly tiled hallway and up the impressively wide staircase to his bedchamber.

It was everything one would expect from an Elizabethan mansion. Darkening oak panelling and heavy furnishings, a four-poster bed hung with embroidered hangings and an expensive looking Persian rug covering the polished floorboards. Comfortable but gloomy and no expense spared. It certainly felt sumptuous in comparison with his cramped room in Emery's London house.

The footman arrived with his bag and said he'd send a valet to him immediately to help him unpack and change for dinner. Nathaniel, who had been a soldier not so very long ago, was perfectly capable of unpacking his own bag and getting dressed but knew better than to say so.

The servant asked if he would be needing to take a rest as his master was a little fatigued from the incessant heat and was lying down for an hour in the cool to recover his strength.

Nathaniel replied that he would wash and change and then explore the house and gardens and the footman said he'd come and find him when his master was ready to see him.

He had a thorough wash, stripping down to his breeches and removing the stubborn layer of grit which had worked its way right through to his skin and was starting to chafe. He then changed into the only other clothes he'd brought with him; he wasn't planning to stay long so he'd brought only the basic necessities. And then he went on a tour of the house.

It was, as expected, ostentatious, purely designed to show off his host's unlimited resources. He thought it beautiful but rather too crammed with glass cases of dead butterflies and birds, collections of iridescent beetles and tiny bleached skeletons and curiously, a viewing cabinet of embroidered and bejewelled kid gloves. It wasn't at all to his taste. He found it vaguely disturbing.

He was just strolling lazily through the Great Hall when the footman came to find him to inform him that his master was now rested and ready to meet him.

* * *

The parlour he was shown into was large and sparsely furnished, the wainscoting highlighted in gold leaf and the tapestries which decorated the walls, garishly coloured. There were stained glass heraldic and animal devices in the large bay windows which cast an eery glow over the room and heavy brocade curtains in rich greens and golds framed the openings; the effect of the whole was dazzling and a trifle unsettling.

His host put down his glass of wine and rose to greet him and Nathaniel was once more slightly amused and irritated by the man's aura of breath-taking conceit; he wore a sense of entitlement like an extravagant and expensive coat, as though it were an inherent part of him. A life of luxury and indolence had removed any idea he may perhaps once have had that others might not be so fortunate as he or that he should, at least pretend to be modest and sympathetic.

Gervase, Marquis of Winterborne, held out a much-bejewelled hand and smiled at Nathaniel, his pale brown eyes, almost orange in the late afternoon sunlight which streamed through the windows.

"Captain Heywood! Welcome, welcome indeed! I cannot tell you how delighted I am to see you. I've had no guests for over a fortnight and life is become tedious in the extreme. Living in the country is not for the faint-hearted. It's good of you to make such a journey in this weather. So terribly enervating, do you not find? I can barely bring myself to venture outside when it's like this. I just don't have the constitution for it any more. Come, sit! Will you take a glass of wine?"

Nathaniel shook him firmly by the hand and made his way to the chair being indicated, a damned uncomfortable looking piece of Jacobean furniture with too much carving and no cushioning. "Thank you, my lord, I must admit to being greatly surprised by your invitation, but curiosity is a besetting sin of mine so, having nothing else to occupy myself for a few days, I thought it might be entertaining to ride right across country in withering heat to see this much-lauded place of yours. I've heard a good deal about it from our mutual friend, Emery Talmarch, who was most eloquent about the house and park, rhapsodising about the maze and the topiary and I think he may even have mentioned a nuttery? From what I've managed to see so far, I cannot disagree. I envy you, as I've no particular abode at the moment having just sold out and my family estates in Derbyshire are, shall we say, encumbered, although finally beginning to improve but I'm not yet ready to settle down, so am content to be a vagabond for the present."

The Marquis poured dark velvety red wine into a glass and handed it to Nathaniel, "You envy my burdens and responsibilities and I find I envy you your freedom! How ironic. Tell me, your parents, they are both gone? Yes, I understood so, from what Talmarch has said. You have siblings?"

"I have an older brother who inherited the estate, poor devil."

"And you joined the army because otherwise the only choice would have been taking the cloth for you?"

Nathaniel laughed bitterly, "No, indeed, I joined because I enjoy a good scrap as much as the next man but unless I want to journey across the Atlantic, there's very little to interest a fighting man here. I thought it was time to put my limited talents to better use. Hence my being here at Winterborne, my lord. I will admit to being intrigued by your proposition and, under Emery's auspices, I was persuaded that there might be some benefit in riding forty dusty miles on a scorching day." He smiled his rather dazzling smile, which everyone of his acquaintance thought to be his best asset and took an appreciative sip of the excellent wine.

"So, Talmarch said nothing about my reasons for asking you here?" enquired the Marquis idly.

"He did not. For a change he was unnaturally tight-lipped. You must have paid him well or threatened him with violence. He's generally prone to squealing like a rabbit at the least provocation."

The expression on Winterborne's face told Nathaniel everything he needed to know. God, what a fool Emery was! He'd somehow been coerced into involving him and although expecting a significant reward for his collaboration, would no doubt now be living in fear that the whole scheme might fall apart, leaving him to bear the blame and continue his precarious life as a pauper. He would probably already be preparing himself for a spell in Newgate Prison. No wonder he'd been so insistent that he visit Winterborne Place as soon as possible. Emery did not deal well with anxiety and was probably at this very minute pacing his drawing room floor with a large brandy in his hand, fretting about Nathaniel's reaction. His relief, when he'd realised that his friend was at least going to test the water, was palpable. Nathaniel had felt desperately sorry for him and had rashly promised to do his utmost to secure what promised to be an enormous and life-altering payment. The moment the words left his mouth he'd regretted them, but Emery's face had promptly brightened so he'd felt unable to go back on his word. He cursed his ready tongue and prepared himself for a wasted journey and almost certain humiliation.

Winterborne was watching him from his oddly coloured eyes and tapping his wineglass with a blunt finger. Despite the heat, he was wearing a heavy silvery-grey wig, much curled and long enough for those curls to rest upon his narrow, bony shoulders. His aquamarine blue coat and waistcoat were much embellished with silver thread and a cravat made from the very finest lace. No more than average height and as thin as a reed with no spare flesh or bulk to fill out the folds of his finely cut coat; his face was gaunt and his eyes sunken, the carved arches of the sockets casting shadows across his deep lids. To Nathaniel he looked like a man who had been gravely ill for many months, only recently recovered and still somewhat ailing after weeks living on gruel and lying abed all day. His attire was oddly outmoded, the English taste having moved on in recent years from the French penchant for extravagant decoration to the more tailored and subdued kind of style that Nathaniel himself favoured.

"All shall be revealed Captain Heywood. In good time, in good time. I know from our previous meetings in London that you're a patient kind of fellow, which will stand you in good stead, but I must ask you not to reveal the purpose of your visit to anyone here at Winterborne."

Nathaniel raised his eyebrows, "It would be exceedingly difficult for me to reveal anything as I know nothing apart from the fact that you have used threats to achieve your objective," he said in measured tones.

"Forgive me, I realise that it must be hard to make sense of any of this and I'm unable to reveal the reason behind it at the moment. Tell me, do you have any experience in the dubious world of business?"

"Absolutely none, I'm afraid. The army has been my only business since university and the Law Courts, which admittedly I didn't much take to. I suppose being a soldier made me dependent upon being part of an organisation which ordered my time, on the most part, with military efficiency and I became lazy and allowed myself to be lulled into a false sense of security. But then, quite suddenly, I'd had enough of it. Enough of sleeping in tents and eating squirrel stew, with no other purpose but to keep the whole regime idling along. It dawned upon me that it was all rather pointless and once I'd opened my eyes and seen the truth I had to act right away. And that's the moment when Emery managed to snare me, when I was at a low ebb. At such a wretched loose end, in fact, that even his rackety suggestion seemed like a good idea at the time, which just goes to show that I wasn't thinking straight."

"I hope that given time you'll think that it's a remarkably good notion, Captain Heywood. I have put a deal of thought into it. I believe you'll find it of interest and will be able to put aside any qualms you may presently be harbouring."

"I must say you make a compelling argument, my lord."

The Marquis smiled and offered Nathaniel more wine, which he refused, thinking it would probably be wise to remain sober at this juncture, until he was more sure of his ground.

Muffled scuffling noises from the other side of the door was followed by murmured voices and a timid knock. Lord Winterborne instructed them to enter.

The door opened and Nathaniel looked around to see who was causing the Marquis to smile so warmly and hold out his hand in a surprisingly welcoming gesture.

A small girl, dressed in white with a blue sash, long nut-brown curls and a cherubic, pink-cheeked face raced across the room and threw herself at Winterborne's knees. He lifted her up and swinging her through the air, sat her upon his lap. She laughed up at him in delight and clapped her dimpled hands. Nathaniel guessed she must be about five years old and recognised her as the child he'd seen running through the garden earlier. He glanced back at her companion, who still stood uncertainly by the door.

"Come in, my dear and meet our guest," said Winterborne, still smiling.

Nathaniel watched as she approached them, and he stood up to face her.

She looked a good deal different now. The scarlet gown had been exchanged for one in a sober slate grey, her hair had been hastily swept up into a fashionably high style, a few curling tendrils having escaped to frame her face, which was captivatingly lovely; her skin creamy and her eyes a darkly serious grey, almost black arched eyebrows, one with a slight quizzical angle in the middle of it, a long straight nose, tip-tilted at the end, and wide mouth which was clamped firmly shut at the moment. And the toes of some very respectable blue embroidered shoes were peeping out from beneath her skirts. She didn't acknowledge Nathaniel, keeping her eyes fixed upon the child who was pulling playfully at the Marquis's wig.

"Grace, Marchioness of Winterborne, allow me to introduce Captain Nathaniel Heywood. And this little handful is my daughter, Lady Jemima, who may look like an angel but is, in fact, the very opposite!" And he ruffled the little girl's hair affectionately.

Nathaniel took a step towards the Marchioness and she met him halfway, holding out her delicate hand. He bowed over it and murmured something perfunctory about how pleased he was to meet her, and she graciously inclined her head.

"I am sorry to be late," she said in a quietly mellifluous voice, "We were unfortunately delayed by having to change our clothes."

The Marquis looked up at her, having rescued his wig from Jemima's insistent grasp, "Ah, yes, of course, it had slipped my mind. The damned portrait painter. He still hasn't finished?"

"Good gracious, no, Gervase — my lord, he's unable to get Jem to sit still at all. Not even for a second. She will wriggle and laugh the whole time, and tease the dogs, making his job nigh on impossible. However, he tries very hard to placate her, coaxing her with sweetmeats and promises that he'll allow her to paint something of her own when our portrait is completed. I fear he will regret his generosity."

"I'm sure it'll all be worthwhile in the end, my dear, when it's in pride of place at the far end of the Long Gallery." He turned to Nathaniel, "Grace and Jemima are being portrayed as something — Arcadian and mythological, I believe. Or was it *à la Turque*? I forget. Anyway, it's been a tortuous sitting, lasting weeks and disrupting everything relentlessly. They're posing in the garden, against the topiary, with the house in the background. I thought they'd be painted inside against a backdrop but apparently the moment the artist saw Grace, he decided he wished to depict her in the open air — a windswept goddess, or some such nonsense. And he has Jemima all in white pretending to be a seraph which, of course, is making his life exceedingly difficult as in reality she's nought but a demon! There's no artist in this world good enough to portray her but thus!" And he tickled the child under her chin until she curled up into a giggling ball.

Nathaniel, who had only ever seen the Marquis at play in his club, drinking copious amounts and playing recklessly at the tables with his degenerate friends, found he was at a loss for words. This person before him bore no resemblance to the roué he had met and so disliked in London. The change in him was quite extraordinary and had he not seen it for himself he would never have believed it. Nathaniel was beginning to think he'd mistaken the man's character. And to find that he was married was even more of a shock. He wondered if the Marchioness had any clue to her husband's other debauched life when he was away from Winterborne. It was all rather baffling, and he had to admit that he was more than a little intrigued. He glanced at her and found her to be staring at him with an expression of cool disdain, which she failed to disguise swiftly enough. She averted her eyes and continued to watch over her daughter warily, clearly not trusting the child not to suddenly tug the wig from her husband's head.

Nathaniel was trying hard to equate this aloof and rather scornful woman with the vision he still had in his mind of her racing barefoot in scarlet through the garden. It was becoming quite clear to him that all was not as it seemed here at Winterborne. The dissolute Marquis appeared to be a doting father and generous husband and the hoydenish gypsy he'd seen earlier turned out to be a haughty and regal lady of the manor — with a daughter. The only character in this strange play he could even begin to understand was the child. Children were, on the whole, uncomplicated creatures who acted on their impulses, revealing their true natures without deception. He had had scant contact with children during his life, his only sibling being unwed and childless. But Jemima was certainly quite an engaging child and seemed to have her father wrapped around her little finger — a notion he was still finding quite unfathomable. He couldn't wait to tell Emery about this miraculous transformation.

"Has the painter finished with you for the day?" asked the Marquis.

"He has. The light has changed apparently and he's now tackling parts of the background which require attention but are not affected by the altered light. We've been most fortunate with the weather although it's exceedingly hot standing for so long in the direct sun. He will not allow me a hat or a parasol, and I know how much you dislike freckles."

Her husband eyed her critically, "Yes, and I think your nose is getting sunburnt which is most unbecoming."

"I'm sorry, Gervase. I will take care to remain inside at all other times to make sure it gets no worse. He's quite the tyrant when it comes to his painting. Oh, will you want supper in the dining room or the breakfast parlour? It's just that Kirby was asking."

"Dining room. Tomorrow I'd like you to show Captain Heywood the maze. I think he'll find it entertaining."

"Certainly, I'd be happy to," responded Lady Winterborne so unenthusiastically that Nathaniel had to smile. She caught his amused expression, and her face became a mask of icy indifference. He wondered why she so clearly resented his presence at Winterborne when she knew nothing about him and was thankful that he was only staying two days.

"But now, if you'd like to leave us, the Captain and I still have much to discuss."

"Of course," said the Marchioness stiffly. She crossed the room and scooped Jemima up into her arms and with a curt nod for Nathaniel, she carried the protesting child out of the room.

"You must be extremely proud of your family, my lord. You're a very lucky man," remarked Nathaniel, whilst feeling much relieved that he wasn't burdened with a family of any kind.

Lord Winterborne looked at him with interest, "You might say that they are everything to me," he lifted his glass and took a mouthful of wine, frowning down into the residue left in the glass as though considering its value. "Jemima has been a welcome addition to the household and as you can see, she's a lively little thing and Grace, well, she's a beauty, is she not?"

Feeling a trifle uncomfortable, Nathaniel agreed, "Lady Winterborne is indeed very striking. May I ask how you met her?"

"Ah, you may not know that Lady Winterborne is my second wife. My first wife died," he paused and closed his eyes, "But I have my daughter."

Light began to dawn, "I see. Jemima is your first wife's child."

The Marquis nodded, eyes still closed, "Margery and I were married for nearly eight years. Her health had always been fragile, but she was keen to have children. To provide an heir, you understand. However, when she finally was with child, she became ill during the confinement and although Jemima was thankfully a lusty baby, Margery never fully recovered and died not many days after the birth."

"My God, you must have been devastated," said Nathaniel.

"It was, for a while, difficult to cope. I was left with a baby who was in need of a mother. A reliable wet nurse was found, and we managed to get through that first year without too many mishaps but there came a time when I realised that I'd have to marry again for the child's sake."

Nathaniel, unused to such candid confessions, was getting more ill at ease by the minute and noted with disquiet that his host had not yet finished his tale.

"After the mourning period was over, I was introduced to Grace, by a good friend, who knew what I was looking for and thinking that she would probably be the perfect wife and mother, I proposed."

"She seems to have taken to the role of mother with ease."

"She was sixteen when we married and at first it was hard for her, but she was the oldest child with five younger siblings, so she understood what had to be done. I must say she took to it with all her habitual poise and has never yet put a foot wrong."

"Most impressive," murmured Nathaniel, hoping for a swift end to the awkward conversation.

The Marquis said nothing, seeming to fall into a pensive state. He stared blindly into space for a long while, leaving Nathaniel cursing Emery for getting him into such an embarrassing fix in the first place. He waited while his companion seemed to brood over the acquisition of his new wife and wondered what on earth he might say next.

When it came, it was beyond anything he could have ever imagined and made him consider the possibility that Lord Winterborne was insane.

"Which brings me to the reason I requested the pleasure of your company, Captain Heywood," mused the Marquis. He seemed to suddenly become very tired as though the effort of speaking was too much for him.

"I would like you to father a child with Grace."

Two

Having entirely lost the powers of speech, Nathaniel was unable to do anything apart from stare at Lord Winterborne.

"You're no doubt thinking I've run mad, but I can assure you that I've never been more serious in my life," said that gentleman with impressive equanimity. "I don't suppose you've ever considered becoming a father as you're not yet even thinking of marriage. It has its rewards — and its disadvantages. However, it's now imperative that I have a son to carry on the name of Winterborne after I'm gone. There is no other way. It must be with the Marchioness, obviously, and I have it on Talmarch's authority that you have no obligations, and, in his own words, you are apparently as good a fellow as I could ever hope to find. Your army career does you justice; I understand it's been exemplary throughout and there are no scandals attached to your name. I believe that you're the perfect person to sire an heir for me."

Nathaniel, coming out of a kind of stupor where he didn't seem to be able to think clearly at all, swallowed hard and put a finger under his neckcloth to loosen it a bit as it seemed to be trying to choke him.

"Lord Winterborne, I'm afraid you've very much mistaken your man! I'm not nearly mad enough to accept such a task. In fact, I can think of no one who would ever even contemplate such a thing. It is complete lunacy."

The Marquis smiled, "I intend to make it very much worth your while, of course. A substantial down payment and then the full amount when it becomes obvious that the deed is done and also, as promised, a payment for Mr Talmarch, which according to my sources, would be very much welcomed."

"That is a well-aimed, low blow, my lord, but I still cannot countenance such a ridiculous and revolting suggestion."

"Revolting? You refer to my wife?"

"Good God, no! Of course not! I find what you're proposing utterly repellent. Why do you not sire the child yourself? You've already had one child so it must be possible."

There was a moment's silence as Lord Winterborne covered his eyes with his hand, and slumped in his chair, "I have led a life of — shall we just say, reckless self-indulgence and, rather too late to do anything about it, I find I am now too incapacitated to complete the task myself. It's imperative that I have an heir, Captain Heywood, before I die, and this is the only way."

"And Lady Winterborne is in agreement?"

"She knows nothing of this. She would never agree — "

"Then how do you propose that this should happen? It seems to me that if the main participant in your scheme has not been taken into consideration, then the plan is hardly likely to succeed. My lord, I cannot think of any female who would willingly agree to this. It's debasing and inhuman."

"Oh, I entirely agree. If she were to find out I'm fairly certain that she'd either leave me or assault me. She's possessed of a very volatile temper and I would not be surprised to find a knife buried between my shoulder blades if she should ever discover what I was planning."

Nathaniel shook his head in bewilderment, "Then, how the hell were you hoping to make this come about?" he demanded.

"You're a handsome young man, Captain, I should think the ladies all flutter their eyelashes at you! I suspect that if you were to put your mind to it you could make Grace fall in love with you in a trice."

"Devil take it man! You can't just engineer for two people to fall in love! It doesn't happen that way."

"Maybe not, but I think you could still make it happen if you wished it."

"No," said Nathaniel irritably. This was really getting out of hand, he thought. The Marquis was talking about it as though it might actually happen. He had to put a stop to it. "Lord Winterborne, there's absolutely no way on earth that I could ever consent to this. I would not be able to live with myself. And I've no desire to find a knife between *my* shoulder blades!"

The Marquis made a slight shrug and pulled down the corners of his mouth, "Could I just ask you to take a little time to think about it and then, if you're still of the same mind tomorrow, I'll let it drop and we'll discuss my other business proposition instead, which I'm confident you'll find a more enticing and less unusual prospect. I have to admit to being impressed that you'll not give up your high principles for a *considerable* fortune. It speaks well of your character — Talmarch was right about you, it seems."

"Emery Talmarch is a fool if he thought that I would ever consider this."

"A fool in desperate need of funds," said the Marquis thoughtfully. "No, don't get on your high horse again! I was merely pointing out the obvious. But I can see you'll not change your mind. Have dinner and then you can sleep on it. You must be tired after your journey and now I've thrown this at you and you're at *point non plus* for which I can only apologise."

Nathaniel rose to his feet and looked down at his host, who was drawn and pale, "I came to Winterborne because I thought I could help my friend and I have a genuine interest in beginning a new career after twelve years in the army, but I cannot in all good conscience be a party to such a scheme. I'm sorry, but there it is. My lord, you're looking a little under the weather. Can I get anything for you? Shall I ring for a footman?"

"Thank you, if you could just call in Kirby. He'll be hovering just outside the door. It's the heat, I find it very draining," and he sank back into the chair as though a puppet with his strings cut and closed his eyes. Nathaniel noted his breathing had become laboured and went to call the butler.

Kirby came in like a man who was expecting something such as this to happen. He calmly helped his master to his feet and guided him out of the room.

Nathaniel watched them go and wondered what he should do next. He sat back down for a moment to ponder what had just happened. It was beyond belief and he was still reeling from the shock. He wasn't quite able to grasp the whole thing, but it was obvious that Lord Winterborne was in earnest. He had the look of a man who knew he had not much time left and wanted to tie up the loose ends of his life. Nathaniel could easily understand that part. What he was having a problem with was the idea that the disdainful Marchioness would ever agree to being impregnated by a total stranger for the sake of keeping a distinguished ancestral bloodline from breaking. A bloodline that was not even her own. He thought of her face as she'd looked at him, a woman of quite startling beauty without a doubt, but he would have assumed she was a cold and austere woman had he not witnessed her racing barefoot across the grass in a red gown, trailing dogs and a small child.

Married at sixteen to a known libertine and then finding herself mother to a dead woman's child; at that tender age, it can't have been easy. It appeared to Nathaniel that Lady Winterborne had assumed a mantle of adult responsibility that belied her years; she could be no more than twenty years old. She had had no choice in the matter. He had no doubt that her father and the Marquis would have come to some sort of gentlemanly arrangement over a glass of fine brandy, and she had been passed between them like a parcel, with no thought for her own wishes and feelings. It was a barbaric but commonly accepted practice. He had to admire the way she had dealt with it, *was* dealing with it. But he couldn't help but wonder what her reaction would be should she discover her husband's plotting. He sighed, the sooner he could politely excuse himself and leave, the better. He would reiterate his decision to Lord Winterborne after breakfast and then return to London in all haste, where he would seek out Emery Talmarch and draw his damned cork!

A short while later a footman came to tell him that supper was being served in the dining room. Nathaniel sprinted upstairs to wash and tidy himself. He had no more clothes to change into so merely adjusted his neckcloth and retied his hair and only then did the apologetic valet arrive. He allowed the servant to brush down his coat and take a cloth to his boots, but then sent him away explaining that he'd be leaving the next day. The valet, eyeing Nathaniel's casual attire, had to be grateful that he wasn't to be tasked with trying to make this gentleman look anything as elegant as Lord Winterborne; it would be an impossible enterprise. He left without regret.

Nathaniel entered the dining room and found it to be empty. The long table was clothed in white linen and the places set with silver and crystal. There were many candles in candelabras and sconces, a vast arrangement of flowers in the centre of the table and an expressionless footman standing like a statue against one wall. Nathaniel clenched his jaw and prepared himself for a tense evening. The footman showed him to his place, and he sat and waited patiently. He was just beginning to think that no one was coming, and he would be dining alone when the door flew open, and the Marchioness hurried into the room. He rose to his feet. She glanced at him and at the table set for three, breathed a sigh of palpable relief and took her place at the table, opposite him.

"Captain Heywood, I'm sorry to be late — again. It's an unavoidable hazard when you have a small child who dislikes going to her bed. She will not accept the ministrations of her nursemaid and insists that I tuck her in every night and tell her a story." She glanced expectantly at the door, "I expect Gervase will be here at any moment."

"He was very tired earlier and the butler took him upstairs to bed, my lady."

"Oh," said Lady Winterborne, and turned to one of the footmen, "Robert, will you please go and see if Lord Winterborne is going to join us for supper. Thank you." The footman slid quietly from the room.

"Would you like wine, Captain?" she asked and when he agreed, she rose and fetched the decanter from the sideboard herself and filled his glass. He thought this unusual but made no remark upon it.

"Thank you. How old is Jemima?"

"She's five," she replied with a half-smile. "She's a law unto herself. Wild to a fault. I blame Gervase for indulging her. He lets her have her way in all things. I'm sure he'll be here soon," and she cast another nervous glance at the door.

"Well, if he doesn't come, I promise not to keep you long at the table; I'm still very much the soldier and have learned to eat fast in case someone else comes along and steals the food from under my nose. That behaviour is *also* an unavoidable hazard. The army teaches you extremely quickly to fend for yourself or you'll suffer the consequences and be forced to go to your bed hungry."

"It must be a hard life?"

"It can be for those who are not suited to the conditions, but I was ideal military material."

"Footloose?"

Nathaniel smiled, "Rootless, I suppose. The army provided me with a home and a family of sorts. It steadied me and gave me purpose."

"You were lacking in purpose?"

"You might say that, having lost my family in various ways, I also lost my bearings for a while, but, once established in the army, I quickly found my way again."

The footman returned and announced that Lord Winterborne had retired for the night and would be taking his supper in his bedchamber and he sent his regrets. Nathaniel saw his hostess flinch and compress her lips, clearly not cherishing the ordeal of entertaining her husband's guest alone.

"My lady, if you'd prefer, I could also take supper in my bedchamber. It makes no odds to me."

He had thought her quite pale already, but she lost even more colour at this suggestion. She hesitated, her breath coming a little fast, "There's no need. I — I am expected — I would be delighted — " she faltered.

Nathaniel caught a glimpse of the young girl beneath the carefully constructed facade and took pity upon her, "I promise that I am able to hold a perfectly respectable conversation without causing any great alarm. Although I've been in the company of soldiers for rather too long, I can still manage a fairly civilised exchange," and he smiled to soften his words.

Before she could form an answer two more footmen arrived bearing an array of silver dishes and began arranging them on the table in front of the silent couple. They waited until the room emptied again before beginning to eat and there followed a silence which neither could fill.

After a few minutes the Marchioness cleared her throat, "I expect you met Gervase in London, at his club?"

"Yes, through a very good mutual friend, about six months ago and we found we had various things in common and I suppose formed a friendship from that."

"Things in common? Cards?"

Sensing a weighted question, Nathaniel shook his head, "No, I'm not a gambler. I never really took to it. I suspect watching my brother, Alexander, become addicted to gambling and throw away most of our inheritance was enlightening enough to make me think twice about following him down the River Tick. My vices are few." He saw again a flicker of some unreadable emotion cross her face and wondered what he had said to cause it.

She frowned, "Is that so?" and for a few minutes said nothing more as she ate her supper of cold chicken and veal, asparagus and buttered potatoes. Nathaniel was famished so, taking her cue, he concentrated upon his plate for as long as she needed to recover her composure.

"I understand, you're thinking of leaving tomorrow," she said, eventually.

"Yes, my lady. I've almost completed my business with your husband and must return to London."

Her eyes widened, "Oh? Gervase's — friends usually stay far longer."

Again, he caught an undercurrent which he couldn't account for.

"I came only to discuss a business proposition with him."

"Business?" she mused, idly pushing her mostly untouched food around her plate. "What kind of business, Captain Heywood?" She didn't meet his eyes and he had an uncomfortable feeling that she was probing for something in particular.

"Well, as yet I'm not entirely sure. We are to finish the discussion tomorrow if he's well enough."

"I see."

Nathaniel had a gut feeling that there was something out of kilter here at Winterborne and he'd somehow become part of a set of circumstances he didn't fully understand yet. He was used, as a soldier, to listening to his instincts, they'd become honed over the years and seldom let him down. He should, of course, have listened to those instincts telling him that Emery was talking nonsense and to beware of his ludicrous moneymaking schemes, but he'd allowed himself to be lured into this harmless looking trap. His desire to help his friend had overridden any misgiving he might have felt when he'd heard that Lord Winterborne was involved. If he'd had any common sense at all he would have backed out then and saved himself from this embarrassing predicament.

The Marchioness put down her knife and fork and stared at her hands which were clasped tightly in her lap.

"I wonder, Captain Heywood, because you hardly seem like the normal run of guests we usually have here at Winterborne. They — are, as a rule, more — theatrical and — less soldier-like. You would seem very out of place if you found yourself in their midst."

Nathaniel laughed softly, "I'm not sure whether I should be insulted or gratified! Your husband has a fondness for the theatre?"

She blushed, the pink rising rapidly and staining her cheeks, "He acquired a taste for all things thespian while he was living in London and quite often invites groups of such people to stay with us." She knitted her dark brows, "They're inclined to be exceedingly boisterous, which I suppose is only natural in their kind. I often go to bed early and leave them to give free rein to their high spirits. I fear I must have a very sedate nature. Gervase often despairs."

Nathaniel saw a flash of scarlet in his mind's eye and lowered his eyes to hide his amusement; she was hardly sedate not from the evidence he'd seen, "It's not a bad thing to be reserved, I think. My brother, Alexander is the very opposite to me; loud and argumentative and easily distracted by any pretty dancer who might be passing by. He makes me look very dull in comparison."

He thought he almost glimpsed the slightest smile stretch her wide mouth a little wider.

"He sounds a good deal like one of my own brothers. He's desperately rackety and, since a child, will mindlessly follow anything which makes a din! He used to bang things with sticks and cause a commotion if he could. Everywhere he goes he is followed by uproar. You can always tell where he is, so he can never be lost. Whereas I have another brother who is as silent as a tomb and lives just to read. One can *never* find him. He will sit beneath a tree for hours, forgetting to eat and drink, forgetting he has a family at all, his nose buried in his book. He writes poetry and sings most angelically. And another who suffers from the most dreadful rashes — "

She abruptly stopped as though suddenly becoming aware that she was talking too freely. She looked back down at her hands.

"Are your siblings all brothers?" enquired Nathaniel.

"I have two sisters as well. All younger. All so very different."

"And you are their keeper, I suspect? The oldest and the one who ended up having to herd them like geese?"

She looked up at him and her eyes gleamed, "Indeed, I was their nursemaid. But I enjoyed it, on the whole. They are, apart from William, quite well-behaved."

"But did you manage to have any kind of a childhood yourself? Or have you always been mother to the children of others?"

He knew immediately that he'd said the wrong thing because she lowered her eyes and her lips compressed into a colourless line.

Fortunately, the two footmen decided this was the moment to clear the table and remove the covers.

She managed, after a moment, to regain her poise and said, "Would you care to remain here and enjoy a glass of port?"

He shook his head, "No, thank you, my lady, I believe I shall retire for the night. I'm not terribly keen on port. And I must be getting old as the journey has quite fatigued me, so if you'll excuse me?" He saw the undisguised look of relief and rose to bid her goodnight. "You are very good to receive strangers into your home, it must be unsettling at times."

She flicked him a guarded glance but said nothing. He bowed over her hand and saw himself out of the room.

* * *

He awoke in the early hours to the sound of shouting and heavy footsteps thudding along the corridor and up and down the stairs. He lay there for a moment, thinking that it was none of his business, but the commotion continued and although he tried to turn over and go back to sleep, he was unable to block out the jarring sounds coming from the other side of his door. With a sigh he kicked off the covers and swung his legs out of bed, quickly pulling on his breeches and shirt, he opened the door and peered out into the dark corridor.

He was greeted by a lantern swaying towards him, held high by the butler and eerily illuminating the man's face.

"Kirby? What's going on? Can I be of any assistance?" he asked.

Kirby stopped and his face was crumpled with concern, "It's Lord Winterborne, Captain! He's taken a turn for the worse and the doctor's just arrived. This heat has been too much for him. I just knew it'd make him bad."

"A turn for the worse?"

"He was taken bad after his supper, Captain Heywood! He sometimes has a funny turn when he's had one or two, but tonight he was in such pain. His valet, Latton, came to fetch me at two and begged me to call for the doctor. One look at him was enough! Never seen him this poorly."

"Take me to him, Kirby," said Nathaniel.

* * *

The bed was lit by a branch of candles which was shaking violently as a sleepy young footman stood to one side holding it aloft. Nathaniel went to him and relieved him of his burden and instructed him to return to his bed and get some sleep as there was bound to be plenty for him to do in the morning. The footman needed no further encouragement and left at speed.

He introduced himself to the doctor, explaining his presence in the house and freely giving his army credentials to reassure him.

The doctor looked up at him, "Glad to have you on hand, Captain Heywood. I'm Richard Morton. Lord Winterborne isn't looking too good at the moment, I'm afraid."

"More than happy to be of service. Just tell me what you need me to do. I've had experience in field hospitals and am used to being instructed and have become accustomed to seeing sickness and everything that goes with it."

"That is good news, indeed. I don't know how much you know about Lord Winterborne's health, but I can tell you that we're dealing with the results of his dissolute way of life. He was warned many times but chose to ignore the advice.

There's nothing more I can do now, except to make him comfortable. If he rallies after this, I shall be greatly surprised but he's a wilful man so may yet pull through. In his previous condition I had given him a year maybe, as long as he stayed away from alcohol and ate a healthy diet and lived a sound life here in the country away from temptation, but I hear that he has not heeded me. I do not hold out much hope, Captain — "

There was a small, strangled sound from the corner of the room. Nathaniel peered into the darkness, moving the candles a little to illuminate the furthest reaches of the bedchamber.

The Marchioness was sitting quietly unnoticed in the shadows. Nathaniel started forward but something in her face made him come to a halt. Her eyes were wide and dark, her face pale and anguished.

"Lady Winterborne, I'm so sorry. I didn't see you there."

She shook her head and looked towards the bed, "Latton came to fetch me as soon as he realised — " she said in a voice he could barely hear. "He said Gervase — called for me."

"Of course. Are you all right? Is there anything I can do for you?"

"Thank you, but no, Captain, I — will stay with him. The nursemaid, Bridie, is with Jem in case she wakes in the night."

Doctor Morton turned to the Marchioness and looked gravely at her, "He sleeps, my lady but his breathing is erratic, his abdomen is swollen and his eyes yellow. It is as I suspected, disease of the liver, otherwise known as gin liver. He simply *must* stop drinking! Although I think it may already be too late. I can give him laudanum for the pain but when you withdraw alcohol from someone who has been dependent upon it — there are always complications. He may become violent and confused, suffer tremors and hallucinations — it won't be easy. You'll need support to see him through this — whichever way it may go."

Nathaniel looked at Lady Winterborne and saw that she was beyond speaking, "Doctor Morton, you'll be able to come regularly to keep an eye on him?" he asked.

The doctor nodded, "Of course, but that'll not be enough. He'll need round the clock care and it might be a good idea to hire a nurse to sit with him. We've no clue how long this may go on so you must make provision for whatever may be on the horizon. I'll gladly advise but to be perfectly frank, Captain Heywood, the coming days will be ugly and there is nothing I can say to ease that."

The Marchioness seemed to be in dream, her eyes fixed upon the doctor's face but quite clearly not taking anything in. Nathaniel sighed, "I understand, Doctor. I've seen this kind of thing before in the army and witnessed how it was dealt with and I will swear to you now that I shall remain here, with the Marchioness's permission, until the worst is over." Even as he heard himself say the words, he wondered what on earth had come over him.

He felt Lady Winterborne's gaze turn to him. She stared at him blankly and then opened her mouth to speak but closed it again without uttering a word.

The doctor exchanged a glance with Nathaniel, "That is good of you. I understand that apart from the servants Lady Winterborne has no relations staying here who might help."

"So, I apprehend," said Nathaniel, "Although she has siblings who might — "

It was as though the Marchioness suddenly woke up, "No, no! They would not come! I could not ask them. They — they hate Gervase and would not lift a finger to save him."

Rather startled, Nathaniel frowned at her, "If that is truly the case, then it's fortunate that I'm here. I will stay, should you wish it, at least until we're sure how serious the situation is, and I'll do my best to help."

Lady Winterborne put out a hand but let it drop as though it were too heavy to move, and she stared at Nathaniel from eyes shadowed with repressed emotion. "Captain Heywood, I cannot ask you to do that! It would be impossible."

"Lady Winterborne, it would be impossible for me to leave you in such a plight as this without being wracked with guilt! I could not, in all conscience, abandon you to such a fate.

Please, accept my offer and I will try my utmost to assist you in any way I can."

She gave him a searching look which he couldn't fathom, "I cannot thank you enough and will gratefully accept," she murmured in strained accents.

He gave a little bow of acknowledgement and turned his attention to the doctor who spent a good while giving him a comprehensive list of instructions and advice. Lady Winterborne sat and listened in silence.

Three

Grace, the Marchioness of Winterborne, woke up from a nightmare and found that she wasn't alone.

It was a very strange feeling, and she wasn't quite sure what to make of it. She warily opened her eyes and looked across the room towards the bed and remembered the real nightmare. Then she recalled a pleasant voice gently telling her that she was only dreaming. She sat up and put a hand to her hair, it was falling down in curls about her shoulders. She must look a terrible sight and she'd no idea if she'd been giving away secrets in her sleep, which her sisters said she had a habit of doing. She stole a glance at the stranger on the other side of her husband's bed, sitting in a comfortable reading chair, which he'd carried up from the library after declaring that most of the furniture to be found in the house was unacceptable for someone who'd been in the saddle for eight long hours.

He seemed to be asleep, his breathing steady, his long legs stretched out in front of him, and his fists thrust deep into the pockets of his breeches. He looked like a man who could fall asleep anywhere, under a hedge, in a barn or in an unknown bedchamber where death lurked in the shadowy corners of the room. She studied his face.

He was, she supposed, rather handsome, in a languid sort of way and yet she had the distinct feeling that he could be energetic and proficient whenever it was necessary but that he was conserving his energy. He said he'd spent twelve years in the army and that surely meant that he'd seen and done all kinds of terrible things in that time but had learnt not to waste effort when it might be needed for more important tasks. He had dealt with Doctor Morton and this crisis with calmness and a confident air of authority, and she was thankful because she didn't seem to be able to gather her wits enough to ask the right questions or even listen to the doctor's advice. Her mother would have told her to stop wool-gathering and rolled her eyes in despair. She knew she'd been a disappointment to her parents even though she'd tried her best to be a good daughter and sister. She'd always been aware of an undercurrent of dissatisfaction in the family and knew that she was the cause of it; to begin with, she'd not been born a boy and then she'd failed to bring any of her proposed suitors up to scratch; they'd all backed down quite quickly and retreated, making lame excuses, leaving her parents eyeing each other in angry frustration. Funds had become a problem and they were in need of a wealthy son-in-law, one who might be willing to ease their financial burdens.

Until Gervase had arrived, the gentlemen callers had been, at first, enthusiastic and then, embarrassingly quickly, they became reluctant to linger and left with unseemly haste, leaving Grace shamefaced and baffled and her parents unable to meet her eye without showing their anger and disappointment. Her siblings were less diffident and told her in no uncertain terms that she was doomed to be a spinster and live out her days as a governess, unloved and unwanted.

She overheard her father talking with her mother about the situation and he'd complained at length about her inability to catch a worthwhile husband; he said that with her outstanding looks she should have snared someone with ease. Her mother had readily agreed and blamed her daughter's inherent wild streak, saying if only she could be more ladylike and biddable then they might be rid of her and be able to save the family from disgrace and certain penury.

So, she had tried. She'd forced herself into a cloak of respectability and submission. She kept her eyes lowered and her voice muted, her hands stayed clasped meekly in her lap and she agreed with everything anyone said to her. She could see at once that her parents were relieved, and they began to praise her as though she were at last their ideal child. As time went on, she died a little inside and began to forget who she had once been. And then, when everyone had given up hope, Gervase had come to speak with her father and a deal was struck. She was told about it after it had been signed and sealed.

In one way it had given her freedom, in another it had imprisoned her. Her family, at last, seemed delighted with her and their futures were secured, and she'd won for herself a kind of independence even though she was still at the mercy of others; she at least was able to occasionally be herself when no one was looking.

Her husband was undemanding in all the ways that truly counted; even in the early days of their strange marriage, he showed no interest in her whatsoever. When he invited guests, it was as though she were on show for them, like one of his exhibits, pinned to the velvet cushion and enclosed in a display cabinet for everyone to admire but not touch.

She graced his table and listened to his guests until they became too unruly and then she quietly retired to her bedchamber and breathed a sigh of relief.

Right from the very first night she'd expected and steeled herself for a nocturnal visit from her husband, but months went by and none came and eventually she realised that she was to be spared. Before the wedding her mother had taken her aside and given her a terrifying talk about what her husband would expect of her. She'd wanted to cover her ears and scream but had meekly listened and pretended that she was amenable. Her mother had warned her that it would be painful and embarrassing, but she should just be still, and do as she was bade, and then everything would be all right and it would be over in a trice. She advised her that the less fuss she made the quicker it would be over.

Grace had run to her bedchamber and bolted the door and then sat on her bed staring into space until she could block out the appalling images which had infested her mind. There was no one she could share it with; her sisters were too young, and she could never even contemplate asking her brothers for their advice on such a sensitive matter.

Then, just when she thought things couldn't get any worse, her father had informed her that she would be a stepmother to a small child of just a year and she'd retreated even further into herself until she almost disappeared.

It wasn't until Jemima was old enough to understand that Grace was in sole charge of her and could be relied upon for comfort and support and finally began to communicate, that Grace had formed a bond with her, and now they were inseparable. Grace needed Jem as much as the child needed her. They were their own little family rattling around inside the huge house, mostly unnoticed by her husband, unless he wished to display them for guests. Surprisingly, he genuinely seemed to love his daughter and spoiled her too much when they were together. Grace, he treated like a much prized but slightly irritating acquisition. He was pleasant enough to her but would occasionally complain about the style of her hair, her choice of gown or her tendency to freckle. He'd eye her in a mildly disparaging manner, and she would know that she'd committed some *faux pas,* which she didn't fully understand but would have to be swiftly rectified, nonetheless. She didn't object to this particular conceit of his, as long as he left her alone in other ways. She'd learnt to avoid unnecessary and unwanted attention so that she and Jemima could live some kind of bearable separate existence where the strangers welcomed into the house could not impinge upon them.

Just recently she'd noticed a sea change in the air and had become nervous that her hard-won contentment was about to alter again. It had started after Gervase had been away from home for nearly four months in London and had returned in a state of exhaustion, and not many months later it had become clear to everyone that he was seriously ill. He was constantly fatigued, and his usually healthy appetite dwindled. He began to lose weight and his hair fell out so that the elaborate wigs from earlier times became *de rigueur.* His temper became easily frayed and the constant influx of people from London, who filled the house with their noisome antics, did not abate because of his health; they seemed to increase, but as they seemed to keep her husband entertained and out of her hair she learnt not to mind as much.

The last group of guests had left Winterborne a fortnight ago and she'd hoped it would be the last for a while, but without warning this man, this stranger, had arrived and she'd thought he'd come to disrupt her life, like the other gentlemen, the ones who were close to her husband and always put him back in good spirits once more. Or the ones who wanted to see if she would respond to their drunken advances.

She had the great misfortune to accidentally walk in on a scene that she still could not make sense of and she was more than grateful that she naturally moved silently, so was able to back out of the room without being seen or heard. She'd tiptoed away and found a quiet corner where she could sit and calm herself before carrying on as though nothing untoward had happened, consigning the memory to the furthest recesses of her mind.

She hadn't dared to ask anyone to explain to her what she'd seen, knowing that the staff were loyal to their master so that she was never able to talk about him in front of them. She and Jem stayed resolutely in their own little world, merely popping in and out of the strange goings on around them when it was unavoidable. They lived alongside Gervase and his friends but not with them.

Slowly, his illness had worsened and even the visitors could not lighten his mood. Then, for no apparent reason he'd become more positive and almost cheerful, and Grace had begun to hope that he was on the mend and that he wouldn't snap at them any more. And then, Captain Heywood had arrived, and she found that he'd met her husband in London during his long absence and she'd wondered if he might be the reason for Gervase's mood lifting so noticeably.

She was surprised upon meeting the Captain because he'd not been at all like the other gentlemen and now, here he was, having very firmly taken charge of this nightmarish situation, looking every bit the soldier — at ease, despite the desperately unusual circumstances.

His face, in repose, was a little less formidable than when he was awake. The straight brows weren't drawn down in a grim frown, his stern mouth had relaxed, and she could no longer see the disapproval in his bright blue eyes, so he looked almost agreeable. His dark blonde hair was a bit dishevelled having come loose from its black riband and softened the general demeanour of a disciplined and serious military gentleman.

His conduct during the night had been exemplary and even though she'd been severely alarmed by the sudden deterioration in her husband's condition, Captain Heywood had remained composed and had taken control of the sickroom and the staff with complete authority but without appearing to usurp anyone else's position in the house. She thought it was quite clever of him. His understanding of what was needed and how best to accomplish it was faultless. After a very short while Grace had managed to sit back and stop panicking so much.

She didn't want to lose Gervase; she was used to him now and the way he liked things to be. If, God forbid, he should die, she would have nothing again and everything would have to change, and poor little Jem would lose the only real parent she had left. She couldn't bear the thought of having to start all over again.

Her thoughts were interrupted by Captain Heywood opening his eyes and looking directly at her.

"Good morning," he said quietly. "You managed to sleep a little at least."

She nodded, "I think you must have had to wake me from a nightmare?"

He smiled, "I was afraid you might disturb the Marquis. I think you were dreaming that you were being chased through the Maze."

She gave him a rueful look, "Ah, yes, that one. A recurring dream I've had since coming to Winterborne. The Maze — frightens me a little. I don't know why."

"I expect it's the fear of being lost. It makes perfect sense."

She put up an automatic hand to her hair to try to rearrange it, "Yes, I suppose it does. I always wake up before I'm caught anyway."

He watched her fiddle with her hair, "Your hair looks nice like that," he said blandly.

She started, her hand fell, and she glanced quickly at her husband, "Has he — ?"

"He's not moved since we gave him cordial at around five. Although, I do think his breathing is a deal easier than it was, which is promising. Why don't you go and have some proper sleep while I stay with him? It will do you no good sleeping in a chair. We must be sensible about this; we shall need the other to be well rested so that we can share the work."

Grace was silent for a minute and then she nodded, knowing it made sense. "All right, I'll have a quick nap and I'll come back in an hour or so and you can then do the same."

"That's a deal, then. Make it two hours, I shall be able to manage here — it doesn't look as though he's going to be much of a problem for a while yet."

"Do you think — ?" she faltered.

"I'll be perfectly honest, my lady, I've no idea. I hate to say it, but time will tell. As a soldier, you quickly learn not to be impatient because time changes everything. We'll just have to wait and hope. But from what I know of him, he's a strong-willed character and will not give up easily."

Grace rose to her feet and approached the bed. She stood looking down at her husband, who was lying perfectly still, his face haggard and as white as the pillow, dark shadows under his eyes and she reached out and briefly touched his hand, which was resting on top of the counterpane. Nathaniel thought it was a strange little gesture, lacking in affection and, he noted with concern, it seemed to show a certain amount of unease, not induced by the gravity of his illness. The situation at Winterborne was getting odder by the hour.

"Are you hungry, Captain? I can send for some breakfast for you?"

"That would be splendid, thank you. They say an army marches on its stomach."

She allowed herself the slightest smile and left the room.

* * *

The Marquis lay in a coma for three days and everyone had given up any hope of him recovering. Kirby, the butler, was already in mourning, dragging himself around the house with very little enthusiasm for his usual tasks, and Latton, his valet, hovered outside the door for most of the day not knowing what to do with himself. Doctor Morton came and went, and Nathaniel decided that he was a man of sound sense, imperturbable and with a dry sense of humour which always helped in cases like this. Nathaniel assisted with any lifting and washing that had to be done, wishing to spare Lady Winterborne the distress. Whenever he could persuade her, he sent her off to be with Jemima, whom, he thought, must be missing her. She was always reluctant to leave but once she was in the corridor, he heard her racing away to find her stepdaughter.

On the third day, he and the Marchioness were just swapping over so that Nathaniel could stretch his legs in the garden, when Lord Winterborne made a small sound and twitched his fingers. Nathaniel moved back to the bed and with Grace's help, they propped him up enough to get him to take some more cordial. Even though he only managed to swallow a very small amount, Nathaniel was pleased, and Grace was able to relax her shoulders a bit. She was so tense that her neck ached, and the pain travelled up into her skull and pounded in her temples.

A day later, their patient opened his yellowed eyes and stared blankly at them. He took a little food and drank some cordial.

Two days after that, he managed to sit up in bed and exchange a few words with Doctor Morton.

The doctor was exceedingly pleased with his progress although he was diligent in warning them repeatedly that even if he recovered from this episode, he would still not be able to beat the disease that was destroying his liver.

Eventually he was well enough for Jemima to pay him a quick visit. This was only partially successful as the child, although happy to see her father, was, at first, alarmed by how different he looked without his wig, and then quickly getting bored, she began to dismantle the room bit by bit until Grace enticed her away with a promise of sweetmeats.

At the end of that week, with the weather still baking the countryside until the ground was as hard as marble, the portrait painter begged that Grace should continue to sit for him and, feeling sorry for the poor man, she'd agreed. It happened that the doctor was with Lord Winterborne and advised Nathaniel to take the opportunity for a stroll in the grounds, so he'd followed Grace and Jemima around to the topiary garden to watch the painter at work.

He had an enormous easel set up, which held a massive canvas, and while he arranged his sitters into their previous positions, Nathaniel took a look at the painting, enjoying the smell of turpentine and oil paints warming in the sun.

It was still in its early stages, some areas merely sketched out and others blocked in, but the main figures were very nearly finished. The whole thing was drenched in hard sunlight, making the house and the topiary sharp edged and a contrast for the two girls. The Marchioness was standing in the foreground in the scarlet gown, which was blowing in the wind and hugged her curves in a loving manner. Her hair was mostly loose and flowing behind her, her arm outstretched as though to welcome someone and her head tilted back a little, showing off her elegant neck. Standing at her feet and leaning nonchalantly on one of the two dogs, was Jemima, all in white, her nut-brown curls clustered about her face, a wicked smile curling her rosebud mouth, and she was looking directly at the viewer from knowing eyes. Nathaniel laughed out loud and peeked around the canvas at the child who was at that moment resisting being put back into her position, insisting on hiding beneath her stepmother's skirts and making growling noises. The painter was beginning to lose patience and was sounding irritable.

Nathaniel grinned at her, "You look wonderful in the painting, Jemima! Quite the best thing in it by far! I can't wait to see it finished and hung in the Long Gallery. You know, if you don't want to continue posing for it, I could always do it instead!"

Jemima came out from beneath the petticoats and gave him a wondering look, "*You?* But you are not a *lady*. *I'm* a lady. You wouldn't fit in my gown, you'd break it."

"Oh, I think I might just squeeze into it, if you help me with the fastenings."

Jemima giggled, "You'd look werry silly in it. Anyway, you have a hairy chin — I don't. An' you're too tall," and with that she threw herself into her place and gave Nathaniel such a worldly look that he couldn't help laughing again.

Lady Winterborne rolled her eyes, "Thank you, Captain, but you should know as a soldier that you must at all times remain in charge or she will ride roughshod over you. She has no finer feelings at all and will leave you thoroughly trampled!"

Nathaniel smiled at her, "I don't think I'd mind that much. I've always had a weakness for fiery characters."

She gave him a curious look, "Oh dear, I fear Jem has already won this round then. You poor man, I will pray for you."

"Thank you but there's no need, I can look after myself and I have always rather enjoyed a scrap even if there's a danger, I might be outflanked by a four-year-old seraph. I have broad enough shoulders to weather a skirmish or two."

"Skirrr—mish," said Jemima, savouring the word like a sweetmeat.

The painter frowned around the side of his canvas, "Please be quiet now! I'm working."

"Jemima is only five so a little patience would be appreciated," said Nathaniel in measured tones. The painter retreated again out of view while the Marchioness, hiding the whisper of a smile, persuaded Jemima to behave herself or else Captain Heywood might decide to try on her gown, and he would be bound to split all the seams. This seemed to do the trick, as the little girl was quite delighted with her new gown and didn't want it spoiled. The dogs, Thisbe and Dancer, were then marshalled back into the picture and convinced to stand still for a few minutes at a time. Nathaniel, who had plenty of experience with hounds, was able to keep them under control for just long enough for the testy painter to add a little more detail to their heads and finish Jemima's hands, which were clutching Thisbe's rough coat rather too eagerly. After about an hour of manoeuvring and negotiations, everyone including the harried painter had had enough and Nathaniel drew the sitting to a premature close. Released from being restrained the dogs joyfully pranced off around the lawn, snapping at bees and peeing on everything and Jemima sprawled on the grass and declared that she didn't want to be an angel anymore because they were *werry* boring and she'd rather be a dog now and pee on things.

Nathaniel cast an amused glance at Lady Winterborne and caught a gleam in her eyes before she quickly turned to run after her stepdaughter who had capered away with Thisbe and Dancer and could be clearly heard barking like a dog.

"That child needs a sound smack, she's out of control!" bleated the painter.

"What she *needs* is her father to recover from his illness and a little sympathy," responded Nathaniel icily.

The painter made a grunting sound and Nathaniel walked away before he said something he regretted.

He followed the mad procession around the garden; dogs bounding around each other, small girl barking wildly and spinning in circles and the Marchioness in the flowing scarlet gown, trying in vain to catch them. As he chased after them, he wondered how on earth it had come to this in just a few short days.

Finally, they cornered them in the parterre and herded them back to the house. They'd just reached the drive when Jemima made another bid for freedom and tore away from them. Nathaniel sped after her and swooped her up in his arms, throwing her over his shoulder and carrying her back perched up high. She squealed with delight, pulling the black riband from his hair and throwing it onto the ground. Her mother picked it up and tucked it into her pocket as they careered up the steps to the house.

Four

Two days before this, Nathaniel had written an urgent letter to Emery Talmarch, with whom he was temporarily lodging, asking him to pack up some of his clothes and belongings and send them on to him as he'd decided, to stay at Winterborne a little while longer. He explained briefly about the Marquis's illness and how he was helping care for him until he either recovered — or didn't. He felt he couldn't leave the Marchioness alone in such circumstances when he knew he'd be able to ease her burden by assisting with the care and organisation. He'd already seen how she and Jemima lived in their own private world, set so carefully apart from the real one and he really couldn't blame them. He'd been loath to get Emery's hopes up, but it couldn't be helped, he desperately needed some of his possessions and clean clothes. The housemaid had taken away his spare shirt to be washed, leaving him with just the one he was wearing. And his neckcloths were looking decidedly worse for wear and although he could not even remotely have been labelled a dandy, he liked to be neat and clean, a remnant, he supposed of being in uniform for so long. Old habits were hard to break.

It was, with some surprise, just two days later, after leaving Doctor Morton with the Marquis, that he was greeted as he descended the stairs, by Kirby, looking unusually agitated.

"Captain Heywood, your — ahem — luggage has arrived."

"That's excellent news, Kirby, thank you," and, astounded by Emery's surprising efficiency, he strolled down into the Great Hall, only to stop dead on the threshold and stare in astonishment.

"Ah, *there* you are, Nate my dear friend!" declared Mr Emery Talmarch, his large pale blue eyes open wide and laughing. "I've been here an age! Anyone would think I was a sideshow in a circus the way I'm being stared at!"

Nathaniel strode across the room to where Emery was standing surrounded by portmanteaus, bags and trunks and warmly clasped his hand in his, "Emery! What the devil? I said to *send* my things! This can't possibly be all *my* belongings!"

"Lord, no! Most of it is mine. I had the brilliant thought that I'd come down and keep you company and well, to be perfectly frank with you, I found that I urgently needed to escape London. It was getting a little too fraught for my tastes."

"Being dunned again? Running away from your responsibilities? Honestly Emery, you're a disgrace."

"Oh, I know. But, enough about me! How goes everything here? Is the Marquis improved at all?"

Nathaniel raised a quizzical eyebrow, "Afraid he might not be around to provide your unjust reward?"

"Not at all! I'm merely concerned for a fellow human being, my dear! That is all. I assume that it's all right if I stay a while?"

"Naturally I shall have to ask Lady Winterborne. She has a great deal on her plate at the moment and I wouldn't wish to add to her troubles. You'd better be prepared to put up at a local inn."

"What a hideous thought! Have you no sympathy for a weary traveller?"

"None whatsoever. We both know you're not here out of the goodness of your heart. You're just seeking sanctuary and hoping to collect your money. We shall be having words anyway about exactly how much you knew before sending me off on this disastrous mission."

Fortunately for Emery, Thisbe and Dancer arrived just then, panting in from the garden and thankfully causing a distracting commotion. Thisbe barked rather lackadaisically at Emery before throwing himself down onto the cool tiles. Dancer circled him, assiduously sniffing the luggage until he'd decided it wasn't a threat. Jemima came racing into the Hall full tilt but came to a sliding stop when she saw the new arrival and stared at him with wide eyes.

"I remember you!" she declared and looked him up and down with a critical eye but then, catching sight of his much beribboned hat, which was perched on top of a trunk, she rushed at it and balanced it on her head; she could barely see from under its brim. She then danced over to Nathaniel, "What a werry silly hat!" she exclaimed.

Just at this inauspicious moment, the Marchioness came hurrying in from the garden, "*Jem!* That's not polite! Oh, I do beg your pardon, she doesn't mean to be rude."

Emery Talmarch took her proffered hand and bowed elegantly over it, pressing it to his lips, "Lady Winterborne, as enchanting as ever! Think nothing of it, she's quite right anyway! Just tellin' the truth after all — wouldn't be right to reprimand her for that!"

"You're too kind, Mr Talmarch," then her eye fell upon the enormous heap of trunks and cases and she became visibly alarmed. "Are — are we expecting Gervase's friends? He didn't say — "

Nathaniel frowned, "No, my lady, it's mostly Emery's luggage and some of mine which I asked him to bring for me. He's — hoping to stay a few nights, if that would be convenient? I know it's a trying time, but he's come all this way —"

"Oh, of course! That would be quite delightful," she turned and made a signal to Kirby who was lurking at the edge of the Hall, awaiting instructions. "Kirby? The same bedchamber as before please and all the luggage — "

"Yes, my lady. And will a valet be required?"

Nathaniel intervened, "I'm happy to share my valet as I have very little use for one and Emery — well, he cannot dress himself without assistance!"

"I will inform Brent, Captain Heywood," said Kirby impassively and he left the Hall to begin organising, thinking that Brent, the valet, would be well satisfied when he set eyes upon the dashing and clearly helpless Mr Talmarch. He had had a good deal to say about the Captain's scandalous lack of vanity and scant clothing and none of it had been complimentary.

Lady Winterborne asked the footman to show Mr Talmarch to his room so that he could wash and change. Emery was effusively grateful and followed Robert from the Hall, with a sidelong glance at his friend as he passed, "Don't let the little minx ruin *mon chapeau!*" he warned.

Nathaniel chuckled as the much-loved piece of headgear pirouetted past him, giggling.

The little minx's mother quickly snatched the hat back from the unrepentant hat thief and handed it to Nathaniel, "I'm so sorry. It's my fault, I don't seem able to keep her under control," she murmured, not meeting his eye.

"I think you're doing a sterling job and deserve rich praise for your efforts. It cannot be easy. She seems a very high-spirited child and knows just how to get her own way. These are difficult times for both of you, but she has no way of understanding what's going on around her. I don't think you need to worry. It seems to me that she's just fearful she may be ignored in favour of our new guest."

Lady Winterborne glanced up at him and considered his words carefully, "Thank you, I suppose I'm particularly sensitive to her wayward moods because she's the only child at Winterborne and she tends to antagonise the adults who are usually here. If they come across her, they immediately suggest that she should go to bed!"

Nathaniel smiled, "Probably because they fear she'll get the better of them in an argument. It would be an unfair contest. That poor painter, by the end of the sitting he'll be fit only for Bedlam. I must say, it's an extraordinary work though. He's caught something — a side of you which is not at first obvious."

The Marchioness quickly turned away, colour rising in her cheeks, "He's made Jem into a seraph — !"

"Yes, but he has captured that mischievous gleam in her eye. I'm fairly certain he has the measure of her, even if he dislikes what he sees. And she quite definitely has the measure of *him*! She thinks him pompous and domineering and is in danger of puncturing his self-esteem. It's no wonder he's so angry all the time. But the painting is exceedingly fine I think."

"It was Gervase's idea. He loves showing us off — almost as though — " her words drifted.

"As though you were exhibits to be displayed? I've seen his collections of beautiful things in their glass prisons," and he observed her profile as she gazed unseeing across the Hall. "I have a desire to break the glass and set them free."

She flinched and her eyes flashed back to his and she frowned, then without saying another word she went to where Jemima was now hiding amongst the mountain of luggage and taking her hand led her from the Hall.

He watched her go and noting her rigid shoulders, wondered if she could see what seemed so very obvious to him. He shrugged and for a moment stood watching two footmen gathering up the bags and taking them upstairs. Emery being here was going to considerably complicate things especially as he was reckless and selfish and likely to cause all kinds of mayhem. Sometimes Nathaniel wondered why he was so fond of him.

He saw the doctor coming into the Great Hall and went to thank him for visiting, "Any improvement in his condition, Doctor Morton?"

"I think he's not at risk for now at least, as far as I can tell, but that doesn't mean that he's cured, by any means. He's in grave danger as long as he keeps drinking. I cannot impress upon you enough that he must give up his addiction or it will kill him even sooner. And you probably have a good idea what that may mean. As I have already said he will suffer badly whilst trying to forgo alcohol and it will not be easy for those who love him. I am much relieved that you'll be here to help Lady Winterborne but even so — "

"I understand, Doctor, I have seen it first-hand and know what to expect. I will be here come what may."

"Excellent, that eases my mind a little. Lady Winterborne, for all her dignity and reserve is but a child herself really, who, by the sound of things, has had adulthood forced upon her. So very young and yet thrust into a life of — well, you will see, I expect."

"I have already seen a good deal in the few days I've been here and can speculate about the rest. It's an interesting setup here at Winterborne."

"It is indeed, Captain, and you don't yet know the half of it, I'm afraid, but it's not for me to say — " and with those oblique words, he said he'd be back in a day or two, said his goodbye and left.

* * *

Jemima was sitting on her mother's bed watching her stare into space. There was something strange in the air which she didn't like. Mama was unhappy. Papa was lying in his bed. Nothing seemed quite right.

Grace herself was feeling even more anxious than usual. The balance of her life was upset as though the floor beneath her feet were tilting. She couldn't quite find the level ground she needed to keep herself from falling. She greatly feared loss of serenity. She needed a sense tranquillity so that the panic didn't rise and overwhelm her. It was almost as though she craved what most people dreaded, a humdrum life. She and Jemima had managed to find their own place at Winterborne where no-one bothered them as long as they docilely did as they were told and appeared before guests as dutiful and beautiful wife and daughter. It was a simple case of keeping some sort of balance. But now, things had tilted, and she was feeling uncertain again. Her hard-earned sense of security seemed to be under threat. The Captain had, at first, alarmed her, his sudden arrival, his military demeanour and her husband's sudden change of mood, which seemed to coincide and was causing her some concern. She was just beginning to suspect that he was perhaps not the man she'd at first feared him to be, although she was still unsure about the reasons for his visit. She supposed it had something to do with Gervase's business interests, but there was something about the Captain which reminded her of deadly undercurrents in a dark, still river, something dangerous and unknowable. And now there was the addition of Mr Talmarch, whom she'd met twice before, but she had, until now, had very little to do with him. He'd come to Winterborne the first time with some of Gervase's friends from London, a loud group of theatrical folk, who drank vast quantities of champagne and disturbed the air of harmony in the house and made her want to hide away in the garden with Jemima. She felt safe in the garden, apart from near the Maze, which had always made her uneasy; the idea of being lost within its confining tall hedges filled her with breathless panic, but in the rest of the grounds she felt free to be herself.

There was a small Grecian temple in the furthest corner of the garden, which caught the evening sun, and she and Jem would go there to find some peace and she'd tell the little girl stories about animals who could talk and children who had wings and could fly above the clouds and a kindly fox who made it his life's work to rescue chickens. She'd tried to read the books meant for the *instruction and improvement of the minds of all good children* which she'd found in the library and found them to be severely lacking in imagination and joy, being mainly hymns and prayer books translated into simple English. So, instead she created the stories herself and allowed Jemima to add any ideas she might have along the way. They'd laugh at the antics of their rather wayward characters and invent outlandish names for them, like Mistress Skipsalot, Lord Verycross and Miss Naughtybreeches. They whiled away many an hour sitting in the temple together, lost in their very own imaginary world.

Mr Talmarch was an odd enough character in real life with his affected manners and outrageous attire; Grace really didn't know what to make of him. She had wondered to begin with why her husband had drawn him into his circle. She now surmised that it was to get closer to Captain Heywood; she didn't yet know the reason why, but she had her suspicions. Mr Talmarch seemed an unsteady sort of person, she decided; she felt he would go wherever the wind blew him, like a dandelion clock. And that meant he could not be trusted.

"Mama?" said Jemima, "Is Lord Werrycross going away like the rabbit in the wood?"

Startled out of her reverie, Grace focused on her daughter, "Lord Verycross — is not at all well at the moment, dearest, a bit like that poor rabbit. And, like the rabbit, I'm afraid he's — not going to get better so we must be very kind to him and make him as happy as we can. Do you understand?"

Jemima looked thoughtfully at her mother and a small frown drew down her brows, "I think so Mama. I promise I won't pull his wig any more."

Grace smiled, "That would be a splendid idea, my love, and would make Lord Verycross less cross which would also be good."

"The *other* man is werry funny," said Jemima more cheerfully.

"Mr Talmarch?"

"No, not *him*! The *other* man — with the eyes."

Grace laughed, "But they both have eyes, Jem!"

"But the other man has *smiling* eyes."

"Ah," said Grace, light dawning, "You mean Captain Heywood?"

"Cap-tin. Yes, *that* man. He says funny things."

"Does he? Like what?"

"Cats is werry tiny tigers!"

"That's true."

"If I sit on his shoulders, I might see the sea!"

"Hmmm. I'm not sure about that one — although he is exceedingly tall."

"He said I might see whales as big as the house, an' mermaids, an' pirates. What *is* pirates?"

"They're naughty sailors who steal other people's gold."

"Can I be a pirate?"

"Very probably! There were lady pirates in the olden days, but they weren't very lady-like! I think you'd make an excellent pirate."

"Is the Cap-tin a pirate?"

"No, he's a soldier."

"Oh," said Jemima, deeply disappointed.

* * *

Mr Emery Talmarch entered the dining room with a decided flourish and paused for a moment so that those gathered there could fully appreciate the magnificence he was bringing to their lacklustre country lives. Grace couldn't help a slight intake of breath as she gazed upon his sparkling person. From the top of his white pigeon-wing bag wig to the tips off his shining buckled shoes, he was the picture of wholly unrestrained elegance. The pale lemon velvet coat was embellished with gold thread and pink lilies and the waistcoat of ivory silk was also much embroidered; his breeches were lemon yellow, his stockings white. His face was delicately powdered and patched and his lips subtly rouged.

"God, Emery! Are you off to the opera?" said Nathaniel, with the ghost of a smile.

Emery made an impressive bow to them both, very much in the grand manner, "Gad, I just thought I'd bring a little light into your lives! Hopefully out here in the wilds of wherever this little backwater is, I can show you all how we townsfolk present ourselves."

"No wonder you're short of funds, my friend. How much did the coat cost?"

"A gentleman should never discuss money in front of a lady. It was worth every penny, no? Will you please examine this embroidery closely! It is exquisite. Of course, you, with your taste for sombre colours and severe style, will never be able to fully appreciate such fine work, such remarkable tailoring! You dress like a clergyman, Nate!"

"Thank you. Coming from someone who is such a dedicated peacock, I find I'm much gratified and believe my rather restrained tailor would be vastly relieved."

"Pshwarrr! You only look remotely well-dressed when you're in full uniform. Lady Winterborne, I hope you will please excuse our raillery — we are like long-lost brothers forever teasing one another," he raised his quizzing glass and peered at Nathaniel, "Although, you must freely admit that we are nothing alike! Truly, I despair! Regard his neckcloth, if you please — he's obviously tied it himself and without the benefit of valet or looking glass. A dire testament to his nonchalant attitude to his appearance and the importance of cutting a dash!"

"I thought him exceedingly well turned out," said Grace daringly, as she took her place at the end of the table.

Nathaniel flicked her a surprised look, "It's fortunate you didn't see me after eight hours in the saddle, coated in a thick layer of dust and with leaves and insects in my hair. My bootmaker would have wept over the state of my top boots."

"You *rode?*" exclaimed Emery, "Well, of *course* you did! I came by post-chaise and was very nearly in a fit state to be seen on arrival. You will always remain a soldier at heart."

One footman poured wine, and another brought the dishes in and placed them upon the table. When all but Kirby and Robert had left the room, Emery asked Nathaniel how Lord Winterborne was.

"He's asleep at the moment. Doctor Morton has found us a reliable nurse to sit with him and tend to his needs for a few hours every day. He is somewhat recovered from his earlier fragile state and I think we may even be able to encourage him to come downstairs for a while each day if he continues to improve. You will be able to talk to him then."

"It can wait," said Emery magnanimously.

"Good, because he's not yet well enough to receive visitors. And he'll certainly not be ready to discuss business matters for some while."

"I will keep my peace, I promise, and dedicate myself to entertaining my hostess. I must say, Lady Winterborne, the house and park are in fine order. Last time I was here it was winter, and I could not fully appreciate the beauty of the gardens. I must beg you to give me a tour," said Emery with his most charming smile.

Grace, who had been hoping to avoid exactly this, graciously agreed to show him around.

Nathaniel, sensing her discomfort said, "I would be happy to do it for you, my lady, as you'll be engaged caring for your husband and chasing after the seraphim."

Grace gave a quiet chuckle, a sound Nathaniel suspected must be quite rare, "Thank you, Captain but I would be pleased to show Mr Talmarch around Winterborne. Gervase would expect it."

"All right then, but may I have the privilege of exploring the Maze with him?"

Grace blushed and cast him a grateful look, "Well, if you insist!"

"I do," said Nathaniel, "I shall endeavour to lose him in it."

Emery rolled his expressive pale blue eyes, "I shall take a ball of string with me so that I can find my way out."

"Knowing you, the string would run out long before you found your way out or you'd fail to attach the end properly."

Emery laughed, "You're unfortunately right. You know me far too well."

"It's a burden I must bear," reflected Nathaniel.

"So, what do you do for amusement here at Winterborne?" asked Emery.

"Other than nurse invalids and care for small children, manage the estate, entertain unwanted guests — ?" Nathaniel eyed his friend cynically, "You'll find no gambling dens and no theatres or taverns filled with your drinking cronies. When in the country one makes one's own entertainment. You ride — you may take a horse from the very fine stables and gallop across the fields. Or go for long bracing walks which will improve your health and temper. You may find a book in the library and read to your heart's content — although you may be in danger of learning something valuable. You could play hide-and-seek with Jemima in the garden or shoot rabbits in the kitchen garden which would please the cook greatly or go fishing for brown trout in the lake. So much choice," he said with a glint in his eye.

Emery who was tucking into a juicy morsel of chicken, nearly choked, "I am not at all used to the wonders of country life!"

"Nobody asked you to come, Emery."

"No. And don't think that's gone unnoticed! I had no choice but to invite myself. A rum do, indeed!"

Grace was listening to this conversation, thinking how nonsensical it was and rather enjoying their light-hearted banter. She was only used to her parents' endless complaints about her behaviour and Gervase's veiled criticism of her appearance, or the boisterous and ribald exchanges of the theatrical types who came every month or so at Gervase's request. She hadn't understood a good deal of what was said at those gatherings but knew some of the comments were aimed at her. They seemed to mainly consist of sexual innuendo and bawdy jokes and as soon as they started to drink heavily, she quickly realised that she had to make herself scarce or become the target for their ridicule. She knew that she should stand up to them but found it too daunting and ran instead, with their laughter trailing after her. Gervase told her she must stay and behave with suitable propriety, but it was impossible, even if by disobeying him she incurred his wrath. She'd found dinner time to be the most strain because she was unable to escape under any pretext; she just had to sit and try not to listen to their awful words. She'd keep her eyes on her plate and answer any questions with as short a response as possible without having to resort to being openly rude.

She desperately wished she could join in this conversation between the Captain and Mr Talmarch, but she didn't know how — it was far beyond her own limited experience.

It sounded at first as though they were insulting each other but beneath the words she could hear the strength of their attachment and she envied them that friendship. She only had Jemima.

She cleared her throat nervously, "Mr Talmarch, as Jem finds your hats so entertaining, you'll always be welcome at Winterborne and I'm sorry to say that she's going to need a replacement hero now having, much to her evident disappointment, discovered that Captain Heywood's not actually a pirate."

She was surprised and gratified when both gentlemen laughed appreciatively and felt an unfamiliar warm glow in the region of her chest, and she smiled.

Five

The Marquis opened his eyes and the first thing he saw, albeit a little hazily, was the newly employed, hatchet-faced nursemaid, sitting beside the bed.

"Brandy," he muttered desperately.

She got to her feet and looked down at him unsympathetically, "There will be no brandy, my lord. I will fetch you some cordial."

He opened his mouth to argue.

"No! You have had your last brandy, Lord Winterborne. And, if you'll forgive me for remarking upon it, look where being a servant to the Devil's brew has got you. You have been exhibiting very poor judgement for someone with a young family who depend upon you. I think after you've had your cordial, we shall pray together and hopefully we may yet have time to save your poor blackened soul," said the nurse in portentous accents.

My Lord Winterborne groaned and closed his eyes again.

* * *

Grace waited until the cool of the evening to escort Mr Talmarch and Captain Heywood around the garden, she was fearful of adding to the freckles she already had as she seemed very much predisposed to acquiring them should she carelessly stay too long in the sunshine. Her father had frequently told her that they were not at all ladylike, being more suited to fieldworkers and dairymaids. She'd tried all kinds of remedies to rid herself of them, but nothing seemed to work. Someone had recommended lemon juice, but it had just inflamed her skin.

Just in case of accidental exposure to the sun, she'd put on a large straw hat which tied with a dark pink riband under her chin and would hopefully shield her face from the glare.

They began by wandering through the nuttery, a large, grassed area on the east of the house, given over to ranks of hazel trees, and underneath them, long grass and wildflowers. There were a few statues set amongst the trees of Greek gods and one particularly impressive one of Pan playing his pipes, right in the centre of the wood; Grace always averted her eyes from it because it seemed rather too suggestive. Ragged Robin, Herb Robert and Cowslips dotted the meadow like brightly coloured stars and Jemima ran to and fro gathering them with artless abandon, pulling them up by the roots or snapping their heads off willy-nilly, until she had a small untidy bunch which she tucked into Dancer's collar. She picked a Meadow Buttercup and presented it to Nathaniel, who threaded it into a buttonhole on his lapel; Jemima considered it with her head cocked on one side and then nodded approvingly. She and her mother made a coronet of flowers and grasses and she wore it slightly askew amongst her brown curls and declared she was Queen of the Nuttery and made them all bow and curtsy to her, telling them imperiously that if they didn't, she'd chop off their heads. Emery warned them that unless severely curbed the child would have all their heads on spikes. Jemima was enchanted with this gruesome thought and danced away trilling a joyous song about a dead and headless rabbit.

They moved through the meticulously laid out Herb Garden, stroking the fragrant plants and admiring the orderly arrangement of the beds and the wide range of different herbs. From there they strolled down the long Beech Walk to the Orchard and back through the Parterre towards the west side of the garden. Nathaniel noticed that as they approached the Maze, Lady Winterborne began to slightly drag her feet and hang back, allowing Emery and himself to go ahead and reach the entrance to the Maze first. He glanced back and although she was showing no obvious signs of her dislike of it and said nothing, she stayed a little apart.

"Why don't you and Jemima run on to the Temple and we'll quickly explore the Maze and meet you there in a short while?"

She nodded and taking her daughter by the hand, walked swiftly away.

"Should there not be a manned tower overlooking the maze to help us find our way out again?" asked Emery.

"That would be too easy. Surely, you're not daunted by a few high hedges? You think you'll get lost and miss your supper?"

"High quality food here, Nate! Worth the damned long coach journey! As is Lady Winterborne! Remarkably beautiful woman, no?"

Nathaniel fixed his friend with a cynical eye, "Yes, Emery, the food is good, and the Marchioness is beautiful. What are you so clumsily alluding to? I think it might be time to tell me exactly how much you knew of this ridiculous scheme. Did the Marquis tell you all?"

"All? I'm not sure — " said Emery slightly apprehensively.

Nathaniel raised a damning eyebrow, "Really, Emery? I think you might want to consider carefully what you're about to say."

Emery swallowed, "Look, Nate, I may have slightly overstepped — but I swear I had your best interests at heart! He asked me — came straight out with it — just like that! What could I say? The *money* Nate! It'll get me out of an awful fix. And I thought you'd be sanguine about it, like you always are. It's not as though you'll have to murder anyone!"

"I would like to murder *you*," said Nathaniel darkly. "What on earth were you thinking? It's out of the question. Did you even consider Lady Winterborne? She's only twenty years old and trapped in what appears to be a very peculiar marriage. She was to have no say in the matter, I suppose? D'you not see what an imposition it is for her to even have to have strangers in her home all the time? But *this*, this is beyond a joke! How could she possibly agree to it? Devil take it, Emery! I cannot believe the mess you've embroiled me in. I'm up to my neck in their woes now. And, therefore, cannot leave until I'm sure that the Marchioness isn't going to have to deal with that cantankerous and dying man all alone. There seems to be no help coming from any other quarter either. Her siblings hate her husband and I'm starting to see that they might have good reason. He's a damned shady cove!"

They were strolling around the Maze as they talked, turning this way and that and coming up against dead ends and twisty turnabouts, the high yew hedges towering above their heads in a rather menacing fashion.

Emery was not enjoying the conversation; his friend could be exceedingly forbidding at times, and it made him a little uncomfortable. He'd always known that Nathaniel had an enigmatic side which could turn in a trice to something quite threatening, even darkly sinister. He'd supposed he'd learnt to be that way in the army, but Emery was beginning to realise that it might be deeper rooted than that. He didn't like being on the receiving end of his ire, especially as he knew that, this time, he was the one at fault. When the offer had initially been made, he'd only been able to see the reward and barely taken notice of the potential pitfalls. Like, for instance, Nate thinking the whole thing was a terrible idea and he had to admit to not really having taken Lady Winterborne's feelings into consideration at all, which had been an oversight. He thought that she'd probably just obey her husband in everything, without question. She was very young and when he'd met her previously, he'd had the impression that, where her husband was concerned, she was rather biddable, although her general demeanour could be decidedly frosty at times. When Lord Winterborne had asked him if he knew of anyone with unimpeachable credentials who might be available for a well-paid assignment, Emery had immediately thought of Nathaniel; he was a soldier after all — he was all about mysterious assignments and derring-do! And there was the money, of course. That had been the final deciding factor. It was a damned fortune. And after all, if Nate could induce the Marchioness to fall in love with him, it was going to happen anyway! Why not make all their lives a little easier in the meantime? He and Nate would be financially secure at last, Nate would have the benefits such a beautiful woman would bring him, and the Marquis would have his heir. It sounded as though everyone won. And here was Nate making the devil of a fuss about, admittedly, the trickiest part of the plan but still, he should be able to talk her around; he'd seen his friend cajole much pricklier types than Lady Winterborne. This would be simple, if he could just make sure Nate overcame his wretchedly inconvenient scruples and then make sure that the Marchioness fell for his undeniable charms. What could possibly go wrong?

'Yes, I've never much liked the Marquis," admitted Emery, "He has some downright odd ideas, and his friends are mostly deplorable."

"I have to agree with that statement," said Nathaniel dryly.

Emery cast him an indignant look, "*Very* amusing. I've only been trying to help everyone and all I get for my trouble is abuse. It seems to me that you could be a bit more grateful. I mean look at where we are! Living in the lap of luxury, surrounded by all this beauty. And we're not even having to deal with the Marquis himself, which I must say is a blessing."

"*You're* not having to deal with him. Lady Winterborne and I have to tend to him. It's not a sight such a young girl should have to endure. He's a living cadaver and slowly dying, in the worst way. She bears it bravely, for he has nothing for her but criticism and carping even when he's at death's door. I don't know how she puts up with it. *This* way, Emery! It's along this path. Come, follow me. You've never had any sense of direction."

"This is poor entertainment, my friend! Life in the country is enough to drive one to drink. One has to feel a good deal of sympathy for Lord Winterborne's plight!"

"One does not. He's taken a path which only leads one way and yet he sticks to it zealously despite his wife and child being there to witness his gradual descent into hell. He has only himself to blame."

Emery came to a sudden standstill, "You sound as though you feel sorry for the Marchioness! Well, that's a step in the right direction, at least."

"Don't be ridiculous, Emery. I feel no more for her than anyone might, seeing how her predicament has her imprisoned. You will never persuade me that Lord Winterborne's scheme is reasonable when it emanates from such an unsound mind. Come along, I see the centre of the Maze ahead and they'll be waiting for us in the Temple."

"One day, you'll thank me, Nate! Of this I'm entirely sure. You will be overflowing with gratitude and blessing the day I chose you to reap the rewards with me — and our fortunes will be made. Is this *it*?" exclaimed Emery, looking around in disappointment at the little garden at the centre of the labyrinth. A statue of some partly clad goddess stood in the middle of a grassy circular space. "How dispiriting! I cannot believe this is to be my recompense for all that effort." He looked askance at Nathaniel, who, in turn, was examining the statue with sudden interest. "What is it? Admiring the sculptor's fine handiwork?"

"No, it's naught but a mediocre piece of statuary. But the face is recognisable nonetheless."

Emery peered at it a little closer, "By Jove! So it is! Well, I never. D'you not think that's a trifle odd? You'd think she'd feel somewhat uncomfortable about strangers coming in here — seeing that. It doesn't leave much to the imagination, does it!"

Nathaniel frowned, "I doubt she even knows it's here. She avoids the Maze, it frightens her. You saw her just now — running away to the Temple with Jemima rather than showing us around. It is strange though. The Marquis is a collector of beautiful things. But something just doesn't add up."

"What are you talking about?"

"I don't know really. Just a suspicion, nothing more."

"Oh, do let us get out of here, it's damned oppressive in this heat! I don't think I'm going to become a devotee of mazes. I wonder what will be for dinner? Last night's veal was truly sublime!"

They approached the little Temple nestling in the far corner of the garden, half-hidden beneath silver birches and surrounded by lavender, the fragrance filling the air. It was domed and had tapered Ionic columns with scrolled capitals and fluting. Nathaniel thought it incongruous and ostentatious. The evening sun bathed it in golden light and as they neared it, they could hear the sound of laughter.

"Ah, there you are," said Nathaniel as the two girls looked up and stopped their giggling. "We have managed to find our way in and out of the Maze without incident, but Mr Talmarch has decided that he much prefers other parts of the garden, the parts with less mystery and opportunity for becoming lost."

"The Maze is horrid. I don't like it," said Jemima, echoing her mother's sentiments precisely.

"Mr Talmarch thoroughly agrees with you. He found it to be too much for his delicate sensibilities and fled."

"Ran away?" Jemima turned and looked at Emery, disenchanted. "He was *afraid*?"

"Terribly afraid. He couldn't wait to get out."

"Oh, now, I *say!* Going too far!" cried Emery. "I merely thought it a little dark and oppressive."

"Ran away," reiterated Jemima, giving him a withering look.

Nathaniel shot him a look of mild triumph and addressed Lady Winterborne, "That is a very fine maze, my lady. I have visited several and this one is extremely well laid out."

"I'm glad you think so," she replied coolly.

He thought of the hidden statue and wondered for a brief moment how accurate it was. He wanted to know if the Marchioness knew of its existence and why her husband had placed it in the centre of a rather public feature in the garden.

It made very little sense. He then realised that he'd been staring at Lady Winterborne in a distracted manner, and she was returning his gaze, her expression bland. He then caught himself wondering what she might be like if she were to lose that air of indifference. He imagined that the girl in the scarlet gown was just beneath the icy, aloof surface of this woman regarding him from cold grey eyes and he found himself wondering if he might release her from her prison of rigid propriety. He had to give himself a mental shake to rid himself of some decidedly unwanted thoughts. No, he was not going to fall into that trap and become a pathetic dupe, beholden to a madman. He would not allow the Marquis to use him in his ludicrous plan.

He smiled at Lady Winterborne, hoping to convey his lack of interest and concern but to his acute discomfort she met his gaze with equanimity and held it. He suddenly realised that, despite her sheltered upbringing and the naivety she retained as a result, she saw more than he first thought, and this was going to make his life even more difficult. In her eyes there was, he felt, some understanding of his situation which made him want to loosen his neckcloth's overly tight grip on his throat. He wasn't used to feeling at a disadvantage; he usually had the measure of anyone he had to deal with. This was unfamiliar territory and strangely unsettling. He was the first to look away, pretending that he was examining their surroundings closely.

"This Temple makes quite a statement. Did your husband have it built or was it already here?"

"He designed it and had it built after his parents died and he inherited the house. He was the only child so there has been no one to challenge him."

Nathaniel's eyes wandered about the temple and alighted upon a frieze which circled the inside of the building. He followed the progress of the story to its conclusion and returned his gaze to the Marchioness who was watching him with mild interest.

"The tale of Ganymede and the Eagle, I believe. An interesting choice," he said.

"He has always been very fond of Greek myths," she replied.

"It's certainly all Greek to me!" laughed Emery, "What does it mean? Some handsome young fellow being carried off by an eagle?"

"The eagle represents Zeus and he's bearing Ganymede away to Olympus to be his wine pourer, if my memory serves me correctly." explained Nathaniel, cautiously.

"Oh, well, perhaps I should have paid more attention to my lessons because I don't remember this particular myth at all. But, I will own, it is a very beautiful fresco. Your husband is clearly an academic sort of fellow. Far above me, I'm afraid."

Nathaniel met Lady Winterborne's eyes briefly but neither of them said anything.

He moved to the back of the Temple where there were niches cut into the walls to display small statues and had his suspicions duly confirmed. He shook his head and wondered how much Lady Winterborne really understood. The Temple was not even very subtle in its significance. In fact, its message was pretty blatant. It was as though the Marquis were daring anyone to mention it; it was a challenge, a glove across the face. Things were gradually beginning to make sense but, although he could see more clearly the reasons why his presence was required, he could not even begin to fathom why Lady Winterborne remained here, the dutiful wife and mother. If she were to flee and take the child with her, nobody would blame her. He most certainly wouldn't. He looked back to where she was sitting, her back so erect, the low sunshine gilding her hair like a halo, her arm around Jemima's waist. They looked like a Renaissance painting of the Madonna and Child. He let out an involuntary laugh as their hopeless situation made a mockery of what he was seeing.

"What do you find so amusing?" asked Emery, noting his friend's expression as it turned quickly to vexation.

"Just the absurdity of life. It's staggering what humans are able to bear sometimes. I suppose we each have our own limits, and some are able to tolerate more than others."

The Marchioness turned to look at him, "Some have no choice about the direction their destiny takes, Captain Heywood. Choices are thrust upon them and they must simply make the best of it," she said quietly.

"But surely every human capable of independent thought can make their own choices and act upon them accordingly?"

The slightest smile tugged the corner of her mouth, "You would think so, but there are times when sacrifices must be made for the common good."

"Ah, I think you quote Plato. But do you not think that there must be times when the common good must be sacrificed for the good of the individual."

"It depends what must be sacrificed, Captain Heywood. Some sacrifices are too great and if they involve others — innocents — then how can one make that choice based merely upon what one selfish individual desires?"

Nathaniel said nothing for a moment but looked from Lady Winterborne to the child in her arms.

"You see," she continued, "For some the answer is simple but what if their decision means others must lose everything — lose their birthright — *their* destiny? Would that be acceptable? Does one individual have the right to alter another's life so drastically — so permanently?"

He considered her face which was, as usual, rather impassive and debated taking the conversation even further but was halted when he caught sight of Emery's bemused expression.

"I suppose that every person must make decisions which they can live with, otherwise life would become untenable," he replied.

"By Jupiter! I'd give a monkey to know what the devil you're both talking about!" exclaimed Emery, throwing up his hands in despair.

Nathaniel laughed, "You haven't even got five pounds let alone five hundred pounds."

"Well, there's no need to draw attention to it. My dignity is already in tatters!"

"And you only have yourself to blame. You chose your destiny by frequenting gaming hells and — "

"What is gaming hells?" asked Jemima, perking up.

Lady Winterborne rose to her feet, "I think we should go back to the house now — it must nearly be time for supper."

They all followed her out of the Temple and across the lawns to the parterre and the front of the house. They were greeted in the Great Hall by Robert, "I was just coming to find you, my lady. Lord Winterborne is calling for you."

"Oh, I shall come at once. Jem can you go with Robert and he'll take you to find Bridie and she'll give you supper. I'm just going to see Papa. I'll come along and tuck you in," promised Grace.

"I don't like Bridie," said Jemima, sticking out her bottom lip.

"I know, darling, but — what about if Mr Talmarch goes with you? He might even allow you to try on his hats. You'd like that wouldn't you?"

The child nodded and looked uncertainly at Emery, who was, in turn looking understandably panicked.

"My — *hats*? I — they're — made by Lock's of St James's! They are — not for children!"

Nathaniel stepped in, "But even so, Emery is more than willing to allow Jemima to try them on if she goes with him to find — er — Bridie. Are you not, Emery?"

Emery made a strangled sound, and nodded, unable to form actual words. He cast Nathaniel a look of violent loathing and held out his hand to Jemima, who took it rather as though it might turn out to be a wet fish.

"I will hold you responsible for any damage done," he muttered and left the Hall with Jemima.

"Oh, dear," said Grace, "That was unkind of me, but I really don't want her to become too aware of the seriousness of Gervase's illness. Thank you for helping."

"Emery doesn't mean half of what he says, you know. He's just become a little bitter because he's unable to control his inherited tendency to gamble and being penniless doesn't suit him at all. Come, we'd better see what Lord Winterborne wants."

Grace looked at him in surprise, "You're coming?"

"Of course! We're in this together, my lady."

For a moment she stood as though frozen, "What I said — before — you cannot — allude to it in front of Gervase! He might revoke what he has bequeathed Jemima and she will not get what should be hers by right."

"You have no need for concern, I will say nothing. You can trust me."

She frowned up at him, "I can trust no one apart from Jemima."

"Well, I'm telling you — you and the child can put your faith in me."

She sighed and turned away, "If only that were true, Captain, but I fear that he's brought you here for some reason of his own and knowing my husband as I do, I know it cannot be for the common good."

Nathaniel followed her up the stairs but remained silent because he was unable to deny her words.

Six

The sickroom was in partial darkness, the sun having disappeared, leaving just a faint rosy glow in the sky. A branch of candles cast a warm light across the room, but the Marquis was in shadow behind the hangings of his bed.

"There you are, at last!" he said testily. "I called for you."

"I know, I'm sorry, Gervase, I had to make sure that Jem was settled before I could come, but I'm here now. What did you want?"

"Do I have to want something? You are my wife! You should be at my bedside. Where have you been?"

"I took Captain Heywood and Mr Talmarch to see the Maze, as you instructed," she explained. "The Captain is here, if you'd like to talk to him about it?"

Nathaniel stepped forward, "Your Maze is indeed a wonder, Lord Winterborne. I'm impressed."

The Marquis tried to sit up so that he could see better, and Grace rushed to his aid, "Oh, don't fuss so! I can manage! So, you liked the Maze, eh? Thought you might! Hoping it would encourage you to reconsider my proposal!"

"My lord, if you are referring to what I think you are, I must reiterate that nothing could change my mind."

"But you appreciate the prize a little better I think."

"It's not really a prize though, is it? And it's not yours to give away. Naturally, I could fully appreciate the beauty of it but must remain true to my principles."

"I will double the reward then!"

Nathaniel narrowed his eyes, "You can offer whatever sum you like, but it will not alter anything. And it's no use trying to bribe Emery to persuade me either because I would never trust his judgement on something as serious as this."

Grace was now sitting in the chair beside the bed, listening to them talk, "What pray, are you discussing? I cannot make head nor tail of it. Reward? Who is to be rewarded and for what?"

"None of your business!" snapped her husband, "It's between me and Captain Heywood. You just need to concentrate upon Jem and your duties. Nothing else need concern you. I've invited a few friends to stay, by the bye."

"Oh, no! I — I mean — " uttered Grace, without thinking.

"When do they arrive, my lord?" interposed Nathaniel swiftly.

"On Friday."

"That gives everyone a few days to prepare the house. I'm sure your cook will not be put out by such short notice. At least, I've met her and she's formidable — but brilliant! Emery was rhapsodising over the veal. Said it was the best he'd ever tasted."

Distracted by the interruption the Marquis turned his attention to the Captain, "I poached her from a good friend. Paid her more to come here. Money well spent. Her previous employer still won't speak to me!"

"I'm not surprised. You certainly have a treasure there."

"*Everything* I own is a valuable treasure," said Lord Winterborne complacently.

Nathaniel opened his mouth to say something but caught Grace's eye and closed it again. He had no desire to make things worse for her, but it was the devil's own job to stay silent when the man said such outrageous things. The look she sent him was a warning, but it was also laced with fear, which he couldn't ignore.

"I must say I find your collections fascinating. The variety of specimens that you have and the sheer beauty of them! What made you start collecting?" enquired Nathaniel, still intending to divert his attention.

"A passion for beautiful things. A love of possessing them. Paintings, sculptures, this house, the garden, my collections, they all belong solely to me and I plan to hold onto them come what may. There are yet more things I desire to collect even now. Things of great value and beauty. Things no one else can afford. Money can buy you anything you desire."

"Not always, my lord, not always," said Nathaniel mildly.

"We shall see, Captain Heywood. I generally get what I want."

"You must understand by now that time is of the essence and in this case, time is something *I* have in abundance."

"The more I get to know you the more I think I've made the right choice for my project."

"Interesting. The more I get to know *you*, Lord Winterborne, the more I realise that I have *also* made the right choice," responded Nathaniel with a crooked smile.

The Marquis laughed, "I think you'll find that your options are best kept open especially when you have a friend as rackety as Mr Talmarch. From what I understand he's a mere hair's breadth away from Newgate! Or worse. I've heard that he owes money to some exceedingly unsavoury characters. The kind that are only really happy when they're lopping off fingers and other appendages."

"Gervase! You cannot mean that!" exclaimed Grace, "Oh, poor Mr Talmarch, he must be in such a state!"

"He is. And Captain Heywood is, as you can see, unwilling to help him."

Grace's burning gaze fell upon Nathaniel, "Why would you not wish to help your friend? It seems unspeakably callous."

"I've tried to help him in the past, but he will not be saved, whatever I do. And the only way out I've been offered is, I'm afraid, out of the question."

"I see," said Grace.

"No, I don't think you do, my lady, but it hardly matters anyway as it is no more than a fanciful notion."

"Well, I must apologise but as your conversation is so hard to comprehend, I think I shall go and put Jemima to bed — she'll be waiting for me. I will come back a little later, Gervase, to sit with you."

He dismissed her with a wave of his hand, and she left the bedchamber, "So, the sight of the statue could not even entice you? You must be made of stern stuff."

"It's made of lifeless marble. Hardly enticing. Cold and hard."

"Not unlike my dear wife, then!"

Nathaniel said nothing.

"Ah! Do I discern the beginnings of a budding sense of loyalty?"

"Loyalty? I barely know Lady Winterborne. I'm barely loyal to Emery, let alone someone I've known but a few days and Emery I've known most of my life."

"You do yourself an injustice. You came here at his behest, knowing nothing of what would be required of you and yet still you remain, despite your obvious misgivings. I think you have loyalty buried deep in the marrow of your bones, Captain, though you may deny it."

Nathaniel clenched his jaw, "My lord, you're looking somewhat pale, may I get you anything? Some cordial perhaps?"

"You can get me some damned brandy! I'll give you my hunting box in Leicestershire if you fetch me a glass!"

"What would I do with a hunting box? I don't hunt and I never have cause to venture into Leicestershire."

"More fool you! What about a small manor in Hampshire?"

Nathaniel laughed, "I'm not looking for any responsibilities at the moment, thank you. I have no wish to be tied down, having been bound to the army for so long, I'm happy to be free of rules and regulations and to finally not have to obey the orders of those for whom I've lost respect. A hunting box or a small manor would mean gardeners and cooks and footmen all clamouring for my attention. No, I'm sorry, I don't plan upon giving up my first real moments of freedom in over a decade just to become fettered to a pile of bricks."

"Your brother inherited everything?"

"He did. I fell out with my parents over his errant behaviour so even the few things which were to be mine went to him. It makes no odds. I'm perfectly content with my life as it is and wouldn't swap it for his. He's in as bad a state as Emery, the responsibility of being Lord of the Manor and head of the Heywood family weighs heavily upon him and he's succumbed to drowning his sorrows in any vice he can find."

"You're not tempted to rescue him?"

Nathaniel eyed the Marquis wryly, "No, he's old enough to look after himself and I'm not much inclined to the role of rescuer."

"And yet, as I said, you are here."

"Yes, I will admit to a momentary lapse in judgment."

"She's a virgin, you know."

Taken aback by the abruptness of this casual remark, Nathaniel took a moment to reply, trying to resist the temptation to rise to what must only be deliberate provocation, "I guessed as much," he said in measured tones, "*Ganymede.*"

Lord Winterborne laughed but it turned into a spluttering cough, so Nathaniel fetched the cordial and helped him take a few sips to ease his discomfort.

When he had stopped gasping for breath he said hoarsely, "You disapprove?"

"I rarely disapprove of anything, especially when it has nothing to do with me. I do wonder though how you can justify your marriage when it's based upon nought but deception."

"Jemima needed a mother. I wanted something beautiful and obedient. We both got what we wanted, and her family were saved from penury. It seems entirely fair to me. Everyone benefits. And before long you'll give her another child which will in turn give her something to focus upon and my family name will live on."

"You're being rather presumptuous. Even if I were to agree, which I won't, you could not guarantee she'd have a boy and as you've already sired a girl — "

"By the law of averages, the next will be a boy."

"You have God's ear then?"

"If you think God would listen to someone as lost to salvation as I, you must be insane! I'm afraid there's little hope that I shall end up on the side of the angels," said the Marquis wryly.

"We all make choices which we may later regret, I suppose. I've made many false steps in my life but fortunately they've only injured *me*. The choices you've made have affected others but at least you will not have to live long with the consequences of those decisions. Although I must say that I doubt it would have altered anything anyway. I fear you're a lost cause, my lord."

"And glad of it!"

"You chose Lady Winterborne only because she was beautiful?"

"Oh, that was certainly part of it. I saw other beauties in my search but when I was introduced to her and saw the conflict in her eyes, the desire to fight back which had to be quashed, I realised that it would always be a battle for her to be obedient, I just had to have her. To watch her fight her own inclinations in order to be the child her parents wanted and rescue her family — it's delicious, no?"

"It's malicious. Inhuman."

"It's entertaining and fascinating to see how far another human is prepared to go to achieve their own ends."

"But it's not for her own ends that she has altered herself, is it? She's sacrificed herself for her family and now for your child. I think that makes her the better person by far."

"You admire her resolve, Captain. She certainly has unflinching determination — I'll give her that. She'll be a good example for my children."

"She's already that. A fine counterbalance to their twisted and alcoholic father."

"You don't shy away from the truth, do you? I'm wondering if you will choose to stay with her once the deed is done. It occupies my mind a good deal while I lie here waiting to die."

"Your fondness for tormenting those closest to you keeps you awake?"

The Marquis chuckled, "You *could* call it tormenting I suppose! I see it more that my way is the only way. Better for everyone. They'd be fools not to listen. Also, if they do as I ask, they will be richly rewarded. There is surely no harm in that?"

"It depends what you're asking them to do for that reward. In this case you're asking your own wife to sleep with a complete stranger to further your own interests. I've heard some pretty vile stories in my time but for God's sake man, she's just a twenty-year-old girl — and an innocent. This could destroy her."

"She's more resilient than you think. I believe, in the end, she will be the victor."

"Well, I hope you are proved right. She deserves better than this."

* * *

The nursemaid had laced Lord Winterborne's cordial with a good dose of laudanum hoping for a peaceful evening and seemed content, despite the heat, to sit dozing by a small fire in his bedchamber while Grace, Nathaniel and Emery took a light supper in the parlour. Forgoing their after-supper discussion, the gentlemen took their port and joined Grace in the drawing room because otherwise she would have been alone. She found she was quite glad to see them arrive earlier than expected as she was used to her husband and his gentlemen friends lingering over their drinks and leaving her to sit with the so-called ladies who shocked her with their bawdy gossip.

Mr Talmarch entertained Grace with amusing tales of his life in London where he was perfectly content to paint himself as the villain or the victim of the piece as long as it caused sufficient merriment. She particularly enjoyed his story of being mistaken for a highwayman whilst making his way to a masked ball. As he described how he'd been forced to explain to the group of bullish public defenders that he was in fact just an ordinary citizen dressed in masquerade costume and they'd felt obliged to search his person for stolen jewellery, she'd laughed out loud and encouraged him to share more stories. He was a consummate storyteller, happy to embroider the tale to make it more amusing and never one to spoil a good story with the truth. Nathaniel, who had heard most of his tales at least once before, was always impressed by how much they changed over time. His version of the highwayman story was now graced by half a dozen burly fellows with fists like hams, instead of the original couple politely enquiring. He listened and said nothing. He couldn't help but watch Grace's face as she followed the ever-changing plot, enraptured, her eyes alight with unaccustomed amusement. Her habitually blank expression changed dramatically, her eyes almost disappeared as she laughed, her smile was wide and she possessed an unexpectedly delightful giggle, which was infectious; she drove Emery on to tell even more outrageous and mostly unashamedly exaggerated stories.

The evening continued cheerfully until gone midnight, when Grace suddenly noticed the late hour and rose hurriedly to her feet, "Oh, my! That cannot be the time! I must leave you gentlemen. Jem has a habit of getting into my bed at dawn and expecting me to be wide awake to listen to her chatter! Thank you so much for — a very different evening to the ones I'm used to. I — enjoyed it. I will see you both at breakfast. I bid you goodnight."

Nathaniel crossed the room to open the door for her and as she reached for the handle at the same time as him, their hands touched briefly and by accident, but she withdrew hers as though she'd been burnt. Her eyes flew to his, her cheeks flushed scarlet, and she practically ran from the room, leaving Nathaniel gazing after her, a bemused frown creasing his forehead.

"What a divine creature!" said Emery, relaxing into his chair and reaching for his glass of port, "She's far more vivacious than I first thought. I think I might be starting to envy you just a little! Maybe if *you* don't — "

"Do not *dare* finish that sentence, Emery, or I shall have to knock you to the ground! She's not some courtesan to be passed around like a damned plaything."

Emery looked at his friend with interest, "No, she's being passed directly to you and you'd be a fool not to take advantage. Better you than some other less trustworthy brute! Don't forget I've met his — *friends* and will readily admit that even I found them to be well below the salt! Gad! He even knows that bounder George Carew, seen them together many times in London," and he shuddered dramatically, "He makes my skin crawl. He was here last time I stayed, and I think you'd want to protect any female from his oleaginous attentions. I'm sure that given half a chance he'd jump at the idea of bedding the Marchioness. He wouldn't leave her alone, fawning over her and touching her all the time. It was hard to watch."

"I've heard a little of Mr Carew and none of it complimentary. Is he not the worthless little worm who drove Sir Nicholas Verney's daughter to kill herself a few years ago?"

"The very man. Refused to lead her to the altar after compromising her in the worst way and spreading calumnious rumours about her. I'm telling you Nate, you don't want Lady Winterborne cast adrift amongst these kind of people. They'd eat her for breakfast and spit out her bones. I've seldom been more shocked. Winterborne left her to fend for herself and seemed to delight in her discomfort. It was beyond anything I've ever seen in the home of so-called respectable folk. And you know me, I'm accustomed to frequenting the haunts of the lowest of the low so I'm not easily scandalised. I make no excuses for my proclivities. But this group of wastrels and fornicators made my blood run cold. They're a strange mix too, all sorts — and the women are mostly as bad as the men. You'd be wise to keep an eye on Lady Winterborne and the child because it seems to me to be open season."

Nathaniel was staring hard at him, "Thank you for your advice, I shall be prepared. Although, as I've said before it's really none of my business. It's only your stupid machinations which have brought me to this juncture and made it impossible for me to leave without being haunted by a lifetime of guilt as a result."

Emery shrugged, "I still think you're the man for the job and even though you rail against it, I think your resolve is already weakening. Would you have her used by George Carew? No! Of course not. You shall see when they arrive. Not the thing at all. I'm hoping to collect my money before the inundation and then I shall be off like a hare before the hounds!"

"Of that I have no doubt! You feeble coward," said Nathaniel without rancour.

"You've always known I'm not Sir Galahad material! And yet still you remain my friend. It never ceases to astound me,"

"You make me look good by comparison."

Emery laughed, "Ah, Nate, you are the very best of fellows! I just have a feeling in my bones about all of this. I think in the end it will turn out to be the making of you in many ways."

"Or, more likely, the death of *you*."

Emery grinned winningly, "Yes, there is always that possibility, but every time I see you and the Marchioness together, I get a little chill down my spine."

"You've probably caught something nasty in one of those drinking dens you frequent!" retorted Nathaniel.

"Very likely! You should have *seen* — no, I won't shock you, you old prude! But sometimes I feel you miss out on life because of your reluctance to let your guard down. You're too tightly buttoned! As is Lady Winterborne. But Gad! She's such a beauty! Are you sure I couldn't simply — ?"

"Emery! I shall be forced to break your damned jaw in a moment to stop you talking, which you would find devilishly difficult to explain away!"

"Hmmm," mused Emery thoughtfully, "Jealous?"

* * *

Grace had been to bid her husband goodnight, although he was in a drugged sleep, and to speak with the nursemaid, Mrs Hawkins, who promised, as usual, to fetch her if anything should happen and then she'd peeped at Jemima, who was, thankfully, also sound asleep. She watched her sleep for a while because she found it soothing to see her breathing gently, her dark eyelashes curving against her plump cheeks, her hair a little damp with sweat where it lay on her forehead. Grace smoothed a curl away and smiled down at this strange little creature, her *daughter*, and prayed that their futures would continue together, wherever they might end up. She lived day to day, with no plans or expectations and at the end of each day she said a silent prayer to thank the Lord for sparing her and Jem yet again. She dropped a kiss on the child's warm sticky cheek and pulled the covers up around her, sighed and returned to her own bedchamber.

Her own abigail, Sally Hopton, helped her undress with her usual devoted care, like a mother hen, but always careful not to be too bustling as she knew her mistress found it vexing.

Sally was a local girl, who'd been hired at the age of thirteen to look after the new Marchioness. Her family had been so proud of her and she'd looked forward with great excitement to working in such a big and important house for such splendid people and earning enough money to be able to send some home to help her parents. It had come as something of a shock to her to find that her lovely mistress was married to someone so peculiar and apparently uncaring. It took a while for her to become used to their strange ways and to learn to listen, without saying anything, to the awful words he said to his wife. She didn't understand it at all, and it made her ever more defensive of Lady Winterborne who bore his neglect and scolds with such dignity. Sally had not been at Winterborne very long before she decided she would throw down her life for her mistress or even kill for her, should it become necessary. She certainly would cheerfully murder the Marquis. The way Lady Winterborne cared for the little child everyone knew wasn't hers, making sure she felt loved and sheltering her from the worst of what went on in the house, well, it made one's heart swell with pride. To be working for such a true lady! She knew her mother bragged about her position to anyone who would listen, and she was determined to keep her job but if it came to losing her precious post or saving Lady Winterborne, she would choose her mistress every single time.

She was taking down Lady Winterborne's hair and brushing it out, so that it shone and then braiding it ready for bed.

"My lady, will you wear the blue gown tomorrow or the silver grey? It might make sense to wear the grey as it is silk and cooler."

"The grey," said Grace, absent-mindedly.

"The weather is unusually warm for early June, so I think the grey would be best. Perhaps it'll rain soon, and it'll cool down."

"Perhaps," murmured Grace.

"Is Lord Winterborne feeling any better today?"

"He is a bit, I think."

"Do you think he'll be able to go downstairs soon?"

"Very likely. The doctor said he might."

"Will that be good, my lady? His lordship being downstairs?"

There was a slight pause, "No, not really. He — cannot see so much from his bed and — then he has his London friends coming — so I suppose he must be with them — his illness is not likely to get any better, but he seems to have rallied."

"That's excellent news," said Sally glumly.

"Yes, it is, isn't it?"

"But it's nice having Captain Heywood and Mr Talmarch staying, is it not? They are not at all like those other people from London. The Captain is very thoughtful, and Mr Talmarch is very funny — he makes Jemima laugh a lot."

"Yes, he does, doesn't he? Although, I think Jem is laughing *at* him not with him sometimes! The Captain — I feel — he's hiding something though. He and my husband are supposed to be going into business together — but there seems to be some dispute between them that is, as yet, unresolved and it hangs in the air all the time. I feel they're each waiting for the other to give in first. I might just be imagining it, of course."

"Would you like me to listen at the door, my lady? I could, without being noticed."

Grace turned to Sally, "Good Lord, no! Please don't! You might be found, and he'd send you away! I couldn't do without you now. I rely upon you — to talk to. I don't have anyone else, but Jem," she said anxiously.

"I won't then but if you asked m'lady, I'd do anything. You'd only have to say."

"I know, thank you, Sally. I truly bless the day you came to me Until then I thought I was entirely alone and wasn't sure if I could bear it. It was such a change from my previous life — so very different. In some — ways not as bad as I was led to believe but in others, so very much worse. And now those awful people are coming again. I dread it so. Even though the Captain and Mr Talmarch will be here."

"We'll manage to come about somehow, my lady. There, your hair is all done. Shall we get you into bed now?"

"Oh, Sally! You're such a comfort. Perhaps, life will soon begin to improve.

Seven

Friday arrived too quickly for Grace. She awoke that morning with a feeling of dread she couldn't place but then remembered in a rush and wished she could stay in bed all day and not have to face what was coming. But there was no getting away from it; she would have to deal with it as best she could and without showing her dismay. The main thing was to keep Jem away from the invasion of guests as much as possible; she would just have to stay in the nursery with her nursemaid and not complain about it. She knew that, if provoked, Jem would not be able to stop herself from saying something and it was bound to be insulting as Grace couldn't seem to cure her of her childlike honesty — and admitted to herself that she didn't really want to. Grace knew the child would hate being shut in; she was so used to having the run of the house and gardens and doing exactly as she pleased, as long as Gervase wasn't watching, being a prisoner was going to test both of them to their limits. She had a feeling that the next few weeks were going to be a kind of living hell that she couldn't avoid however hard she tried.

Sally helped her into the inconspicuous pale grey dress in watered silk which Gervase hated and made her look washed out but thankfully allowed her to blend into the background. She had perfected her ability to meld with the shadows, keeping very still and barely breathing, in the hopes that she would be overlooked by the visitors. She was relying upon Gervase being too ill to really notice what she was doing; in which case she would be able to slip from the room without him noticing.

At breakfast she was even less talkative than usual, allowing Captain Heywood and Mr Talmarch to dominate the conversation, and silently ignored the food on her plate.

"Lady Winterborne? You seem rather distracted this morning!" declared Emery.

She glanced up, "I'm so sorry, Mr Talmarch. I was just wondering if everything has been properly arranged for the visitors. Gervase is very particular."

"Of course, he likes things to be just so. It must be quite a trial for you. Still, you have Nate and me for support this time!"

"That is certainly a comfort. I've been thinking, gentlemen, as you will both be here for a while yet, would you please call me Grace? It would be so much easier, and I've never really felt much like Lady Winterborne — it feels as though I've stolen someone else's name and it doesn't really fit me properly."

"Of course, with pleasure, eh, Nate? Call me Emery!"

"Grace," said Nathaniel softly, "It couldn't be more apt. You can call me Nate, if you wish, although I'm more commonly addressed as Nathaniel. Emery's just too lazy and uses the shortest version he can."

"What about Nathan?" she asked him.

He smiled, "Alexander used to call me Nathan, so yes, that would also be most acceptable."

"Well, now that's all so politely settled — how shall we handle this influx of unwanted incomers? I vote that we just ignore them and carry on as usual!" announced Emery cheerily.

Grace laughed, "I only wish that were possible, but as you already know, having met them before, they are hard to ignore."

"Will Lord Winterborne be coming downstairs to receive them?"

"Yes, he wants to take up residence in the withdrawing room for now. He will hold court and entertain there. There's a very fine spinet and plenty of room for them to act out their plays and so on."

"That sounds grim," said Nathaniel.

"They're inclined to caterwaul into the early hours, under the illusion that they're singing!" exclaimed Emery, "You'd think, with a house this size, that you wouldn't be able to hear them upstairs but somehow the sound carries through the thick walls. I had a permanent headache the last time and had to excuse myself in the end and retire to my bedchamber and cover my ears with a pillow!"

"I can only apologise. It is beyond my very limited control," murmured Grace.

"We shall present a united front and see them off at the drawbridge. Would that we had a moat! With crocodiles in it!" said Emery, warming to his subject, "Or castellated turrets we could shoot arrows and muskets from. It would be such excellent sport! They're not exactly hard to spot. All those jewels and feathers. And their loud voices!"

Nathaniel rolled his eyes, "I expect you can tell that Emery wished to be on the stage when he was a child? Quite naturally his parents forbade him to ever go near a theatre, but he paid them not the slightest bit of notice, of course. He's always had the liveliest imagination and is keen to entertain people with his stories and antics. He likes to be the centre of attention which is the real reason he didn't take to your husband's friends, as they are scene stealers *par excellence*. If he is eclipsed, he storms off in a fit of pique."

Emery cast him a fulminating glance.

Grace smiled, "And you, Captain — Nathan, are you not interested in being the focus of attention?"

"No, indeed. My brother was the inveterate show-off in our family, and I was considered to be the introvert and therefore the oddity."

"I find that hard to believe. You seem to be exceedingly — sure of yourself."

"Twelve years in the army will help rid one of any lingering reservations. I quickly learnt to assert myself and take control — or be trampled upon and relegated to the ranks."

"It must have been hard if you were a reticent sort of boy."

"To begin with, yes, but as with everything, one eventually becomes inured to violence and deprivation. Otherwise, armies could not exist — which, of course, might be a good thing, now I come to consider it."

"We all become used to change but it doesn't always mean it's a good thing. I always wish things would just stay the same, but they never do."

"Change can lead one to other things that in the end might be beneficial," suggested Nathaniel.

Emery perked up, "Is this not exactly what I've been saying to you all along, Nate? You need to be more open to change. You're far too guarded. Look at me! I'm a fine example of someone who doesn't refuse at the first fence. If I come off in a ditch, I dust myself off and get back on the horse."

"You wouldn't be seen dead on a horse, Emery. You might get your coat soiled and that would never do."

Emery laughed, "All right, I will own that riding is not perhaps my chosen method of travel, but you must see that my analogy makes sense."

"Very little of what you say makes sense," remarked Nathaniel equably.

"*Why* are we friends? I shall never understand it!"

"Me neither."

Grace was enjoying this light-hearted exchange and had for a moment forgotten what the rest of the day was about to bring.

"I wish *this* would not change," she mused.

Her companions looked at her and she realised that she'd spoken her thought out loud and blushed, "I — I mean — well, I suppose I *do* mean that. This — is nice. Talking. Listening to you — " she faltered to a halt.

"You enjoy the spectacle of me being insulted by my dearest friend?" asked Emery indignantly.

She smothered a grin, "Well, yes, I must admit that I do! Is that very bad in me?"

"Not bad at all. I think it shows great perspicacity. Emery was made to be the target of jokes; he never really gets offended, and his behaviour is mostly laughable," responded Nathaniel with an amused glance at his friend.

"Oh, you see, now I am beginning to feel sorry for him," said Grace, her grey eyes gleaming.

"By Jove!" cried Emery hotly, "I'm right here in the room! Will you please stop talking about me as though I were invisible? And I am compelled to point out that I have feelings just like the next man, so your words can cut me! *If you prick me, do I not bleed?*"

Nathaniel shook his head in despair, "Misquoting Shakespeare now. Have you no shame?"

Emery let out a bellow of laughter, "No, absolutely none! As you are fully aware!"

"Actually, I'm impressed you can quote Shakespeare — you're not exactly bookish."

"Which is good because otherwise I'd prose on endlessly about the latest novels like you do, until everyone falls asleep in their porridge!"

Grace turned her still sparkling eyes upon Nathaniel, "Oh, do you read much? I thought perhaps as you were a soldier that you wouldn't have had much time for books."

Momentarily taken aback by the liveliness of her expression he paused briefly to regard her face, which in its habitual stillness was beautiful, in a distant sort of way, but when animated, was utterly bewitching. He cleared his throat, "I've always read whenever possible. It was a convenient way of removing myself from the tedium of army life although it wasn't always easy to obtain the books I wanted to read when billeted out in the wilderness."

"Oh, well do help yourself to the books in the library; Gervase has very well-stocked shelves with a gratifyingly wide variety of subjects," said Grace eagerly. "I could not be without books. I'm hoping to get Jem interested in them too, but to be frank the books written for children are dismal. It's no wonder they're not interested."

"Thank you, Grace, that's very generous and I'd be delighted to see what the library holds, especially as we may be here a while and Emery didn't bring any of my books with him even though I particularly asked him. I may even manage to get Emery to read something — if it has illustrations."

"Very amusing," said Emery looking much put upon.

"Mind you, I doubt there would have been room for any books with the vast number of coats and hats you elected to bring with you. Just as though we'd be going to the theatre every night."

"One can but live in hope."

* * *

Grace and Jemima walked slowly down the huge staircase, holding hands rather tightly. Jemima had been reluctantly put in her very best gown with the blue sash and had her hair furiously brushed until it fell into shining curls onto her shoulders, and she'd been lectured *ad nauseam* on how to behave until she'd wanted to throw something. Then, she'd had her face washed for the *second* time that day which had been the last straw and outraged tears had welled up and coursed down her face. Her nursemaid, Bridie had roundly ticked her off and told her to stop being so childish, which Jemima thought was a ridiculous thing to say. She'd stated mulishly that she *was* a child! At which point Grace had flown in and gathered her into her arms and hugged her and Jemima had cast Bridie a look of triumph over her mother's shoulder. Bridie had told Grace that she spoiled the child and would one day be made to regret it and Grace had ignored her and kissed away Jemima's tears.

At the bottom of the stairs, was a group of servants all awaiting the arrival of their guests, whose carriages had been spotted in the distance, making their way down the avenue towards the house. The staff were straightening their wigs and adjusting aprons and cravats, then lining up on the steps before the house like statues, just waiting for the order to leap into action.

Gervase had been carried by the footmen in a chair from his bedchamber to the withdrawing room and was now settled in front of the open bay windows, with a rug over his knees, ready to receive his friends.

Grace smiled down at her daughter who looked cross and took a deep breath. Her hands were shaking slightly and her heart thumping loudly in her ears.

She had done this before so she could do it again, she thought, as she heard the foreboding sound of carriage wheels on the gravel drive. She just wanted to run away.

There was a quiet movement beside her and she glanced around to see Nathan looking down at her and, moving to her other side, Emery, wearing the most dazzling coat of purple satin. She took a shuddering, relieved breath and smiled at them vaguely and then her attention was drawn to the sound of carriage doors opening, horses whinnying and the unwelcome sound of strident voices. She moved forward, flanked by the two gentlemen and with Jemima clutching her hand, to greet the first of the visitors.

"Gad! George Carew! As I live and breathe! What a delight to see your disagreeable face!" cried Emery, with not an ounce of sincerity.

Nathaniel saw Grace flinch and he too stepped forward to block Carew's path to his hostess.

"We haven't met, Mr Carew but I have heard a great deal about your exploits so am naturally thrilled to finally meet the gentleman behind all the gossip." They shook hands and Nathaniel saw the man's eyes slide sideways to Grace and whilst still managing to stand in his way, he allowed Carew to briefly bow over Grace's hand and then Nathaniel was moving him resolutely onwards into the Hall.

Grace watched as he was led inexorably away. George Carew, self-made businessman, was of above average height with excellent proportions, a handsome countenance and a good head of sandy coloured hair and pale freckly skin. He had a habit of thrusting his head forward and staring from his pale, almost silver eyes and wherever she was, she could always feel those eyes upon her. He made her desperately uneasy, and she loathed his limply wandering hands, wishing she had a knife to chop them off to stop him touching her flesh.

She turned to hold out her hand to the next visitor and managed somehow to look as though she were pleased to see them again. Emery stayed by her side and deflected any of the party who needed to be steered past Grace and the glowering child.

"Ah, Marcus Delamere! Good to see you. You know Lady Winterborne? Yes, I thought so, and this is their daughter, Lady Jemima. A footman will take you to your bedchamber in a moment. Is that Peter Leventhorpe? Haven't seen you in years!" said Emery, not pausing to draw breath. "*Thankfully!*" out of the corner of his mouth, *sotto voce*. "What have you been doing with yourself; you look a bit rattled! Hiding from that deplorable wife of yours? Don't blame you! Oh, what's that? She's *here* with you! Ah, Mrs Leventhorpe, you look radiant! Come, there are refreshments, you must be parched after such a journey. A footmen — ah, there, *off* you go! Curse it, Peter what in God's name made you *bring* her?"

"Had no choice!" responded Leventhorpe gloomily. "She insisted upon coming with me. Never get married, is my advice. Going to ruin all my fun."

"Not planning to, dear fellow, not planning to!" said Emery as he pushed Leventhorpe further into the Hall after his wife. "This is like a party made in Hell!" muttered Emery under his breath to Grace.

"Oh, I thought just the same earlier! Oh, no! Look, it's Lady Cheyne, how awful! She hoped Gervase might choose her daughter instead of me, so she hates me. I began to wonder if she didn't rather fancy him herself," whispered Grace.

"What a hideous picture that conjures up! Oh, do allow me! Lady Cheyne! I'm trying desperately to recall your elder daughter's name — Joan? Jane? Ah, of course, Agnes! Is she yet married? No? Such an adorable girl! So, graceful in the dance and the voice of an angel," as he turned to lead Lady

Cheyne away, he made a face at Grace, curling his lip and crossing his eyes and Grace had to choke back a giggle.

"That won't do, Grace," said a pleasant and most welcome voice at her side and she found Nathaniel had taken Emery's place. "Where are your manners?"

"I'm sorry but it was Emery — " she breathed.

"Of course it was. He's despicable. He has no care for propriety and can barely be civil if he's caught by one of his mischievous whims. I daresay that this sort of thing will all be too much for him and he'll test us to our limits. He's very likely to insult everyone so badly they'll all leave early."

"Oh, I do hope he does then!" said Grace hopefully, "For this is more than we can bear. Poor Jem, having to stand here being silent and still. You're doing so well, darling, it won't be long now and then you can go and play in the garden."

Jemima frowned, "I want cake, Mama."

"You shall have some, as soon as we've done what Papa wants," she bent down and whispered in her daughter's ear, "We can go and paddle in the fountain if you'd like?"

She was rewarded with a beaming smile, "Yes. That would be werry nice. I'm hot."

"It won't be long now. Just a few more visitors to greet. Then cake and paddling!"

"Heaven forfend!" said a grating voice, "Is that a *child*?"

Grace clenched her teeth as she heard the sound of someone approaching and looked up into the almost black, lifeless eyes.

"Lady Standon, we're so glad you could come. This is our daughter Jemima and Captain Nathaniel Heywood."

Jemima twisted her mouth into a small knot and glowered even harder, but Nathaniel turned his most devastating smile upon the woman. She had once been very beautiful and still thought she could bring men to their knees with just a look, and she favoured Nathaniel with what she obviously thought was a coquettish smile and was gratified to find that he immediately responded with a smouldering glance.

"Captain Heywood, you weren't here last time. I would have certainly remembered your handsome face!"

Nathaniel took her hand in his and dropped a lingering kiss onto it, "Ah, Lady Standon, tales of your famed beauty have had me yearning to meet you. And I see that it was all indeed true. You're a veritable goddess. I count myself most fortunate to be here, able to gaze upon such radiance."

Lady Standon smacked his arm with her fan and giggled girlishly, "We're going to have such frolics, you and I, Captain! I simply cannot wait."

Just then a small crowd of people all arrived in the Hall together, jostling each other and all seemingly talking at a once.

"The Theatricals," said Grace faintly.

Eight

They were like a flock of preening, shrieking peacocks she thought, and involuntarily moved slightly closer to Nathaniel for safety.

Nathaniel, aware of her surreptitious shift towards him, glanced down at her, "What a damnable rabble! But don't worry, I won't leave your side."

Grace couldn't take her eyes from the dreadful vision making its way towards her. A group of actors and actresses, dressed up to the nines, fans and feathers fluttering, voices shrill and unrelenting even as they approached their hostess, seemed to be in some kind of collective choreographed ballet, arms waving, heads nodding, skirts swishing and advancing upon her all at once like an appalling tidal wave of ostrich feathers and silk, cheap glittering jewellery and even cheaper overpowering scent; she took a step backwards but felt a resolute hand in the small of her back, supporting her and she stopped and stood firm, facing her foes with all the fortitude she could muster.

'Excellent," said Nathaniel quietly and she held out her hand again to continue greeting the nameless and faceless creatures before her. Afterwards she could recall none of them; their features were so heavily disguised with the blank white of Venetian ceruse and their cheeks rouged and patched, they were more like puppets than humans, apart from the constant noise they made.

It took perhaps ten minutes to speak to them all and to allow Nathaniel to encourage them through into the main part of the Hall, but it felt like a lifetime to Grace. She could feel their eyes boring into her and knew they were whispering about her behind their hands. She just wanted it to be over. She caught Bridie's eye, as she lurked on the edge of the room, waiting for instructions and asked her to take Jemima away to the nursery and for once the little girl went willingly, glad to escape.

Still being shepherded by Nathaniel, she moved into the melee of assorted people and attempted to speak with some of them, with what she hoped was the kind of stately dignity expected of the lady of the manor.

All the time she felt the still but insistent presence of the Captain beside her and for the first time since she'd arrived at Winterborne, she felt sustained and not alone. It was a very curious feeling after years of neglect and isolation.

She spent an hour or so exchanging pleasantries and asking what she thought were inane questions or listening to Nathaniel and Emery talking and laughing with her guests — her terrible, hateful guests. The crowd gradually thinned out as they made their way to their bedchambers to rest and then wash and change and prepare themselves for dinner. Some had already found their way into the withdrawing room and were kicking up a rumpus with their host; she could hear the spinet being tunelessly tinkled.

Then, finally there was a moment when they had all gone and she was feeling a little overwhelmed, her chest was constricted and her breathing shallow. She just knew she had to run and hide, even if it was only for a short while, so she dashed up the stairs and along the corridor to her bedchamber but saw, coming out of one of the guest rooms, several of the Theatricals, all chattering mindlessly and laughing, and she stopped in her tracks and panicked, not wishing to be seen in her current state of wretchedness.

Then suddenly, she found herself being grabbed around her waist and swept out of the corridor and into the darkness of a nearby linen cupboard. She opened her mouth to scream but a laughing voice told her to be quiet. She snapped her mouth shut.

The raucous voices continued outside in the corridor, just a few feet from the cupboard and they could hear them talking.

She started to say something angrily.

Nathaniel put a gentle finger to her lips, "Ssssh. Be still."

Grace held her breath, listening. There wasn't much room and she realised that his arm was still around her waist. She knew she should protest but didn't dare, it wouldn't do to be caught in a linen cupboard with anyone but her husband. She could feel the strength of him and for some unfathomable reason felt entirely safe, which shook her as she had never felt safe with anyone other than perhaps Jem and Sally. There was no light at all, but she could hear him breathing. She could smell him. He smelt faintly of something musky and spiced. He smelt clean and warm and comforting. She had the sudden inexplicable desire to rest her head against his chest; to just rest and let him make the decisions, to take away her worries. Disconcerted by her own treacherous thoughts, she pulled away, trying to get some distance between them.

"We can't be in here — they might find us! What if Gervase — ?"

"Hush."

"*Nathan!*"

He pulled her closer to him and stopped her whispering with his mouth. She gasped but he just pressed his lips harder against hers. He pulled her tightly to his body and held her there, his kiss becoming a little more insistent and urgent.

The voices faded away outside.

She turned her face away and kicked his shin as hard as she could through her skirts, and he gave a muffled groan which wasn't entirely pain and reluctantly let her go.

"How *dare* you!" she hissed into the darkness.

"I was just trying to keep you from being found *in flagrante delicto*! It seemed the only way to stop you giving us away and causing a monumental scandal."

"Oh — I — you're *insufferable*! Vile, *odious* creature!"

"First kiss, I'm surmising?"

She was silent.

She knew he was smiling as he said quietly, "I thought so, although I'll admit I'm somewhat surprised. Well, I'm gratified to have been your first, would that I could also take the next as well."

She made an infuriated sound somewhere between a sigh and a growl and pushed at the door with her fists.

He opened it and released her, like an escaping wild thing, back into the corridor. He watched her storm away with a glint in his eye and then cursed, "Damn it all to hell. You utter blockhead."

"Who's a blockhead?" asked Emery coming upon him leaning against the linen cupboard door and gazing distractedly down the now empty corridor.

Nathaniel straightened up and adjusted his neckcloth, "*I* am. Just gave into my not-so-worthy instincts without thinking it through first and am now, I've no doubt, about to be thrown out of Winterborne on my ear."

"What the devil have you done, Nate?"

"Hmm? Oh, I just kissed the Marchioness in the linen cupboard."

"You — *you what? Kissed?* Grace? How? Why?"

"Because I felt a sudden urge to do so. So, I did. Which might possibly turn out to be a mistake."

"I should *say* so! You utter dolt!" Emery paused in his rebuke, "What were you *doing* in the linen cupboard in the first place? Seems damned smoky to me!"

"As I say, it was merely an impulse. One which I'm already regretting."

"What if she goes to Lord Winterborne?"

"She won't, of that much I am certain. But I may have shot myself in the foot as far as she's concerned."

"You don't say!" said Emery sarcastically. "And what of the Marquis's grand scheme?"

"That may have been brought to *point non plus*, I'm afraid."

"So, because of your insatiable appetites, we're destined to be penniless for the rest of our days?"

"I *kissed* her. I didn't rape her. Her first kiss, by the bye, which is interesting."

"Her first! Surely not! How can that be? Oh. Are you saying — ?"

"I'm saying that Grace has never been kissed before — even by her husband of four years."

Emery said nothing for a moment and Nathaniel watched as he tried to fathom things out in his head.

"Ganymede?" he offered helpfully and waiting patiently for the light to finally dawn.

Emery's eyes suddenly opened wide, "Oh! *Oh!* Hell and damnation! Are you *sure?* But how can that be? They are *married!*"

"The Marquis desperately needs an heir as his health is now failing fast. This was to be his way of achieving those ends, but his previous way of life has put a stop to his plans and that, my slow-witted friend, is where you and I come into it."

"He's — he's — "

"Yes, Emery, he is, well done, and so are several of this joyous bunch of people he has staying. Which is all well and good, but Grace and Jemima are caught up in the middle of it and it isn't right for them to be here alone. That Carew has his eye on her for sure. If we're not evicted forthwith, we will have to stand guard and not let her be alone with any of them."

"Or *you*, by the sound of it! Gad! What an adventure this is turning out to be!"

"Emery, you know I wouldn't hurt her? Not for the world. She's — she — "

Emery eyed his companion shrewdly, "Ha! I knew it! She's growing on you. That's absolutely fascinating. The biter bit. Don't you *dare* hurt that girl or you'll have me to answer to and I have a fairly sound right hook!"

Nathaniel laughed, "No you don't. You punch like an old lady. You were a laughingstock at the Ring. And, you know damn well that I don't mean to hurt her. It was just a kiss."

"Just a kiss to *you* maybe, but to *her?* When she's been starved of affection? And she's in such obvious need of comfort and support despite that impressively serene facade she hides behind."

"Since when did *you* become so compassionate or perspicacious? God, you think I don't know all of this, Emery? I'm not a complete idiot. Anyway, you're the one who's been pushing me to take her to my bed. After all, that's why we're really here. To make her fall in love with me and sire a child and for you to get paid your damn blood-money so that you can buy more purple coats. None of it reflects particularly well upon either of us. None of us come out of this covered in glory apart from maybe Jem and Grace. Are you now backing down and saying that you don't want me to complete the task?"

"No, I — well, I suppose we *must* or else I'll end my days in Newgate and will bring shame upon my family and when I finally wither away and die in a miserable cesspool of a prison cell, you'll have to live with the guilt of having done nothing to save me and I'll have to dress in filthy rags and the other prisoners will steal my wig and my quizzing glass and my father's gold pocket watch, which has a great deal of sentimental value for me," he said confidingly.

Nathaniel took his friend by the shoulders and gave him a friendly shake, "Firstly, I would *never* let you die in a prison cell and secondly, I'd bring you a change of clothing and naturally I'd keep all your valuables safely until your release and thirdly, do you want me to complete this assignment or not? You need to make up your mind."

"If I say yes, would you be able to bring yourself to do it? And if I say no, could you leave her now that you know how she must live and what her future might be?"

For a long moment Nathaniel said nothing and then, "Say yes," he said quietly.

* * *

Grace sat on the edge of her bed and tried not to think. She tried to block out everything. All the people in the house. All the dangers that were circling her like peckish vultures. And the changes which were all happening too suddenly for her peace of mind. She didn't like change. She liked steadiness and not being taken by surprise. She liked ordinary. She liked being kissed.

She stared blindly out of the window across the garden, the verdant green distance shimmering in the unaccustomed June heat, two gardeners working hard at pruning shrubs, Dancer and Thisbe lying in the sun, panting.

She saw only darkness. She smelt only clean linen and a faint musky scent. She felt only safe and comforted. She felt unfamiliar stirrings somewhere deep inside, which she considered for a long while and hoped it wasn't desire. She had never felt anything like it before. It was as though she were frightened, hungry, happy and excited all at the same time. It was horribly confusing. She had wanted to slap Nathan but at the same time she'd wanted him to kiss her again. And again. She was angry with him. She didn't want her routine to be changed; she didn't want the balance of her life to be disrupted by emotions she couldn't control. Although the sudden surge of passion she'd felt in the darkness of the linen cupboard had taken her by surprise, she was afraid of it and what it might bring to her strangely ordered life. She'd turned it into anger; anger against Nathan and now herself. She was used to suppressing her resentment. Despite all of that, she still wanted to run and find Nathan and beg him to hold her again. To risk everything for a few moments of what would be in the end just meaningless joy.

She buried her face in her hands and moaned softly. What was she to do? How could she cope with the next few weeks? She wanted desperately to order Nathan to leave Winterborne so that she could breathe easily again. She suddenly found that she wanted all kinds of things that she'd never even considered before. It was as though she was waking from a deep sleep.

Just as though she'd been in a dream, where she'd already drowned and was floating lifelessly downstream, all hope lost. Then as her eyes could no longer see and her ears no longer hear, her skin numb and her memory erased, she was being hauled from the cold water and back into the warm, scented air. In that linen cupboard she'd taken her first breath. But now, she was terrifyingly alive and feeling far too much. She wanted it to stop. But, at the same time, she wanted more.

She moaned again.

There was a tapping at the door and Sally let herself in. She took one look at her mistress and dashed to her side and threw her arms about her, "What's happened, m'lady? Is it terrible bad?"

Grace nodded mutely and leant her head on Sally's shoulder.

"Has Lord Winterborne — ?"

Grace shook her head, "No. It's me. I've done something so appalling."

"Whatever it is, I'll gladly take the blame!" cried Sally defiantly.

Grace let out a small puff of laughter, "No, you can't. I — I've done something so stupid — so dangerous — "

Sally gasped, "You've *killed* his lordship! Oh, m'lady! This is *such* good news!"

"No, *Sally!*" exclaimed Grace, "Don't be ridiculous! Of course I haven't killed him!" The look of disappointment on her maid's face was enough to make her go off into helpless peals of giggles and fall sideways onto the bed. "I'm so sorry to let you down but I couldn't *murder* anyone! I can't even squash an insect. Your *face!* Imagine trying to get away with killing him in a houseful of people! It would be impossible."

"I could find a way," said Sally, sullenly.

"I'm sure you could but there would be no point as he's dying anyway. I don't want you to go to prison or to the gallows."

"Well, if you say so but just say the word — ! But, then what did you do that's so bad, m'lady?"

Grace sobered and closed her eyes against the powerful images in her mind, "I — I allowed Captain Heywood to kiss me in the linen cupboard!"

Sally's chin practically hit her chest as her mouth opened in a soundless gasp of surprise, "*My lady!*" she breathed, "Captain Heywood? In the linen cupboard?" Her cheeks flushed a delicate pink, "That's so — *romantic!*"

Grace's eyebrows went up and her eyes opened wide, "Romantic? No, no, no! It wasn't at all. It was peculiar and disturbing and — and — "

"Passionate? Tender? Loving?" suggested Sally happily.

"No! It was — frightening and I wanted to hit him."

"*Did* you hit him?"

"I kicked him!"

"Oh, my lady! You are so funny! But, if I may ask, why were you in a linen cupboard in the first place?"

"He pulled me in there to save me from being seen by some of those horrid Theatricals. But — it was dark and he — well, he held me — so close — and kissed me so — nicely."

"*Oh!*" sighed Sally ecstatically, "He is so very handsome! His eyes! So laughing! His voice, oh, so like treacle!"

"*Treacle?*" marvelled Grace, falling into laughter again. "Anyone would think you were in love with him yourself!

Sally grinned sheepishly, "No, m'lady, not me! Although, he's even nicer than the footman, Robert."

"Robert? A footman has caught your eye, has he?"

The young maid stood up and busied herself with folding up some clothes thrown over the back of a chair, "No, m'lady. Not at all. I would *never*, not with a footman!"

"Well, not until he puts a ring on your finger I should hope!"

Sally pouted, "That ain't never going to happen, he's far too pleased with himself, so he is!"

"Puffed up with his own consequence, is he?"

"Yes, he is, he thinks he's the crown jewels ever since he came here to work."

"And remind me, what does Robert look like?"

"He's not too tall and not too handsome," said Sally, twisting her mouth to one side as she considered. "He has blue eyes but not as blue as the Captain's and a broken tooth at the front."

"He sounds absolutely delightful. I must try to make his acquaintance so that I can see what all the fuss is about," she smiled, "You're right, the Captain does indeed have very blue eyes."

"Oh, m'lady, do you like him?" asked Sally, clasping her hands together under her chin.

There was a long pause while Grace stared into space, "Yes, I suppose I do, in a way. He — makes me feel safer — even when he captures me and drags me into a linen cupboard. I suppose I'm beginning to trust him, which I must say is a very new and pleasant sensation for me. I'm so used to being wary of everyone. I *was* suspicious at first, when he arrived out of the blue, I thought that he must just be another of Gervase's odd friends from London — but he seems to be as wary of them as I am and today when they arrived, he stayed beside me and protected me. It was wonderful."

"Oh, I can just picture it," sighed Sally.

Grace frowned and shook her head, "This won't do at all! I'm a married woman! I have a child. Oh, my! I've let the heat go to my head. What a fool I am. What was I thinking? Now I have to face him at dinner! I must make sure I don't give him the wrong ideas."

Sally went to the press and pulled out an open gown in a rich Chinese cerulean blue silk with a floral pattern woven in silver thread and triple frills on the elbow length sleeves and a low square neckline, "This one, I think for tonight, my lady. We want to make our entrance on the very first night and show them who is the lady of the manor. I'll do your hair simple, with just a silver riband and that nice little pearl clip and perhaps just the pearl necklace?"

Grace looked at the as yet unworn gown and knew that it would make a declaration of intent nobody could mistake and would show that she was not to be trifled with, "Yes, I'll wear it," she said with a slight smile.

Nine

Nathaniel and Emery were in the withdrawing room and neither were happy. They exchanged a glance across the congested room which said as much and although Emery was holding forth and being as entertaining as ever, Nathaniel's smile went nowhere near his eyes. He'd been cornered by an actress and a ballet dancer and other than pushing them to one side and making a run for it, there was no escape.

Others from the company were gathered around Lord Winterborne, as he sat in state at the other end of the room, in the bay window as though on his own stage. The spinet was being idly played by another of the Theatricals who was humming a vague tune.

Emery was trapped on a sofa with Mrs Leventhorpe, who was looking so disapprovingly at the dancers and actors; she looked as though she'd been sucking a lemon. Emery was trying desperately to keep her amused by telling her fanciful tales of his exploits, but her gimlet eyes continued to roam the room alighting with distaste upon the various eye-catching costumes and the glittering jewels, the towering wigs and the shocking amount of flesh on show. She was longing to get her husband alone in their bedchamber and give him a thorough scolding. She was able to see him out of the corner of her eye, eagerly leaning in towards a very buxom lady of middle years, wearing an outrageously low-cut gown of eye-wateringly yellow satin; she was coquettishly flapping her fan in front of her heavily made-up face and stroking his arm suggestively. Mrs Leventhorpe was simmering with poorly disguised rage.

Lord and Lady Standon and Mr Marcus Delamere were circling the room talking to various members of the company and already drinking rather too much.

In a chair beside the fire slouched Mr George Carew, brandy in hand and his gaze pinned upon one of the voluptuous young actresses swaying to the music. Nathaniel, catching sight of him from across the room, was uneasily aware of the man's predatory air and he knew he'd be looking for weaknesses he could exploit, so that he could then insinuate himself closer to his prey. Nathaniel realised that it was going to be the devil's own job to keep him distracted and away from Grace. He felt that the other ladies in the group were perfectly capable of looking after themselves, having spent a lifetime in the theatre fighting off unwanted admirers, or — not fighting them off. He glanced at the clock and was just wondering where she was when a footman opened the double doors, and the Marchioness entered the room.

Nathaniel wasn't the only one to catch his breath. There were several audible gasps around the room, some filled with admiration, some laced with jealousy. He glanced quickly at Lord Winterborne and caught his expression of pride at the appreciative reception his wife was receiving, she being the crowning glory of his collection.

She stood on the threshold for a moment and surveyed the faces all turned towards her. There was an infinitesimal pause before she smiled, just long enough to make sure everyone knew who she was and that she really didn't think much of the company. It was perfect. The pause conveyed a good deal, the smile was cool and her bearing regal. As she crossed the room, he watched her progress with fascination. This was the haughty woman who had greeted him when he'd first arrived when she'd shown none of the warmth, he now knew she possessed. And underneath the carefully constructed facade was just a young girl pretending to be lady of the manor, wife of a Marquis. The gown spoke volumes. It spoke of a long line of aristocratic ancestors who metaphorically stood behind her and of her present elevated position and the abundant wealth at her fingertips and it said, above everything, keep your distance. It said look — but don't touch.

He suddenly had an almost uncontrollable desire to disobey that order and had to crush the thought very firmly. Whatever happened, he had to make sure that he kept his distance too; the last thing he needed was the burden of another man's wife hanging around his neck. If he were to complete this preposterous task, he must be able, at the conclusion, to disappear without any regrets or added responsibilities attached to him like leeches. He had no need for a ready-made family or to be encumbered with anyone so obviously in need of someone to watch over her. He knew that although she was studiously ignoring him that she was well aware of his presence and he had to admit that he couldn't blame her for treating him so. He'd acted like a complete idiot and in just one reckless moment he'd undone any good he'd previously managed to achieve. Now she was bound to give him a wide berth and Emery would probably have a better chance of making headway with her. He had burnt his boats.

He was still observing her as she reached her husband and held out her hand for him to kiss.

It was at that point Emery, watching the gentle drama unfold as well, saw his friend turn away, repulsed by what he'd witnessed, and he couldn't help a slight smirk as Nathaniel resolutely returned his attentions to the simpering ballet dancer and the brassy actress, his expression rigid. Emery knew that face and it could only mean trouble ahead.

* * *

Grace made her way around the room, graciously making an attempt to include everyone in her welcome. The gown swished heavily around her feet and the bodice was pleasantly stiff, holding her up and supporting her like a firm embrace. She felt as though she could not be vanquished whilst wearing it. When she finally reached the fireplace, George Carew got to his feet with no urgency at all; he stood waiting for her to reach him and bowed courteously. She stayed a few steps away and was reluctantly drawn into a stilted conversation with him. Her frosty reception to his flattering words was plain to see and she answered his questions with a brevity bordering on rudeness. He didn't seem to notice this slight and continued on conversing as though they were the very best of friends.

Nathaniel was listening with one ear and found it hard to believe that anyone would be prepared to be treated so shabbily by their hostess and not show some displeasure.

Eventually she broke away from Carew and had no choice but to stop and talk to Nathaniel and the actress and dancer. She couldn't have been any stiffer had she been frozen solid. His mouth twisted into a wry smile as she approached him, and her cold grey eyes reluctantly met his. The only sign of their previous meeting was a delicate, telltale pink flush across her cheekbones. If anything, it made her look even more beautiful.

"Lady Winterborne, you've already been introduced to Miss Elvira Dean and Mrs Mary Redman? They were just regaling me with some very — detailed descriptions of their lives in the theatre. It's probably not for your ears. I'm not even sure it's fit for mine."

"Oh, Captain Heywood!" cried Miss Dean, "You are such a lark! As *though* we'd say anything which might offend such a very proper lady! We know how to behave in society, don't we Molly?"

"Indeed we do!" declared Mrs Redman, her voice harshly nasal, "We mix with the best of 'em! Royalty comes to our theatre to see us perform. We rub shoulders with 'em. They've always liked a bit of playacting and I've acted with the best, y'know! I've had my share of standing ovations and bouquets, *I* can tell you! And the gentlemen callers after the show! Oh, dear, perhaps I shouldn't have said that! They only come to leave little *billet-doux* and flowers and sweetmeats, which is what I like best of all. Flowers only last a short while and then have to be thrown away. At least I can get some lasting pleasure from a box of stuffed dates!"

"But what about the sentiment behind the flowers?" asked Grace quietly, "Each flower holds a different message. For instance, violets mean loyalty and marigolds, despair."

"Well, ain't that a thing! Who'd have thought? Perhaps I'll look more closely at them from now on then!" said Mrs Redman, flashing Nathaniel a saucy look.

Grace was slightly dismayed to see him return the glance with a flirtatious one of his own. She surreptitiously studied the actress and thought she was a good deal older than she was pretending to be and there was something so grasping about her that she wondered at Nathan's rather surprising lack of judgement. But she thought crossly, perhaps he liked women to be so blatantly available, to be so forward. He was a soldier after all and used to having lewd camp followers within easy reach. She inwardly shuddered as she considered his previous life and decided that she'd made the right decision to snub him. She had no wish to become just another one of his conquests and was determined to teach him a lesson on how to behave with decorum.

Nathaniel was aware that Grace had suddenly drawn herself up and looked, if it were possible, even more distant and unapproachable. She was clearly not impressed by his high-spirited companions. She was exuding frost like an early morning in January. What a strange woman she was, like no other he'd ever met. He realised that he had no idea how to handle her. He tried to meet her eyes to convey his true feelings about the company they were being forced to keep but her gaze shied away, leaving him frustrated. How was he to convince her that he was sorry for his impulsive actions when she wouldn't even look at him?

The ballet dancer was staring at Grace intently, "You have a daughter? You don't look old enough to have a child! How old are you? Eighteen?"

"Twenty," replied Grace briskly. "My daughter, Jemima is five."

Elvira Dean laughed loudly, "Well, even *I* can do the arithmetic on that! Did you give birth when you were *fourteen?* Heaven forbid! Were you a child-bride?"

"No. She's my step-daughter."

More laughter, "Oh, that makes more sense! Molly and I were wondering, but Gervase hadn't explained. You're his *second* wife?"

"Yes."

"Ah, I see. I must say I was quite surprised when I discovered he was married at all —"

"Elvira! No, *really!* Too far, my love! Not our business, eh?" protested Mrs Redman, smacking Miss Dean sharply on her arm with her fan.

Miss Dean glared at her friend and rubbed her smarting arm, "How was I to know? Common knowledge, surely?"

"No, it's not. Anyway, your daughter, Lady Winterborne, will we be able to meet her or is she to be kept away from such unsuitable company?"

Grace blushed and flicked a glance at Nathaniel, "Gervase will require that she come and make her curtsy at some point soon, I expect."

"I can't wait! I love children. Do she look like her mother?" asked Miss Dean.

"I'm sorry to say that I never met her mother but, apparently, she does resemble her, a little, although she has Gervase's colouring. Brown hair and brown eyes. There is a painting of the first Lady Winterborne in the Long Gallery which you can see tomorrow if you wish."

"We'll take a look at that, won't we Vira? Is there one of you too?"

"Not yet, it's just being painted but won't be finished for a while yet. Jemima's in it too."

"It sounds lovely. You're certainly very beautiful — ain't she Captain Heywood?"

The Captain studied Grace's face for a second, "Yes, she is, very beautiful," he said softly and watched her mouth tighten as his gaze lingered upon it. And then suddenly he just laughed out loud, the whole ridiculous situation making him realise the absurdity of this life that had been thrust upon him, leaving him at the total mercy of deranged strangers. He thought of the logic and order of his army existence and laughed even more. What the hell was to become of him? What was he *doing* here?

"What's so funny, Captain?" demanded Mrs Redman, querulously.

He shook his head, still grinning, "I was just thinking that life is like that cursed Maze out there in the garden — all twists and turns and dead ends and very little real reward at the end of it."

"I've heard of the famous maze. I cannot wait to take a peek. Did you enjoy it?"

"Enjoy is rather a strong word. I endured it for the sake of my friend, but I found it to be a bit dismal with very little to show for all the effort one must put into finding your way through it. Much like life."

"Can you tell us what is at the centre of it?"

"No, madam, I cannot, for that is part of the — er — "fun". Finding the treasure at its heart."

"Well, now you *have* got me all excited!" declared Mrs Redman, pouting her pinched mouth at him. "It really doesn't do for me to get all of a flutter! Bad for my nerves!"

Grace was beginning to feel slightly queasy and very deliberately looked over at her husband, "Oh, I'm dreadfully sorry but I simply must go to Gervase. He has signalled for me," she lied and quickly moved away from them but not before catching the barely audible snort of derision from Nathaniel.

A footman brought wine and champagne and Nathaniel downed one glass of wine as though he were parched, replaced the empty vessel back on the tray and took another. If he stayed at Winterborne much longer, he mused, he was in danger of becoming a drunkard.

Lord and Lady Standon sauntered across the room towards Nathaniel and once more he was looking around for an escape route but seeing none, steeled himself to make polite conversation with them.

"Captain Heywood, I was telling my husband all about you! Obviously not in enough detail to make him jealous but just enough to pique his interest. You must tell him all about your army career — he always yearned to be a soldier."

"Did he indeed? And what stopped you, my lord?" asked Nathaniel, with a disarming smile.

Lord Standon returned the smile but with much less charm whilst eyeing Nathaniel with some reservation, "I come from a long line of army stock — father, grandfather and two uncles. Expected, y'know? I alway thought I'd buy a commission — but my health, y'know? Very poor. My lungs. Not suitable soldier material."

Nathaniel, observing with interest, the robust-looking individual before him, couldn't help a slight sneer curling his lip, "That's most unfortunate. You must have been devastated. Although, it must be said that the army life isn't for everyone. It can be brutal and has been known to break many a stouthearted fellow who thought it would be child's play, leaving them face down in a waterlogged ditch with splintered wagonwheels and worn-out and discarded boots."

Lord Standon's smile faltered and was replaced with uncertainty, "As you say, Captain, a hard life but one I would have gladly chosen had I been able. My lungs, you understand, weakened by serious childhood illness."

Nathaniel said nothing, leaving Lord Standon to flounder. He'd heard it all before and had very little sympathy left. The army wouldn't have benefited from someone of Standon's calibre, but he should just be honest and admit he wasn't cut out to be a soldier – there was no shame in that. It was the lying he couldn't tolerate. The pretence. Then he heard the sound of his own hypocrisy and felt momentarily abashed. He was lying to Grace about why he'd been invited to Winterborne and lying about why he was remaining. Unfortunately, he would have to continue to lie to her as well, until he could come to some definitive decision about Lord Winterborne's plan. Time was running out; Lord Winterborne might be putting on a splendid show for his guests, but the doctor was adamant that he had only a few months at the most and Nathaniel had seen enough sickness and death amongst the troops to know that this was the truth.

"Well, in that case, it's probably for the best that you managed to steer clear of such an arduous career. I'm sure that your dear wife must be much relieved to have you by her side all the time. It must be such a comfort."

Lord Standon gave him a doubtful glance, as though he suspected he couldn't quite trust what the Captain was saying, but not wishing to make a fool of himself, he kept his suspicions to himself, "There is always much to do on the estate, as you surely know yourself!"

"Not at all. I have no estate, my lord. I don't own a house or any land, nothing apart from my horse," said Nathaniel blandly.

"Good God! Can this be true? But — are you not Viscount Heywood's son?"

"You could say that, although my family have taken the trouble to disown me. And I'm the *second* son. My brother Alexander inherited."

Lord Standon's eyes opened wide in dawning comprehension, "Ah! So, Drayton Hall goes to your brother?"

Nathaniel smiled, "It does and with my blessing too. I've no desire at all to be chained to that wretched place. Nor has my brother, but he has no say in the matter, poor devil. It has brought little joy to anyone's life."

"But to be rootless! How can you exist like that?"

"I lodge with my friend, Emery Talmarch and find that the nomadic life suits me very well. I am restless by nature," replied Nathaniel, enjoying himself.

"It seems a mighty odd way to carry on to me! Can't understand your reasoning at all. In my day we'd have given our right arm for a house and some land to call our own. Otherwise, what is to become of you? Are you expecting to marry into money?"

Nathaniel scoffed, "Marry money? I certainly hope not. What an appalling idea. I'd rather live in a cow byre or stay in the army and billet in a draughty tent. You may think me unnatural, my lord, but not everyone has a burning desire to be tied down to a lifetime of ruined harvests, collapsing roofs and outbreaks of foot-rot. It has never been my ambition to become either a glorified farmer or an employer of shepherds and housemaids."

"It seems to me, Captain that your ancestry means little to you, which says much about your character, I fear," said Lord Standon with some asperity.

"Why *should* it mean anything to me? I didn't know them. They have done nothing to earn my admiration or loyalty. Some of them, in fact, were decidedly inferior human beings. All we have in common is our name."

"But surely that is enough. Your name, Captain should be everything to you and you should defend it with your last breath like any proud Englishman!" exclaimed Lord Standon.

"It's just a name. I've willingly defended my country for twelve years and would continue to do so but there is little opportunity at the moment to prove one's allegiance, so I've decided to find another occupation," said Nathaniel in measured tones.

Lord Standon considered his companion, "And you mean to go into business with Gervase, I understand? I would have thought that there was very little security in doing that — at this juncture!"

"You're right. He offered me an opportunity and I've merely been deliberating my options and weighing up Lord Winterborne's generous offer whilst enjoying his lavish hospitality. It seemed like an offer I couldn't refuse. I have nowhere else I need to be at the moment." He glanced up and much to his relief saw Emery making his way towards him. "Emery, dear friend, come and defend my honour!"

Emery, wearing a coat of emerald green with silver braiding, joined them and bowed elegantly to the group, "Gentlemen, Ladies, charmed, as ever. Why am I to defend your honour, Nate? What is being said?"

"My patriotism is being called into question and my devotion to my family name."

Emery's face lit up, "I would never dare question your love of country but must reluctantly agree that, although you may still have a residual fondness for Alexander, you have next to no love for your ancestry or heritage or for anything which might mean that you cannot just pack a bag and ride away as soon as things get too vexatious, and people start expecting you to settle down."

"Thank you, Emery. I'm profoundly grateful for your stalwart support," said Nathaniel wryly, "I knew I could rely upon you."

Emery laughed, "Always! Lord Standon, your place is in Hertfordshire? It has a very fine deer park I'm told."

Lord Standon inclined his head smugly, "The finest in the south east of England. You must come and shoot with us, Mr Talmarch, be happy to put you up."

Devil take it, thought Nathaniel, here we go.

"I don't shoot," stated Emery very clearly and with a mischievous twinkle, "Or hunt. I barely ride. Not really the outdoor type."

Nathaniel wondered if Lord Standon was going to have a seizure, his mouth opened and closed several times and he'd turned an impressive shade of purple.

"I do own a very nice little townhouse though," continued Emery happily, "In Duke Street. Present from my grandfather."

Nathaniel taking a sip of his wine, tried not to choke.

Lord Standon appeared to have temporarily lost the powers of speech and was staring at Emery as though trying to fathom what he might really have said. "Duke Street, y'say? I knew your grandfather. Good man. Rode to hounds like a dashed Valkyrie!"

"Valkyrie? Were they not *female* warriors?" murmured Nathaniel, eyes gleaming.

Lord Standon cleared his throat, "No need to be pedantic, Captain! It hardly matters now anyway, fellow's been dead years."

"True, although I would remind you that Emery was exceedingly fond of him."

"I most humbly beg your pardon, Mr Talmarch. I did not intend — "

"Oh, devil a bit! None taken! He was a handful, my grandfather, I am not in the least like him. He thought nothing of riding from London to the south coast and catching a boat to France, on the merest whim. Or risking his life in any number of escapades even when he was in his eighties! I know that he was disappointed in me and felt I'd be safest settled in London so bought me the place in Duke Street to keep me from shaming him amongst his county friends."

Nathaniel, feeling a sudden prickling on the back of his neck, turned and saw Grace looking across the room at him. He glanced quickly at her husband and could see that he was slumped a little in his chair. Without a word of apology to his companions he strode across the room, weaving in and out of the guests, to reach her side as swiftly as possible.

"He became agitated and confused and then — this," said Grace in a low voice.

Nathaniel immediately summoned two footmen and ordered them to take his lordship back to his bedchamber.

Ten

It took a while to achieve the transfer from the withdrawing room as Lord Winterborne stirred himself enough to become irritable and did not wish to leave the gathering and was voluble in his displeasure. The footmen were roundly abused for their disloyalty and threatened with dismissal, as they bore him away in his chair and Grace somehow managed to ignore his swearing at her although her cheeks became a little pinker.

Once in the bedchamber, Nathaniel organised everything with military efficiency and Grace had nothing to do but watch.

As soon as his lordship was ensconced in his bed, Nathaniel sent one of the still lingering footmen to fetch the doctor and told the Marquis in very direct language that he'd better stay in his bed or suffer the dire consequences. Lord Winterborne, who was beginning to shake and feel sick, said nothing and closed his eyes.

The nursemaid, Mrs Hawkins, had been called and she came at once to assist.

Nathaniel suggested to Grace that she return to her guests, but she seemed understandably reluctant. The haughty Marchioness was gone, to be replaced by a nervous young girl who was clearly out of her depth but hiding it well. She looked tired and afraid, so Nathaniel just gestured to the seat beside the fireplace, and she obeyed, sinking into it gratefully.

Doctor Morton arrived an hour later and could only offer laudanum and much the same advice as before and left after conducting a brief examination of his patient.

Grace and Nathaniel were talking in the corridor outside the room, "I will go down and explain to everyone what has happened and tell them that you are detained in the sickroom. They will understand, I'm quite sure," said Nathaniel quietly.

Grace's eyes met his, "Thank you, Nathan. I will come down for dinner, of course."

He held her gaze for a moment, "If you're sure? Naturally, I will be there, and Emery, to provide support, should you need it."

She attempted a smile but when it didn't work, she gave up and pressed her lips together into a tight line, "That is a comfort because I find even under normal circumstances that so many people can be overwhelming," she took a deep breath, "Dinner will be in the Great Hall, not the dining room, which is like dining in a cathedral, and I find it rather intimidating."

"I can understand that. But this time you will have me at your elbow, and I will not allow anything untoward to happen."

"Last time — " she began in a whisper.

"No, do not think about it. Grace, I know — that you may be inclined not to trust me — after — "

She lowered her eyes, "The linen cupboard."

"Yes, I gave in to a regrettable impulse, but I want you to know that it will not happen again."

Her eyes darted back up to his and then she looked away in embarrassment, "I see," she said softly, "I suspect that, being a soldier, you're used to making decisions for everyone else?"

Nathaniel's eyebrows snapped together, "I thought this would certainly be mutual."

Grace stared hard along the dark corridor, "*Did* you?"

From inside the bedchamber, they both heard the Marquis calling for her in his delirium.

"Was I wrong?"

Grace said nothing. She put her hand on the door latch and paused for a second, her back to him, "Perhaps you shouldn't assume, Nathan."

"Grace — ?"

But she had gone, and he was left looking at the closed door in some confusion.

* * *

Grace stood with her back against the door looking blindly across the bedchamber at her dying husband. Her breath was coming in small, snatched gasps and her hands were shaking. What on earth had come over her? In just the briefest moment she had become someone she barely recognised. Mrs Hawkins glanced up at her and Grace was sure that she'd be able to see right through to her blighted soul. The nursemaid was ferociously God-fearing and, having heard all the rumours, had been longing to get her hands upon Lord Winterborne to try to bring him to God's glory and save him from Hell.

"Lady Winterborne? Are you all right?" asked Mrs Hawkins.

"Oh, I'm absolutely fine, thank you Mrs Hawkins. Just anxious."

"Well, of course you are. You would not be human if you were not suffering terribly over Lord Winterborne's tragic condition. Although, he has no one to blame but himself."

"That's a little unkind! He has his reasons — " began Grace defensively.

"Yes, my lady. Reasons which we cannot discuss but which God already knows because He is all-seeing."

"And surely — forgiving?"

Mrs Hawkins cast her a look of profound pity, "There are some things which can never be forgiven, my lady. Some sins are beyond even the powers of the Almighty."

"Is that so?" asked Grace coldly, "Then we must all look to our own souls because each one of us must be lost."

"You think you too are damned, my lady? I find that hard to believe. You seem so — virtuous."

Something in the way the woman said the word made Grace uneasy. "I would hardly say that I am virtuous — I doubt anyone but a child could be called that in all honesty."

Mrs Hawkins turned back to her sleeping patient, "I see things, my lady. I've noticed how things are here and even though I cannot find it in my heart to blame you, it is against the word of God and He will smite those who defy His word."

"You've noticed — *what* precisely?"

"I have seen how you are with Captain Heywood. And I have seen how he seeks to protect you, which is commendable, but you are a married woman, and your husband still lives," said the nursemaid as she carefully neatened the bedclothes. "I have also seen how your husband treats you and although he only uses words, those words are sometimes cruel. He does not deserve you. You're a good mother to the child which says a good deal about you. And the Captain — he's quite clearly a kind man and has your best interests at heart. But there is something about him — it's not my place to say — but you should be cautious about whom you trust when your judgment is impaired by grief and distress. This much I have learnt in my years looking after my patients."

Grace realised that she should not allow Mrs Hawkins to speak to her in such a familiar manner but although it went against what was acceptable behaviour, she was almost glad just to be able to talk to someone other than Sally even if the nursemaid was managing to make her even more unsure about Nathan and his reasons for being at Winterborne and about her own conduct. Everything had been so ordered and almost bearable before; she had finally managed to arrange her life so that she and Jemima could find some happiness together, but now it was all topsy-turvy and she'd lost control of everything that had brought her a small measure of reassuring stability.

She raised her chin, "You're quite right, it's not your place, Mrs Hawkins. I thank you for your concern but I'm perfectly able to cope."

Mrs Hawkins nodded and turning away, put a hand to Lord Winterborne's forehead, "Yes, my lady, of course. And I apologise if I have offended you. I have a daughter about the same age as you and I would wish someone to keep an eye on her if they thought she was in trouble."

Feeling guilty for reprimanding her, Grace smiled warmly, "I too beg your pardon, for I'm sure your sentiments come from an honest desire to give assistance, but I do assure you that my only consideration is the health of my husband and the welfare of my daughter. They are my prime concern."

"Yes, my lady, I understand. Lord Winterborne is calm now, the laudanum has worked. You could go down to dinner if you wished, and I can always send for you if necessary."

Grace could think of nothing more daunting than facing her husband's guests *en masse* but knew that she would have to go down at some point and the later she left it the worse it would be. The last time had been unbearable, and she had no wish for a repeat of that evening.

"If you think Lord Winterborne has settled now, I shall go and tidy myself and return to the party but please call me if anything changes."

"Of course," responded Mrs Hawkins.

* * *

Nathan knew that Grace would have been standing outside the Great Hall for several moments before having the courage to enter the enormous room. He had to give her credit though because she showed none of that fear as she came into the Hall. She looked every bit the cool matriarch and he went immediately to her side and escorted her to the head of the table.

Eventually, the footmen had ferried in the numerous dishes and everyone seated themselves. Grace bravely stood to address her guests and briefly explained that Gervase was now sound asleep and would no doubt feel well enough again to see them all in the morning.

There was a murmur amongst the gathering and some sympathetic looks. Grace was much relieved to see that she was flanked by Nathaniel on one side and Emery on the other. They were like guard-dogs and they made her feel a little more secure.

The dinner seemed to go well, everyone complimented the cook and the talking never ceased, the babble of voices rising up and reaching the arched beams supporting the high ceiling. For a moment Grace recalled how she'd quite blatantly led Nathan to believe that she wouldn't object to him kissing her again and even though she didn't regret what she'd said, she realised that it might complicate her life even more.

"Lord Winterborne? He hasn't regained his senses?" he asked.

She shook her head, "No, not yet," she said, and looked around to see if anyone was listening to their conversation, "He's still unconscious. I received a sound scolding from Mrs Hawkins."

Nathan raised an eyebrow, "Over what exactly?"

Another glance around the table, "Why, you, naturally."

Both eyebrows went up, "Fascinating. What have I done to incur her wrath?"

She smiled slightly, "As far as I can tell you've done nothing at all apart from be a man, which is apparently entirely forgivable, whereas I have somehow made God exceedingly vexed."

"Oh, dear. I can only apologise if I have, in any way, made your situation even more uncomfortable."

She paused while a footman filled her wine glass, "It's become vastly more uncomfortable recently, which I very much dislike, but I find I would have it no other way. It's been extremely enlivening, and I believe Jem is a happier child because of you and Emery being here. It was too stultifying before and not at all good for her. It's as though we have been deliberately living in a soap bubble."

Emery, leant over the table towards his hostess, "Did someone mention my name?"

Grace laughed, "I did indeed and for a change it was something complimentary!"

Emery laughed too and Nathan smiled.

"I'm so used to Nate's constant barrage of fraternal abuse that I allow it to glide over me and take not the slightest bit of notice any more," said Emery, cheerfully, "I am inured to insults."

"That is most fortunate," said his friend with a belligerent gleam in his eye, "Considering the disturbing colour of that coat."

Grace looked from one to the other, "No, please! Pray, do not act like little boys! It's very disconcerting to be in charge of *three* small children. I fear it's more than I'm able to competently govern!"

At the other end of the long line of tables, the members of the theatre company were clearly beginning to feel the effects of all the wine they had consumed and were becoming quite lively. Voices were raised and their actions were expressive and expansive. Grace glanced at them nervously and prayed they wouldn't become any worse before the night was over.

"They can do nothing to harm you while I'm at your side," murmured Nathan under cover of a sudden surge of riotous laughter.

Grace kept her eyes fixed upon her plate, "You cannot always be at my side, Nathan."

He watched her intently for a second, "Just say the word," he said, under his breath, his gaze not leaving her face. He had no real idea why he said it, he just wanted to push her, to see how much she would give — to test her. There was something so restrained about her, so unreachable, he wanted to shake her, to loosen her hair again, until it tumbled about her shoulders, to see her cheeks flush with some other emotion than embarrassment, to see her as she was that first day, running barefoot across the garden in a scarlet gown. She reminded him of a wild deer which had been tamed against its will and trained to behave and obey and she was now in grave danger of forgetting that streak of wildness in her desire to please and keep out of trouble.

He saw faint colour flood her cheeks and felt an intoxicating thrill in his chest which took him by surprise.

"What are you two conspiring about?" demanded Emery, who had been paying particular attention to their expressions during the *sotto voce* exchange of words.

"Nothing that need concern you, my dear inquisitive friend," said Nathan.

Emery looked wounded, "But Nate! You know you can trust me!"

"Only until someone is foolish enough to admire your coat or promises you riches beyond your wildest dreams and then you forget your true friends in the blink of an eye. You're exceedingly weak-willed when it comes to loyalty."

"So untrue," said Emery sulkily.

At this point a commotion at the end of the table drew their attention away from their trivial altercation. One of the actors, bewigged and wearing a long embroidered oriental robe of turquoise satin was climbing rather drunkenly onto his chair and once in position proceeded to perform, surprisingly creditably, the epilogue of the play they were rehearsing:

"Thus I begin: "All is not gold that glitters, Pleasure seems sweet, but proves a glass of bitters. When Ignorance enters, Folly is at hand; Learning is better far than house or land. Let not your virtue trip; who trips may stumble, And virtue is not virtue, if she tumble."

There was rousing applause and cheers from his rowdy companions and he bowed to them all extravagantly and jumped down from his impromptu stage and returned to his place at the table.

"Could not have been more apt or more timely, I'd say," said Nathan darkly, the pertinent words ringing in his ears and very aware that Grace had paled and would not meet his eyes.

"She Stoops To Conquer," announced Emery smugly, much to his friend's surprise, "Ho! Well may you gape at me! I'll have you know that I attend the theatre on a regular basis. I'm not merely a wit and a dandy, y'know!"

"God preserve me," groaned Nathaniel, head in hands.

A very sober Mrs Leventhorpe leant forward to catch Grace's eye and raised her voice assertively, "A tempting opening gambit perhaps for what is to come? Shall we be seeing some of the famous Winterborne playacting while we're here? I do hope so, having heard so much about it."

"I doubt I could stop them, even if I had the power," responded Grace impassively, "They need no encouragement, only alcohol and a captive audience."

"I hope Gervase will be well enough to watch. He does so love a performance," added Marcus Delamere.

"Yes, he does. I'm sure he'll rally again, he's very determined."

"Will you be participating Lady Winterborne?" asked Mrs Leventhorpe with a sly look.

"Good gracious, no. Naturally, I will be in the audience."

"But you're young and full of vitality, would you not enjoy pretending to be someone else for sport?"

There was a slight pause before Grace replied, "No, indeed, I would not. I've never been at all interested in showing off. Or pretence. I fear I've always been rather reserved, Mrs Leventhorpe." She felt Nathaniel's bright blue eyes upon her and carefully avoided them in case she saw her lies reflected there. Since becoming the reluctant wife of Lord Winterborne she had assumed a different personality in order to cope with her new life. She'd been in hiding until she'd found herself coming back to life, in a cupboard, of all things. It was ridiculous but she felt as though the feeling were just returning to her limbs; her fingertips, her toes were tingling into life. The all-pervading numbness was fading. It frightened her but also fascinated her; being numb had been ideal. She'd thought she was beyond saving. She thought she didn't want to be saved, because to feel emotions meant one must suffer. Then, she'd been unexpectedly kissed in that cupboard and everything had started to change.

Mrs Leventhorpe narrowed compassionless eyes, "Oh, and Lord Winterborne seems so theatrical, does he not? I would have thought — "

She didn't finish because Nathan ruthlessly interrupted her, "This is your first time at Winterborne, Mrs Leventhorpe?

But your husband has been many times before, no? You must be a remarkably trusting wife."

Grace couldn't help letting out a small, astonished gasp.

Mrs Leventhorpe flushed to the roots of her impressively high powdered hair and made a spluttering sound as she fought to find the words, "Why — why would I not trust my own husband? This is a perfectly respectable house and despite — not really ever having anything to do with people from theatres — surely Lord and Lady Standon wouldn't be here if there were anything untoward."

"I hardly know the Standons having only just met them."

"But Lady Cheyne! She is a stickler for the type of company she keeps."

"And George Carew?" said Nathan maliciously.

She stiffened, "Mr Carew is another matter altogether. He's a well-known reprobate but I fancy his being here is merely an unhappy oversight. Lord Winterborne has not been himself of late, so cannot be blamed for an unusually inferior guest list."

Nathan laughed, "In that case, I'm relieved to be able to point out that Emery and I are not included upon that guest list. We are here by mischance, so therefore cannot be lumped together with those inferior persons you so understandably despise. We must count ourselves fortunate indeed not to be in your bad books, Mrs Leventhorpe."

She looked at him askance, "Captain? I'm not sure that I understand!"

"Emery and I were here in the beginning merely to discuss a business proposition with Lord Winterborne, and we stayed because he suddenly fell ill. It would have been exceedingly ill-bred to have just abandoned Lady Winterborne in that moment, d'you not think?"

"A business proposition?" questioned Marcus Delamere, leaning forward with sudden interest. "You're talking about his shipping business I expect? I have heard very little about it, but it sounds intriguing."

Nathaniel regarded him gravely, "Shipping? We've not been able to take the conversation further as his illness interrupted us."

Delamere raised his heavy eyebrows, "I understand that initially he had a very substantial inheritance and that gave him a solid foundation for dabbling in various businesses. He's certainly been remarkably successful at keeping the whole thing under wraps; the name of Winterborne is as yet unsullied by association with anything in the least bit questionable. He's unequalled when it comes to keeping his cards close to his chest."

"I must disagree," said Emery, "I know of one even more inscrutable than Lord Winterborne when it comes to keeping a guard upon his tongue."

Grace glanced from Emery to Nathan and wondered what he meant and why the somewhat innocuous comment had induced the Captain's brows to knit together briefly and for him to cast a swift warning glance at Emery.

An actress, her face heavily painted, and barely able to stand up without slowly toppling sideways, began to sing a rather wavering aria in a high piercing voice and a ballet dancer left the table to twirl about the Hall in a flurry of orange silk. The other actors thumped the table in unison rattling the glasses and the silverware and making the candle-flames tremble.

Grace watched them with growing alarm knowing that more was assuredly to come.

"Why should Gervase need to keep his business under wraps?" she asked Nathan anxiously, whilst keeping a watchful eye on the singer.

"Pay them no heed," he replied. "Everyone in business is the same. They guard their sources and are jealous of each other's success. It makes them mistrustful of the motives of anyone who might show the least interest in their dealings."

"But what does Gervase deal in? I have never heard him talk of it at all. I just thought he was loathe to discuss such things with a female. Is it more? What does Mr Delamere mean by *questionable*?"

"Grace, I assure you, there's no need for concern."

"Is he involved in something disreputable?"

Nathaniel, who was thinking to himself that the Marquis had been decidedly reluctant to divulge the nature of his business right from the start, felt uneasy about reassuring Grace but he was discovering that he didn't like to see her so visibly distressed.

"Well, if he is, he hasn't mentioned what it might be to me," he said softly.

She looked at him intently, "You'd tell me if he did?"

An infinitesimal pause, "Of course."

Eleven

The carouse went on long into the night and Grace had to grit her teeth to endure the increasing din and exuberance of the Theatricals. As the evening wore on, she wanted to put her hands over her ears and weep but instead she sat regally in her chair and pretended to be mildly entertained by the antics of the troupe. She had perfected a half-smile which didn't reach her eyes but seemed to satisfy her guests. She concentrated mainly upon everyone other than the Theatricals, making sure that they were well cared for and that the footmen were attending to them even though it was sometimes a battle for them to get through the ebullient throng of revellers to the table. The actors seemed to know no bounds and continued to down their drinks with gusto. A few glasses were broken by careless drunken elbows, too-vigorous toasting and dancing whilst trying to sip champagne and she could see a silver knife embedded in one of the very fine and ancient tapestries and hoped it could be repaired before Gervase saw it.

She could see George Carew halfway down the table and knew that his eyes strayed in her direction far too regularly for comfort. She hated him being in the same house as her, let alone the same room and resolved to be on her guard at all times. He was being exceedingly attentive to the pretty young actress sitting next to him and Grace wanted to warn the girl, worried that she might be in danger of being ill-used, even though she appeared to be returning his teasing behaviour with a good deal of excitement. She averted her furtive gaze and tried to listen to the conversations going on around her end of the table.

Lady Cheyne and Lord Standon were deep in a heated discussion about transportation to the colonies versus corporal punishment and Marcus Delamere was slowly drinking himself into oblivion.

Grace noted that neither Nathaniel nor Emery were drinking at all and she refused to touch her own glass as she needed to keep her wits about her.

At one point as dessert was being served, two of the troupe span giddily to her end of the table and tried to grab her to make her dance with them. She attempted to tug her hand free, but they were relentless and were pulling her out of her chair when Nathan firmly laid his hand upon the arm of the nearest girl, a solidly built young lady, who was being the most insistent and almost pulling Grace's arm out of its socket as she resisted.

The girl looked down at the hand gripping her arm and then back to the owner of it. "You want to dance with me instead?" she asked archly.

"No, indeed I do not, Miss — ?"

"Weston, Peggy Weston. You can call me Peg! Or, if you should prefer, Dinah, which sounds grander doesn't it? Miss Dinah Weston. That's my stage name."

"I'll call you whatever you please but kindly unhand Lady Winterborne, she has no wish to dance."

Miss Weston removed her hand from Grace's with an artistic little flourish, "There! She's free! Will you dance with her instead? She looks like she could do with a good — *dance!*"

Grace rose to her feet and looked at them disdainfully, "I think that it's time I went upstairs to see how my husband is. I should not have stayed away so long."

"Oh, m'lady! Do you not like to dance?" cried Miss Weston, rolling her eyes dramatically at her friend, who giggled loudly.

Grace felt the heat flooding up her neck and into her cheeks, "I do not dance," she said emphatically.

"But you're so young! Course you dance! It'd be a crime for you not to. Captain Heywood will you not dance with 'er?

You looks like you could do a tidy little country dance. I'll bet you'd like nothing better than to dance with 'er!"

Nathan pushed back his chair and with the greatest civility steered the two inebriated girls away from them and deposited them back amongst their troupe and said with a regretful shrug, "Lady Winterborne is overcome with anxiety for her husband's health at the moment so you must forgive her."

Miss Weston gave him a suggestive nudge with her elbow, "You should see to 'er! She's wound as tight as a watch spring! If she don't let go, she'll bust!"

"Thank you most kindly for your advice, I believe she's managing very well without any er — interference from me or anyone else."

Grace watched them and wondered what they were saying. She remained standing until Nathaniel returned to her side, "I think as things are becoming a little too wild for me, I shall go up. Thank you for interceding."

"She meant no harm, Grace, it was just the champagne talking."

She cast him a look which begged to differ and said goodnight to those at her end of the table who were still in a condition to understand her. The gentlemen rose unsteadily to their feet and there was an excess of effusive gratitude and polite bowing. She waved away their thanks and, with a sigh of relief, she went out.

* * *

Nathan caught up with her at the bottom of the stairs. She looked over her shoulder at him, "There's no need — " she began hesitantly.

"There is, which is why I'm coming with you. Anyway, I've had enough of Theatricals at play, they're rapidly becoming boorish. Are they always like this?"

She shrugged, "Often very much worse. Sometimes I've been unable to get away and — well, things have got out of hand — Gervase does nothing. I don't know why. He seemed to delight in my discomfort."

"Emery is there to curb the worst of their behaviour if it becomes necessary. He's being abstemious which is very much against his nature but, to my astonishment, he offered willingly to do what he could to help."

"I noticed his self-restraint. I wish I understood why you're both being so kind."

"Kind? Emery is one of the most selfish creatures on earth. He would sell his own grandmother for a new waistcoat."

Grace laughed quietly as they approached her husband's bedchamber, "I think you're exceedingly unjust to him! He always seems to be most thoughtful. Why he even allows Jem to wear his hats although she might ruin them with her grubby little hands!"

"He's scared of her," said Nathaniel with a wry smile.

"I was too, when I first met her. She was so small and helpless. I thought I'd drop her on her head or break off one of her tiny fingers by accident. I barely dared to touch her."

"But you have younger siblings."

"I do but the wet-nurse looked after them when they were babies, so I missed out on that part. My mother would look at them after breakfast and before dinner but otherwise they were left to their own devices. She was not in the least — motherly."

"Well, in my opinion you have well and truly made up for that with Jem. You appear to me to be the very best mother she could possibly have. And she clearly adores you."

Grace blushed and was thankful for the lack of light in the corridor.

"I am all she has. Poor child. She will not have liked being left with Bridie this evening and will be in a dreadful sulk tomorrow. Bridie can be a bit harsh with her sometimes."

"Perhaps we could take her out for some frolics in the garden tomorrow? Perhaps a paddle in the fountain?"

Grace nodded, "That would be kind although she and I will have to pose for the wretched painter again, I fear. Unless it rains, of course."

"At the moment it doesn't look as though it will ever rain again, I don't think I can remember such sultry weather at this time of year." He opened the door to the bedchamber and stood back to allow her to pass. The hem of her beautiful cerulean and silver gown glided over his booted foot and again he felt something unwonted stir somewhere in the middle of his chest. He followed her into the room and Mrs Hawkins, clutching her bible to her chest, rose and after reassuring them that the Marquis had not stirred all evening, she left to have something to eat and snatch a few hours' sleep.

Grace sank into the chair beside the bed and studied her husband's sleeping face, "He looks a better colour now," she whispered.

Standing just behind her Nathaniel caught himself gazing at the exposed nape of her neck. He promptly removed himself to the other side of the bed.

They could hear the sound of distant singing filtering along the corridor and sneaking under the door. Neither remarked upon it. They merely sat in silence while Grace tried to regain her composure. Her neck was sore from holding herself so rigidly and her shoulders ached, she tilted her head back and forth trying to ease the stiffness. A sharp pain at the base of her skull made her wince. She closed her eyes and leant back into the chair and tried not to think about the coming days and nights in the company of Gervase's friends. She wondered if they might leave once they realised that their host was severely incapacitated by ill-health. Surely they wouldn't wish to be around to watch him deteriorate right before their eyes? She listened to the faint noises coming from downstairs and wondered if they had any idea how serious his condition was and if they even cared. She had a feeling that they were like parasites clinging to a sickly animal and would only leave when their host died. She sighed. She heard a movement from the other side of the bed and then a soft voice beside her murmured, "Lean forward, Grace."

Startled, she opened her eyes and looked up at him. She had no idea why, but she obeyed his order. She sat up and turned a little in the chair. At the light touch of his hands on her shoulders, she very nearly let out a cry but just managed to bite it back. The only person who ever touched her was Jem so, apart from her first kiss in a linen cupboard, she was unused to casual human contact. Nathan squatted down on his haunches and carefully began to ease the tension in her back; his long fingers gently kneading the muscles and working the knots out until she began to relax. However, he soon became irritated by the inconvenient design of the gown's neckline and without asking permission he slid the wide band over her shoulders. Grace opened her mouth to object but then closed it again without saying anything at all. As he pushed his fingers up the nape of her neck and into her hair, she let out an entirely involuntary but ecstatic little sigh. Although it was barely audible, Nathan heard it and smiled. But because he was getting to know her, he knew what would happen once she came out of this state of absent-minded weariness. She was under an immense amount of strain and was not thinking as clearly as usual. Her skin was soft and warm and faintly scented with jasmine. He could feel her giving into his touch, the tension tangibly seeping out of her as he moved his hands over her neck and shoulders.

Grace allowed herself to drift for a few minutes, just letting the unfamiliar sensations take away all her anxieties. She had never before been touched by another person in this way, and she'd no doubt in her mind that had anyone other than Nathan dared to be so familiar with her, she would have slapped them. But, as his hands circled her neck and his thumbs stroked the aching muscles there, she came to a sudden and horrifying conclusion and as that unbidden idea took hold and settled into her stupefied mind, she opened her eyes and looked blindly at her husband's face, half-hidden in the shadows, grey and gaunt; and she slowly pulled away from Nathan and perched on the edge of the chair as though poised for flight. She rearranged her gown about her shoulders.

"Grace?"

"I must be mad," she breathed.

"You're tired not mad."

She closed her eyes again and tried to hold back the wave of emotion that washed over her, "I cannot — I must not —"

"There's no question of you having done anything wrong. You just needed a little attention, that's all."

She twisted round to look at him, her eyes wide and dark in the half-light, "*Attention*? Is that what this is?"

"It's no more than a brother or sister would do for you."

She inhaled a kind of sobbing breath, "You have some very strange ideas about siblings then! I only remember having my hair pulled and being pinched by William on a regular basis but other than that I don't recall anyone touching me in such a — such a — close and overfamiliar manner since — well, ever!"

Nathaniel, who had known this reaction would come eventually because she could not allow herself to *feel* anything in case she began to question her life at Winterborne, sat back on his heels and let her steadily withdraw from him again. He could still feel the warmth of her, and his fingers tingled from applying pressure to her skin. It was as though something had transferred from her to him, and he was powerless to stop it spreading.

"I'm sorry, Grace. I wasn't thinking. It's my fault entirely."

She bit her bottom lip hard, leaving imprints of her teeth, and fought the desire to run away. She had to stop running away. "No, I shouldn't have allowed you to — I wasn't thinking straight," she got suddenly to her feet, "If you will stay here for a while I would like to go and make sure Jem is sleeping soundly." She moved across the room to the door, "I'll come right back." She glanced up at him, "It's my fault. I've been alone so long. I think I'm becoming a little unhinged."

He smiled at her, "I think you're remarkably sane considering what you've been forced to endure. I know of no-one else who could have coped as you have."

She just shook her head and left the room.

Nathan sat for a moment and contemplated his hands. They were still tingling.

There was a slight movement from the bed, "You're making some progress with her, then?" muttered Lord Winterborne hoarsely.

Nathan was jolted back to reality. Just for a moment he'd forgotten the real reason he was at Winterborne. Just for a moment he'd allowed himself to believe that he was a decent sort of man and that his growing interest in Grace was rooted in honest feelings that didn't carry a sense of shame and guilt with them.

"I wouldn't say that, my lord. Grace is bound by a rigid sense of propriety and loyalty and if she got the slightest inkling that I'd come here out of a need to make some money I would again be at *point non plus.* And, if she discovered your real reason for inviting me here — there would be no chance that she would ever speak to me again and I'd be banished forthwith. I should not get your hopes up. Your wife is a woman of high integrity and knows precisely what she owes the name of Winterborne."

The Marquis seemed to be having trouble catching his breath and Nathan fetched the glass of cordial and propped him up a little with a bank of pillows and helped him take a sip or two.

After a moment Lord Winterborne said, "She fights her true nature every day as do we all in one way or another." He chuckled but it made him choke, "I decided long ago to stop fighting mine. I wonder what your true nature is, Captain Heywood. We have yet to find out. Perhaps we shall all be surprised. Ruthless but loyal soldier? Gentleman? Callous and unscrupulous womaniser?"

"You like to manipulate the emotions of others for your own ends which doesn't exactly make you a paragon of virtues, my lord."

"Ah, but I do it for good reasons though."

"Others might not think those reasons so pure. I feel absolutely certain that Lady Winterborne would be revolted by them. And quite rightly."

"Nevertheless, I believe you're breaking down her barriers which is a start at least."

"I'm not deliberately trying to do anything. I suppose I have shown some sympathy which she is unused to."

"I look forward to seeing the desired results before very long."

Nathan silently ground his teeth and returned to his chair. He knew he was putting his head on the block and willingly so, but he also knew that if the worst came to the worst, he could always just leave. There was nothing keeping him here apart from some misplaced loyalty and the flimsy promise of a new career. He could do without a career and could always justify his feelings of burgeoning loyalty as the result of an extraordinarily beautiful face; he was after all just a soldier with simple desires. The secondary reason was merely the raving of a dying madman who wanted to prove his absolute power over people to make him feel more alive in his last months on earth. Nathan should have felt sympathy for him, but he felt nothing but loathing and contempt.

An hour later Grace returned and confirmed that Jem was sound asleep, but that Bridie had had quite a battle to get her into bed and was still fuming about it and had to be calmed down. She'd been a little surprised to see that Gervase was awake and sitting up and tried not to look alarmed as she wondered when he'd woken up and what they'd been talking about while she'd been out of the room. She caught Nathan's reassuring glance and somewhat relieved, she then settled herself down in her chair for what promised to be another tedious and uncomfortable night.

* * *

The next day Grace missed breakfast. Nathan made her excuses, and everyone seemed to accept that after a long night sitting with her husband, she was bound to be tired. But he had his doubts. He was fairly certain that she was avoiding him.

After breakfast when she still hadn't appeared he went to find Jemima. He discovered her throwing a spectacular tantrum in the nursery. He walked in just as she lifted a standish from a small wooden desk and hurled it with surprising strength and accuracy at the door, which he was in the process of opening. He saw the missile and ducked out of the way just in the nick of time and it soared harmlessly over his head and smashed into the door.

"I want *Mama!* I will *not* do my sewing! I am *werry* cross!" she howled.

Bridie was standing with her arms folded across her chest looking severe and as though she might explode with pent-up frustration.

Jemima saw Nathan and stopped howling immediately. She glowered at him, "Where is my Mama?" she asked in a quavering voice.

"Good morning, Jem," he said politely, "Your mother is still asleep. She was up all night looking after your father."

"Oh," she said, scrunching up her mouth into a furious pucker, "I want to *see* her."

"I'm sure you do but we shall have to wait a bit. You wouldn't want to wake her when she was so tired, would you?"

She considered this for a moment, "Yes, I *would*. I *need* her!"

Nathaniel laughed, "I'm sure you do but I think we shall leave her to sleep for now and perhaps if you've had your breakfast, we could go out into the garden with the dogs and see if we can find something interesting to do."

She looked at him from under frowning brows, "And Mr Talmarch too?"

He grinned down at her, "Yes, and Mr Talmarch too, if you insist."

"I do! He says funny things."

"I heartily agree," said Nathan.

Jemima cast her seething nursemaid a dark glance and approached Nathan with her hand outstretched. Nathan took it in his and with an apologetic look at Bridie he opened the door for the child.

Jemima watched as the bits of broken glass were pushed aside by the door, "Did it hit you?" she enquired with ghoulish interest.

"No, your aim was poor," he said cordially.

"If I practice it'll get better," she replied cheerfully and with a skip in her step she pulled him along the corridor and away from an astonished Bridie and some unfinished cross-stitching.

On the way out of the house they collected the two dogs and a yawning Emery who was suffering from a thundering headache and a desire to be left alone in a darkened room. Instead, he was dragged by his beautiful coattails out into the bright sunlight, which instantly made his head even worse.

"No, I'm sorry," he said in failing accents, "I can't do this. I must return this instant to the house."

"But the Captain *promised* you would come with us! He *said!*"

"*Did* he indeed!" growled Emery looking daggers at his friend and clutching his head.

"I may have been coerced into roping you in. Can I just remind you that we are ruled by Jemima The Terrible and she takes no prisoners!" said Nathan trying to keep a straight face.

"I'm quaking at the knees," reflected Emery pitifully.

"So you should be. It's a wise man who knows his real enemies."

"It's hard to fight fair when your enemy is only three feet tall and looks so harmless," mourned Emery.

Jemima, sensing something peculiar in the air, put her hands on her hips and stuck out her bottom lip, "Captin! You *said!*"

Nathan quickly realised they were heading for deep water, "Mr Talmarch is very sorry, and he promises that you can try on all his hats to make up for his exceedingly poor behaviour."

Emery groaned and wished he'd not been foolish enough to come to Winterborne, it wasn't turning out quite as he'd envisaged.

"So, fair Lady Jemima, where shall we go?" asked Nathan with a broad grin.

Jemima thought hard and then her eyes lit up, "The fountain! Come on, let's race!"

Twelve

And so, Grace, looking out of an upstairs window, observed her young daughter, skipping and twirling, leading a mad cavalcade racing across the lawn, followed by two galloping, overexcited dogs and Nathan laughing as he ran and, bringing up the rear, a ponderous looking Mr Talmarch crossly holding onto his wig.

Her eyes widened and an inelegant snort of laughter escaped her. She'd stayed hiding in her bed for a while instead of braving the crowded dining room — and Nathan. She chewed the inside of her cheek and wondered how on earth she'd permitted him to touch her in such a way that had rendered her unable to order him to stop. Once in bed, after Mrs Hawkins had taken over again, she'd lain awake reliving those few moments of bliss. She could still feel his fingers stroking her neck and couldn't help a shudder of delight and a delicious tingle of goosebumps running down her limbs. She closed her eyes and tried to shake the perverse feelings away like dust from a cleaning cloth. When she opened them again Nathan had caught up to Jem and lifted her off her feet and was swinging her around in the air, blue silk swirling, while she shrieked with furious joy. As she watched, Grace pondered the discovery she'd made. She loved Nathan. It was infuriating and inconvenient and terrifying. She had been managing so comfortably before he arrived at Winterborne with his dangerous laughing eyes and stern mouth and beautiful hands and intoxicating kisses. Everything had been perfectly under control. Her life had, in its own peculiar way, been her own. Now, the reins had been snatched from her grasp and she felt as though she were careering towards a cliff edge and there was absolutely nothing she could do about it.

She watched them disappear from view and knew jealousy. She examined the strange feeling for a second and then picking up her skirts ran along the corridor and down the stairs.

She quickly kicked off her shoes and raced in her stockinged feet across the lawn after them, through the parterre and along the arched walkway of wisteria to the fountain. She arrived panting for breath and flushed, to find Jem splashing about in the fountain pool, her skirts soaked, Nathan, also paddling barefoot and Emery perched delicately on the stone edge, bemoaning the fact that they were ruining his coat and that his head was throbbing.

Jem looked up and saw her, "Mama! Look! We're paddling! The Captin cheated in the race and picked me up! It wasn't fair! You must tell him so!"

Nathan stood very still, hands on hips, and watched her approach their comical tableau in the fountain. She was looking tired and yet still as beautiful as ever, but there was something altered in her eyes — she looked different, she looked alive.

"Grace? Is everything all right?"

She smiled. "Perfectly, thank you, Nathan." She turned to Jemima, "So, the Captain cheated, did he? How ungentlemanly of him. He does not like to be bested especially by a female! It shows very poor character, in my opinion. A man who must always win cannot be trusted."

"I *would* have won, Mama! I am werry fast."

"I know you are, my love. You are part rabbit, I think."

Nathan waded to the edge of the pool and held out his hand to Grace, "Are you coming in? It's surprisingly warm. However, you may get splashed — accidentally."

"I think I shall just sit on the edge here with Emery, if you don't mind. I must go and change soon; I saw the painter setting up his easel and sadly it's not looking like rain and he does get so very vexed if I'm late."

She rolled off her stockings and sitting on the edge of the fountain, swung her legs around and put her feet into the water; it felt wonderful. She caught Nathan's swift glance, which deliberately lingered upon her bare ankles and had the temerity to smile up at him. He held her gaze for a second and then laughed.

"What is funny, Mama?" demanded Jemima.

"Just the feel of the water on my feet, it tickles!"

Suddenly, Dancer decided it would be a good thing to be in the water too and leapt over the wall to join in with the frolicking. In the general chaos, everyone got thoroughly drenched and Emery fled the scene to hide behind a tree.

"Oh, no! My *hair!* The painter will murder me!" cried Grace, her elegant coiffure coming down in bedraggled dripping ringlets.

Nathan contemplated her from appreciative eyes and thought she looked absolutely ravishing. Emery catching this unguarded moment from his hiding place, thought, "Oho!" to himself, "Finally! He's well and truly lost!" What a to-do there was going to be now. He knew his friend too well to think that he'd behave like a gentleman and give Grace a wide berth and he recognised, sadly, that he was very likely to ruin all their hopeful expectations by blundering into this, whatever it might be, blindly. And if he were to fall in love with Grace, then all their plans could be wrecked. He could read something undeniably reckless in Nate's eyes and sighed lustily at the thought of all the money he might have one day had in his hands and mourned the rosy future he'd pictured for them both. "Damn and blast!" he said rather louder than he'd meant to.

Jem, pricking up her ears, said with relish, "Damunblast!"

"Jem!" admonished her mother, with a disapproving glare at the tree Emery had guiltily ducked back behind.

Grace caught Nathan's eye and tried desperately not to laugh but the sound just burst out and she collapsed in a fit of uncontrollable giggles. She threw back her head and just gave into helpless laughter until her sides ached and the tears were joining the water dripping down her face.

Jem had gone quite still and was watching her in astonishment, "I don't think Mama is feeling well," she said anxiously.

Nathan put a reassuring hand on the top of her damp head, "Mama is absolutely fine, I promise you; she's just been out in the sun for a bit too long."

"Does sun make you go mad?" asked Jem.

"It can do if you're in it for days and days with nothing to drink but I think in this case Mama has just got a little too warm and it's made her forget there are people watching."

"Will she get better?"

"Yes, in a few minutes she'll be fine again. Come, help me lift Dancer out of the pool and get him to run around so he dries off."

Together they managed to get the large, bedraggled dog out of the water and onto the grass and then Jem ran around and around the little lawn until the dog was almost dry and her sadly ruined gown wasn't dripping. Nathan sat beside Grace and stared at her as she tried in vain to calm herself down. She was still bubbling with mirth and had started to hiccup a little wildly.

"You've been swallowing air," said Nathan and patted her back helpfully. "Hold your breath and they'll go away."

Grace took a big gulp of air and held it for a few seconds but failed to control it and started laughing again and hiccupping at the same time. She buried her face in her hands and gave herself up to hysterics. She felt the hand stop the fraternal patting and begin stroking the small of her back rhythmically and the laughter died away.

"There now," said Nathan comfortingly, "Hiccups all gone."

Emery reappeared from behind his tree and approached them warily, "I'll have you know that this coat was made by a genius called Hawkes! It's a work of art!"

"Then you shouldn't have been fool enough to wear it to go paddling," said Nathan scathingly.

"I had no clue that I would *be* paddling."

"You should always be prepared for the worst," remarked Nathan.

Grace waited for the hand to stop its circling. After a few more circles, it slowed and then stopped but stayed for a moment on her back. Her whole being was focused on it. On the slight pressure, the warmth, the strange feeling of intimacy. Finally, it moved away, and she felt bereft. Such a small thing, but it was both companionable and yet unsettling and she was completely thrown off balance. The day was not going how she'd planned while she was in her bed and able to think clearly. She'd been so sure that she would be cool and dignified and in control of her unpredictable emotions, but she'd practically had a seizure whilst laughing. She was being utterly ridiculous, and she found it hard to care.

"So, my Lady Jemima! Where goeth we next?" said Nathan cordially.

"Tree climbing!" announced Lady Jemima.

"Ah, now that may present some problems as we're not really dressed for climbing, m'lady."

Jem considered him carefully, "You're afraid I might beat you again," she said in disgust.

Nathan chuckled, "No, indeed, I swear I am not afraid, but your gown is already sodden, and if we climb it may well also get ripped. Imagine what Bridie would say."

"Well, I don't *care!* Bridie is always cross anyway."

Nathan sighed and looked at Grace, who shrugged, "Perhaps a small tree?" she suggested.

"Aha! Of course, one of the old apple trees. Perfect. Let us sally forth then to the orchard. Come, Emery, you can watch from a distance where you and your coat will be safe."

"Oh, I'd really rather not — " he began but on seeing Jem's contemptuous expression, he was forced to change his mind, "But, only as long as I'm not made to climb up a tree in all my finery, I will come — but to observe only."

And, as they all set off to the orchard, Jem grabbed Nathan's hand and said confidingly but sadly, rather too loudly, "Mr Talmarch is a fop, isn't he, Captin!"

"Yes, I'm sorry to say that he is, Jem."

"It's werry — dispiritin'," said Jem earnestly. "But you're not a fop, are you?"

"By Jove, no! I cannot abide being all togged up in finery, it's so very hampering," exclaimed Nathan, in mock horror.

"You can't run properly in a gown, can you!" said Jem, swinging his hand happily back and forth.

"No, indeed, gowns are the very worst for hampering one's running," replied Nathan, suppressing a grin.

Emery and Grace were walking quite sedately behind them, as Grace's gown was so wet, the material kept tangling itself around her legs and slowing her down. Eventually, after she'd stumbled a couple of times, Emery offered her his arm, which she gladly took.

"I'm so pleased you're here, Emery. It's made all the difference in the world to Jem and me. I've never had friends of my own before, even though I realise that Nathan came here at Gervase's invitation, I feel that you've both perhaps stayed for us, which is such a wonderful feeling."

Emery had a sudden desire to loosen his perfectly tied neckcloth but didn't dare in case it made him look guilty. "Ah, Grace, how kind. Wouldn't have missed this whole adventure, not for love nor money," then he almost choked as he realised what he'd said quite inadvertently.

Grace looked at him with concern, "Are you all right, Emery? You seem rather agitated."

"Gad! I'm fine! Just emotional, y'know! Delighted that we can be of service. Damsel in distress and all that!"

Grace watched Nathan and Jem ahead of them, "Nathan is used to being with children?"

"'Pon my soul, no! Never seen him with children before now! It's quite enlightening, I can tell you! Had no idea that he even liked 'em. Never showed any interest at all."

"Really? He seems so natural with her and she adores him, I can tell!"

"Probably imitating her mother," said Emery, without thought.

Grace came to a sudden standstill. "I beg your pardon!" she said haughtily.

Emery coloured and stammered, "N-no! I meant — *forgive me!* But — it's true ain't it?"

"*What* is true, Mr Talmarch?"

Emery swallowed convulsively, "Your feelings for Nate have undergone something of a change."

"I have no idea what you're talking about!"

Greatly daring Emery put a hand on her arm and said quietly, "It's all right, I won't say anything. He don't deserve you anyway."

Grace covered her cheeks with her hands to hide the telltale blush. "Oh, dear God! I can't *bear* it! *Please* don't tell him! I never meant to fall in love with him. It just happened. He must never know! It's humiliating. If Gervase were to find out — !"

He'd be thrilled, thought Emery gloomily but nevertheless, calmly responded, "No-one will tell him, you have my word. Nate has no clue. He's not very bright when it comes to sentiments. Ruined by his family and their rigid sense of decorum. Old-fashioned types. Drove poor Alexander to drink and worse. Nate escaped but I'm afraid he's no burning desire to go back to a life of domesticity. He'd rather be free to escape again if needs be. He has nothing to tie him down — likes it that way. No house, no family, no dependents of any kind. He lodges with me and lives as he wishes. He doesn't gamble and drinks very little. Actually, he's a dead bore now I come to think about it! He makes an exceedingly poor friend."

"But you love him, Emery, so surely he *must* have some good points?"

"Oh, yes indeed, he does. He's loyal, when it suits him. He's excellent with his fists, a punishing left hook and displays to advantage. I'd always back him in a fight. He doesn't womanise much; never really been in the petticoat line myself either, can take 'em or leave 'em. Oh, beg pardon! Perhaps shouldn't have mentioned that. He ain't of the first stare, mind, don't give much thought to the cut of his coat which is a shame because he'd shine up well given half a chance. He's got a fine brain, often surprises me. Seldom loses his temper either. Looks splendid in uniform."

"Well, goodness me! What a catalogue of virtues! I'm astonished he hasn't already been snapped up by some simpering little heiress!"

Emery wasn't sure if she was serious or not so decided he'd probably already said enough in defence of his friend and firmly closed his famously uncontrollable mouth.

They entered the orchard and could see Jem already picking out the tree she wished to climb and Nathan trying to persuade her to pick another much smaller one. But she was determined and paying no attention to him. Nathan looked up from their gentle bickering and saw Grace and Emery strolling towards them arm-in-arm and for a moment, all coherent thought left him, until he saw that Grace was looking a little exasperated.

"Grace! Come and bring your daughter to order please," he called out and she schooled her face into a smile as she drew nearer.

"If *you* can't make her obey, then what chance do I have?" she said.

"Help me up, Captin! I can't reach."

Nathan turned away from Grace and Emery and with a resigned shrug, he hoisted Jem up in his arms and swung her onto the first branch, where she clung on like a monkey. He guided her tiny hands and feet into the safest places and assisted in the climb as much as she would allow. She had a habit of trying to smack his hands away when she thought she could manage by herself. He held her skirts bunched up in one fist so that she could move more nimbly and steadied her with the other hand just in case she tumbled. She was so surefooted she didn't slip once.

"I don't think she's part rabbit, Grace, I think she's part mountain goat," said Nathan over his shoulder.

Grace agreed with a short laugh and sat down in the long grass to watch them from a safe distance. She spread out her skirts around her to dry in the sun. Emery tentatively sat down beside her, fanning his coat-tails out behind him so that they wouldn't get crushed.

"He won't guess. He's dreadfully slow," said Emery under his breath. "There's no need to be afraid."

"I'm not *afraid!* I just don't want anything to change. Everything has already been much altered, and it makes me uncomfortable. If he thinks — if he should suspect that I have feelings for him, he'll leave. You said he likes to escape. It's been so — different since you both arrived, and I find that I like it like this. Jem has been a changed child; she's become more adventurous and less argumentative."

Emery raised his eyebrows in disbelief, "Really? She seems *excessively* argumentative to me!"

Grace smiled and watched her daughter fearlessly sitting on a branch, swinging her bare legs, just as though she'd spent her whole life in a tree, "I can assure you that although it may not seem so, there has been a marked improvement! She is just generally a much happier child."

"I think you're a saint," said Emery reflectively.

"Indeed, I am not! Far from it. My first instinct was to run. I wanted to escape, just like Nathan, when I first realised that I was not only to be a wife to a complete stranger, but also a mother to another woman's child. I couldn't understand how I would be able to manage and not go quite mad! But somehow one learns along the way and before long things slip into place and the problems become not so insurmountable. I quickly realised that although I may be suffering, that Jem was completely lost without a mother and to have only a father who — did not, perhaps, behave quite as one would expect was so sad for her. My mother left a good deal to be desired so

I understood how Jem would benefit from having someone to care for her — to love her. It can make all the difference."

"A *saint*," said Emery.

Grace laughed and responded by giving him a playful shove, so that he toppled sideways into the long meadow grass where he closed his eyes and pretended to be asleep.

"Mama! Why did you hit Mr Talmarch? Was he bad?" called Jemima from her high perch.

"Yes, very bad!" replied Grace.

"He must go to bed with no supper!" declared Jem joyfully.

Emery, lying sprawled in the grass, heedless of his superior attire, opened one eye, "Marked improvement, eh?"

Grace shrugged, "A month ago I couldn't get her to have her hair brushed without her having a fit of screaming. Now, I only have to suggest that your hats will be out of bounds or that Nathan might not want to spend time with her, and she is all angelic smiles. It's a small miracle."

"Catch me!" shrieked the angelic one and with no further warning threw herself out of the tree and into Nathan's waiting arms. He caught her deftly and carried her across to Grace and Emery and dropped her between them like an unwanted package.

"Safe and sound. Although I think she's dislocated my shoulder," he said with a grin.

Grace grabbed her daughter by the waist and pulling her into her lap, kissed her cheeks soundly, "Have you thanked the Captain for being so kind, Jem?"

"Thank you Captin for being so kind," said Jemima obediently and then threw her arms about Grace's neck and hugged her tightly, her face buried against her mother's shoulder, but peeped up at Nathan from under her eyelashes, "I *like* fun. And I'm werry sorry for throwing that thing at the door and nearly hitting your head."

Grace frowned, "*Jem?* What did you throw?"

"The pen thing," muttered the child, "It broke to bits."

"Oh, dear! I'm so sorry Nathan."

"But, Mama, I missed the Captin! My aim was bad," declared Jem more cheerfully.

Mortified, Grace shook her head and looked at Nathan ruefully, but he merely chuckled and shrugged and then sat down next to them and lay back amongst the lush grass and closed his eyes.

"I'm worn out now," he said, "I'm not cut out to be a nursemaid, it's exhausting. It was far easier being a soldier and being shot at."

Jem sat up, "You could teach me how to *shoot!*"

"Absolutely not," said Captain Heywood.

"Oh," said Jem and collapsed back against her mother without further argument.

Grace caught Emery's incredulous eye and smiled triumphantly.

* * *

The painter stood glaring at them impatiently from the wisteria arbour.

"Lady Winterborne, you're late and still not dressed!" he stated tetchily.

Grace scrambled inelegantly to her feet, apologising incoherently. She'd completely forgotten the beastly artist.

"I'll run and change at once!"

The artist frowned, "Well, be quick about it, my lady! The light will alter soon and then all the shadows will be a completely different hue. Really, I've never had such trying sitters before!" he complained.

Nathan got to his feet and gave the painter a quelling glance, "That's quite enough! Either treat Lady Winterborne with the respect she's due or you can pack your brushes up and leave, painting unfinished and unpaid for."

The artist gulped and backed nervously out of range of the rather powerfully built gentleman with the icy blue eyes. He then turned and made his way hastily back to his easel, muttering darkly to himself.

Grace and Jemima dashed back to the house to change into their costumes, followed by Dancer and Thisbe.

Nathan looked down at his friend who was still sitting on the grass, "So, what were you two talking about?" he asked quietly.

"This and that," replied Emery without meeting his eyes.

"Emery."

"We were talking about Jem and how she's taken to you."

"Is that all?"

Silence.

"Emery."

"Sworn to secrecy, Nate!"

"You've never kept a secret in your life."

Emery rolled his eyes, "Only because you're relentlessly inquisitive and must know everything!"

"So, what did Grace say?"

"No. I will not divulge. I *swore*."

"Did she mention me?"

"Not *everything* is about you!"

"So she did?"

"I didn't say that — !"

"Yes, you did. You're a terrible liar, which is why you lose so much at the tables."

"Nate! It's not fair to her. She trusts me."

"She doesn't know you otherwise she wouldn't have been so foolish."

"She's an absolute saint and a darling and you mustn't hurt her. She's too good for you."

"What the devil do you think I'm going to do? I only need to know where we stand. I'm not planning to do anything other than see which way the wind blows. We may yet have a chance of coming out of this with our pockets full and our dignity intact."

"And Grace unhurt?"

"Naturally. I — I regard her with — great respect."

"*Do* you? I think I've noticed signs of you thinking of her with something other than respect."

Silence.

"Nate?"

"It's no more than an understandable attraction to a beautiful woman."

"Aha! I thought so! I could see the cracks appearing in those barricades of yours!"

"My "barricades" are still intact and unlikely to be breached anytime soon."

Emery grinned knowingly, "So, you say, Nathaniel, so you say!"

Thirteen

The next few days passed without incident and Grace began to relax a little. A routine emerged and she found she was, with Nathan and Emery's help, even able to endure the terrors of dining with the guests. Jemima was surprisingly biddable, and she wondered if Nathan had had a quiet word with her normally capricious child. Her husband recovered enough to be allowed downstairs once more and, with a great deal of fuss and comings and goings, was made comfortable in the withdrawing room and although his pallor was enough to send Doctor Morton into a bit of a flap, the Marquis insisted that being in bed was only making him worse. Mrs Hawkins remained in attendance, much to his lordship's disgust; she would perch on a hard chair in the corner of the room, clutching her bible like a talisman to ward off evil.

Grace managed on the whole to avoid being alone with Nathan because she was frightened that she might give herself away with some careless gesture or expression. She stayed dutifully beside Gervase when he demanded her presence but otherwise was to be found with Jem or occasionally, Emery, as long as the Captain was elsewhere. She stayed well out of the reach of George Carew and his intimates and as June continued warm and sunny, she reluctantly posed for the artist, which she found gave her far too much time to think about Nathan — and spent the rest of her time trying to organise the gardeners and staff. The head gardener suggested that some of the wilder bushes beside the river, which wound crossed their estate, should be cut back and the small lake, which fed from the river, cleared of weeds and she'd agreed although she really had no idea if that was the right thing to do; she just had to trust to his superior knowledge.

The most exciting thing to happen all week was that Thisbe somehow contrived to pick up a thorn in his foot and had been limping and whining. Grace was all for sending for a groom to see to it, but Nathan waved away her suggestion and said he was perfectly capable of dealing with it. This he did, with great calm and efficiency, the dog quite content to surrender its paw to his firm but gentle touch. Within a few minutes the thorn was removed, and the wound area had been liberally doused with vinegar water and although Thisbe limped for a day or so, he was soon to be seen gambolling about the garden as usual. Grace noted that after this, the grateful hound seemed to develop a marked preference for the Captain's company and if Nathan sat down, the dog would rest his muzzle on his thigh and gaze up at him adoringly, his whiskery eyebrows twitching. Grace smiled to herself and thought it must be nice to be able to give into one's basic instincts without fear of embarrassment or rejection. She thought, with an inward groan, that she'd quite like to rest her head on that perfectly formed thigh and have her head stroked by those long absent-minded fingers. She spent the rest of the day in hiding, in case her indecent thoughts betrayed her, and Nathan saw how she was longing to be near him.

The Theatricals continued to entertain themselves, steadily drinking their way through the Marquis's well-stocked cellar, singing ribald songs and acting out various scenes for their own amusement. Lord Winterborne seemed to take great pleasure in their performances and Grace was astonished to see him laughing at their jokes, which she privately thought remarkably unfunny.

The problem was that there were so many of them that they seemed to be everywhere and were hard to avoid without causing offence. Her instinct was to turn and run if she saw them approaching but she had to compose herself and meet them with a gracious acknowledgment and as much false warmth as she could muster. She found them mostly reluctant to encroach as long as they remained sober and she discovered the actress, Miss Weston, to be rather thoughtful and unassuming when not with her companions, although she had the distinct feeling that she could detect a measure of sympathy in her eyes and wasn't quite sure how to cope with that. She didn't want anyone to feel sorry for her.

She was just beginning to think that things had settled rather nicely and that everything would be all right when The Fates decided to give her a sharp little tweak again.

* * *

Sally was just finishing arranging Grace's hair and chatting about the things which were going on in the house when there was a knock on the door and a housemaid entered and announced that there was a visitor just arrived and demanding to see the Marchioness.

"Who is it?" asked Grace anxiously.

The maid shook her head, "Never seen them before, my lady. I'm sorry I didn't catch their name."

"Oh, goodness, who on earth can it be? I've had no letter. Oh, dear. Thank you, please tell them I'll be down in a minute."

The maid went out and Sally watched her mistress's face in the looking glass. "There's no need to fret, m'lady. No harm can come to you while the Captain's here."

"No, I know. But I never have visitors. Not a single one since I've been at Winterborne. I don't know anyone locally apart from the Reverend and he never comes near the house any more because he thinks we are beyond redemption and Gervase was so rude to him on his last visit. Am I dressed appropriately? Is this gown good enough?"

Sally smiled, "All your gowns are good enough and as we don't yet know who the visitor is, how are we to know? I think you look lovely, as always," she tucked the last curl up into the coiffure, "Would you like me to fetch the Captain for you, so that you're not alone?"

Grace rose to her feet and shook out the creases in the indigo silk and adjusted the gauzy white *buffon* around her shoulders and Sally retied the turquoise sash and fiddled with it until it was perfect.

"No, thank you, I can cope without Captain Heywood," said Grace firmly.

"Yes, m'lady," murmured Sally, thoroughly unconvinced.

* * *

Grace descended the stairs as though she were going to her own execution. Every step was painful and the desire to turn and run was overwhelming.

Entering the Great Hall, she had no idea what to expect but was holding herself rigidly, expecting the worst.

She skirted around the carved screens and looked around.

Standing before the empty fireplace was a stocky young fellow, resplendent in an extremely close-fitting coat of vivid cherry red, a quantity of lace at his throat and a neat bagwig with artfully curled pigeon wings over his ears. In his hand he held his gloves, hat and ebony cane and his boots shone like jet. He looked up as she entered the huge room.

She almost stumbled and then collecting herself, she flew across the room to him.

"William! Oh, my *William!* Is it *really* you?" she cried, the tears starting from her eyes.

Dropping his accessories heedlessly to the floor, he opened his arms and welcomed her into them, lifting his sister off her feet and giving her a rib-crushing hug.

"Grace! Of course, it's me, you silly goose! Who else has this much effortless style and elegance?"

She laughed and as her feet touched the ground again, she gazed at him with undisguised joy, "What are you *doing* here? You swore you'd never cross the Winterborne threshold unless the moon turned red and as far as I know it's still white!"

"Well, I've had a change of heart."

"Is everything all right at home?" she asked nervously examining his face.

"Everyone's still alive — unfortunately!"

"*William!*"

"Oh, don't be such a hypocrite Gracie! I'm sure you've very little love for some of them."

"No! I love them *all* — just — some more than others! How is Hester? And Clara? And Henry and Arthur? Are they well? How are Henry's rashes? And Arthur, is he still reading all the time?"

William laughed heartily, "Oh, Gracie! You haven't changed a bit! Yes, Arthur still has his nose pressed into a book all day and thankfully Henry must at last be growing out of his rashes. Hester is still just as annoying as ever and Clara is in love with the new parson!"

"New parson? What happened to Reverend Rawlin?"

"Carriage collision. Broke his neck."

Grace covered her mouth with her hands, "That's terrible! Poor man. Oh, his wife!"

"She's gone to live with her sister in Surrey. She looked quite happy."

"He could be a little — harsh at times!"

"Anyway, enough about home! My dearest sister, what about you? How are you and how is that — daughter of yours?"

Grace took a step back and considered him from disappointed eyes, "William, she *is* my daughter. She cannot help being his child, it wasn't her choice. I love her with all my heart."

"Of course you do! You're a very loving creature — always were. You still haven't answered me though. How are *you?*"

"I am perfectly well, thank you."

"Oh, *so* polite! You look tired."

"Thank you again. It's always reassuring to know that one is looking one's best."

'It goes without saying that you look beautiful, but that's nothing new. You *always* look beautiful — but there's something different about you."

"I have a houseful of guests, almost an entire stage company, invited by Gervase and it's exhausting. There's too much going on."

"You never did like a commotion! I remember, you used to hide in the library under the desk until it had all died down and it was safe to come out again."

"I still mostly feel like that." She smiled rather sadly at him, "It seems I haven't changed at all."

"I wouldn't want you to change."

"What are you doing here, William?"

"Ah. Yes. That's a splendid question. And difficult to answer. Except, that it's Mother, of course."

"Of course. What has she done to drive you out of the house?"

"Catherine Wingfield."

"Oh, no! She cannot still be angling for that connection!"

"It's even worse than before. She's informed Catherine that I am to offer for her."

"That's so cruel! How could she? I'm so sorry, Will. So, you've run away?"

"As they say, out of the frying pan and into the fire." He looked round him at the vast and glorious Great Hall, "A very fine fire too, by the looks of things. You've done well for yourself."

"Not my choice either," said Grace bitterly.

"No, you felt obliged to make the Grand Sacrifice. Have you at least been able to find some happiness?"

There was the slightest hesitation, "I'm very happy. I have Jem."

He took her by the shoulders and gave her a little shake, "Dash it, Grace! Look at me! Has he been good to you?"

"In his way. He's good to Jem."

"That's not good enough. I *knew* it! Father should never have made that bargain with him. We would have survived without his damn money. He had no right — "

"He did what he thought best. You cannot blame him entirely. Anyway, we both know it was Mother who pushed for it. She was always the power behind the throne!"

"It's still just the same and, what's more, getting gradually worse. Although, of course, the money has helped a good deal so at the very least the girls won't be forced into marriage because of our reduced circumstances. We are now living most comfortably, due to your self-sacrifice. But it makes me angry that you should have been made to marry such a man! I don't think they realised just what an oddity he is, but I've since heard — "

"No, no! William! Please, don't say more. He's very ill and — I'm afraid he doesn't have long to live. He suffers most terribly."

"Good," said her brother callously, "He deserves it."

"You mustn't say that! It's so unchristian of you."

"I don't know how you can talk of being Christian when you're married to such a foul individual!"

"I try to remember that he was the one who gave me the best thing in my life — my daughter. Without him, I would still be living with Mother and being made miserable by her malice. But this way I have my own life, of sorts and someone to love and to love me. She's only five Will, and purely an innocent — most of the time."

"I cannot wait to meet her! Anyway, dearest one, I'm come to stay for a while until the dust settles at home and I'm forgiven for some of the unforgivable things I said to our parents, when I lost my temper. Have you room for me?"

"Always! We have plenty of bedrooms even with some twenty guests already! It's the most ridiculous house and normally Jem and I rattle around in it like loose marbles and the remotest parts of it never get visited from one year to the next! Oh, I'm so pleased you're here, it couldn't be more heaven-sent. I was just — " she paused as she heard a commotion outside the main door to the Hall and looked across the room to see Jem skip in, followed by Nathan carrying something in his arms.

Jem ran to her mother but kept a critical eye upon the newcomer, "Mama! See what we have! Come and see! We found it! In the stables. Can I keep it? *Please?*"

Grace, dragged by a small insistent hand, approached Nathan, and looked in lively astonishment at the tabby kitten nestling against him.

Jem danced around them, "See? It's just a baby cat. Can I keep it? The horse man said I could."

Nathan gave Grace an apologetic look, "I'm so sorry. We stumbled upon it whilst looking at the horses. Its mother is the chief mouser, and the head groom says they have plenty more. Perhaps I should have put my foot down right at the beginning?"

Grace laughed and took the kitten from him, holding it in her cupped hands and looking it in the eyes, "You look like an intelligent sort of beast. Girl or boy?"

"I've been reliably informed that it's a boy."

"All right, then you may keep him, but he'll need a name and he cannot sleep in your bed! Do you understand Jem?"

Jemima nodded fervently, "I really promise."

Grace turned to her brother and gestured for him to come forward, "William? Come and meet Lady Jemima Winterborne, my daughter. Jem, this is my brother, your Uncle William; he is the eldest of your three uncles."

William held out his hand and Jem rather uncertainly put hers in his and let out a delighted giggle when he bowed over it and kissed it with a formal flourish. "Lady Jemima, I am enchanted to make your acquaintance!"

Smiling shyly, Jem retreated slightly and pulled her mother's skirts around her.

"And this, is Captain Nathaniel Heywood, a — friend — of the — family. Nathan, this is my brother Mr William Edgerton. The one I was telling you about. The noisy one."

William grinned and shook Nathan's hand vigorously, "Captain? How splendid! Did you see any action?"

Nathan returned the smile, "Not as much as I'd have liked which is one of the reasons I sold out."

"Oh, that's too bad! I would have loved to have bought a commission but wasn't allowed."

"I'm afraid he'll quiz you to death, Nathan, he's a very typical young man and has always longed to be in uniform, hence, I suspect, the rather dazzling scarlet coat! He'd probably have been charged with banging the drum for the troops to march in time!"

"I would warn you that it's not a glamorous life, the army. It's usually just long days and nights spent in either the cold and wet or in unbearably hot weather in foreign lands, with all manner of insects to nibble at you and the worst food you can possibly imagine. Nothing really to recommend the life at all apart from the odd pointless skirmish or a long march in knee-deep mud to keep one from murdering one's fellow soldiers. And the much-glorified comradeship is not all its purported to be. You find yourself billeted with the type of fellow you would normally cross the road to avoid and certainly wouldn't wish your sister to marry."

"It would still be a more tolerable life than living at home with my mother!" said William with some asperity. "It's no wonder Gracie took the first chance she had to escape. She made off like a startled deer and never looked back."

"You *know* that's not true, William! I miss you all dreadfully. I didn't want to leave you."

William put his arm around her shoulders and gave her a rough squeeze, "Lord, you think I don't know! I was only teasing. So, Captain Heywood, how long do you stay?"

Nathan glanced at Grace, "As long as your sister will have me or until I can be of no further use to her."

"Lending a hand, eh? That's good to hear. I worry about her being here entirely alone. It must have been a difficult period, after the wedding, removing so far away and to this enormous unfriendly pile. We live in a fairly modest manor-house, Captain, which, compared with this, is rustic and — snug. We certainly wouldn't be able to accommodate as many people as Winterborne. How many rooms does this have?"

Grace shrugged, "I have absolutely no clue. I've never asked or bothered to count them. Too many to keep clean and free of mice that's for certain! Let us hope this little creature takes after her mousing mother! Which reminds me, Jem, what are you to call the kitten?"

Jem who had been twisting this way and that amongst the indigo silk folds of her mother's gown, popped her head out and looked at the small creature in Grace's arms, "Barker," she said.

The three adults exchanged glances, "But, he's a cat, Jem, not a dog. He doesn't bark, he meows."

"Oh," said Jem. "But Meow would be a silly name. I want to call him Barker."

"Very well, he is your kitten, after all, so you may call him what you wish. Barker it is." She handed the kitten to its new mistress and showed her how to hold it properly.

"Tomorrow the Captin is going to show me a kingfisher by the river."

"The Captain is more than kind. I haven't ever seen a kingfisher."

"You can come too then," said Jem nobly. "But you have to be werry quiet. I'm not allowed talk *at all* or they'll run away."

Nathan suppressed a chuckle but made the mistake of looking at Grace, who was holding a hand to her mouth to stop herself laughing out loud, her eyes wide and sparkling. He was forced to turn away so that he couldn't see her, his shoulders shaking.

William was watching and wondering. He'd never seen his elder sister like this; it was eye-opening, and it was giving him a whole new perspective on this strange new life of hers. She suddenly seemed to have become even more vivacious and if he hadn't known her better, he'd have said, happier. He looked from her to the handsome, mysterious stranger, Captain Heywood, and drew some rather interesting conclusions. Since, the Captain had entered the Hall, his sister's demeanour had undergone something of a change and remembering her as she'd always been when at home with her siblings, she'd seldom been anything other than the serious elder sister. She organised them and instructed them and loved them but she'd never, as far as he could recall, giggled with them or spoken in this particular way; the words tumbling softly, her eyes dancing. No, this was a very new and surprising Grace, one he barely recognised.

He remembered her on the distressing day of her wedding to Lord Winterborne, so stiff and dignified, so lifeless and resigned. It had broken his heart but although he was only a year younger than her, he'd been unable to do anything to rescue her. He'd always felt that he'd let her down, weakly allowing her to be taken away to a life of unspeakable torment but here she was, positively vibrating with joy. He was astounded and hugely relieved. Perhaps, after all, she'd found some well-deserved happiness. It may not be the life she would have chosen for herself but somehow, she'd managed to find the love she craved. And it wasn't just the love one has for a small child; it was more, and he knew for certain that it wasn't for her husband. Watching and wondering, he was beginning to see quite clearly, and he worried that if he could see it, then others would too. It appeared that Grace was living dangerously and if she didn't take care, everything would come tumbling about her ears.

"How did you travel, William?" she enquired, "I'll ask the footmen to bring in your luggage."

"I came in Papa's carriage, with Shawe and stayed overnight at post-houses along the way. Three days we've been on the road."

"Papa lent you the carriage?"

"Good Gracious, no! I stole it."

"Oh, *William!* Please tell me that's not true!"

"Of course, it is. How else was I to get here? Don't worry, I left them a note. I told them I was going to Winterborne, to you and not to expect me back. And also, that I'd taken

Grandpapa's gold pocket watch to pawn to pay for the journey. I haven't had a chance to do that yet so am rather short of funds."

Grace gasped and the colour left her cheeks, "This is just dreadful. Father will have convulsions! And *Mother!* Mother will have you hunted down and thrown in prison. Oh, William, what have you *done?*"

William grinned at her, "Gad, Grace! You're as fidgety as ever you were! What *can* they do? They wouldn't ever risk alienating the source of their wealth. They depend upon Lord Winterborne's largesse, but he unnerved them *so* severely at the wedding that they'd never dare challenge you either especially as I'm seeking sanctuary — I believe I shall be safe. I can always send Shawe home with the carriage if the worst comes to the worst."

Nathaniel, who was hugely enjoying this frank exchange, said cheerfully, "Jem and I shall take Barker to the kitchens to get him some food, and leave you two to try to work out this hornet's nest. I shall send the footmen to deal with the luggage, Grace, so that you can concentrate on being overwrought."

She glared at him, "I'm *not* — overwrought! I just know my parents will already have written countless letters accusing me of kidnapping their son and will probably be consulting their attorney at this very minute! They won't take kindly to being outwitted by one of their own children. Oh, it's just too awful to think about!"

"Well," said Nathan soothingly, "Don't think about it then. Why don't you see your brother to his room, and I'll deal with Barker and Jem and the luggage and we can meet back here in half an hour or so for breakfast."

"That sounds like an excellent plan!" said William, "I'm absolutely famished! Haven't eaten for *hours!*"

"I don't believe that for a moment!" said Grace, "I've no doubt you had at least two breakfasts at the last posting house and you probably have a hunk of bread and some cheese in your pocket. I've never known you go hungry. I shall have to tell the cook to order in extra supplies just as though we're having a battalion of soldiers to stay!"

"All boys his age eat as though they've been starved for days," said Nathan. "I was the same. I ate every meal as though it might be my last and that stayed true in the army, when it very well might have been my last."

"Did you really Captain Heywood? I say, I can't wait to talk to you about soldiering! Come on Gracie, let's go and find my bedchamber — I finished that bread and cheese *hours* ago! And two large apples!" admitted William with a shameless grin.

Grace laughed at him and led him away to the stairs while Nathan, Jem and Barker went to find sustenance in the kitchens.

Fourteen

William threw himself onto the bed and bounced on it to test its softness while Grace looked around the room to make sure that it was satisfactorily clean and diligently checked the bed linen to make sure it wasn't damp.

He watched her with a wide grin creasing his amiable young face. "You certainly have become unexpectedly housewifely. And, I must say that it suits you. You seem to be happy too and I don't think I'd anticipated that. I thought that you'd be living in misery, hidden away in a dark and depressing mansion with surly servants and ivy covering the windows and roof — but I find you looking remarkably cheerful and accompanied by a rather dashing looking soldier who seems to have your daughter in tow *and* has a winning way with animals."

"He doesn't *accompany* me! He's a business acquaintance of Gervase's who just happens to be staying at Winterborne with his friend, Mr Talmarch, amongst all manner of other people including dancers and actors and very bad singers and a handful of people of high social standing who are mostly unbearable!"

"Dash it, I'm *so* glad I came!"

Grace sat down on the bed beside him, "I am too. I really am. It couldn't be more fortuitous really. You can help me entertain everyone."

"Gervase cannot help?"

"He's far too ill and although he's able to go downstairs at the moment — the doctor says it won't be long before he is overcome by his illness."

"What illness is he afflicted with?"

Grace looked away, "Disease of the liver."

"Ah," said William knowingly, "I see."

"Don't be too harsh on him. He's had a hard life and you've no idea how he suffers. Nobody, however sunk in wickedness they may be, deserves to die in this way. He's still Jemima's father and that's the important thing."

"That don't excuse him his poor behaviour! Why he practically *bought* you! Just like that. Saw you, fancied you and made an offer that couldn't be refused. Just as though you were a thoroughbred horse. I'm surprised he didn't examine your teeth and fetlocks!"

She lay back on the bed and closed her eyes. "Jem saved me."

"I can see that. And — Captain Heywood? How does he fit in?"

"I told you. He's just a guest."

"He seemed very — at home, for a guest."

"He's been here quite a while — since the day Gervase became really ill. Nathan has helped me care for him and is wonderful with Jem."

"And he treats you well?"

"Oh, very well indeed, just as though we'd always been friends or siblings. He's a wonderful support and makes Jem laugh."

"Does he make *you* laugh?"

"Yes, he does, and he allows Jem to order him around but somehow manages to keep her under control almost without her noticing and that makes my life so much easier."

William lay down beside his sister and said nothing for a while.

He sighed deeply, "Travelling is so fatiguing. I feel quite sleepy — but ravenously hungry at the same time. You know you can tell me anything."

"There's nothing to tell, William."

"Every time I ask about the Captain, you change the subject back to Jemima. I've not exactly been blessed with a great intellect but even I can see something in you has altered."

Grace turned her head away, "I've no idea what you mean. Nothing has altered. I'm still the same person I was before but I just have more responsibilities. Honestly, William you're being quite ridiculous."

"Am I? I think that I know you exceedingly well and even though I haven't seen you for a few years, I can still sense when you're evading the truth." He propped himself up on his elbow and looked hard at her, "'Pon my soul, Grace you deserve some happiness. Don't be ashamed to admit that you've found some, even though it may not have been where you were expecting to find it. It hardly matters anyway. If Gervase is — well, not around for much longer then surely — ?"

Grace sat up suddenly, "Oh, you mustn't speak like that! I'm his wife, and his child is in my care. *My* daughter! You just don't understand."

"Balderdash. You wouldn't be getting so agitated if I were that wide of the mark. Anyway, it matters not to me! I'm delighted and relieved to find that you're not a wretched prisoner with no hope at all of a better future. I can't tell you the guilt I've suffered these last few years. I wanted to come before but was far too scared. It took only the much more terrifying threat of Catherine Wingfield and I was able to forget all those fears and sneak out under cover of darkness and escape in Father's beloved carriage. I have to say that Shawe was excessively keen to come, he does love an adventure! He was carriage driver and says he can stand as my valet as well — he's an absolute Trojan! I even explained that until I'd pawned the pocket watch I wouldn't be able to pay him, but he merely waved that away and demanded to know the route we were to take."

"He always was very reliable and used to get you out of endless scrapes! I'm glad you had enough sense to bring someone trustworthy with you — at least you haven't lost *all* your wits."

"He's a jolly good fellow. I remember him standing foursquare before Mother's wrath and me quaking behind him holding onto his coattails. He wouldn't hear of me leaving alone and I must say that I was grateful because I'd never travelled far before especially by myself and had no clue how to go on at the post-houses and so on."

"I can imagine! Mother kept you close by at all times, afraid of just this sort of thing — you escaping her clutches and having some fun! Oh, she's going to be so angry! I feel desperately anxious for the others — they'll be caught in the teeth of the storm, poor things. I wish there was something I could do to rescue them."

"Arthur won't even notice because he'll be reading some dry-as-dust book and Henry just won't care. Clara is too taken up with ogling the parson so it's only Hester who'll bear the brunt and frankly, she deserves to suffer, she's so frightful."

"She cannot help being so, she takes after Mother because she was the most impressionable of us all. We must count ourselves fortunate that not more of us followed in her footsteps."

"I suppose you're right. Having said that, Clara is almost as bad, there is very little worse than a girl in the first throes of an infantile infatuation. She weeps into her handkerchief all day. The sound of melancholic sniffling is hard to escape. And she writes dire poetry about him and his "skin of ivory and raven's wing hair"! It's intolerable! She dangles over the garden gate all day hoping he'll ride past. He must think her quite demented."

"Oh, poor Clara, she was ever the most emotional of us. She'd fall in love with a gatepost if it were sunlit from just the right angle. You were always very unkind to her though and far too inclined to pinch her rather than being understanding."

"She constantly wails that he won't wait for her to reach a marriageable age! Him being some fifteen years older than her and, of course, a veritable Adonis! It's enough to make you tear at your hair!"

Grace laughed, "How you must have suffered! I'm so sorry that I abandoned you to such torment."

"Well, I've escaped it now, thank heaven!" He flicked her a sideways glance, "So, the Captain — ?"

Grace jumped to her feet and smoothed down her skirts, "Come, let us go down to breakfast or we'll miss it. I'm afraid you're going to have to meet all the guests at once, which will be rather grim. They're quite daunting *en masse.*"

William smiled to himself, as his sister blatantly avoided the subject yet again, "Right, I'll just wash the dust from my hands, and we shall set forth to face our dreaded foes!"

* * *

As William's gaze fell upon the assembled visitors, he wondered if he'd made the right decision coming to Winterborne. A naturally gregarious sort of boy, who was usually more than happy to talk to anyone, even *his* heart quailed a little when he realised the ordeal he must face. The babble of voices did not let up as he and Grace entered the room, and he was mildly shocked by how few of them acknowledged their hostess. He was introduced to those nearest to them and, as there was no room elsewhere, invited to sit next to a gentleman dressed like a peacock, who turned out to be, rather surprisingly, the Captain's dearest friend, Mr Talmarch. After sharing an initially polite exchange with him, Mr Talmarch soon became merrily loquacious about the company they were keeping and quite quickly reduced William to having to suppress his schoolboy giggles.

Grace, seeing her young brother being so royally entertained, was able to relax a little herself and enjoy Nathan talking about the next chapter in Barker's unexpected new life at Winterborne. Apparently, he had very much enjoyed his meal of scraps from the kitchen and the irresistible combination of kitten and adorable child had apparently so enchanted the staff that the creature was not in imminent danger of being rejected or starved.

He had a particular way of telling a story which showed him to a disadvantage and made the whole tale far more amusing and she found she was powerless to resist his gifted narration, frequently giving into laughter. Concentrating on the sound of his pleasant voice, she was able to ignore the tumultuous noise coming from the other end of the long table, which under normal circumstances, would have rendered her mute with apprehension.

"Jemima has demanded that the kitten should have a basket of its own and I've persuaded her to allow him to sleep in the kitchen in the warm. So, I have therefore requested that one of the gardeners find a suitable cat receptacle and he seemed to think he knew where to lay his hands upon one. But for now, Barker is being ruthlessly carried about the place and is in grave danger of losing the use of his legs if he's not put down on the ground more often. He is, at present, with Jem in the nursery, being shown her desk and much-despised sewing frame. He, of course, being a kitten, immediately tried to unravel the dangling threads and has succeeded in making his first enemy: Bridie, who's already threatening to banish him from her domain for the rest of eternity. I fear there will be even more reason for her to complain once she realises that he's not yet been adequately trained to be anywhere other than the stables."

"Oh, dear! What a calamity! You seem to be rather adroit at setting the house on its head and then walking away denying all knowledge of the chaos you so carelessly leave in your wake," said Grace.

Nathan smiled a little ruefully, "I think you're rather too severe. You must surely take into account that I'm merely a poor bachelor, unused to being in a household containing children and small animals and therefore must be afforded *some* leeway for learning as I go along, and also given some credit for transforming from soldier to nursemaid without turning so much as a hair."

"Oh, I do indeed give you much praise and thanks! It's most impressive how readily you've left behind your brutish army ways and allowed us to turn you into a nanny and governess."

"Thank you. It's certainly nice to be appreciated. And today, as part of our schoolroom lessons, we're to go kingfisher watching. I sincerely doubt Jem's ability to stop talking for long enough to let the poor birds settle though. They're beautiful but exceedingly shy birds," he said, studying her face pensively.

She caught the considering look and swiftly averted her eyes.

He continued to look at her with gentle amusement. Watching the emotions chase each other across her lovely face was fast becoming one of his favourite things to do. He would have to bestir himself to make some kind of decision about his future at Winterborne before he became much more entrenched. Emery had been plaguing him and although he'd thought things would soon become more easily resolved, he was finding that as each day drifted by everything just grew more complicated and the more reluctant he was to make a final choice. Emery considered that Nathan was being cowardly and constantly made him aware of his feelings of disappointment. But he felt he was justified in his procrastination because whatever he decided would be detrimental to somebody here: Grace, Jem and Lord Winterborne all stood to lose out one way or the other and of course, Nathan himself was on that list and was slowly discovering that he also had a good deal to lose either way.

Grace could see that William was tucking into his habitually sizeable breakfast, whilst he listened keenly to Emery chatting about the excellence of his tailor and the importance of a hat which *said* something. Her brother was devouring everything within his reach: an array of excellent cold meats and cheeses, including a rather fine sage cheese, boiled eggs, kippers, bread rolls, toast and preserve, coffee and chocolate, followed by an enormous wedge of plum cake served with thick cream. She would be utterly astonished if he were still able to walk afterwards and felt quite faint when she saw the quantity of food he was able to consume in one sitting, especially as a large dinner was not many hours away.

Nathan leant forward and murmured, "Don't worry, we shall take him out later and make him run around the park a few times with Dancer and Thisbe."

"You'll have to push him in a wheelbarrow!" replied Grace and was delighted when Nathan let out a crack of laughter. She went quite pink with pleasure at the thought of him finding her remark amusing and then had to turn her face away so that he didn't see her ridiculous delight.

As they were leaving the dining room after breakfast, Miss Weston held Grace back saying she wished to have a word with her, so Nathan, Emery and William went on ahead, intending to prepare for the Great Kingfisher Expedition.

"What is it, Miss Weston? Can I be of any assistance?"

Miss Peggy Weston was looking rather serious, which was unusual, as she was more often to be found with a broad grin upon her wide face and a ready laugh upon her lips.

"Well, my lady, it's just that I'm in a bit of a pother about my good friend, Jenny — Miss Robbins!"

"Oh? And which young lady is that?"

"Y'know, the actress, the little one, with the golden hair an' the big blue eyes! She's a really good actress but not very — clever? She's forever bein' led astray by gentlemen — well, perhaps *not* gentlemen — who have a way with words an' a pleasing way about them, but I'm afraid there's one here who has a little too much danger about 'im!"

"Ah," said Grace, "I believe I know where this is going now. You are concerned about a certain — *gentleman* — who has his eye upon her?"

"That's it *precisely*, m'lady! How clever you are to understand! It's that Mr Carew. He's — makin' a nuisance of himself an' Jenny cannot or *will* not see that he's up to no good! I've managed to pull her out of hot water before but this time she won't pay me no heed. She's set her sights on 'im an' thinks that he's in earnest. I think he's a — right shuffler — a regular thatch-gallows! He ain't to be trusted. Jenny, she's such a silly little thing an' is always hopin' for love an' she's so *very* trusting. She was brought up in a small village in the middle of nowhere an' should have wed some jolly cowherd an' born a dozen babies but she fell into the theatre world by accident an' now — now she's heading for more trouble an' I just thought you might be able to talk to the — gentleman an' persuade him to leave off!"

Miss Weston looked at Grace with such respect and belief in her eyes that Grace found herself nodding, "I'll see what I can do. Although I fear Mr Carew is unlikely to heed anything I may say but I will try," she thought for a moment, "Or, I might get Captain Heywood to have a word. Mr Carew might be more inclined to listen to him!"

"Oh, thank you so much, m'lady! I *knew* you wouldn't let me down! You're a rum mort, so you are!"

"I have no idea what a "rum mort" may be, but I suspect thanks are in order. Although, I cannot promise a result which will satisfy you, Miss Weston."

"It's bloody marvellous! I've told the others that you're as fine as five pence."

"I'm delighted to be thought so! I'm sorry but I must dash now as I've an urgent appointment in the garden with my daughter and, hopefully, a kingfisher."

"A proper adventure! I have to go an' rehearse my lines for the play we're puttin' on in a few days. I'm playin' Miss Kate Hardcastle. It's the best part I've *ever* been given!"

"I'm so glad to hear it. I'm sure you'll be splendid in the role."

"Oh, I will! I've been studyin' *you!* Miss Hardcastle is hoity-toity, so I have to speak just like you do."

"Goodness gracious!" said Grace, thoroughly lost for words.

* * *

The sun was so dazzling that it took a moment for Grace to become accustomed to the brilliance of the great expanse of sky above her and she had to blink her eyes a few times as she stood on the terrace at the front of the house. The garden was just beginning to show signs of suffering from the lack of rain, the grass bleached to palest ochre in places and the shrubs looking a little limp and weary. Far away the hills were painted in soft blues and violets and hazy in the heat, their outlines gently rippling as though under water. Somehow the sultry heat felt ominous to Grace, although she loved the ferocity of it and enjoyed the scent of baking earth and the rich heaviness of the air. She could hear voices, one high and excited, and saw that standing in the shade of a large topiary peacock was a small gathering of aspiring ornithologists, one being already rather too lively at the prospect of being allowed to join what must seem, to her, to be an exhilarating quest. Jem had been blessed with a vivid imagination and sometimes Grace felt that she wasn't able to keep pace with her high-spirited daughter as well as she should. She felt that she was too prosaic and lacked the required inspiration to keep Jem amused and out of trouble. As she approached the little group, she could see the child's upturned face as she was saying something to Nathan and thought, not without a pang of unwonted jealousy, that she seemed to have found that inspiration in someone other than her mother.

She noted that Jem didn't even really take much notice of her arrival apart from a quick smile, so focused was she on whatever Nathan was now saying to her.

William shouted out to her and gave her a friendly nudge, "Mr Talmarch has declined our invitation to lie in the dusty grass and wait for hours for some elusive bird to maybe appear or not, depending upon its whim! Mr Talmarch said he rather thought his tailor would cast him off if he ruined yet another coat. He's terribly amusing! And his coats are first-rate! I shall be able to learn a thing or two from him on how to be more modish. He's very willing to help me, giving me guidance and tips."

Grace looked helplessly to Nathan, who had been listening with half an ear. His lips twitched as he cast her a swift sympathetic glance.

"I think you already have a unique style all your own, William! And Mr Talmarch — has a flair with rather more outlandish fashions," said Grace as diplomatically as she could.

William laughed, "He *said* you'd be politely averse to me taking his advice! Don't worry! I shall not be covered in gold frogging and flaunt a purple lace handkerchief! I mean merely to learn about the *cut* of a coat and how to recognise when something is *too* dandyish!"

At this Nathan could not prevent a derisive snort of laughter escaping and quickly took Jem by the hand and strolled off towards the river before he disgraced himself.

Watching him walk away, Grace privately called him a few uncomplimentary names to his cowardly back.

Grace and William caught up with them as they neared the riverbank.

Jem turned to them and in a piercing stage whisper scolded them for not tiptoeing silently. "Ssshh!" she hissed, a dimpled finger to her lips, "You're far too *noisy!*"

William made a comical face at her and began to tiptoe stealthily and over-theatrically, as though he were a burglar, which made Jem giggle, clap a hand over her mouth and frown at her ridiculous uncle in feigned disapproval. She shook her head in grown-up despair and looked up at Nathan expecting a show of support and that gentleman just had time to wipe the grin from his face before giving his indignant companion a look of serious and like-minded understanding.

They were forced to make their way some distance along the riverbank because the gardeners had, with Grace's inexpert permission, cut back a good deal of the cover the birds might have used, until Nathan spied a still area of water in a small, overgrown oxbow lake. He gestured to a comfortable spot in a nearby spinney where there was a convenient fallen tree trunk to perch upon and a good, but disguised, view of the pool.

Nathan pointed out the opposite sandy bank where there were several holes and whispered that they might be kingfisher burrows. He'd already told them that they must listen for the bird's distinctively high-pitched call and warned them that they may see nothing at all even after waiting for an age so must be prepared for disappointment. Jem nodded wisely and from then on stayed alert and silent, her eyes watching hopefully for any sign of their tiny quarry.

Grace was astonished to find that her usually restless daughter was sitting as still as a stone, every line of her small figure, tense and expectant. Looking down at her, Grace had never loved her more, and was filled with an overwhelming desire to scoop her up into her arms and cover her face with kisses. Tears sprang to her eyes and she dashed them away impatiently but not before Jem had heard her sniffle and hushed her severely.

Nathan had also witnessed her moment of maternal pride but chose to pretend he'd been looking the other way.

They waited. And they waited.

* * *

Forty minutes later, nothing had changed. The sky was still blue and cloudless, there was not a whisper of wind, other far less exotic birds came and went and were dismissed as not worthy of special attention; a squirrel busily dug up a tasty nut and nibbled it prettily, spinning it around in its tiny human-like paws. There was the occasional soft splash of a brown trout as it left the river for a second to snap at a dragonfly and returned again to the cool shadowy water. The buzz and hum of insects, like a strange orchestra, filled the muggy air with their hypnotic music.

Grace was finding it difficult to keep her eyes from closing. She dug her nails into the palms of her hands to try to stay awake. Jem felt obliged to poke her in the arm several times to wake her up even though she wasn't actually asleep; she'd been drifting, allowing the heat and the somnolent sounds to lull her. William seemed to be in an open-eyed trance, but she suspected that he was cleverly, actually asleep, and Nathan, with a soldier's long experience, was relaxed but vigilant.

She was just wondering how long they'd be sitting there when Jem's sharp intake of breath roused her. The child was pointing a stubby finger. Grace turned just in time to see a jagged flash of turquoise. Jem grabbed her mother's hand and squeezed it hard. Then, as they stiffened with anticipation, Jem let out a muted squeal. They followed the direction of her jabbing finger further across the lake to where a group of alders crowded the edge of the riverbank and some of their branches hung low over the water.

On one branch, sat a kingfisher with two of its young; the adult suddenly took off and dived like a swift blue dart into the still water beneath the branch and seconds later emerged with a wriggling minnow in its beak. It returned to its perch and beat the fish on the branch to stun it and then fed it to the first of its infants.

Grace found she was holding her breath as she observed her child watch the colourful and dramatic display.

Then, they were gone.

Jem let out a sigh of pure joy.

"We *saw* them," she whispered. "The Captin *said!* And they were here. I wish Mr Talmarch had seen them; they wear coats just like his!"

Grace gathered her closer and squeezed her rather too hard until she complained she couldn't breathe, "I think Mr. Talmarch will be very sorry he missed them. Although I don't suppose he would have been able to sit still for as long as you and Captain Heywood did."

"Yes, we were best, the Captin and me. We *really* wanted to see the kingfishers because they're the best thing but not as best as Barker," declared Jem happily.

Grace kissed the top of her curly head and looking at Nathan, murmured a slightly wobbly "Thank you," at him.

William gave himself a shake, "Did I miss anything?" he asked rubbing his eyes.

Fifteen

Lord Winterborne was eyeing his young brother-in-law dispassionately. The boy stood before him, his mouth set firmly and his expression defiant. William was determined to have his say, and had waited a whole day before gathering the courage to do so. Even though Grace had warned him to be respectful and not antagonise her husband, William possessed the bombastic swagger of youth, certain in the knowledge that he was right and that everyone would be able to see that if they'd just listen to him. Unfortunately, he had not encountered anyone quite like the Marquis before, apart from brief glimpses of him at his sister's wedding, where Lord Winterborne had failed to endear himself to the fifteen-year-old boy, who'd thought him far too old and sinister to be a suitable bridegroom. He hadn't liked the way he had treated his sister or his parents so imperiously, as though they were somehow vastly inferior. He'd just expected to be given anything he desired without argument because he was titled and wealthy and they were in desperate need of his riches with nowhere else to turn. He'd assumed that no member of the Edgerton family would stand in his way and none did. And this, William had bitterly regretted for the last four years. He was now set upon a course which he knew would probably end badly for him but the fifteen-year-old boy in him still felt hard done by and was seeking some kind of justice for his favourite sister.

The withdrawing room was thankfully empty of the Theatricals and other guests and William was able to put forward his case without the embarrassment of having an audience to witness his humiliation. And, even knowing that he was bound to be humiliated, he squared up to the Marquis and tried to speak clearly and not become emotional.

Lord Winterborne heard him out and for a moment said nothing, just staring at him from narrow, yellowed eyes.

When he spoke, his voice was surprisingly strong, considering his precarious state of health, "You have overstepped, boy. This is none of your business and I'll thank you to keep your opinions to yourself."

William swallowed, "Yes, I'm sure, my lord, but she's my sister and it would be unforgivably remiss of me — in fact, outrageously *irresponsible* if, I the eldest male Edgerton, after Father, of course, should neglect my duty to any of my siblings. I therefore feel it to be my bounden duty to inform you that I must take you to task for your unforgivably shabby treatment of both Grace and the rest of my family. I know there's nothing I can do to change past events now, because I've left it too late to make my feelings known and I was far too young at the time to protect Grace, but I still feel obliged to make you aware of the depth of my disapproval."

There was a moment's silence as Lord Winterborne digested this carefully rehearsed but rather hurried speech.

"You're a brave boy, William Edgerton, and I think more of you because of this show of courage. I despise cowards. Therefore, I applaud you. You've more of your sister's admirable qualities than I first thought."

William, completely taken aback and with the wind comprehensively knocked out of his sails, rendering them limp and useless, opened and closed his mouth several times, unable to think of a suitable rejoinder.

Lord Winterborne looked upon him with an expression bordering admiration, "Yes, indeed! It doesn't do to make assumptions about people when you have nothing but unsubstantiated allegations against them. I may have faults and they may be legion, but I don't think you could ever accuse me of not being able to recognise a stout-hearted fellow when I meet one."

"Well — I'm — you — by Jupiter — "

"Lost for words, eh? While you're trying to think of something pertinent to say, be a good lad and hand me a drink from the sideboard."

William looked across at the array of decanters on the sideboard and then back at his lordship. "They only contain cordials of various types, my lord. There's no wine or brandy."

The Marquis frowned at him for a moment before giving a short, mirthless laugh, "*Naturally!* Fetch me a glass of damned cordial then! My throat is dry from all this talking."

"Yes, my lord," said William and did as he was bade. He was shaken and needed a second to recover his wits. As he poured the dark crimson cordial into the engraved glass, he pondered his predicament. This man, whom he'd sworn to hate, had utterly confounded him, making him doubt his own long-held convictions. He knew that he was dealing with a duplicitous and clever man and had expected his incompetent argument to be met with either violent outrage or dismissed with chilling brevity but the almost affable riposte he'd been accorded had left him floundering. He'd planned to storm out of the room and slam the door on the Marquis's coldly callous words but as none were forthcoming, he was left bobbing about in an ocean of uncertainty, looking helplessly for rescue or the very least, an explanation.

He handed the glass to Lord Winterborne, who took it in a pale, trembling hand and lifted it to his mouth with the utmost care. He took several sips but then seemingly overcome with the effort it took, he held out the glass to William.

"Took the brandy away, eh?" said his lordship, bitterly. "That meddling sister of yours probably. Can't think why she bothers. As good as dead already. *Both* feet in the grave."

"Oh, *no*, my lord! There is *always* hope!" William heard himself say, much to his astonishment. "You *mustn't* give up!"

A laugh of sorts left his lordship's grey lips, "Hell and damnation! Am I now to be hounded into the family vault by some bleeding-heart schoolboy? I can only wish for a quick and merciful death if that's to be the case!"

William smiled a little wanly but noting the deterioration in the Marquis's already pale aspect said, with genuine concern, "I think I shall go and fetch Mrs Hawkins, my lord — you're looking somewhat fatigued." And before Lord Winterborne could argue, he'd dashed to the door and called the hovering footman to find the nursemaid at once.

* * *

Later that evening, William found himself, most gratifyingly, to be seated comfortably beside Captain Heywood in the parlour, while the Theatricals rehearsed their play in the withdrawing room, and he felt compelled to say something about his meeting with the Marquis to this fine gentleman because he had the feeling that the Captain had a very good understanding of the lay of the land at Winterborne. He himself, had heard nothing but baseless rumours and Grace had never mentioned, in her infrequent letters, anything in the slightest bit negative about her life with her new husband and stepdaughter. But then, he thought, she wouldn't; she'd never been the sort of girl to complain about her lot, unlike Hester who did nothing *but* complain! It was extremely hard being an elder brother, it was certainly not for the faint-hearted but deep down he knew it had been even more of a trial being the eldest sister in the Edgerton family.

"Captain Heywood?" he began diffidently.

"Yes, William? By the bye, I do wish you'd call me Nathan, constantly being reminded that I was in the army is not conducive to being at ease with the world."

William cast him a look of ill-disguised adulation, "*Thank you!*" he breathed, "What an *honour!*"

"Nonsense!" said Nathan briskly, "Now what troubles you?"

William took a steadying breath, "It's Lord Winterborne."

"Ah," said Nathan, and gave the young man his undivided attention.

"I was wondering what you thought of him. You've had the opportunity to speak with him more than I have, and I was hoping that you might share your conclusions with me."

"*Did* you? I take it that you've spoken with him?"

"I have. You see I meant to tear him off a strip, but he thwarted me! I managed to tell him that I utterly *condemned* his having bought Grace as though she were a prize heifer at an auction and all he said in response was that he admired my *pluck!* The interview did not go at all the way I'd planned."

Nathan allowed himself a slight smile but treated the boy's concerns with due solemnity, although he had his doubts about Grace enjoying being referred to in any context as a prize heifer. "So, he got the better of you in this altercation?"

"I don't know, to be honest! It just seemed that one minute I was stating my case, and the next he was telling me that he despised cowards and that I was 'a stout-hearted fellow!' Well, you could have knocked me down with a feather! Never have I been so — *crushed!*"

Nathan hid his amusement, "I can imagine. There's nothing quite as disconcerting as having the rug unexpectedly pulled out from beneath your feet. So, what was the outcome of the encounter?"

"Why, I ended up offering him sympathy for his condition — which is, as we are all aware, *wholly* his own fault — and telling him not to give up! I couldn't believe the words coming out of my mouth! It was as though I had no control over my own thoughts."

"That is quite understandable, he's a very compelling individual and is used to getting his own way in everything. Don't feel disappointed. At least you made the effort. On behalf of your sister, I presume?"

"Yes," said William gravely, "It was my duty as her brother. Someone should have saved her right at the beginning, stepped up and fought for her, but no one did. *I* didn't."

"You were fifteen, little more than a child. You cannot blame yourself. Anyway, I suspect that nothing you could have said or done could have stopped the wedding from going ahead. And, looking at it another way, your sister has found a reason to be grateful for her marriage — Jemima. That little girl has become the most important part of her life and I believe if you gave her the choice of being able to change the outcome, to *not* marry and *not* have Jem, I am absolutely convinced she would still marry Lord Winterborne, even being forewarned."

William was much struck by this notion and took a minute to consider it. "I suppose you're right. I hadn't thought of it that way."

Nathan saw the boy's shoulders relax a little, "I take it you left the Marquis on good terms then?"

William shrugged, "I might have done had I not called in Mrs Hawkins when I thought he needed help! He was most severely put out!"

Nathan laughed, "That will serve him right for being so awfully reasonable. He loathes Mrs Hawkins with a deadly passion — she prays at him in the vain hopes of saving his ruined soul."

"Oh, no wonder he looked so very pained!" exclaimed William, stricken.

"It's good for him to suffer, I think, he may learn something — albeit too late to make any difference. Do you know what, William, I think you might be good for the Marquis! I believe he's going to find it refreshing to have such an honest, good-natured young man around to keep him in order."

William wasn't sure what to make of this statement but was very much heartened that the Captain thought that he might have some beneficial effect on Lord Winterborne and was mightily relieved that nothing he could have done would have altered the course of Grace's life because it had haunted him, and he'd been unable to properly enjoy any moments of success or pleasure in his own life because of the overwhelming sense of guilt he felt. He had decided, aged sixteen, that he'd take up the Cloth and become a priest or a monk, in order to atone for having let Grace down. When he turned seventeen, he changed his mind and vowed to become a soldier so that he could kill Lord Winterborne with military efficiency and an indifferent shrug. Then at nineteen he'd been threatened with an imminent betrothal to Catherine Wingfield, so he'd run away from home. Looking back on these last few years he decided that he'd not covered himself in glory but at least Captain Heywood — *Nathan*, seemed to place some faith in him and that gave him heart.

At this point Emery wandered over to join them and demanded to know what they were talking about as he'd been cornered by Mrs Leventhorpe for the last hour and was so bored, he was ready to shoot himself, having not been allowed to insert one single word into the conversation; not that he'd wanted to contribute to a diatribe which mainly consisted of her complaints about everything from how to deal with lazy footmen to the correct seating arrangements for dining with royalty. He had absolutely no interest in anything she said and was hard-pressed not to yawn throughout the whole tedious monologue and as soon as he could politely manage it, he escaped.

"Gad, Nate! That woman could stupefy a herd of rampaging bullocks with her dreary, droning blather! I've never been so close to feigning sudden death! You might have come to my rescue! Just left me to her tender mercies! Abominable! So, what have you been discussing, you both looked uncommonly serious?"

"Capt — *Nathan*, has been giving me some sound advice," said William, "It's been most enlightening."

Emery gave his friend a doubtful look, "Has he indeed? That's fascinating. I had no idea that Nate had any knowledge outside being a soldier. Is he advising you to buy a pair of colours? Don't listen to him! You'd be better off taking Holy Orders. Far safer! Unlikely to get shot at whilst giving a sermon."

"No, we were talking about my sister."

A candid look at Nathan, "Well, there's a thing! Grace, eh? Remarkable woman. You must hold her in high esteem."

"I do. She's admirable in every way."

Emery glanced around the room, "I wonder where she is, I haven't seen her since breakfast."

William frowned, "She had to talk to the cook, I think, and then she was going up to the nursery to find Jem." He cast an eye at the bracket clock on the mantelpiece and rose to his feet, "I think I shall go and look for her — she should be here by now." And with that he went out, leaving Emery free to question Nathan about the advice he'd been so readily handing out.

"He merely needed me to lend a fraternal, nay, *paternal* ear to his concerns. It was nothing of import. Although, it seems that he has managed to pierce the Marquis's armour and made him something of an ally," said Nathan blandly.

"I find that hard to believe. I had thought Lord Winterborne to be impervious to all forms of blandishment."

"I think that's the point. It appears that William stood firm and spoke the unvarnished truth and the Marquis approved of his backbone. It's interesting to find that he's some conventional human qualities. William, of course, could not be more likeable or trustworthy. One would have to be pretty hardhearted not to fall under his endearing spell. It would be like not warming to a doe-eyed puppy."

"But still — *Lord Winterborne*! Not exactly known for his conviviality."

"No, but everyone has their weakness. Even cold-blooded devils like Winterborne. There is always hope for even the most lost soul."

"Sounds like you're going soft, Nate!"

"Maybe I am," reflected Nathan.

He had just glanced up at the clock when the door opened and William stood on the threshold, ashen-faced.

Nathan quickly got up and went to him, "William? What is it?"

"Grace — she can't find Jem *anywhere!* Bridie left the nursery for just a moment she said and when she returned Jem had gone. They've been looking all over the house and have set the footmen and gardeners to searching the grounds but — "

"Why the hell didn't she alert me sooner? Come, Emery, Marcus, Peter! The terrace *now!*"

* * *

A party of the male guests spread out and began to methodically search the nuttery and orchards and kitchen gardens, the Maze and the meadows beyond. Nathan organised the stable lads to thoroughly comb the stables and the numerous outbuildings and he found Grace still frantically going through the house, checking and rechecking all the chambers and antechambers, the cupboards and sculleries and realised she was fast becoming incoherent with anxiety. He stopped her in her tracks and took her by the shoulders.

"Grace! Look at me. Take a breath. We shall find her. I am certain of it. But you must stay calm — this panicking will get us nowhere. Did she say anything? Give any clue to what was in her thoughts?"

Grace shook her head wretchedly, "*No!* She said nothing apart from her usual nonsense! Oh, where can she *be?* She never runs off! She's been gone for ages now. Oh, God, Nathan! I can't bear it! If I lose her! If something has happened to her!"

Still holding her by the shoulders he shook her gently to try to halt her growing agitation, "Stop it! This will do no good." He looked up to see Bridie hastening down the corridor towards them, "Any news?", but the nursemaid shook her head. "Then, we must look further afield. Bridie, did Jem say anything at all to you that might give us a clue as to what was on her mind?"

"No, Captain Heywood! I told Lady Winterborne, she was just as she always was, talkative and unwilling to do anything I told her! Nothing out of the ordinary. She wouldn't let go of the kitten despite me saying that it wasn't suitable to be clutching an animal when sewing — "

"Is the kitten still in the nursery?" interrupted the Captain.

"No, he's — gone too."

Nathan knitted his brows, "She's taken Barker," he murmured to himself, eyes narrowed, "Bridie, stay here in case she returns. Grace come with me." He took her hand and pulled her along the corridor, "I think I understand. She's taken that damn kitten for an adventure."

* * *

They made their way through the garden, Grace scrambling to keep up with Nathan's long stride, as he still held her hand firmly in his, dragging her along behind him.

"Where are we — *Nathan!* Slow *down!* I must take off my shoes for I can't run in them!" And she hopped along for a few steps inelegantly prising off the despised footwear and leaving them heedlessly in the long grass, followed by her stockings, Nathan slowing just long enough for her to tug them off and drop them in their wake.

They skirted the Maze and continued on through the fields beyond and finally came to the river.

"Oh, dear God! She *wouldn't* — !" gasped Grace breathlessly.

Nathan's narrowed eyes were raking the scene, "I've an idea that she may have decided to take Barker birdwatching and if that's so she may be anywhere along the riverbank."

Grace put a shaking hand over her mouth to keep from crying out and Nathan gave her hand a squeeze, "You stay here, and I'll head downriver to look."

'No, I'm coming with you."

Nathan didn't stop to argue; he strode away in the direction they had taken on the day of the Kingfisher Expedition and Grace stumbled along after him, but he was soon out of sight around a wooded bend, and she was forced to stop to catch her breath. She could hear him calling for Jem.

She looked around blindly, the blood rushing in her ears and her heart pounding uncomfortably under her ribs.

Then she saw it.

A tiny scrap of harebell blue caught on the weeds dangling over the edge of the river.

"Oh, no, no, no!" whispered Grace, as she pushed her way through the reeds to the riverbank. She reached out and snatched at the blue riband. Jem's blue riband.

Then, through the sound of her rising panic, she heard something.

The faintest sound.

She stood very still and listened. Trying to sift the sounds, the hum of bees, the water hurrying past, the sigh of the trees —

There it was again.

She eased her way forward and peered out into the swirling water.

The sound carried to her — a soft mew.

"Barker?"

Clinging onto the undergrowth, she lowered herself down the incline, praying as she went. Her skirts caught on the brambles and she ripped them away.

"Please! *Please!*" she begged God, or anyone who might be watching over them.

Then, remembering, she called out, "Nathan! *Nathan!*" but her voice was stifled, her throat tight with fear.

She felt her foot slip and grabbed a handful of reeds to steady herself and then saw, just a short distance away, under the bank's overhang, half in the water and wedged between some tangled twigs, the kitten, bedraggled and terrified. She looked all around for any sign of her daughter but seeing none, she anchored her bare foot into a sturdy looking bush and wrapped her arm about one of its thicker branches. She leant out over the water and made a grab for the tiny animal.

On the second attempt her fingers found a purchase on slippery fur and with a grunt of relief she hauled Barker out of the eddying waters.

But, as she edged backwards, holding the limp creature none too gently, her foot lost its precarious grip and shot forward and she slid, wildly snatching at the weeds as she fell, and plummeted into the river.

She somehow managed to keep the kitten above water, just holding it clear but struggling to keep her own head from going under.

Her heavy skirts started to drag her down, caught in the current, which even though not as fast as usual was still strong enough to pull at her clothes, preventing her from being able to get hold of anything solid, drawing her inexorably out into the middle of the river.

The water was too deep for her to find a foothold and she'd never learnt to swim. She knew she didn't have long before she was pulled under. She lunged at the bank but ended up being submerged and came up spluttering, spitting river water. The weight of her gown was too much, and she found she hadn't the strength to fight it. Her head went under again and her hair, coming down in wet strands, wound itself about her face, blinding her.

She kicked out and made one last effort to reach the reeds. The pitiless, swirling water closed over her head. She opened her eyes and saw nothing but muddy green; she came up again into the air, gasped and choked and, face-to-face with her fate, screamed with what she was certain was her last breath, "*Nathan!*"

Sixteen

Nathan, having happily come across a sobbing Jemima, forlornly dragging a long thin branch behind her, was trying to decipher amongst the tragic hiccupping and incoherent babble of words, what she was trying desperately to tell him. It appeared that she really *needed* a stick and after a few moments he ascertained that it was to rescue the kitten. She was unable to explain where the kitten might be because she'd become quite lost, the ground by the river being bewildering for someone so small, the bushes and trees all blending into a terrifying jungle towering above her head. She said she'd let Barker have a walk while she sat down to rest and he'd disappeared into the river and that she'd gone to fetch a stick to help him out again.

"That was a brave thing to do, Jem. But if you're ever in trouble again you must seek a grown-up to come and help you. Now, let us see where that wretched kitten is, shall we?"

It was as they made their way back the way he'd just come, that he heard the faint cry.

His skin prickled, a cold chill raising gooseflesh.

He scooped Jem up and began to sprint as fast as he could over the uneven, treacherous ground. He had no time to reassure the child, intent on finding the source of that blood-curdling sound. His eyes were scouring the land for clues and eventually spotted the trampled grass, broken reeds and a significant blue riband; he quickly looked about him and put Jem down on the grass, instructing her very firmly to sit and not to move an inch whatever happened. She nodded obediently sensing the seriousness of the situation.

As he was swiftly pulling off his boots, he spotted out of the corner of his eye someone racing towards him along the riverbank and was deeply grateful to see William heading his way at full tilt. He yelled at him to mind Jem and followed the tracks down to the water's edge.

He could see nothing at all, just the river going about its usual business. His breath caught in his throat. He steadied himself and forced himself to scrutinise the water's surface.

All he could hear was his own heartbeat thumping.

All he could think was that he'd lost her.

Then, a slight change to the pattern of ripples caught his eye and he dived in.

He struck out to where he'd seen the telltale sign and plunged down. Something wrapped itself around his arm and he grabbed at it. He had a handful of sodden, swirling material and then another. He hauled at it and finally had her in his arms.

Somehow, he managed to drag her to the bank and William was there with his muscular young arms to heave her out onto dry land.

He didn't even take a second to catch his breath but clambered out immediately.

William was rolling Grace onto her side.

Then, Emery was there, carrying a now wailing Jem away from the upsetting scene.

Nathan knelt beside Grace and saw the limp kitten still held in her hand; William was frantically slapping her back but looking to Nathan for support. His eyes were wide and terrified and his face colourless, all his usual ruddy complexion faded to chalky grey.

"Is she — !"

Nathan could already see that Grace's pallor was alarming and if she was breathing at all, it was very shallow. He removed the kitten which wriggled slightly as he dropped it onto the grass.

He suddenly had a vision of an army camp follower, a young woman, who had unfortunately become pregnant by a soldier and had been forced to give birth by the side of the road during a long march. Another older woman was helping her and when the child came into the world, it was blue and not breathing and he'd been astonished to see the woman put her mouth over the baby's and breathe into it. She did this several times until the baby took its first breath and eventually began breathing and it turned a healthier shade of pink and lived.

He didn't stop to think, he just put his mouth to Grace's and breathed into hers. He wasn't sure what else to do. Nothing happened. He tried again and saw to his relief her chest rise and fall. He breathed into her mouth again and then looked up at William in despair.

There was a long moment of just silent nothing. Of Nathan thinking it was too late and of William suffering an agony of anguish.

Spurred on by nothing more than the fear that he might never see her smile again, Nathan caught hold of her and shook her so hard that William let out a gasp of protest.

Nathan shook her again, "Grace! Don't you dare die! Wake up damn you!"

William was sobbing silently, "She's gone. She's *gone!* It's too late. Oh, God!"

Nathan put his mouth to hers again and breathed hard into her mouth.

As he lifted his head, there was the slightest movement and an inhaled breath.

Every part of Nathan's being was focused on Grace. He gave her another purposeful shake.

She coughed and spat up water. She took another breath. Violent and deep.

Then another.

Nathan gathered her into his arms and held her against his chest, "Come on, Grace, Jem's waiting for you. She needs you. For God's sake, keep breathing."

William watched as his sister took another shuddering breath. He wiped his face on his sleeve and looked at Nathan. The Captain was visibly shaking.

"Grace, please open your eyes!" said Nathan, in a suffocated voice.

William let out a tremulous sob.

Just then they were joined by Emery, Marcus Delamere and two footmen carrying a litter.

When Nathan looked up at him, Emery feared the worst; he'd never seen anyone look so devastated and William was crumpled over Grace's body seemingly wracked with grief.

"God, *no! Nate!*" cried Emery.

"She's — alive," said Nathan, barely audibly.

Emery went quite weak at the knees with relief and turned to order the footmen to lay the litter down beside Grace.

"Give me your coat," demanded Nathan, and Emery shrugged himself out of his beautiful coat without a second thought and handed it to his friend. Nathan wrapped it around Grace's inert body, holding it in place for a few seconds before standing up and helping William and Marcus Delamere lift her onto the litter.

Marcus then spotted the feebly mewling kitten and picking it up, wrapped it carefully in his handkerchief.

William held Grace's icy hand as the footmen bore her away. Nathan just stood and watched them go, overcome with a wave of exhaustion so depleting that he thought he'd have to sit down or risk collapsing.

Emery put an arm about his waist and supported him, "Come, dear fellow, she needs you," and he helped his friend walk back to the house behind the slow-moving procession.

"Never mind that — I need *her*," murmured Nathan bleakly.

"I know you do, Nate, I know you do!" responded Emery a little unsteadily.

*   *   *

Back at the house, after instructing Kirby to send for Doctor Morton, only to be told that a groom had already set out at speed to fetch him, Emery went to find Jem, to hopefully persuade her that everything would be all right. He exchanged quiet words with Bridie, explaining what had happened and the outcome and saying that it would probably be best to keep Jem occupied and away from her mother until the doctor had been. Bridie, casting aside all her previous complaints and their frequent squabbles, gathered the little girl into her arms and hugged her.

Nathan followed the litter up to Grace's bedchamber. A silent and stony-faced Sally was already there and a brisk and efficient Mrs Hawkins, and they ushered the footmen and Nathan out so they could quickly get Grace out of her dripping clothes and into a warm bed.

Nathan had nothing to do but go to his bedchamber to change his own clothes. He closed the door behind him and slid down onto his haunches, his head in his hands and for a moment struggled with some strong emotions. He felt as though he'd been winded, and his heart ripped out of his chest.

* * *

Doctor Morton muttered something about the Winterborne's keeping him exceedingly busy at the moment as he entered Grace's bedchamber, closing the door behind him and leaving Nathan kicking his heels outside in the corridor for half an hour. Emery was beside him and doing his level best to calm him but on suggesting that his friend might benefit from taking a few deep breaths, he had his nose bitten off for his pains.

"There's no need to take it out on me, dear boy! I am but an innocent bystander. The doctor will no doubt be doing his best and he did say that as Grace was pulled from the water quite quickly and her colour returned within minutes that he felt sure she would recover with no lasting ill-effects."

Nathan rubbed at his tired eyes with the heel of his hand, "What if he's wrong?"

"God, Nate! What if he's *right?*"

Nathan eyed him blankly, "Emery, when I heard her cry out — I *knew* — immediately, that she was in dire trouble — and in that moment, I also realised that we must leave Winterborne as soon as we possibly can. I *cannot* stay."

Emery studied his companion's drawn face in the corridor's poor light, "Well, if nothing else, I believe you've learnt a salutary lesson today. You've — *we've* learnt that you're capable of putting others first — and that you're able to feel *deeply* for someone. I've always had serious doubts that your heart was a proper functioning organ. It seemed to me that you're quite content to be — numb. Well, I'd say that now you're no longer numb! Of course, the problem with *not* being numb is the unwelcome introduction of *suffering!* Suffering is something you'll not be familiar with, Nate, and I can tell you, it can be — unbearable."

Nathan, who had privately decided that he was done with suffering, had no desire to prolong the visit which was causing him to question his own sanity and was bound and determined to leave the reason for his sudden discomfiture behind; the minute Grace was well enough to be safely left he would ride away and not look back. He forbore to question his flimsy excuses for not quitting Winterborne sooner but reassured himself that he had only done what any decent human being would do in the same circumstances.

Watching him, Emery could see the battle he was having with his conscience and realised that until a very short while ago, he'd been convinced that Nathan was wholly disinterested in anyone other than himself. Naturally, he was prepared to give his unstinting loyalty to his fellow soldiers but when not with them, shoulder to shoulder, he was able to forget them and consign them to the Devil: out of sight, out of mind.

Emery had a fiendish desire to push Nathan right to the edge of whatever cliff he was relentlessly backing away from and suppressing the mischievous glint in his eye, he asked, with all the appearance of innocence, "So, are we to leave without having completed the — er — task and return to certain penury and probably a crowded and rat-infested cell in Newgate?"

"Yes. We are. We'll somehow survive. We did before and we will again. It was a damned ludicrous idea in the first place. I must have been out of my mind to listen to you. I blame you for persuading me that it might be a sound prospect because it's brought me nothing but headaches and misfortune and we've gained not the slightest benefit from all our travails. I might just as well have stayed in London and returned to the army for all the good it's done me."

"Just for the purposes of idle curiosity and playing the role of Devil's Advocate, could it be that since you arrived at Winterborne and heard the *real* reason for the invitation, that you've undergone some kind of change of, well, I want to say *heart*, but that would be incorrect; a change of *sentiments* — no, that's still not quite right either for you're not prone to having such things — I'll just *say*, you've discovered a convincing reason to keep you here: dancing attendance on a sick and twisted old man, entertaining a demanding and maddeningly precocious child, oh, and rescuing a ridiculously beautiful and bewitching girl! Ha! I begin to see wherein lies the stumbling block!" Perceiving the look in his friend's eye, he took a hasty step back but continued rashly, "You've found a hitherto undiscovered penchant for caring for the infirm!"

"If you don't bite that evil tongue of yours, Emery, I shall be forced to knock you onto your backside."

It was at this fortuitous moment that Sally popped her head out of the bedchamber, "Doctor Morton says you can come in now," she said, and Nathan noted that although she was still very pale, that she managed the ghost of a smile and even that small indication that things were not all bad, made him breathe a sigh of relief.

Doctor Morton, beginning to have suspicions about the oddity of the whole situation, took Nathan to one side, "I should, of course, be addressing Lord Winterborne, but he is, as you know, not capable of dealing with any information I might give at the moment. So, I've decided that you are, by dint of being an officer and here at the Marquis's particular request, standing in as the head of the family in lieu of his lordship."

Nathan looked aghast, "You're much mistaken Doctor. I'm fairly certain that Lord Winterborne would not approve of my taking his place."

"Well, it matters not, for now, you can always pass on the pertinent information to him, but someone needs to take responsibility for Lady Winterborne," said the doctor, emphatically.

"In that case, I'll naturally, do my best," said Nathan, his eyes sliding to the still figure in the bed. "Is she — ?"

"She's still in a state of shock. I've seen near-drowning several times before, mostly in children, and although I'm optimistic about a full recovery, I must warn you that I've witnessed patients who have having nearly drowned ended up with permanent damage."

"Damage? Like, what precisely?"

"They sometimes develop pneumonia and never recover or if they do survive, they have problems thinking clearly and sometimes even have difficulties with movement. Some are bed-ridden, some become entirely helpless. I'm just warning you, Captain Heywood, of the worst that might happen so that you're forewarned, just in case she doesn't pull through."

"But — you're hopeful?"

"From all accounts you succeeded in retrieving her from the water very quickly and then got her to breathe again just as speedily. This is unusual in these sorts of cases. It's more common for panic to set in, or for the rescuers to be too slow, or to have no knowledge of how to help but I suspect that your career as a soldier helped you remain calm and good instincts helped you do the right thing. There's no point giving her any laudanum as she's sleeping peacefully at the moment and is probably not in any pain. But, if she becomes agitated, you can give her a few drops. My advice is to keep her warm and calm and have someone with her at all times until she hopefully makes a proper recovery. It's quite possible that she may be sick again, which would be good as it's getting rid of the river water she swallowed. She may become thirsty, give her lemonade or cordial, not alcohol, and I wouldn't give her anything to eat for at least a day or so. I wish you all the luck in the world, Captain. She's always been, even in the most trying of circumstances, very pleasant to deal with and I pray that she comes through this. Don't hesitate to send for me, if anything should happen."

"Thank you, Doctor Morton, I'll do my utmost to ensure that nothing untoward occurs."

* * *

After the Doctor had left and Mrs Hawkins had returned to her duties with Lord Winterborne, it was just Nathan and Sally, standing beside the bed and looking down at Grace's unnervingly lifeless form, buried beneath a mound of eiderdowns and counterpanes, a wrapped hot brick at her feet and a fire lit in the grate.

"She'll be all right," said Sally, as though if she willed it, it would be so.

"She has to be," murmured Nathan in a colourless voice.

'Thank you, Captain for rescuin' her. If she pulls through this, it'll be due to you."

"I shouldn't have left her alone on the riverbank. I should've known she'd do something reckless."

"How could anyone know what she might do? She has a wild streak, which she keeps well hidden — "

"Running barefoot — "

Sally gave him an understanding look, "She's just a rascally girl underneath all the finery. She'd far rather run barefoot with her hair flyin' behind her than go to a ball in the very best gown."

"I think I'm beginning to understand that." He sat down, perching on the edge of the bed and took Grace's cold fingers in his, looking down at them, resting in his palm, with something akin to despair, "She's not like anyone else I've ever met. She's loyal and loving and — impossible."

"I know. She's never had the chance to really be herself. Her mother — y'see? Then, the Marquis. She's always been at someone else's beck an' call — a sort of servant really. She loves Jem though, with all her heart, she does!"

Nathan nodded, remembering the blue riband caught in the reeds, "That's why she risked her life today — she saw Jem's riband and thought she'd gone into the river."

Tears sprang to Sally's eyes, "Oh, isn't that just like her! I shall give her *such* a set down — " The tears trailed down her face and she sniffed loudly as she realised that that may not be possible if Grace's health didn't improve.

Nathan's fingers closed around Grace's and he just sat there in a kind of exhausted stupor until a gentle knock on the door heralded the arrival of William, in clean clothes, but still looking strained.

"I just came to say that I'll happily sit with her if you have things to do, Nathan."

"I think I'll stay for now, if it's all the same to you — I wouldn't be averse to some company though. Sally and I have been talking about Grace and her more unusual qualities."

William smiled a trifle wanly, "She's the best sister you could ever wish for."

"She'll come through this."

"Shall we bring Jem in to see her yet?"

"I think it may be a little too early. Let's wait until hopefully there's been some marked improvement. I don't want Jem to be frightened."

"Nathan?"

"Yes, William?"

"I'm so glad you're here."

"Well, I never thought I'd say so, but I'm glad I'm here too," said Nathan, and knew it was the truth.

As he spoke, the fingers held gently in his hand, made a small convulsive movement and Nathan looked down at them and then at Grace's face and saw that she was looking back at him with incomprehension in her eyes.

He tried to take a breath.
"Grace?"

Seventeen

Grace was unable to make even the smallest sound, her throat was so very sore, and she found that her limbs were reluctant to move at all; they felt sluggish and heavy as though they didn't belong to her. Her chest hurt, her eyes smarted and she was having difficulty remembering what had happened in the last few days. When she'd opened her eyes the first thing to come into view was Nathan. For some reason he was sitting on her bed holding her hand, which was nice, and she found she didn't object in the slightest, but she couldn't think why he might be doing so. It was very odd. He looked — different, his eyes were shadowed, and he seemed to be rather subdued. She wondered if Gervase had been causing more trouble. She looked around hoping to see Jem's smiling face but found another wan countenance staring at her from tragic eyes: Sally, as pale as a goose, and tear-stained. What on earth was going on? And there, in the background, coming slowly into focus, was her darling brother, William. He too appeared to be suffering from some kind of melancholic affliction. His bottom lip was trembling. She turned her gaze back to Nathan hoping he might be able to enlighten her and found he was looking at her with such — well, she was hard-pressed to describe it — relief or was it gratitude? She frowned at him and he reached out and stroked away the puzzled crease on her brow. Something was very peculiar indeed! Why didn't someone explain? He still held her hand in his, so she squeezed his fingers in an attempt to make him understand. He lifted her fingers to his lips and kissed them. Good Lord, she thought, has someone died? Was it Gervase? She began to feel rather agitated and tried to press his fingers harder but found she barely had any strength. Where was Jem? Why wasn't she there? A terrible thought struck her, and her eyes filled with panicked tears.

"No, no, don't cry, Grace! Everything's all right. Jem's safe. The Marquis is as well as can be expected. But — you've been in an accident. You fell into the river when we were looking for Jem and — well, you're safe now and you're going to get better. You just have to rest. You may feel weak and rather ill for a while, but Doctor Morton assures me that with the proper care you'll fully recover. You're not to worry about anything, we have it all in hand. Are you thirsty? Can I fetch you a drink?"

She managed the slightest nod and Sally handed him a cup and between them they were able to get her to take a few sips, but the effort of swallowing made her choke. Sally gently mopped her face and they lay her back against the pillows.

How had she come to fall into the river? Looking for Jem. Why were they looking for Jem? She had so many questions but was suddenly too tired to try to convey her concerns. She closed her eyes and drifted. After a few seconds she opened them again and made sure that Nathan was still there; he was, so she allowed herself to slide away into a dreamless sleep.

Nathan felt her hand go limp in his and for a brief moment watched her, his heart in his mouth, until he saw she was still breathing.

He was still sitting there when she woke up again some two hours later.

* * *

The following day Jem was allowed into the bedchamber to see her mother; she'd been severely warned by Bridie to behave herself and not tax Grace with her nonsense and she'd promised faithfully to behave. Jem had been positively angelic for the first ten minutes, partly because she wasn't used to seeing her mother in such strange circumstances: *she* was usually the one in bed. Also, Mama wasn't saying much, she seemed to be not quite — *Mama*. But when Jem had glanced up at the nice Captain, he'd given her a wink and an *excellent* smile, and she'd felt a good deal happier. She perhaps shouldn't have climbed onto the bed, but she was keen to give Mama a hug and the Captain had whisked her back onto the floor very smartly, which she hadn't minded because he made it like flying which was fun.

Two days later Grace was able, with assistance, to get out of bed and sit in an armchair for a while and even managed to exchange a few words with William, although her voice was hoarse and faint. William did most of the talking, telling her in elaborate detail about the adventure she still couldn't recall. It seemed as though it was something that had happened to someone else and had nothing to do with her. She was soon to realise though that she'd come very close to drowning and had only been saved by Nathan's quick thinking.

And the description William had so vividly conjured up of Nathan breathing life into her, on reflection, made her feel as though he'd become a part of her, and every breath she took she somehow felt they shared.

She wanted to thank him but couldn't find suitable words. How *did* you thank someone for giving back your life? It seemed such a trivial, trifling word, said too often for so little. She was finding it exceedingly hard to meet his eyes.

A tiny posy of glossy golden buttercups was brought in by Sally who said they were from Miss Weston and for some inexplicable reason this made Grace cry. And Jem brought a much-recovered Barker to visit, and he was allowed to roam freely across the bed because he'd also had a near-death experience, but Grace couldn't remember jumping into the river to save the kitten so had to pretend that she knew why the creature was being treated like a deity of some kind.

William fretted about his sister's emotional state to Nathan and Emery but was promptly and convincingly reassured that she was bound to be a little shaken by events even if she couldn't recall the actual incident itself. He was advised to be patient and not to try to rush her.

William was hardly famous for his patience, but he even surprised himself by spending hours each day sitting with his sister regaling her with amusing stories about her other siblings and how Jem had found multiple new ways of tormenting Mr Talmarch and that poor gentleman was powerless to stop her.

Sally had to be sternly ordered to leave the bedside to catch up on her sleep because she was so reluctant to abandon her mistress to anyone else's care. And Nathan was content to just to watch Grace sleep.

Downstairs the Theatricals continued to rehearse their play but had been made aware that the noise must be kept to a minimum as Grace needed to rest. They seemed happy to oblige having recognised in the Captain a man who would not care to be defied. Miss Elvira Dean gave a delighted little shudder when Nathan issued his orders and told Miss Robbins that he could ride roughshod over her anytime he liked and Jenny Robbins, looking rather shocked, had slapped her arm and giggled and admitted that he was indeed a very handsome man, but Miss Dean said that she was sure Jenny liked William rather more than the Captain and Miss Robbins had blushed rosily.

When Lord Winterborne had been informed of the accident and its aftermath, he'd not had much to say about it other than demanding to be kept abreast of any further developments. Emery shared his thoughts on the matter with Nathan, saying the Marquis was probably only concerned about the continuation of his family name but William had been thoughtful enough to spend some time with him filling in the gaps and knew that although his lordship was renowned for his coldness, that Nathan's part in his wife's rescue had not been unappreciated. William was convinced that Lord Winterborne must possess some redeeming qualities and because he was young and was blessed with a positive nature, he was determined to bring about some kind of miracle. Nathan didn't like to dishearten the boy, so kept his own counsel.

The weather continued much in the same vein, providing no relief, every day more oppressive than the last; the air was choked with veils of blue smoke from accidental fires and the gardeners were starting to despair, endlessly carrying buckets of water from the depleted lake to try to save the most important shrubs and trees. The desiccated leaves fell early and crunched underfoot. The mote-laden air was bustling with insects and darting, well-fed swallows and swifts.

Nathan took Jem to the fountain for a paddle every day even though they both agreed that it wasn't quite the same without Emery crying over his spoiled coat and hiding in quaking terror behind a tree.

Finally, the day came when Grace was declared well enough by Doctor Morton to go downstairs and she was escorted by a small coterie of well-wishers to the parlour at the front of the house, with a good view of the garden. One of her first visitors was Miss Weston who'd been devastated to hear of the accident and was beyond thrilled to see her up and about again. She kindly recited some of her part in the play for her entertainment and hoped that Grace would be well enough to be in the audience. Grace said, quite truthfully, that she wouldn't miss it for the world and Miss Weston had blushed with pleasure and gone off to tell the rest of her troupe that Lady Winterborne was an absolute angel and they'd better put on their finest ever performance for her.

Grace was nibbling half-heartedly on some buttered toast, a tray perched upon her lap and Nathan sitting beside her.

"I was wondering, Nathan, how to thank you for — saving my life— ?" she said, not meeting his eyes.

"There's no need to say anything at all," he replied with a casual shrug.

"Oh, you *say* that but — if it weren't for you, I'd be at the bottom of the river."

"No, you wouldn't, we'd have fished you out by now," he countered.

She smiled slightly, "You know very well what I mean! Please, allow me to say how I feel — "

"I apologise, Grace, I didn't mean to make light of it."

She looked at him directly for the first time, her grey eyes, tired but steady, determined to have her say, "If Jem could understand, she'd also thank you because without you she'd be motherless. William has told me what you did, in *gruesome* detail, and I know I owe my life to you. I will always be in your debt."

"Well, don't be. I'm not planning to hold you to account, I swear."

"I wish you would. It's a heavy burden to carry. You must say if there's anything I can do to repay you."

"Oh, don't tempt me," murmured Nathan, with a disquieting glint in his eye.

Grace thought she'd misheard at first but seeing the telling gleam, she coloured faintly and looked away afraid of what he might see.

"Nathan, please — "

He stood up and took a turn about the room, raking his hands through his hair and filled with a desire to kick the furniture. He came to a standstill in front of the window, looking across the parterre to the hazy hills beyond and he came to a decision, "Grace, I must tell you something. I wanted to tell you before but then Jem went missing and in all the commotion I didn't have a chance but — "

The door banged open, and Jem bounced into the room wearing a cocked hat with a daring cockade of roughly tied pink ribands, followed by Emery with a bundle of ostrich feathers adorning his Rococo wig and William in a long black velvet cape and a tricorne.

Nathan took one look and sank down onto the window seat, knowing that anything he might have been going to say would have to wait. He silently cursed his reluctance to reveal his real reasons for being at Winterborne. He had to admit that he was becoming more reluctant by the day to admit his duplicity and ensuing guilt as each of those days passed. The more he got to know Grace the less he wanted her to find out that he'd actually considered her husband's outrageous proposal even if only for a very short time. In his nightmares he saw her face beneath the water, disappearing into the murky green depths and as he reached for her and found nothing but handfuls of riverweed, he woke up gasping for breath.

He watched Jem lead the ridiculous parade around the room and was tempted to laugh out loud at the appalling mess he was making of his life. There was no escape from the ramifications which had been set in progress by his foolish decision to try his luck at Winterborne. He'd lost on every count and there was no going back to how things were. He would either have to escape or stay and weather the storm and see if he could salvage something from the wreckage.

He listened to Grace laughing at her daughter's antics and wondered how he was going to come out of this latest adventure unscathed.

A light supper was later laid out in the parlour so that Grace wouldn't have to exert herself too much and she shared it with Jem who was allowed to stay downstairs because it was such a special occasion. Then Bridie came to lead Jem away to her bed and Sally was there fussing over her mistress saying that it was high time that she too was back in her bed.

Grace was wilting a little after her first real sortie since the accident and rose to her feet to do as she was told, but as she stood her legs buckled under her and she collapsed back into the chair. Nathan let out a muffled curse and crossing the room in two strides, gently swept her up into his arms and carried her to the door. Sally raced ahead and opened it and then ran up the stairs ahead of them to prepare the bed.

"I *can* walk, Nathan!" said Grace in a shaky voice.

Nathan took no notice of her protestations and bore her up the stairs and into her bedchamber. Sally excused herself with a sly smile, saying she was going to fetch some hot water and Nathan lowered Grace onto the bed, and swiftly took off her shoes and stockings despite her indignant gasp. He ignored her and pulled the counterpane around her and on impulse bent and kissed her lightly on her surprised lips.

She said nothing but put a hand up to cover her mouth as though to hide the evidence.

Nathan shook his head, "I cannot think, for the life of me, why I did that! I apologise, sometimes my inclinations get the better of my common sense. It's been a stressful few days so you'll have to forgive me. I'm prone to make poor decisions when overtaxed and you must admit that you've done your very best to stretch me to my limits recently."

Grace let out a trembling sigh, "I wish you'd stop talking and do it again," she said softly.

Taken aback, Nathan studied her face intently, "Grace! You don't know what you're saying."

She reached out and tugged at his sleeve, drawing him closer, "Yes, I do. I know *precisely* what I'm saying, Nathan!"

"Damn it, woman!" he said with barely suppressed violence and sliding his arm around her waist, pulled her hard against him. He tipped her chin up and with a low moan, kissed her again, only this time he was completely unable to control the fierceness of his passion and felt her soften under the pressure, her mouth perfectly eager and giving under his.

He tried to lift his head and stop the madness, but she held him by the lapel of his coat and looked up at him, her eyes drowsy with ardour, her lips parted and swollen, her soft skin reddened by his stubble.

"Nathan," she whispered longingly and put her mouth on his. He was powerless to stop her — he didn't want to stop her.

His fingers slipped inside the neckline of her gown and sought the silvery, satin-smooth skin of her breast and she pressed herself closer to him, arching her back.

A slight sound at the door made Nathan spring back and he turned to see Sally entering the room bearing a large pitcher of steaming water.

She grinned at them, "I never saw a *thing!* I'm as blind as a mole!"

Grace, rearranging her gown, let a small gurgle of laughter escape and put her hands to her flushed cheeks, "The Captain was just — just — " she faltered.

"Removin' an eyelash from your eye? Yes, I thought so! They hurt like the very devil! If you'd rather I left — ?"

Nathan got to his feet and looked down at Grace who had collapsed back against the pillows with all the appearance of someone who had just been thoroughly ravished. She was laughing at him, a finger to her bruised lips, her hair tousled, and he thought she'd never looked so exquisite.

"No, Sally, I'm just leaving — " he said rather huskily.

Sally smirked, "Well don't feel you have to leave on my account, Captain! I'm as silent as a tomb, so I am!"

"I'm sure you are but I really have to — leave," reiterated Nathan, starting to feel uncomfortable.

Sally sent him a sympathetic glance, "I'll bet you do!"

He regarded Grace whose eyes were dancing, and he chuckled, "Well, you're both vastly amusing! Kind of you to mock."

He quit the room to the sound of girlish giggles and was forced to take a moment, leaning against the wall in the corridor, to regain his control. Then he went to his bedchamber to splash his face with cold water, which didn't really help much.

"Nathaniel," he said to himself, "You're in deep trouble."

* * *

Grace buried her face in her pillows to muffle her laughter and Sally leant on the back of the armchair, her head hidden in the crook of her elbow, making undignified snorting sounds.

Eventually Grace surfaced biting her lip hard to stop herself from going off into stitches again, "That was — so cruel! Poor man! I took advantage of him when his guard was down and then you laughed at him!"

"You did too!" cried Sally.

"Oh, he'll never forgive me! I was so brazen! He'll think I'm no better than the Theatricals! And perhaps I'm not. I *so* wanted him to kiss me again it made me feel quite faint with longing. Honestly, I had to do something about it, or I'd have been in danger of losing my mind. I've never felt that way before. As though I were on fire and covered in gooseflesh at the same time. It's very peculiar."

"It's lust, my lady," said Sally sagely.

Grace looked horrified, "*Lust!* Oh, no! But — isn't that the Second Deadly Sin? Oh, this is perfectly *dreadful!*"

"I shouldn't worry! You've so many of the Seven Virtues that they must surely cancel out just the one triflin' Sin! I'm sure you'll be forgiven. He is so *very* handsome! And, after all, when one thinks about it, you could reason that as God made him that way, it's His fault anyway!"

Grace sank back against her pillows, "Oh, Sally, how very sensible you are."

"I know, my lady, it comes of havin' so many brothers and livin' on a farm! One gets to know how things go on very quickly — once you've seen a cow and a bull — !"

Grace clapped her hands over her ears, "*Sally!* Don't say another word! Oh, what a frightful image! How could you? And just when I was feeling so — romantic!"

"Lustful, my lady," said Sally, with a snort.

Eighteen

The heat got no better even at night, seeming to press down on everyone, making the gentlemen wish they could remove their coats and neckcloths and the ladies yearn to undo their stays. Sweat trickled down backs and foreheads were beaded with glistening dewdrops, hair was damp and curling of its own volition, or hanging in unmanageable tendrils, unwilling to be restrained. Heads itched under wigs and palms were unbearably clammy. The high-starched points of modish collars wilted and drooped, refusing to stand to attention for any amount of coaxing. Emery had borrowed one of Grace's fans and was working it hard, trying to keep the perspiration from trickling down his face. Eventually he could stand it no longer and he ripped off his wig, throwing it to the floor and stamped on it, telling the company that he was going out into the garden to hopefully find some cooler air.

Lord Winterborne had stayed in his bedchamber as he was finding the heat intolerable and Mrs Hawkins had thoughtfully provided him with a bowl of cold water to soak his feet in, which helped him feel a little less nauseous.

Grace had stayed upstairs with Jem, telling her stories and stroking her damp forehead in an effort to get her to sleep. It took over an hour to achieve it and finally certain that her fractious daughter was sound asleep, she went down to supper, knowing that most of the Theatricals and guests would be in the withdrawing room by then. A few still lingered in the dining-room and after she'd exchanged pleasantries with them, she wandered into the Great Hall and saw Nathan in conversation with Marcus Delamere and William and she hesitated, not knowing quite what to do with herself. Nathan glanced up and seeing her, smiled, just happy to see her, despite everything. She, much to her chagrin, blushed right up to the roots of her hair and turned away quickly and went out into the garden, where she thankfully found Emery sitting on the terrace wall, fanning himself and sipping his wine crossly. His short pale blonde hair was plastered to his head and he'd loosened his neckcloth. He looked uncharacteristically dishevelled.

"This is *outrageous* weather!" he expostulated, "Is the world on fire? Have you ever known anything like it? I'm melting. I feel I should go and immerse myself in the lake, fully dressed! And, if it weren't for a strong fear of frogs, I damn well would!"

Grace laughed and sat down beside him, "You could paddle in the fountain. No frogs there."

"Do you know what? That's not a bad idea! I think I might just do that."

They watched as some footmen arrived bearing lanterns and placed them around the terrace, the flames immediately attracting an array of demented moths and insects to flap senselessly about the lights.

"I don't like moths," said Grace, eyeing their frantic fluttering with consternation, "Or spiders."

"What a pair we are!" declared Emery.

They sat in companionable silence for a moment watching some bats swoop low over the garden snatching up the unwary moths.

"I kissed Nathan," said Grace, apropos of nothing.

"Good God!" exclaimed Emery, much taken aback.

"Well, to be perfectly truthful, he kissed *me* first, in a very half-hearted sort of manner which infuriated me so much that *then* I kissed *him* — in *not* such a half-hearted sort of manner!"

"Good God!" repeated Emery, lost for words.

"Of course, I probably shouldn't tell you this, but I suddenly have the most urgent desire to talk about it to someone. His kisses are very nice — not that I've anything to compare them to, really."

"No, Grace, *please!*"

"I expect you think my behaviour is wanton, but I can assure you that Nathan is the first man I've ever kissed or been kissed by. Oh, I know that I'm married but I might as well not be! And, since the — accident — I have begun to realise that my life might have ended there in the river — I might now be *dead!* You can't do *anything* when you're dead. And I suddenly thought that I was allowing life to pass me by and that perhaps I should be more daring and take some risks instead of hiding away like a scared rabbit afraid to put its foolish head out of its burrow." She laughed at her companion's stricken expression and patted his knee, "Don't worry! I won't do anything *too* scandalous! I just mean to experience what other people probably take for granted. I suppose very nearly dying has made me realise that I've allowed myself to sleepwalk through the last few years and although I'd never swap Jem for *anything* — I think I'm ready to escape the shackles that have held me prisoner for so long. Are you *very* much shocked?"

Emery shook his head but nevertheless still looked bewildered, "No, indeed — not shocked at all. Happy for you, m'dear! Been thinking that you were wasted on Lord Winterborne but Nathan — he's by *no* means perfect, y'know! He's — well, I wouldn't set store by anything he says — I mean, he's inclined to think only of himself, always has. He has his reasons for being here, for — oh, dash it, I'm making a fearful mull of this! He's a good friend but he's — flawed. That's it. Flawed," concluded Emery with some satisfaction.

"Aren't we all flawed in some way? There's no such thing as absolute perfection."

"I'd say you come pretty close Grace!"

"Oh, Emery! You toad-eater!" and she subsided against his immaculately clad shoulder, leaning on him amicably, "I *do* love you!"

Emery was getting a little hot under his collar and loosening his neckcloth even more with his free hand; he unwound it and tugged it off. "Dashed thing! Nearly strangling me!"

Nathan paused in the doorway and took in the scene before him. He knew it was innocent but still couldn't prevent a surge of some strange and unwelcome sensation rising and threatening to overwhelm him. He firmly shook it off and stepped out onto the terrace.

"There you are. Hiding away from your guests, Grace?"

Grace quickly sat up and put a guilty hand to her hair, "Not *hiding!* Merely having a rest."

"Are you feeling tired? You're still not fully recovered. Perhaps you should retire for the night, Doctor Morton says you mustn't strain yourself — "

Grace smiled, "You sound like my nursemaid!"

Nathan raised a quizzical eyebrow, "I doubt you treat your nursemaid as shockingly as you've treated me!"

She lowered her eyes in confusion, "I've no idea what you're referring to — "

"Yes, you damn well do! However, I'm too much the gentleman to allude to such improper behaviour in front of Emery, who is, despite appearances, something of a prude."

"I'm *no* such thing!" declared Emery, "And anyway, we've just been discussing Grace's apparently lamentable behaviour and have concluded that if she makes any rash decisions in the future, we must blame her new-found desire to live life to the full, having so very nearly been deprived of it."

"Is that so?" said Nathan, softly, "So, not only have you used me and carelessly cast me aside, but you've now resolved to ruin what is left of my tattered reputation by sharing my shame with Emery and then you have the temerity to blame your impetuous behaviour upon the whims of Fate? I begin to see that I'm in even deeper trouble than I'd first thought!"

Grace was forced to bite her lip to stop herself giggling, "No, really, Nathan! *Used* you? That's going *too* far! You know the truth of the matter!"

Emery looked from one to the other in growing dismay, "I'm beginning to feel a little as though I'm playing gooseberry. Shall I make myself scarce?"

"By Jupiter, no!" retorted Nathan, "She can no longer be trusted to behave with even the smallest amount of decorum.

You'd be putting me in mortal danger, and I fear I'm too weak to resist."

There was a sonorous rumble of thunder far off across the county and all three looked up to the sky.

"Is it to break at last?" said Emery hopefully, mopping his forehead with his neckcloth.

Grace cast a measured glance at the horizon which was lit only by the faintest smudge of pinkish grey where the sun had long since set. She hoped the storm, if it were to come, might avoid them. She had no great love of them and although she was longing for the insufferable heat to let up, she did not look forward to the uncontrolled tumult of a thunderstorm: they often gave her migraines, and she found the spectacle distressing rather than spectacular.

"This kind of steamy heat is always followed by a storm. That's just Nature's way," remarked Nathan.

"It seems rather unfair that we should be made to suffer so much before being released from such torment. My valet cannot keep my shirts from crumpling like a tortoise's neck! I look an absolute disgrace! It's fortunate that none of my more fastidious acquaintances are here to see my shame. The invitations would cease immediately!"

"How exceedingly shallow your friends must be then."

"At least I *have* some friends! You're sadly lacking in that department. I'm the only friend who has stood by you in spite of your deplorable character."

"That's rich coming from you, my dearest and only friend. You only keep those friends who can be useful to you and are happy to cough up some blunt when you've run out of paper to write your vowels upon."

Grace listened with interest to their raillery and noted how often the teasing came down to their lack of funds and she wondered just how hard up they were and why, if that was indeed the case, that her husband should have made the effort to invite Nathan to Winterborne; he was seldom interested in anyone who couldn't give him something in return for his condescension. What did Nathan have that Gervase wanted? Nathan had mentioned a business proposition but had never elaborated. She studied his face for a moment as he conversed light-heartedly with Emery and as he sensed her scrutiny and turned to look at her, his eyes lingered on her mouth for rather too long and she felt her cheeks begin to glow; his soft laugh just added to her discomfort and she was relieved when she saw William strolling towards them with Miss Weston clinging to his arm.

"Grace! Miss Weston — *Peggy* — wanted to come and see how you were! She's all agog to hear about your adventure, and even though I've already given her my best version of it, she's determined to hear it from your perspective!"

"Lady Winterborne, I'm so glad that you're recovered! I must say we was quite worried for a while until the Captain assured us that you was on the mend!"

"Oh, thank you, Miss Weston and thank you so much for the pretty buttercups. One of my favourite flowers. How could one not be cheered by their jolly golden faces? How are the rehearsals coming along?"

"Very well. I know all my part now and we've done a dress rehearsal n' all which weren't too bad although Jenny don't seem able to keep her lines in her head and she's hardly got anythin' to say anyway bein' just the maid! But we're hopin' as she's so very pretty that no one will notice. She can just stand there and flash her lovely eyes! That should do! Oh, my, it's so swelterin' hot!"

"Isn't it just! But I think a storm is coming so we may get some relief at last. Poor Jenny! Perhaps it'll all come good on the night? Does she suffer from stage fright?"

"No, m'lady! She never has but she's used to bein' on an actual stage and not havin' people quite so close to her. When we set it up in the Great Hall, it's bound to make a difference and she'll calm down a bit. Also, nod to the wise, you'd best keep this lad out of her sight! She's taken quite a fancy to him!"

"To *William?* Surely not! He's just a boy!" said Grace in astonishment, frowning at her grinning brother.

"Well, Jenny's nought but a girl! She be only sixteen."

"Good Gracious! She's a *child!* She shouldn't be — " began Grace but stopped when she realised what she'd been about to blurt out.

But Miss Weston gave her a knowing look, "No, m'lady, she *shouldn't* but I tries to take good care of her and not let her fall into the hands of rakehells and no-goods! It's hard though because she's so very pretty. Like you! Temptin' to the gentlemen!"

"I heartily agree, Miss Weston. *The spirit is willing but the flesh is weak,*" quoth Nathan with a crooked smile. "Temptation comes in many forms and one never knows when it's going to strike you down."

"Bible quotes now, Nathan? Have you no shame?" asked Emery rolling his eyes.

"William, you must not forget that you're practically betrothed to Catherine Wingfield."

"I'm jolly well *not* as you're fully aware! I mean imagine, Gracie, if I returned home with Miss Robbins as my bride! Mother's *face!*"

"William! Don't be so disrespectful," gasped Grace, horrified by her brother's rare lack of tact.

"Excellent brandy they serve here, no?" said Nathan blandly.

"Oh, yes, indeed! I've never had better!" replied William, falling artlessly for the bait.

"You've been *drinking!*" Grace glared at him, "No wonder you're saying things which tomorrow I hope you will bitterly regret. Please apologise to Miss Weston for being so discourteous and go to bed!"

Another rolling growl from the sky made Grace look apprehensively over her shoulder into the encroaching darkness.

"I think I shall take you upstairs William before you completely disgrace the family."

William attempted to protest but the look in his sister's eyes made him swallow his words. He bowed a little unsteadily to the company, raised Miss Weston's fingers to his lips with a theatrical flourish which made her giggle, and allowed Grace to lead him away, followed by a dogged Miss Weston who was asking about the accident with ghoulish delight.

"Will you come back down, Grace?" enquired Nathan casually.

"No, I shall retire I think as I can feel a headache coming on. I bid you all goodnight and hope that the storm doesn't keep you awake."

Nathan watched her go, her back as rigid as ever.

"What are you about, Nate? I thought you'd decided against his lordship's proposition!" said Emery uneasily.

"I have. But that doesn't mean that I can't be responsive if a lady flings herself at me!"

"She doesn't know what she's doing."

"Strangely enough, that's what I told her, but she said that she knew *exactly* what she's doing."

"You're more of a fool than I thought then if you believe her! She's as innocent as a baby. Don't ruin her, Nate!"

"God, I don't plan to. I'm not that far gone."

"But you *are* trifling with her. I can see you have that look in your eye. It never bodes well."

"What would you say Emery, if I told you that I think far too well of her to — *trifle* — with her?"

"I'd say it was time we took our leave and returned to London expeditiously."

"And if I'm not ready to leave?"

"I shall drug you and throw you into the carriage by force!"

"I'd like to see you try. But, seriously, Emery, I can't leave yet. I — I have to — to — "

"Gad, have you lost the powers of speech? What the hell is going on, Nate? You're behaving like a damned ninny-hammer. One minute you're saying we must quit Winterborne immediately and the next that you can't leave! I don't even know you any more."

Nathan rubbed his eyes, as the sky rumbled again, this time a little closer, "*I* don't even know who I am any more. I just know that I can't leave her."

"Because — she needs you? Or you need her?"

"Because I can't imagine not seeing her every day." Nathan stood up and looked out into the blackness as a streak of lightning stabbed the horizon line. "When I thought she'd gone — after we pulled her out — my first feeling was anger. Anger that I'd found her, and she'd just given up and left me. The next feeling was abject terror. Terror that I'd have to go on without her. I don't even know what it all means. The situation is quite simply — impossible. I came here to make a business deal — to make money in order to save our pathetic necks. But I was offered a proposition which, as you know, was very tempting. Sire the next Winterborne heir. What could be simpler? Take the money and run. I could have done it with ease. But stupidly I got to know Grace — and admire her and in so doing have ruined *all* our futures."

"'Admire' is an interesting word, Nate."

"It is, isn't it? I could use all kinds of other words. But I don't ever remember regarding another women with so much respect or having ever felt such a prodigious need to protect them. I was usually just fighting boredom and if I felt the slightest urge to continue an affair beyond its natural demise — I left."

"Ran away."

"Call it what you like. But I've no desire to run now. Which fills me with a different sort of terror. An unknown terror."

There was the sound of voices behind them and they looked around to see George Carew, Marcus Delamere and Peter Leventhorpe coming out onto the terrace.

"Wondered if you'd care to join us for a few hands of cards, gentlemen?" said Marcus. "The ladies have all turned in for the night and so we've the run of the house. A little brandy nightcap and a round of vingt-et-un or piquet?"

"Perfect," said Nathan, thinking he needed something to take his mind off his concerns — one particular concern having gone to her bed leaving him to reflect upon her uncharacteristic behaviour. Cards and brandy were precisely what was called for.

* * *

Seated next to George Carew, Nathan, never much of a gambler, was finding it difficult to concentrate on the hand of cards he held. His mind kept wandering and he'd already lost two rounds and was in danger of losing a third.

"Damnable weather, ain't it!" said Carew, rearranging his cards with awful precision.

Nathan looked up from blindly staring at his cards at the man's pale silver eyes, "I beg your pardon? Oh, yes, — damnable."

"Storm's coming though. Listen to that thunder. Getting closer now. Summer storms have a habit of getting trapped in the valley and just rolling around for hours. Been caught in one here before. I've been many times to Winterborne."

"So I understand."

"Lady Winterborne and I have spent many a pleasant evening together. She throws all the other ladies into the shade, does she not?"

"I'm fairly certain she doesn't give a damn about that kind of thing."

"No, she's above the ordinary. I've often wondered how she came to be with Gervase, though. Seems a little odd, no?"

"I've no idea, she hasn't taken me into her confidence," said Nathan tersely, hoping to end the conversation.

"Oh? I had thought you to be in Gervase's pocket!"

Nathan eyed him with disdain, "I'm not sure what you mean by that but as I only came to discuss business and stayed out of compassion — I'm in *no one's* pocket."

"Is that so? It seems to me that Gervase has very particular plans for you. Or — so I've heard."

That checked Nathan and he narrowed his eyes, finally paying proper attention, "What have you heard, Carew?"

"Oh, this and that. I like to keep my ear to the ground. It can come in useful — when one is least expecting it. You know, when one finds a chink in someone's armour."

Marcus reminded Nathan it was his turn to put down his cards and he chose randomly and laid them on the table. Marcus shook his head, "Don't think your mind is on the play, Nathan. You're not going to even win back your stake at this rate."

Nathan's mind was certainly not on the cards — it was racing as he tried to work out precisely what George Carew was insinuating. His face remained utterly inscrutable as he feigned interest in the game, while his mind went back to his talk with Emery on the terrace and wondered just how long George Carew might have been in the doorway before he'd been joined by the others. If he'd happened to overhear the conversation — Nathan knew he'd have a hold over him and that he could not allow. The idea that Grace might find out about Gervase's plan from Carew was abhorrent to him. He cursed the fact that she'd already retired for the night and determined to speak to her first thing in the morning come what may. He would have to risk her wrath or worse still, her bitter disillusionment in him but at least then it would be over, one way or another. This uncertainty was hard to bear.

"No good can come of eavesdropping, Carew," he said cordially, "I should have a care if I were you in case you find yourself out of your depths. I cannot think of anyone likely to rescue you."

George Carew just smiled, and Nathan downed another large brandy to try to stamp out the creeping feeling of foreboding.

* * *

The storm approached in soft kid slippers with lengthy gaps of muffled stillness between the mute lightning and the thunder's grumbling response. The mugginess continued to increase until Nathan felt he couldn't breathe with ease. Emery declared he'd had more than enough and went to retrieve his discarded wig and then took himself off to bed. The other gentlemen all threw in their hands, counted up their winnings or losses and strolled away upstairs.

Nathan shut the door of his bedchamber and let out a deep breath. He had not much enjoyed the tail end of the evening and was a good deal more inebriated than he'd have liked. He blamed it on the heat. One should never indulge in such weather. He paced the room rather unsteadily for a while and then stood looking out of the window at the animated sky. His head was a little woolly and he wondered if Grace was managing to sleep through this ominous prelude to the storm. She had quite clearly not been looking forward to it and he suspected she'd be in her bed with her pillow over her head. The thought of her in her bed brought him up short and he couldn't help but recall their recent encounter on that same bed. He grinned and shook his head as he felt again her tugging on his lapel. So insistently. He slammed his fist into the wall as though he could drive away the memory with pain.

Another wave of thunder rolled around the valley.

Nathan thought he could probably do with another brandy or two or he would never get to sleep but he knew that he'd have a thumping head in the morning if he did, so he shrugged himself out of his evening coat and changed into his top boots. A breath of night air would be the thing, clear his head, straighten out his confused thoughts. Rid himself of the image of Grace's languorous eyes looking up at him with — He went quietly down the stairs and ignoring the stern warning voice, he snatched up the brandy decanter from the sideboard and went out onto the terrace where the lanterns still burned; he picked one up and headed off through the parterre towards the Maze. He may not be able to enjoy the sight of her in the flesh, but he knew where he could see her beautiful form carved in marble and that would have to do until he'd sobered up.

Nineteen

For the third time Grace sat up in bed and stared hard at the shutters which were still firmly closed and securely battened. She was starting to seriously doubt their power to resist the weather and feared that if the storm were to break her window, that the shutters would give way and she would be at the mercy of the wind and the lightning.

She lay down again and pulled the counterpane tightly around her and pressed the pillow over her head to block out the distant sound of thunder, but the noise penetrated the ancient and sturdy oak panels of the shutters and even two thick layers of goose down. She heaved a furious sigh and sat up yet again and stayed like that staring into the darkness for a few moments watching out of the side of her eye as the gap between the shutters lit up in a streak of icy blue. She waited for the thunder. When it came it was still far off and no more than a polite growl.

She was wide awake now and feeling increasingly fidgety. She knew she wasn't going to be able to sleep so she swung her legs out of bed and perched on the edge for a few minutes wishing she'd given into Sally's request to sleep in her dressing room in case she needed company, but she'd foolishly said that she was perfectly capable of enduring one stormy night alone. She'd had everyone fussing over her for over a week now and she was glad to be rid of them and just have some time to think without constant interruption. She dangled her legs and huffed crossly. She just wanted to be asleep so that the endless thoughts would cease plaguing her. She wanted to be blank and empty again, she would welcome the void with open arms.

She thought she'd just go and take a peek at Jemima and make sure she was sleeping soundly. She pulled her wrapper on over her nightgown of white lustring and, picking up the unlit candle, padded barefoot out of her bedchamber and down the corridor to her daughter's room, stopping only to light her candle from one in the sconce outside her room. She tiptoed into Jem's room and saw that Bridie had made up a truckle bed to sleep on so that she could keep watch over the child during the storm. Bridie made a good deal of noise about her recalcitrant charge, but Grace knew that she would always have her best interests at heart despite their petty differences.

She backed out quietly and set off to her own bedchamber but stopped as she passed the Long Gallery and was drawn into it by some instinct which she had no sway over. Holding her candle up she crossed the gallery, which stretched the whole length of the western aspect of the house, she found herself in the large bay window from where she would have had, had it not been dark, a view of the garden, the meadows and a vast expanse of the land beyond. She could just make out the first bend of the river, the intermittent lightning silvering the surface of the water and, closer to the house, the looming darker shapes of the topiary trees and hedges. Pulling her wrapper around her as she felt the chill of the huge room, despite the clammy heat, she turned to leave but something caught her eye.

There was a dim light showing beside the Maze. A faint golden glimmer, like a glow-worm. She watched it for a moment but found if she focused upon it too hard that it was more difficult to see.

Wondering if it was one of the gardeners out making sure that something was securely tied down before the storm, she decided that it wasn't her business. But then it moved, disappearing suddenly as though it had been snuffed out. Grace frowned and then jumped as a loud crack of thunder exploded closer by. She quickly hurried from the Gallery and shut the double doors behind her as though that might keep the storm at bay.

But who was near the Maze at this time of night and what were they doing there?

As she walked back along the corridor, she pondered the question and thought it suspicious but could find no satisfactory answer. She decided that she wasn't fool enough to go out to see for herself so she settled upon the next best thing — she would send someone else.

And the only person who came to mind slept at the far end of the long corridor and probably wouldn't mind being awoken because he'd been a soldier and must be used to keeping odd hours.

She tapped on his door. There was no sound from within, so she knocked with more vigour. Still nothing. The thunder crashed somewhere over the estate and she ducked nervously.

Suddenly desperate to have someone to talk with, she opened the door a crack and whispered his name. Then, when there was still no answer, she knew for certain the room was empty.

Her first thought was that he'd left Winterborne. Then after swiftly stilling the ridiculous surge of panic, she realised he wouldn't have gone without saying something to her and Jem. She just knew. Then, the thought occurred to her that some of the actresses and dancers were very pretty and quite saucy, and, to her consternation, had shown a marked preference for his company, flirting provocatively with him, and he'd often readily engaged them in amusing and appreciative conversation. Perhaps he had an assignation with one of them. Perhaps he'd been teased enough and wanted some release. He was only human, and she couldn't blame him.

Then another, more reasonable, thought occurred to her. Maybe he'd needed to cool off and had just gone out into the garden. Or maybe he liked thunderstorms and wanted to see one from outside in the open air. Soldiers must like being outside — it was what they were used to.

She stood contemplating her options and found herself thinking of the river water as it closed over her head. That might have been, had it not been for Nathan, her last moment, then there would have been nothing more to feel, to laugh at, to hold tightly in her arms, to kiss, to love. No Jem, no Nathan. Just the endless darkness.

There was another throaty rumbling, ending in a loud crash, which rattled the windows and made her clench her teeth. Before she even realised what she was doing, she started walking steadily along the corridor, down the stairs and out onto the terrace, where she grabbed the only lantern left still burning and headed out across the lawn towards the Maze.

* * *

She hated the damn Maze. It was dark and menacing and the only time she'd ventured any distance into it, when Gervase was first showing her around the grounds, she'd found herself backing out in a cold sweat. It was as though the towering hedges had a life of their own and were crowding in on her, and would suffocate her, squeezing the breath out of her, crushing her in their poisonous embrace. She knew it was ridiculous, but she'd always had a fear of enclosed spaces (although she didn't seem to mind cupboards so much any more) and felt that the Maze had merely been built to torture people. She knew the key to it because she often had to enlighten her husband's visitors if they weren't keen on deciphering the puzzle for themselves. But even so, as she approached it, she could feel her skin crawling.

Jagged lightning pierced the darkness and thunder thumped over her head in acknowledgment making her cower.

She paused at the entrance and tried to justify her actions. After a few moments of internal argument, she carelessly tossed her tumbled hair and took a deep breath. She was determined to change her way of thinking; she was going to make the most of the life she'd taken for granted and make sure that she didn't live her remaining years full of regrets. She stepped over the threshold, the soft grass warm beneath her bare feet.

She held the lantern up, its yellow light brightening the dark green walls of yew as she passed and followed the map in her head, carefully carrying out the instructions she'd been given by Gervase. Trying hard not to think too deeply about where she was and what she was doing, she pressed on into the dark heart of the labyrinth.

There was a moment when she stopped and considered and couldn't help but worry that it might not be Nathan at all — it might be any one of the staff or guests and she was perhaps being exceedingly stupid to endanger herself. She shut her eyes and the river water closed over her head once more. She continued along the sinister avenues of hedges and ignored her palpitating heart and the warning voices whispering in her head.

Ahead she could see a light, a faint blur of gold dusting the end of the last corridor.

As she reached the corner, she swallowed anxiously and gave herself a stern talking-to and then forged on into the centre of the Maze.

* * *

It was not how she had envisaged it at all. She wasn't even sure what she'd been expecting but the reality was disappointing. It was just a circular lawn, surrounded by hedges, a lone statue in the very centre and nothing else of interest at all, apart from, leaning against the base of the statue, a figure, dishevelled, legs stretched out in front of him, chin sunk onto his chest, eerily lit by the glow from his lantern which sat beside him. She noted the empty brandy decanter, tipped carelessly onto its side.

Several lightning flashes illuminated the sky, casting intimidating black shadows across the scene and the thunder chose this auspicious moment to announce its presence with a deafening drum roll, followed by an ear-splitting explosion right above them. Wincing nervously, Grace's eye was caught by the statue, as it was suddenly brought into strong relief and she gasped out loud.

Moving around the plinth, she came face-to-face with herself, it was her countenance without a doubt but as her astonished gaze took in the rest of the smoothly hewn marble, she realised that the figure, which was barely concealed by an artfully draped but flimsy piece of cloth carved from marble, was based upon some other model and she laughed.

"So, this is why some Maze explorers could not meet my eye as they took their tea afterwards! Well, how — *embarrassing*. What on earth made Gervase think of such a thing?" She looked down at Nathan who had opened one bleary eye and was peering up at her as though he could not quite believe she wasn't some figment of his fevered imagination. She was smiling serenely at him, so he closed his eye for a moment and then opened them both. She was still there.

"*G-Grace?*"

"Yes, 'tis I. Are you *very* foxed?"

"N-no more than a trifle — *disguised*," he replied, slurring his words.

"Well, how unfortunate. I thought you said you didn't drink much!"

"I sh-eldom touch the stuff b-but — tonight — I felt an *urgent* need."

"Really? And why would that be precisely?"

"I can't quite — *remember*. Something I wanted to forget — I think."

"So, it worked then?"

"It did — until jusht now."

"Oh? And what brought the memory to mind again?"

Nathan raised an eyebrow and allowed his sleepy gaze to travel slowly down her figure to her bare feet peeping out from beneath the diaphanous nightgown, "I-I can't *think!* It's a — myshtery to me."

"You're being very silly. What in heaven's name brought you into the Maze?"

"Need you ask?" he said with a rueful smile. "Although, I'll readily admit — it's no c-contest for the real thing."

"Nathan, are you deliberately trying to shock me?"

"I'm not sure. I'm — *foxed*, y'see!"

Grace laughed, "I think my lantern is about to go out. Ah, I see you at least had the good sense to bring an extra candle." She opened his lantern and took the spare candle, lit it and fixed it in place on the remains of hers and shut the metal door. Another dramatic roll of thunder boomed overhead. Grace, flinching, took a step closer to Nathan's prostrate form. "Are you just going to lie there all night?"

"Yes, unlesh — you want me to do something d-different?"

"I think perhaps we should return to the house. If you stay out here, you might catch your death."

"It's far too warm for that."

"You're being obstreperous."

"*Am* I? It — musht be the brandy. I'm usually *exceedingly* good-natured, as you know."

"I believe one's true nature appears when one is castaway. Shall I help you up?"

"No, I'm — quite h-happy where I am, thank you."

They both looked skywards as the night was split asunder by what sounded like a hundred barrels of gunpowder igniting.

Grace's whole body started to shake as the first heavy drops of rain tumbled lazily out of the darkness, hissing as they hit the lanterns. Within seconds it was a deluge.

She held out her hand to him and he took it and struggled to his feet. He could feel her trembling, "No need to be afraid."

"That's easy for you to say," she said crossly.

"I don't even have my — c-coat to wrap you in."

"How thoughtless of you to discard it when you were bound to need it! Can we please *go!* I'm getting drenched!"

He smiled crookedly at her, "I can *see!* And *very* — nice it is too."

"Nathan, will you stop being so — so — inappropriate! Come on, I want to get out of here."

He stood looking at her, the rain running in rivulets down her face and her nightgown clinging to her fondly. "Why have *you* come out to the Maze?"

She tried to release her hand from his, but he held firm, "I — I saw the light of your lantern and thought it might be someone up to no good, so I went to wake you — "

"Good *God!* Are you — *deranged?* You went to my *bedchamber!* I think I'm sobering up now. What if someone had *seen* you?"

"There was no one awake. The whole house was asleep. Nobody saw me."

"That's interesting — *nobody* knows you're out here with me? That's — remarkably f-foolish of you," said Nathan with a roguish glint in his eyes, "You're entirely at my mercy."

"Or — you're at *my* mercy," she replied audaciously.

"*Don't* Grace. It's not amusing. You could be *ruined*. As it is we're g-going to have to be — careful getting you back into the house without being seen." He pulled on her hand and began to lead her rather uncertainly through the Maze, as the storm continued to rage above.

Another ferocious crack of thunder made Grace pull her hand away so that she could cover her ears, dropping her lantern to the ground and extinguishing the candle. She closed her eyes and doubled over, allowing an involuntary moan of fear to escape.

Nathan, still quite unsteady on his feet, stopped, put his lantern carefully on the ground and turning back to her, took her by the shoulders, "*Look* at me. No need to be — afraid. *I'm* here with you."

"You're inebriated and therefore utterly useless," she said shakily.

"I may be — but I've a *d-damned* good excuse — for the state I'm in."

She looked up at him, as lightning lit her face, and thunder rumbled, the rain warm and falling in heavy drops, "And what *is* your excuse?"

"You," he answered simply. "Just *you*, Grace."

She blinked up at him and saw the lightning reflected in his eyes.

"Nathan — "

He slowly drew her towards him expecting her to resist, so that he could then arrest his inevitable descent into Hell. But she continued to look him in the eye almost with defiance; he held her pressed against his chest and it wasn't only her trembling. He pushed the wet tendrils of hair away from her face and traced her lips with his thumbs until they parted, and he bent and took possession of her mouth with his. Murmuring her name between her lips and swaying back against the nearest hedge, he pulled her with him.

The hedge gave beneath their weight, like a mattress; rain thudded on Grace's back, thunder snarled and every few seconds the lightning lit Nathan's face, his shirt soaked and sticking to him.

She slid her hands beneath the material, across the slick of his wet skin and around his waist to his back, exploring the hard mass of him with inexperienced fingers, fascinated by the solidity, the unshakeable sturdiness of his body. He was athletically built, his muscles well defined, and she gave into an overwhelming desire to dig her fingers into his pleasingly vigorous form and quickly discovered from his instant response that he *liked* her touch, which made her smile through his increasingly impatient, brandy-flavoured kisses. He was holding her so tightly she could hardly breathe but had no immediate wish for him to release her, so deeply thrilling was the feeling of his arms crushing her ribs. She laughed out loud at how wildly out of control she was fast becoming.

He raised his head and looked at her from drowsy, darkened eyes and she stretched up onto her tiptoes, reaching eagerly for his mouth again, craving his nearness. Pulling her nightgown up out of his way, he clasped strong hands under her bare backside and lifted her; she spread her legs and instinctively entwined herself about his hips and her arms went up about his neck.

"Are you *sure?* I can — stop. I don't want — " he muttered disjointedly.

Grace laughed again, with undiluted joy, "I *am* sure. *Please* don't stop! I *do* want — more than anything!"

"God, Grace, I think I'm too — *drunk!*"

"Well, just do your very best then! I won't complain!" she giggled, no longer hearing the wrathful storm and only vaguely aware of the rain tumbling down between them like a waterfall.

"You don't — *understand!*"

She took his face in her hands and covered it in little butterfly kisses, "I *do*. Sally told me. She knows about such things!"

"D-devil take it," said Nathan hoarsely, "This is — madness."

"And I don't care."

"But I need — to *tell* you — *something* — " he faltered, unable to quite recall what he had to tell her.

"Not *now*, Nathan!"

And with that, everything else skipped his befuddled mind and he threw every bit of his rather unsteady energy into the pressing task in hand — for which they were both about to be exceedingly grateful.

For one of them, the storm continued unabated and for the other, it gradually faded away.

Grace looked up at Nathan, a playful smile on her lips and when he was unable to meet her eyes, she turned his head very firmly so that he had no choice but to look at her.

He sighed, "I-I can do *much* better than that — I *swear*. The brandy — I shouldn't have drunk so damned much — "

She leant against him, her head on his chest, her arms about his waist and listened to the wild thumping of his heart with a kind of wonder, knowing that its beat was so feverish because of her. It made her feel quite powerful but at the same time she wanted to reassure him, "Well, as I'm exceedingly happy with what just occurred, I don't think there's any reason for you to be concerned. Sally made the whole business sound very — perfunctory and I now see that she may have left out some of the more pertinent details! Mind you, as I have no experience in these matters, you might be the worst lover in the world, and I wouldn't know any better — !"

Nathan clasped her even more tightly, "Y-you — impudent *minx*. How dare you impugn my abilities!"

She rubbed her cheek against the hair on his chest, his sodden shirt having been removed and discarded at some point during the storm, which was now more muffled and distant.

"I didn't *know* — " she murmured, her lips trailing idly across his midriff, "I'm so glad it was you."

"Are you really? I feel I've taken advantage of you — the storm — this damn Maze — "

Grace smiled up at him, "I think as you were the one who was in a sorry state that it was *I* who took advantage. You really had very little say in the matter. But let's not quibble! I *must* ask though — and *please* tell me the truth — I expect that with all the other ladies you've — known — that I must seem very — "

"Damnation Grace! D-don't you *dare* mention those — females in the same breath! You have no idea how — how d-delightful you are — how *sweet* — I can't even *begin* to tell you — "

She looked at him from under her eyelashes, "Then could you *show* me please?" she said breathlessly.

"*Again?* What now? Here?" He suddenly laughed out loud, "Perdition! I think I may have met my match! Yes, I'd be happy to prove to you that I'm not usually quite so — inept."

His breeches hung loosely open on his hips and Grace, with another enticing look up at him, slid her hands into the waistband and began to ease them down.

"I shall be having a stern word with Sally about — some of the things she's been teaching you," he said with a despairing shake of his head, just as the candle in his lantern flickered and went out.

* * *

A while later they made their way back across the lawn, hand in hand, keeping as much as they could to the areas with the topiary in order to afford them some concealment. The storm had finally moved on and all they could detect was the odd faint shimmer of lightning and a few faraway grumblings of thunder on the far edges of the county.

Their clothes were soaked, and Nathan's hair was hanging loose, another black riband long gone and Grace's nightgown was wrapping itself around her legs and making it difficult for her to walk. She hoisted her skirts up impatiently and cast an uncertain glance up at her companion.

"If you're worried about me seeing your lovely legs," he remarked casually, "May I remind you that I've just been privileged to feast my eye upon some other extremely beautiful parts — "

"*Nathan!*" she whispered, coming to a sudden standstill, "You mustn't *say* things like that! Someone might hear you! Oh, Heaven's above, you're not going to blurt it out in front of people, are you? You must be cautious and keep your indelicate tongue under control!"

Nathan pulled her to him, "That's *not* what you were saying just moments ago — "

She tried to prise herself out of his embrace, pummelling his chest with her fists, "*No!* You can't say things like that! It's too shaming."

"Well, *I'm* not ashamed. I've never felt so — exultant."

"That's the brandy talking!" snapped Grace.

He tenderly smoothed her tangled hair, "No, it's you. *You* intoxicate me. You make me feel as though anything is possible, as though life is worth living."

"You're being very irresponsible. Let me go!"

He released her suddenly and she stood unsteadily a pace away from him, frowning in a puzzled fashion for a brief moment before flinging herself back into his arms and he let out a husky laugh and kissed her fiercely until her knees buckled. He swept her up and carried her the rest of the way back to the house.

"Put me *down!* You odious bully!"

"Really?" he laughingly enquired.

She buried her head in his neck, "No. Don't you *dare.*"

* * *

He carried her as stealthily as he could through the dark house, across the Great Hall, up the stairs and along the corridor to her bedchamber. With some difficulty, he took the still burning candle stub from the sconce in the corridor, pushed the door open and allowed Grace to slide down onto the floor, where she leant against him as though she had no strength to stand up. Reaching out, he managed to fix the candle onto the spike on the nearest wall bracket. She was giggling into his chest and he was worried that someone might hear. He tilted her head back and put a finger against her lips, "Shhh," he whispered, "Go to bed."

"Only if you come too," murmured Grace.

He shook his head, laughing, and lifting her slightly off the ground, he edged her towards her bed. "You're a disgrace," he quietly laughed.

"I'm disgraced Grace!" she said with a grin.

"Oh, God! *Bed!*" He gave her a little push and she fell back onto the four-poster, where she lay gazing up at him, her eyes dancing in the candlelight and he knew for certain that he was absolutely lost.

"Nathaniel — ?"

"Good night, Grace."

And he turned on his heel and went out.

Twenty

Sally knew the moment she saw her mistress the following morning that something was different. Grace could barely look her in the eyes without blushing and covering her face with her hands. There was also the muddy nightgown thrown over the chair and a pair of telltale dirty feet. She suggested a bath might be in order but when the bath had been filled, there was a pause while Grace stood and looked at it mutinously, reminding Sally strongly of Jemima.

Sally pursed her lips, "You cannot go down lookin' like a filthy ragamuffin, m'lady. There would be questions an' talk."

Grace glowered.

Sally folded her arms across her chest, "No argument."

"But — I don't want — " faltered Grace hopelessly.

Sally shook her head, "Yes, I know *why* you don't want to! I'm not stupid."

Grace looked at her enquiringly.

Sally grinned, "You don't want to wash his smell off you."

"Oh, Sally! How can I be so ridiculous? But what if — ?"

"What if he never touches you again? Well, I doubt there's any chance he *won't!* You've got under that poor man's skin. But I have to say m'lady that I can't allow you to parade about lookin' as though I don't take good care of you. What would people think of me? And anyway, his smell will soon fade and then you'll just be *filthy*. Look at your feet! They're a disgrace."

She then wondered why Lady Winterborne collapsed back onto the bed in giggles.

Grace eventually had to capitulate and step into the hip bath and allow Sally to scrub away all evidence of her edifying night in the Maze. She wept softly as any remaining signs of Nathan were ruthlessly removed.

* * *

Downstairs, Nathan was waiting impatiently to see her, pacing the Great Hall and nursing a crushing headache. He thought he'd probably never eat again and had certainly drunk his last ever mouthful of brandy. The night came back to him in vivid flashes and kept disrupting his thoughts and he found himself brooding on his spiritless behaviour. He'd willingly allowed himself to be beguiled into leading Grace astray and it mattered not that she'd been a keen participant; he should have known better, even through a confusing haze of alcohol and lust; he should have saved her from herself. He should have saved himself. He was now so deeply entrenched in the Winterborne affairs that he could see no way of extricating himself without a good deal of pain and complication. And, when he thought about it, he realised that he'd no desire to extricate himself. He would talk to Emery and see what he had to say on the matter. But first he had to see Grace and explain.

* * *

Grace selected her gown with more than usual care, in the end choosing a round gown in deep rose-pink silk and Sally took extra pains with her hair, coaxing a few more shining curls to fall onto her shoulder. She stood back to assess her handiwork, nodded, and gave the cream sash a final tweak.

"That should do," she said, "I think you're ready."

Grace shook out her skirts and turned away from the looking glass.

"I'm so nervous."

"There's no need. He's seen you soakin' wet and muddy and wearing nought but a shapeless nightgown — I don't think he's going to really care what you're wearin'. Anyway, you always look lovely."

"What if he's changed his mind overnight and now regrets what happened? Maybe it really was just the brandy!"

Sally fixed her with a pitying look but said nothing.

"I feel a little queasy."

"Oh, go on with you, m'lady! That's just excitement. As soon as you see him, you'll feel better."

Grace sighed and went to the door. As she approached it, she spotted something on the floor and picked it up, "A letter," she said and opened it. A slow smile spread across her face and she laughed in delight.

"Is it from the Captain?" asked Sally.

"Yes, it is. He writes that he wants to meet me in private because he has something to tell me. That's what he said last night! Oh, Sally! What could it be?"

"Well, you won't know unless you meet him! What time does he say?"

"He says he'll wait for me before breakfast in the Buttery but says I'm to leave the house by the rear door — how odd. Oh, I suppose he's worried that the guests might gossip about us."

"Very wise of him. Would you like me to come with you?"

"No, thank you, I'll be all right, don't worry. Are you sure this gown is — ?"

Sally rolled her eyes and gently guided her mistress out of the door, "Good luck!"

Grace quickly went down the back stairs, past the servants' quarters, tiptoeing by the housekeeper's room and along the corridor to the rear door which opened into the yard and the kitchen garden. Skirting around the busier areas, she crossed the drive and ducked through a gap in the surrounding beech hedge, a shortcut which led to the Nuttery. She was intent on not being seen and had to wait a moment beside the hedge while a gardener pushing a laden wheelbarrow ambled past so slowly, she wanted to shout at him to go faster. She watched him disappear and then lifting up her skirts, practically skipped around the edge of the orchard of hazel trees, her eyes eagerly searching for the familiar figure. She couldn't see anyone and wondered if he'd given up and left already.

"Good morning," said a voice behind her and she span around, shyly smiling. The smile froze and faded away.

"*You!*" said Grace, taking a step back.

"Who were you expecting, my lady?"

Grace looked into the pale silver eyes of George Carew and her breathing quickened. She felt light-headed and looked around for help, but the gardener had long gone and there was no one else in sight.

He was just standing there, staring at her like a predator watching its prey.

She knew she couldn't outrun him and the Nuttery was far enough away from the house for her cries to go unheeded. She tried not to panic but her mouth was dry, and her voice came out in little more than a whisper.

"*You* wrote the letter. What do you want of me?"

He laughed, "Oh, so much, my lady, so very much. I hardly know where to begin."

Grace's heart was thumping loudly, and she was trying desperately to think of some escape, but her mind was being horribly disobliging. She could only try to hinder him, in whatever plan he was hatching, and hope that rescue might come in time.

"Perhaps we could return to the house and discuss this in a civilised manner," she suggested as calmly as she could.

"It won't be a discussion — more of a revelation."

"Well, pray don't keep me in suspense, Mr Carew, I have much to occupy me today and really must be getting on. What is this all about?"

"The Marquis and Captain Heywood — and you."

"Ah, about their business deal?" nodded Grace, "I already know about that. It's common knowledge at Winterborne."

George Carew continued to observe her from coldly calculating eyes, "Really? I'm surprised by your fortitude then. You must be an *exceptional* female."

"My husband keeps me informed about such things."

"How very — broad-minded the Winterbornes are then. I'm all astonishment. Indeed, I'm staggered that you should be so forbearing. I remember my last visit and you were not quite so accommodating then."

"You tried to rape me," said Grace in a colourless voice.

"That's not quite true. I was under the impression that you were amenable. It was a forgivable misunderstanding."

"If it hadn't been for my maid arriving at that moment — "

"Yes, she quite spoiled my day. I'd been looking forward to it for a long time."

"You *disgust* me."

George Carew pulled down his mouth in *faux* disappointment, "And yet you're *not* disgusted at the thought of being used as a brood mare. That seems a trifle peculiar to me."

Her breath caught in her throat, "I — don't understand — "

"But I thought you said you knew! Allow me to enlighten you, my dear. To make sure he doesn't die without a male heir to carry on the family name, Lord Winterborne has thoughtfully procured someone's services, for a substantial sum. But it can come as no surprise to you — as you say he keeps you abreast of his business deals."

Grace was beginning to feel faint.

"I suppose it's a stroke of good fortune that you actually seem to *like* the man chosen to do the deed. Of course, *I'd* have been willing had you only said — "

"What are you *talking* about? Have you lost your mind?" interrupted Grace.

"But Lady Winterborne, you said that you were *au fait* with your husband's business. Surely, as it affects you, you must be aware that Captain Heywood was hired to do what the Marquis cannot — for reasons probably best left unmentioned."

Grace's knees were shaking, and she wanted to collapse onto the grass, but somehow managed to stay upright, and somewhere in the back of her mind she began to pray, begging God to make this a lie.

"You're mad," she whispered.

"I think you're already realising that there's some truth in what I say. I can see it in your eyes. You look scared."

"I'm not scared of you."

"No, but you're afraid that you've been duped by your beloved Captain. He seems so honest and true, does he not? But it turns out he just needs the money and will stoop to anything to achieve his ends — it appears that he's intent upon earning that payment, come what may, so that he can move on as quickly as possible."

Grace couldn't help the colour draining from her face, "It's not true."

He smiled, "You say that, my lady, but I can see you doubt your own words." He gave her an appraising look, "Or, perhaps — its already too late and Captain Heywood will soon be looking forward to collecting his hard-earned reward and riding away from Winterborne and your husband will be able to die a happy man, safe in the knowledge that the name of Winterborne will continue. I think that you have much to consider, my lady — may I escort you safely back to the house?"

Grace felt as though everything had come to a standstill and she was watching what was happening from a great distance. She couldn't quite grasp what he was saying to her but at the same time she felt her life was coming unravelled and would never be the same again.

His eyes were fixed upon her and she knew he was revelling in the pain he was causing. This was revenge as much as anything. She had spurned his repulsive advances and now he was going to make her suffer for humiliating him. By stupidly falling in love with Nathan, she had exposed herself to Carew's devious intrigues; she'd let her guard down and begun to believe that her life might be changing for the better but all she'd done was allow this man's poison to seep in and now everything would be tainted and ruined.

"Lady Winterborne?"

"Leave me alone!" she said frostily.

He moved closer to her, leaning in, "Perhaps we could come to some arrangement? I'm perfectly willing to take up where Heywood left off. I don't mind used goods."

Grace closed her eyes.

Then she heard another voice and opening her eyes, saw the gardener returning with his wheelbarrow, now empty, "Mornin' m'lady. Sir. Fine day, again. Garden'll be glad of all that rain though. Bit of damage here an' there but not too bad, all in all."

Grace managed to smile, "Ah, — Sam? I — I wonder if you could show me where the damage is?"

Slightly startled but delighted that his mistress remembered his name and wanted to accompany him, he nodded, "Yes, m'lady, the worst bit's some flooding. I'll show you."

Without further ado and without acknowledging George Carew she quickly joined the astonished gardener and, keeping up an unusual flow of chatter, she allowed Sam to escort her out of the Nuttery and to safety.

* * *

Nathan glanced at the empty chair at the head of the table and wondered where the hell she was. The dining room was already teeming with yawning, hung-over Theatricals and one or two of the other guests, but there was still no sign of Grace, so he backed out again and went in search of her.

After checking every room downstairs, he came across Bridie and Jem on their way to the kitchen to collect Barker. Bridie said she'd last glimpsed her ladyship much earlier going down the back stairs. So, Nathan went out to the garden to find her.

He eventually spotted her sitting by herself on a bench in the shade of some silver birch trees. But as he approached her and she looked up, his heart sank. She immediately rose to her feet and began to walk away from him.

Lengthening his stride, he caught up with her easily.

"What's wrong, Grace?"

She didn't respond.

He put a hand on her arm to stop her, but she shook it away.

Grabbing her again, he pulled her to a standstill.

She turned her face to him, dead-eyed and ashen.

"Keep away from me," she whispered in stifled accents.

She fought him but he gripped her arms tightly, "What the hell is wrong? What's happened?"

She stopped struggling and became very still.

"Grace! Talk to me."

Her eyes came up and met his and he knew. He released her and took a step away, "So — you've heard. I'm assuming it was Carew as he has the most to gain and obviously overheard me talking with Emery last night. I wanted to tell you — I tried — "

Grace stared blankly at him, "There was no need for you to pretend to like me, you know. You could have just raped me like he tried to last time he was here. That would have achieved the same thing, but without the need for all the lying. You went to far too much trouble to win me over when brute force would have been the answer and so much quicker. You could have had your money weeks ago and now be far away — I might already be — " She faltered and put her hands over her face. "Oh, God in heaven. I might be — "

For the first time in his life Nathan had no idea what to say or do. He felt as though he were sinking into quicksand.

"Please — you need to listen to me. It's true, I did come to Winterborne initially because of your husband's offer but at the time it was just a straightforward business proposition — and it was only when I got here that he gave any hint of the real reason he needed me. When he told me, I thought he was deranged and refused him. I only stayed on because he suddenly became ill, and I thought I couldn't abandon you to care for him alone. And then, I — got to know you — "

"I trusted you and you lied to me."

He paced further away from her, so that he wouldn't be tempted to seize her again, "Yes, I know, but it wasn't long before I didn't want to leave at all, but I knew if I stayed that

I'd be risking being denounced and then before I could tell you the truth you nearly — drowned — and I stayed — because — "

"Because you knew I'd be grateful to you and therefore more easily manipulated."

He looked at her, hating the way she was regarding him with such desolation in her eyes and knowing that he was the cause of it.

"I stayed because my feelings altered. When I thought I'd lost you — "

"You couldn't lose me. I was never yours to lose."

"No, I suppose that's true. But, Grace, it was never my intention to hurt you."

"You haven't hurt me because I never cared for you."

He said nothing for a moment — just watching the face he'd covered in drunken, passionate kisses not many hours before and wondered how it had come to this. He could see a muscle clenching on her jawline. Every line of her body spoke of her anger and distress and he wished she would shout at him and hit him instead, this dignified restraint was difficult to contend with when he was ready to admit his own guilt and wanted nothing more than her forgiveness.

"I've no excuses. I'd no idea that Lord Winterborne would make me such an extraordinary offer — and, in my defence, I didn't know you then, so of course the thought of the money was tempting but only for a very short time, I swear. I quickly dismissed his proposition and would have left then, had he not become ill. I only stayed to help you."

"How *chivalrous*. But then you decided the money might be useful after all?"

He held up a hand, "Wait a moment! You came to *me!* I was just sitting around admiring the artworks and, as you know, was far too inebriated to — to acquit myself as I should have. You cannot accuse me of coercing you into anything because I could barely stand up at the time."

"How will I ever know now *why* you — and to think I so stupidly *gave* myself to you — of all the people to choose! I might as well have allowed George Carew to — It would have felt no more repugnant and mortifying, looking back."

"Don't be ridiculous, Grace. You know that's not true."

"How would you know what's true and what isn't? You're just a liar! You've done nothing but lie to me since you arrived at Winterborne and, even more unforgivably — you've lied to Jem, making her think that you were here for benevolent reasons — making her believe that you're kind-hearted and that you stayed to help us."

Nathan was silent. He couldn't deny the accusations because he had indeed lied, perhaps not barefacedly, but by the sin of omission. He had been reluctant to tell her the truth because of just this sort of reaction. He'd been cowardly and had attempted to avoid the inevitable. Now he must accept the punishment for such spineless behaviour. He must face up to the fact that he was going to lose the only woman he'd ever loved.

He looked at the ghostly pale face in front of him, knowing, too late, far too late, that he'd do anything for her, that he'd kill for her, that he'd give up his life for her — he'd never felt like this before about anything or anybody and even as the realisation took root, he understood that everything he had ever wanted or desired, everything that he would ever want to treasure and protect and love, was standing right here in front of him; so broken and yet courageous, so beautiful and so proud and desirable, and now, never to be his. He suddenly realised that his whole life had come down to this moment. All those years wasted in the army were just him trying to escape situations which might, as Emery would say, bring him suffering. His parents, his brother, his lovers — they could all have potentially wounded him, and he'd decided at an early age that he preferred to be, again as Emery would put it, numb and to stay well away from responsibility and anything that might bind him to one place.

"Have you nothing to say?" demanded Grace.

He shrugged, "What would be the point? You've made up your mind about me. In your eyes I'm guilty. And to be perfectly honest I cannot blame you. Had I thought it through properly I'd never have even come to Winterborne in the first place, let alone got myself so inextricably embroiled in your woes."

Grace's breath was coming in tight little puffs between her pale lips as she fought her lacerating emotions, "I wish you *hadn't*. I was perfectly content before you came and ruined everything."

Nathan raised his eyebrows incredulously, "Is that so? It didn't seem that way to me. You were cold and lifeless and trapped in this travesty of a marriage. You'd hidden yourself away so that no one could find you. Why did you allow me to — ?"

She looked away, a faint tinge of pink smudging her pale cheeks, "I'd been alone so long — I thought — I *hoped* — but I was mistaken."

"What if you weren't mistaken?" He took a step towards her.

"It's too late, Nathan. It's ruined. I know it was Gervase who — created all this chaos — who thought he could turn your greed and my loneliness to his advantage, and he was successful. He's an extremely clever man and determined to make certain his lineage continues unbroken. He cares more about his possessions and his name than anything else. I know that he's made provision for Jem but if I had a boy, he wouldn't mind in the least how it came about as long as he got what he wanted, and I was forced to bend to his will. If I did anything to anger him now, he might withdraw his support for Jem just to teach me a lesson. She might be the one to lose out in all of this and he knows that I couldn't bear that and is willing to exploit my love for his daughter to force me to capitulate. Well, I did capitulate but only because I was foolish enough to be tricked into it."

"God, Grace, I'm sorry. I wish there was something I could do to convince you that last night had nothing to do with the

Marquis and his Machiavellian scheming and only to do with the fact that, since the accident, I've been plagued by thoughts of you and have wanted to tell you but because of my initial reasons for being here, I found it impossible to say anything."

"How convenient. And now, it's too late, of course. The foul deed is done and — oh, I suppose there must be proof of success! So, you cannot escape until Gervase is sure that you're worth your price. I hope it's all been worth it and that you've earned enough to keep you in comfort for the rest of your life."

Nathan gently shook his head, "If you think I'd take the money now, you're as mad as your husband. I won't be the one to tell him about last night, so he'll be unaware that we — were ever together."

"If I should be — if I — we — *then* he'll know." She suddenly covered her face with her hands and let out a stifled sob.

Nathan moved quickly to her side and took her by the shoulders, "I won't let anything happen to you and Jem, I swear."

"It already has, can't you see? It's too *late!* Oh, I wish I were dead!" came the muffled reply and then she pushed him away and ran down the path back to the house.

Nathan watched her go from expressionless eyes.

Twenty-One

"Perhaps we should leave immediately," said Emery, looking thoroughly perturbed.

"After what I've just told you, you know that we can't leave. We have to make sure that Grace is going to be all right. I've brought all this trouble to her door so now I must do my utmost to straighten things out."

"Oh? And how are you going to do that exactly? Have you even considered that she might be *enceinte*? If she is — what will you do? Carrying *your* child and married to that — twisted man. The child will be named for Winterborne. You have nothing to offer either of them, Nate. No house, no career, no money and no future. A fine prospect you are!"

"You don't think I've already considered all of this? Of course I have. I'll stay until she doesn't need me any more."

Emery tugged uncomfortably at his shirt points, "You're in love with her."

"Much against my better judgment, yes. And, of course, she now hates me. You should've seen her face, Emery," said Nathan wearily. "Carew has made absolutely certain that Grace finds herself alone again, which makes her vulnerable. She cannot turn to the Marquis to shield her as he has his own devious agenda and I'm now an unwelcome encumbrance and cannot be trusted. If Carew stays, she's in grave danger from him. How the hell am I to keep her safe if she won't let me near her?" He paced the parlour, looking as though he wanted to tear the tapestries from the wall and stamp on them. Then, he suddenly smiled, "Do you know what her reaction was when she saw the statue in the Maze? She laughed. She thought it ridiculous and amusing. I thought for sure that she'd be outraged and upset. God, I loved her in that moment. I should have told her then, but I was too drunk to think straight — too drunk to do anything other than adore her. What a damn fool."

"We should leave. Get away from all these complications and return to our simple old life."

Nathan was silent, staring out of the window, brow furrowed.

"Nathaniel? What are you thinking?" asked Emery nervously.

"I was thinking that I have to tell William. He ought to know the truth so that he can keep an eye on his sister too. The more people she has guarding her the better it will be. Carew must be kept away from her."

"Can we not make Lord Winterborne aware and then he might have Carew removed?"

Nathan shook his head, "No, the Marquis seems to enjoy Grace's discomfort and likes to toy with her emotions. He would see it in a very different light."

"We could abduct her… and Jem too, of course."

Nathan eyed his friend cynically, "And take them — where, exactly? Your place in London? I have no home. Look at how she lives. How can she be happy in a depressing hovel?"

"Hovel! How dare you? My house is small but perfectly proportioned for my needs!"

"A philandering bachelor with a tendency to drink far too much and squander his meagre inheritance at the tables. I'm sure Jem would find that vastly entertaining. No, there's no way around it. I could never give her what she needed and will never be able to win her back now."

Emery rolled his large expressive eyes, "Fallen at the first hurdle then? Given up? May I just say how very dispiriting it is to have such a craven friend? It makes me look bad too and I deeply resent that."

"My sincerest apologies. But I am decided — I'm going to talk to William. He's a sensible head on those broad young shoulders and will perhaps be able to persuade Grace to — forgive or, at the very least, he'll be able to help protect her, if he's made aware of the dangers. Who better to keep watch over her than her brother? He can stay close without arousing suspicions."

* * *

Grace was lying on the four-poster and staring at the canopy while Sally searched the linen press for a clean petticoat. The silence between them was tense. They never usually argued, having become firm friends when they were both so young, forming a bond almost like sisters. Grace, alone for the first time in her life and missing her siblings had found someone who was sympathetic and relentlessly cheerful and above everything, kind, and Sally, expecting to be working for someone far above her station and unapproachably haughty, had been relieved when Grace had turned out to be so warm and appreciative of anything she did for her. They had quickly established a rapport which sustained them both. But Grace was very aware that if it were discovered they were so close that it would be severely frowned upon not only by Gervase but by some of the more traditional members of staff and Sally might be removed so, outside the bedchamber, they behaved as though they were merely mistress and abigail, politely friendly but no more.

Grace had arrived back from the incident with George Carew in the Nuttery and the dreadful talk with Nathan and hidden herself in her bedchamber to try to come to terms with what she'd been told. Sally had come upon her staring blankly into space and attempted to divine what had put her into such a state. She didn't cry, which was somehow even more disturbing; she just sat dry-eyed and drained of colour, her eyes fixed upon some far-away place, unresponsive to anything that Sally said to her.

Sally began to wonder if she'd had some sort of relapse caused by the near-drowning and thought she should call for the doctor to come, but when she mentioned that was what she would do, Grace seemed to wake up from her trance. Then, when pressed, she'd been reluctantly forthcoming about what had happened. Sally had been shocked by Carew's revelations and disappointed at the Captain's part in the affair, but she had a handful of unruly brothers who constantly stretched her sympathy to its limits and made her wonder why men were thought to be so clever and the only sex capable of rational thought. She thought her brothers were mostly idiots and wasn't really surprised the Captain had been discovered to possess feet of clay. She was inclined to be very forgiving of him because, after all, he'd refused the Marquis's horrifying proposition and heroically saved Grace's life and had very fine laughing eyes. Oh, and he was marvellous with Jem! And, according to Grace, kissed like a god! She really was having a problem with her mistress's rather feeble objections. Yes, he was human! Yes, he was penniless and had come to Winterborne for purely selfish reasons, but he hadn't gone through with it in the end and had several times tried to tell Grace about it. It sounded to Sally as though Captain Heywood had already done his very best to rectify the situation.

Grace, however, just wanted Sally to support her and was put out that her usually faithful abigail seemed to think that she was making a mountain out of a molehill. She was terrified that her night of insanity in the Maze might turn into something all too tangible — a child she would not be able to explain away. Everyone knew she and Gervase didn't sleep together. It was hard to hide the evidence of their separate lives. But she was incandescent that she should have been used in such a contemptuous fashion and just wanted Sally to agree with her and to make her feel better about her poor decisions.

So, she lay on the bed ignoring Sally's cross little sighs and rolling eyes, knowing that she was in the right. Nathan had been treacherous; he'd used her callously for his own ends and had quite obviously never cared for her. She couldn't help the voice reminding her that he'd never yet told her how he felt, and she knew from what her own mother and Sally had let slip, that men were readily able to make love without having any deep feelings for the female. It apparently made no odds to them if they even knew the name of the lady — they were only intent upon the deed itself. She'd found it a repulsive idea and had thought that Nathan could not have behaved as he had in the Maze without feeling something for her. But George Carew had quickly disabused her and left her feeling like a fool. It was humiliating.

Oh, she loved Nathan, that wasn't in doubt, but she would now never be able to tell him that. He had ruined everything.

Sally slammed the door of the press shut and turned to face her mistress, "Well, I can't find the petticoat, it must still be on the line. I shall go and look. Is there anything else, my lady?"

Grace knew from her flat tone that her abigail was unprepared to give in and she became worried that she'd have no one to talk to for a long time if she didn't say something conciliatory and make amends, even though she knew that Nathan was wholly in the wrong.

Sally had her hand on the door latch and Grace watched her open the door and then sighed loudly.

"The Theatricals are putting on their play tomorrow."

Sally stopped but didn't turn around, "I know, m'lady."

"Some of the staff are coming to watch. Would you like to see it?"

An olive branch, thought Sally, "Yes, m'lady. I would. I've never seen a play before."

"Well, you can come and watch them perform in the Great Hall, if you'd like."

"Thank you, m'lady, I'd like that."

"Oh, *do* stop calling me my lady with every breath! I'm sorry that I've been criticising your perfect hero! I cannot help it that I feel he's let me down. He *lied* to me."

"He only lied, my — because he'd no other choice. What would you have done had he told you he was here at Lord Winterborne's behest and was thinkin' that he might get you with child for a large sum of money? It doesn't matter how you puts it, it sounds bad. See, I think that, although he didn't mean to, he fell for you and then couldn't go through with it.

I think last night proves that his feelings have changed. Why was he in the Maze in the first place? To see the statue of you! And, anyway, it was *you* who went to *him!* And, he may have been drunk but he still walked you home afterwards, which is the act of a true gentleman in my opinion."

Grace closed her eyes, seeing again Nathan's expression as he looked at her, after he'd sobered up a little and was gazing into her eyes with such intensity. She'd been so hopeful. She'd never felt so thrillingly alive. Every part of her had quivered with excitement and she'd just wanted to stay all night in his arms.

But now her mother's ugly words came back to haunt her, and she realised that she'd been telling the truth after all. Men were capable of heinous acts, even the most seemingly charming of them. In order to get what they wanted they could feign affection and then just throw it off afterwards like a snake sheds its skin.

She felt she would never trust anyone again; it was too painful when they inevitably let you down. The problem was that having let her guard down just long enough to sample such bliss and, for a moment, allowed herself to believe, she now had to face the rest of her life alone and with the bitterest memories to keep her awake at night.

"I don't want to talk about him any more. Or think about him. We shall return to our usual way of life and hopefully he and Mr Talmarch will soon leave, and we can forget they were ever here."

Sally wanted to argue but knew she was on shaky ground so reluctantly buttoned her lip and nodded. She left the room thinking that they'd both better start praying that the night in the Maze was not going to prove fruitful because then the real problems would begin and life at Winterborne would very likely become unbearable for all concerned.

* * *

There was a last moment flurry of activity from the Theatricals as they rehearsed the play for the final time. They had all suddenly become rather serious and the main actors were to be seen with their noses buried in their scripts, muttering to themselves in dark corners of the house like lunatics in Bedlam. They were unusually subdued at dinner and very little wine was consumed, as they were all keen to keep clear heads for their performance on the following day and Nathan was a little surprised to see how earnest they were and assumed that they must be being paid a considerable sum to do a private performance.

Lord Winterborne remained in his room, conserving his scant energy and William, who had been every day to see him for a short chatty visit, told Grace that the Marquis was in a high state of excitement looking forward to the entertainment.

Grace made an appearance at dinner and sat regally in her place at the head of the table, not once looking at Nathan, or even attempting to make conversation with anyone and eating not even the tiniest morsel. Emery made a forlorn stab at drawing her out of her sullen mood but was treated to the most blood-chilling stare, so gave up and applied himself to his food.

Thankfully no one could tell from her coldly impassive exterior that her heart was thumping in her throat, and she was finding it hard to breathe without breaking down into heartbroken sobs and bolting from the room. She was hard pressed not to constantly remember, in alarming detail, every vivid moment of the night in the Maze and had to ruthlessly crush her rebellious thoughts so as not to allow Nathan to see how weak she really was where he was concerned. She stared fixedly down the table at the epergne, avoiding all eye contact and being extremely careful not to look at George Carew, who, drink in hand, was leaning back in his chair and watching her almost all the time. She could feel his gaze upon her, and it left her feeling defiled. She wanted to bury a knife in his chest and watch the life drain out of his pale silver eyes.

Nathan sat in silence, occasionally acknowledging William's schoolboy chatter, but not being very forthcoming about the army which is what the boy was questioning him about.

Eventually William sighed deeply, defeated by the monosyllabic responses, "I'm sorry to pester you, Nathan, I expect you don't wish to discuss your life as a soldier, having sold out. I've no doubt that it was not always terribly enjoyable. I'm sure there were times when the life was hard to bear. It's just that living with my family was so unspeakably grim and I spent years longing for some real excitement."

Nathan brought his distracted gaze to bear on his eager young companion and apologised for being so preoccupied and politely begged him to continue with his idealistic inquisition.

It was nearing the end of the interminable dinner and Nathan watched covertly as Grace quietly excused herself and left early on the pretext of visiting her husband to make sure he'd eaten something.

As she climbed the stairs with a weariness, which didn't stem from anything other than the emotional strain she was under, she paused for a moment to catch her breath and steady herself. That dinner had been such a painful trial that she'd bitten a hole on the inside of her cheek, trying desperately not to show how distraught she was. She could still taste the blood. She missed the luxury of having Nathan to talk with during the meal, sad not to have his amusing descriptions of the guests, murmured *sotto voce*, just for her amusement. She wanted to scream with frustration when the other ladies flirted with him, leaning in and flaunting their beautiful décolletage for him to admire, their delicate hands resting possessively upon his broad shoulder, or fluttering like pale butterflies between them. She was sickened by their very obvious attempts to capture his interest and wanted to shout at them that he belonged to her, but she'd just bitten down hard on her cheek instead until the pain brought her back into the awful reality where she remembered how he had betrayed her.

* * *

She found her husband propped up in bed, a tray upon his lap, the food mostly untouched.

"Ah, at last! Take this damn tray away. The sight of food is making me feel thoroughly ill. That woman keeps trying to force me to eat!" His voice had lost some of its usual vigour and sounded reedy and frail.

"Mrs Hawkins only has your best interests at heart. She's a very capable nurse, if a little too pious for my tastes." She drew the chair nearer to the bed and taking a spoonful of the nameless grey broth she held it out to him. He turned his head away like a small child might. "If you don't eat, my lord, you'll become much sicker and then where shall we be?"

He looked at her, eyes narrowed, "How can you always be so calm? It's infuriating. Why do you never lose your temper and throw a candlestick at my head?"

She contemplated his waxy, emaciated face for a long moment, "I suppose it's because I don't really care for you, Gervase. I do not feel angry about the terrible things that you do. I merely feel dispassionate and know that the cruelty comes from some place within you, which no one can reach, and no one can alter. It's something which attached itself to you, like a parasite perhaps, when you were a child. I know that you had the most dreadful childhood and one can hardly blame you for being — tainted by what you suffered. But we all have our crosses to bear. Some people are affected more by their experiences, both good and bad, and the bad ones stop them being who they should have been; and there are others who are able to carry on as though nothing happened and reach their full potential. Just look at William! We had the same parents, the same upbringing and yet he is wholly unaffected by the constraints put upon us as children. My mother's evil tongue left him relatively unscathed as did my father's relentless bullying and he's exactly who he was always meant to be. And yet, poor Hester, she's a sad, squashed and bitter little creature because she was unable to protect herself from the poisonous words that my mother exuded. She's very much to be pitied, as are you. It would be the same with a dog, whipped and starved and ill-treated from birth. It would be fit only for life chained in a kennel, for it wouldn't know not to bite the hands of its rescuer. But the same dog, brought up by loving owners — would be an amiable and loyal pet. One cannot blame the dog."

Lord Winterborne closed his eyes and lay in silence, and Grace thought she'd gone too far but was finding, in her present state of wretchedness, that it was hard to care about his volatile temper and what he might say or do. Nothing seemed to matter any more. The things that had once scared her and held her fast, no longer possessed the same terror for her. It was as though she'd been set free from the shackles that had bound her because nothing could be as bad as the pain she was already experiencing. She supposed she should be grateful to Nathan for that at least.

"You've never questioned me about my motives, Grace. Have you never wondered why I should have chosen you when I had half the county flinging their daughters at my feet and why I found none but you acceptable to be the next Lady Winterborne?"

Grace gave a slight shrug, "I've never cared about your motives. Once you had decided upon me, I couldn't change my fate because my family practically had the bailiffs at their door, and I was their only recourse. It was my duty. And then I met Jemima and again, I had no choice, once I knew her and quickly came to love her. I could not then leave her — I was firmly caught in your net and it was easier not to struggle against the inevitable. What would be the point of asking why you should be so manipulative, or why you should wish me to suffer? It would have made no odds to my life at that point. It was best for everyone if I just did as I was told without complaint." She cast him a concerned look, "But why are you asking me this now, Gervase? It's a little late in the day."

He made a sort of coughing sound, which she suspected might have started off as a laugh, "Thank you for reminding me! Being at Death's door has a way of putting things into perspective, I find. I'm very fond of Jemima, you know. She has spirit — unlike Margery who was — sweet but insipid and I — of course, never loved her, as I'm incapable of that kind of love, as I'm sure you've already concluded."

Grace nodded, astonished by the Marquis's unexpected candour.

"You were not shocked to hear of my iniquities?"

Grace didn't answer immediately. She considered his words and tried to recall what emotions she'd felt when she'd finally understood her husband's preferences, through various snippets of gossip and unkind innuendo and eventually when the telling frieze and statues in the Temple had confirmed her worst suspicions. She hadn't felt outrage, which she supposed she should have done, having been tricked into marrying him, and she hadn't exactly been revolted by the truth either. She'd been confused, then saddened, and anxious that Jem should have the most happily unremarkable childhood that she could give her and that she should know that, above everything, she was loved. She'd done her best to protect the child against anything which might adversely affect her by creating a separate world for them, where they could live without fear of the ugliness of real life encroaching upon their imaginary world. It had become an obsession, protecting Jem.

"I don't think so. I'm more appalled by your casual cruelty. It really makes no difference to me how or who you love but when you are needlessly cold and vicious then I must try to protect myself and Jem too."

He frowned, "I wouldn't hurt Jemima. She's a Winterborne."

He made no attempt to deny that he would often deliberately set out to antagonise Grace. He didn't know why he felt compelled to wound her, but there was something so contained about her, so controlled, that it was like a small boy prodding a rolled-up hedgehog with a stick until it unfurled and ran away.

"I know. Even you have your limits." She took a deep breath, "Gervase? I know all about Captain Heywood."

A quick appraising look from her husband, "Heywood? What of him?"

Grace took the tray from his lap and placed it on the table beside the bed; he still hadn't eaten anything. She straightened the counterpane with fidgety fingers, "I know the real reason he's here."

The grey lips thinned, "For a business deal."

Grace looked him directly in the eye, "*You* might call it a business deal, but I'd call it utterly callous and inhuman."

The door suddenly opened, and Mrs Hawkins marched in, a bundle of clean linen in her arms.

"Get *out!*" bellowed the Marquis and she scurried away again, looking terrified.

"Poor woman," said Grace.

"She's in league with God — she'll be all right."

Grace folded her hands tidily in her lap so that he wouldn't be able to see them shaking, "I know why you invited Captain Heywood to Winterborne. There's no point in being evasive."

The Marquis sneered, "My, you've become very bold, my lady! I wonder what has made you suddenly so audacious. So, you've somehow heard about my little scheme? Not from Heywood himself, I assume, as he's hardly likely to endanger his reward."

"George Carew was absolutely delighted to inform me of your plans."

"George, eh? He always was a devious beggar. I'd rather thought I might use him to provide the service to begin with, but you showed such a marked dislike for him that I abandoned the idea pretty quickly. Then, I heard about Heywood through Emery Talmarch and met him many times in London over the months and decided that on the evidence I saw, not many women could resist his fatal combination of good looks, rakish charm and brooding air of mystery. Women are so predictable. I know you've formed a bond with him and then, of course, he had the great good fortune to be able to save your life. How romantic! How heroic! How could you not be swayed by his manifest attributes? I think I chose exceedingly well. The perfect candidate for the job."

Grace rose and walked away to the window to stare out into the garden, gilded by the early evening sun, each shrub and tree haloed in warm light.

"Oh, you chose better than you will ever know, my lord! It was masterly. And you came very close to succeeding in your endeavours but I'm afraid that now the truth has been revealed it's rather spoiled your carefully laid plans."

"Has it?" countered Lord Winterborne, "I think not."

Grace turned to face him, "What do you mean by that?" she asked quietly.

"You didn't think I'd just allow Fate to hold the reins when so much is at stake? Oh, my *dear!* No, I've had you watched from the very first moment. I needed to know if my scheme would bear fruit," he said with a triumphant smile.

She looked at him with undisguised loathing, "So — you know everything. Well, I hope it gives you much pleasure. It must make you feel exceedingly powerful, being able to control us all from what is essentially your deathbed."

The smile faded from his yellowed eyes, "You may not understand yet, Grace, but one day you will. You'll see that not only have I ensured my legacy will continue but I have provided you with a suitable mate and Jemima with someone who will make a decent step-father."

Grace couldn't help laughing, albeit a bitter and mirthless sound, "You're a fool if you think that Captain Heywood will be staying on here and also, that I would wish for an immoral, mercenary liar such as him to be allowed anywhere near my daughter."

"Oh, I think you'll become quite resigned once you finally see how I've left the estate entailed. No, don't look so concerned! Jem will be well provided for, I'm not one of those men who believe the female line should be ignored in expectation of them making an advantageous marriage. I do not, on the whole, approve of child brides — unlike your oh-so-charming parents."

"But you were quite happy to take one for yourself."

The smile reappeared, "Yes, but I knew you were in no danger from me. I never have been any threat to females. I believe that you will find all the arrangements to be wholly satisfactory and I can die safe in the knowledge that Winterborne will continue hopefully for centuries to come."

Twenty-Two

By the time Grace finally got downstairs the following morning, having procrastinated for as long as she possibly could in order to avoid the inevitable crush at breakfast, the Theatricals had already eaten, their dishes had been cleared away and they'd left to finish their final preparations for the play. There were only a few of the other guests, Marcus Delamere, Lord and Lady Standon and Emery in the dining room.

Emery, rising to his feet, as she entered the room, smiled at her hopefully. She nodded at him in such a stiff and unfriendly manner that he sank back into his chair and put his head in his hands in despair. Grace cast him an uncertain glance and sat down. A footman poured coffee and passed her a bowl of bread rolls and then retreated to stand against the wall just behind her chair.

Neither of them said anything for a few moments and then Emery raised his head and let out a sigh so dramatic that Grace had to suppress a smile. Emery, in an undertone, said "I have absolutely no idea how to make this better Grace. I'm entirely at a loss. I'd have you know that all of this can be laid squarely at my door. It was I who introduced Nate to your husband, and it was I who encouraged him to take up the offer to come to Winterborne to discuss what he thought was a legitimate business proposition. He truly had no clue what it entailed. I'm afraid I *did* though. Lord Winterborne had quizzed me about Nate's character and his life, and I soon realised that it was no ordinary proposal. Of course, I should have said something — given him some warning, but we both had such pressing debts — it was paramount that we found a way out of our financial woes. And I'm deeply sorry that I didn't take your feelings into consideration — I was distracted by the tempting thought of not spending the rest of my life in a squalid cell in Newgate. I persuaded Nate to come to Winterborne, he only did it to please me. You should blame me, not him."

Grace was making a pretence of eating some bread and butter, but it tasted like ashes.

"But, Emery, *you* didn't deliberately make me fall in love with you in order to comply with a madman's wishes. He could, at any point have told me, or he could've left — but he didn't. Just as I was tricked into marriage with Gervase, Nathan tricked me into loving him. How am I supposed to forgive him? I'm sorry, but I can't."

Emery glanced around the long dining table and noted that those still breakfasting were taking no notice of their murmured conversation, "I realise that it's no excuse, but Nate's been shown very little real affection in his life. His parents were only interested in Alexander and the type of women who gravitate towards him tend to be keen only until they realise that he's inherited nothing from his father's estate and will have no title. You should hear their pathetic excuses when he candidly announces to them that he's no residence to call home! He only had his army pay and that's not enough to keep most ambitious females interested for long. He'd become cynical and resigned to life on the margins of society but since he's been here, he's changed. I swear to you. I've never seen him like this before. It's a revelation. Please, just give him another chance!"

Grace looked into her companion's earnest eyes and wished she could grant him this wish, but it was too late. She couldn't go back.

Emery, seeing the look in her eyes, knew his words had fallen upon deaf ears and that his valiant efforts had been in vain. So, for the time being, he gave up his campaign to bring some sort of harmony back to Winterborne.

* * *

The chairs had been arranged in rows and dozens and dozens of candles lit and despite the sultry heat after the storm, a fire had been kindled in the fireplace; the Great Hall, with its cavernous ceiling, was inclined to be chilly in the evenings, even though the low sun was still flooding through the newly cleaned windowpanes, highlighting the odd forgotten cobweb in the hard-to-reach corners.

An impassive footman showed Grace to her seat right at the front of the rows of chairs which were all facing the minstrel's gallery at the south end. She glanced around and saw that there was a large comfortable armchair next to hers with a footstool placed in front of it. And on her other side, three more chairs.

She was reassured that Jem was safely out of the way in her bed and would hopefully already be asleep and that Bridie was keeping watch over her. She observed, with some relief, her brother strolling towards her, a broad grin on his affable face. He threw himself down into the chair indicated by the footman guiding him, right on the end of the row, and eyed the part of the room designated to be the impromptu stage, with his usual boyish enthusiasm and wide-eyed interest.

He leant forward to talk with her, "'Pon my soul, Gracie! This is just the thing to cheer his lordship up! He truly seems to love all of this sort of glamour and nonsense, does he not? I'm beginning to suspect that he may have chosen a life in the theatre, had he not had other more pressing obligations."

Grace glanced at him, wondering how much he knew about his peculiar brother-in-law, "It certainly is an obsession with him. I mean, he pays them far more than they could ever possibly earn in London, on the stage or at the fairs, acting in the drolls. Peggy was telling me all about it. She was terribly excited to have been selected because it meant that she wouldn't have to worry about paying her rent for a while."

"They must fall over each other to get chosen for this particular venture. Even if it brings no lasting prestige with it, the money must be compensation enough. Ah, look, here comes Gervase! He looks well this evening."

Looking up to see her husband being carried towards them on a chair, by two footmen, she considered for a moment telling William that the colour in the Marquis's cheeks was rouge and his long, curling silver wig concealed a scalp with only a few sparse strands of hair left. The disease was taking a dramatic toll on his appearance, which he had once held so dear. Although he still managed to look extremely impressive in an oyster satin coat with embroidered bronze waistcoat, large, engraved bronze buttons and a flamboyant neckcloth of the finest Brussels lace fastened with a dazzling diamond pin, the ostentatious gem the size of a quail's egg. He looked every bit the lord of the manor and she was pleased to see that even though his eyes were still stained yellow due to his illness, that they contained some signs of life, which she hadn't seen for a very long time. She rose as they manoeuvred the chair around and then carefully transferred him to the more comfortable seat, where there were cushions and a warm rug for his knees. As the footmen retreated, Grace stepped forward and twitched the rug into place, but he hissed at her under his breath, "Don't fuss so!" so hastily she backed away and returned to her own chair.

Lord and Lady Standon seated themselves next to the Marquis on his right-hand side and behind them sat the Leventhorpes and Lady Cheyne and behind Grace were Marcus Delamere and George Carew. She was horribly aware of Carew and felt that he would be staring at the back of her neck from his hateful pale eyes.

She was also nervously aware that the two chairs on her left were still empty and that the only guests left to arrive were Nathan and Emery. Why they had been seated next to her she'd no idea; she hadn't thought to advise the staff that they ought to be placed further away from her. She could feel her neck beginning to ache already as she tensed herself for the evening ahead and then was unable to rid herself of the unbidden memory of Nathan's fingers easing away the tension in her shoulders. She shivered. And then, as though she'd conjured him up — he was there beside her, with Emery and, with what sounded, above the growing hubbub, like a quiet apology, he sat down next to her.

"Would you prefer William to — ?" he murmured but she merely raised her fingers from the arm of the chair, and he took that as a request for him to be silent, so he sat back and wished he was anywhere but there in that cathedral-like room with a crowd of mostly strangers and with Grace studiously ignoring him.

Those members of the household and garden staff fortunate enough to be favoured with an invitation, were seated at some distance behind the distinguished guests, including Mrs Hawkins, rigid with disapproval and quietly mouthing prayers, and Sally, who could only just make out her mistress's elbow right down at the front, but knew even without being able to see her face that she would be as stiff and cold as an icicle in February. She didn't envy the Captain having to sit next to her; she knew it was going to be a long, frosty night for him and she felt very sorry for him. It seemed to Sally that someone with an axe to grind had made those seating arrangements and suspected Lord Winterborne had had a meddling hand in it. It would be just like him to make sure that his wife was uncomfortable throughout the performance, which by all accounts would last for above two and a half hours. The only acting she'd ever been lucky enough to see before were the Mummers, who came door to door at Christmas and she'd thought them rather silly as they were mostly drunk on homemade cider anyway, singing out of tune and wholly unintelligible. She was very excited about the evening ahead. Her eyes roamed around the Hall and she saw that awful Mr Carew sitting just behind Lady Winterborne but thought at least, in such a crowd, he'd not be able to do or say anything that might upset her mistress. She saw that some of the outdoor staff had been allowed to stand at the back to watch; there was that nice Shawe, Mr Edgerton's valet — such a jolly, wise sort of fellow — and Kirby was marshalling the footmen with his usual dissatisfied frown. Some of the older housemaids had been given permission to attend, as well as the cook, flushed with the thrill of expectation, and a few of the senior kitchen staff. She caught sight of Robert, the young footman, who'd come to Winterborne just after her, and much to her surprise, he caught her eye and winked at her. She put her nose in the air and tried to look as haughty as the Marchioness; he really shouldn't be so forward right in front of everyone! But secretly she was delighted because he was very tall and handsome and an excellent footman and probably bound for a promotion to butler one day in the future. After all, Kirby couldn't live forever, he must be at least fifty!

Gradually, the candles were extinguished, the candelabras lowered, and their candles quickly snuffed and, as the sun sank slowly behind the distant hills, a mysterious and quivering darkness fell like a magician's cloak. In the minstrel's gallery three local musicians struck up a low but jaunty tune and an expectant silence fell upon the audience.

* * *

One of the more mature actors in the troupe, Mr Owen Bray, emerged portentously from the wings and stood just to one side, behind the row of glowing lanterns which edged the stage. He was possessed of a sonorous voice, which made the wine glasses chime and sounded as though it came from the bowels of the earth, a barrel chest and a large purple nose, which dominated his face and betrayed him as a heavy drinker. He cut an impressive figure, entirely clad in black and, sniffing despondently into a handkerchief, he looked up at the faces all turned towards him and dimly lit by the light from the lanterns and the candles upon the stage.

A voice offstage, announced, "She Stoops to Conquer (or, the Mistakes of a Night) by Oliver Goldsmith. And here, read by our wondrous Mr Bray, is The Prologue, writ by the great David Garrick Esq."

"Excuse me, sirs, I pray — I can't yet speak —
I'm crying now — and have been all the week.

*"'Tis not alone this mourning suit," good masters:
I've that within" — for which there are no plasters!
Pray, would you know the reason why I'm crying?
The Comic Muse, long sick, is now a-dying!
And if she goes, my tears will never stop;
For as a player, I can't squeeze out one drop…"*

…intoned Mr Bray, injecting drama into every word. He continued with the monologue on how the play would hopefully arrest the death of comedy and then, having finished his speech, he backed slowly away into the shadows again.

The Hardcastles (played by Mr and Mrs Redman) *appear on the stage and Mrs Hardcastle talks about her son, Tony, and how difficult he can be especially when inebriated. She thinks he's consumptive, but his stepfather says he's just a drunk. Tony enters and declares he's late for an urgent appointment at the local alehouse, The Three Pigeons. His mother tries to stop him leaving so he drags her out with him as he leaves.*

Their daughter, Miss Kate Hardcastle (played by Peggy Weston, trembling with first night nerves, but otherwise surprisingly accomplished and dressed in swirling clouds of amber silk and lace) *enters. Her father tells her he's chosen a bridegroom for her and that he's sure she'll be delighted with him: the son of his old friend, Sir Charles Marlow. He describes him as young and brave, very handsome, with an excellent understanding, and Kate decides, on this recommendation, that she'll accept him.*

Grace, on hearing the description of young Marlow, was made even more aware of Nathan sitting on her left-hand side and tried desperately to gain control of her unsteady breathing so that he wouldn't hear how affected she was by his nearness. She was desperate to return to the icy disdain she'd affected before he came into her life. She'd been safe then, hidden away behind the barriers she'd so carefully erected.

Emery, in between laughing uproariously at the actors exaggerated antics, was making audible comments about what was about to happen next in the play. Grace glanced nervously at her husband, who was leaning forward slightly, eager to hear every word of the dialogue. He turned to look at her and smiled, his bloodless lips sticking to his teeth; Grace, reading a mixture of triumph and anticipation in his eyes, serenely tried to return the smile, but failed miserably, her face frozen into a mask to hide her growing fears.

Hardcastle tells his daughter that the prospective groom is a reserved sort of fellow, which she fears will make him a suspicious husband and she begins to have some doubts. Hardcastle leaves the stage and their niece, Miss Constance Neville, enters (played by Elvira Dean, who, taking her role very seriously, swished across the stage, making full use of her undulating hips, whilst still managing to make eyes at Nathan in the front row) *and the two girls discuss Kate's potential bridegroom. Constance says he's great friends with her admirer, Mr Hastings, and also that Kate's mother has been trying to get Constance interested in Tony by telling her that he's perfect. Constance reveals that if she marries Tony she'll come into her inheritance — a fortune in jewellery — and says that, although she loves Mr Hastings, she's allowed Mrs Hardcastle to believe that she loves Tony in order to get hold of the inheritance.*

In the next scene, in The Three Pigeons, as an inebriated Tony sings an amusing song to his loudly drunken friends, the landlord enters and tells them that visitors have arrived who are lost and looking for somewhere to stay the night. He leaves and returns with Marlow and Hastings whom Tony proceeds to trick into thinking that his stepfather's house is an inn and his stepfather the landlord, and directs them to it for a joke.

The audience, who were slowly catching on to the twists and turns of the plot, laughed appreciatively and applauded as the scene changed again. There was a little buzz of excitement in the Hall as views on the plot were exchanged and events anticipated.

The action returns to the Hardcastle's home, where he's training reluctant farmhands to act as house servants and, above all, to be calm and professional. There's the sound of a carriage arriving and the servants, ignoring his careful instructions, nervously scatter in all directions.

The servants in the Hall chuckled in sympathy and there was a ripple of clapping from those at the rear of the room and

Emery slapped his hand against his thigh and wiped his streaming eyes.

Marlow and Hastings enter, convinced the house is a splendid inn. Hastings teases Marlow on his shyness with women of breeding, and Marlow agrees with him, saying fine ladies petrify him. Hastings says that it's odd that he was so much at ease with barmaids. Hardcastle enters and is shocked by his two guests who, with many asides to the knowing audience, criticise the "inn" as the confusion deepens. Hardcastle and Marlow leave the stage. Hastings is on his own when Constance appears, and she soon realises that Tony has tricked them, and Hastings admits that he's used his friend's visit to gain admittance to her family and she tells him that she and her inheritance will soon be his, but he reassures her that he wants only her. Hastings says that they must keep up the pretence or Marlow will leave.

Grace stirred uncomfortably in her chair, her palms were sweaty and yet she felt chilled to the marrow. She just wanted the interminable evening to end. It was like torture. The minutes dragged by as though Time had slowed almost to a standstill.

Marlow returns and on hearing that Kate and Constance have come to the "inn", he desires to leave immediately. Kate, having been out for a stroll, arrives in her walking clothes with a bonnet on and they're introduced, but Kate finds Marlow to be awkward. Marlow speaks to Kate with Hastings's helpful asides, and with more words of encouragement he and Constance leave them alone. Marlow is covered in confusion again, reduced to stammering inanities and Kate is bewildered.

The audience revelled in the raillery and misunderstandings and are impressed by the unexpectedly accomplished performances. It turned out that Peggy Weston was, as Sally joyfully pointed out to a scandalised Mrs Hawkins, an exceedingly talented actress. Mrs Leventhorpe, in a piercing whisper, announced to most of those around her, that despite their obvious lack of refinement the actors were really quite good in their roles. Grace closed her eyes and hoped that the actors hadn't heard the double-edged compliment.

Marlow, hopelessly floundering, leaves to talk with Constance, and Kate is left alone to ponder his bashful nature and wish she could instil him with some confidence. She leaves the stage. Tony, Constance, Mrs Hardcastle and Hastings arrive, and Hastings discovers that Mrs Hardcastle wants Constance to marry Tony, but that Tony's so against the idea that he promises to help Hastings elope with Constance and recover her inheritance. Mrs Hardcastle and Tony argue about Constance and then they leave. Hastings admits that he likes Constance despite Tony being disparaging and he and Hastings make plans for the elopement.

This development received a roar of approval from the rowdier element at the back of the Hall. Grace gritted her teeth until her cheekbones began to ache and wondered if she were the only one seeing parallels between the play and what was happening in her life.

Act Three begins with Hardcastle wondering why his friend, Sir Charles, should have recommended his son for Kate when he is so rude. Kate returns plainly dressed and they discuss Marlow but as though he's two different people. Hardcastle thinks him brazen and not fit to marry his daughter, and Kate thinks him shy and awkward. They both conclude the other is wrong and leave the stage.

Meanwhile Tony finds the Hardcastle jewels and gives them to Hastings. Constance meanwhile asks her mother if she can wear the jewels, but, as instructed by Tony, Mrs Hardcastle tells her they've been lost. Kate finds out about Tony's deception but chooses to perpetuate it as a way of putting Marlow's nature to the test.

Jenny Robbins made her appearance as the maid and, with only a few whispered prompts from the wings, when she was overcome by the sight of everyone watching her expectantly, managed to be quite convincing in her role, her golden hair and pretty face winning the audience around to her side.

The maid helps Kate take on the role of barmaid to deceive Marlow.

As Jenny left the stage, she made a saucy little curtsy, flicking up her petticoats and winning a laugh all her own and a few whistles from the footmen, who'd been surreptitiously helping themselves to the wine and were beginning to lose their inhibitions and thoroughly enjoy themselves.

Nathan, determined to ignore the uncomfortable echoes in the plot, tried hard to relax and enjoy the performance, but found it extremely difficult to forget the woman sitting so still next to him. He could feel the tension in her and could tell that her neck was already aching and her shoulders stiffening up. He had an overwhelming urge to reach out a hand to her and had to clench his fists to stop himself. Emery, like an over-excited child, kept up a constant commentary on the action being played out in front of them. He'd seen the show before and despite not being particularly scholarly knew what was about to happen and foreshadowed every scene with murmured asides which gave away the storyline. Nathan didn't really mind, being grateful for any kind of distraction. Time and time again, he asked himself why he had stayed and could find no satisfactory answer.

Marlow, thinking that Kate is a barmaid, flirts with her and complains about Kate being an awkward squinting thing and then tries to kiss her.

One of the footmen, his tongue loosened by wine, shouted out that he wouldn't mind a kiss too and was shushed by those at the front of the audience.

Marlow leaves and Hardcastle enters. Having witnessed what happened, he accuses Kate of allowing Marlow to manhandle her and she promises to prove to him that her nominated bridegroom is respectable because she now likes him.

The Fourth Act begins with Hastings and Constance discussing the imminent arrival of Sir Charles Marlow, and their elopement. They exit and Marlow and a servant enter, discuss the whereabouts of the jewels and, after the servant leaves, Marlow exclaims that he must have the maid, who is really Kate in disguise.

Hastings returns and Marlow tells him of his fancy for the maid and Marlow says he'd come across the jewels and, thinking them mislaid, had given them to the landlady and Hastings is distressed, thinking the inheritance has been lost and he and Constance must now elope without it.

Some wag called out that Hastings didn't deserve such a beauty as Constance and Grace shrank slightly further down into her chair. She knew that Gervase occasionally cast her a furtive glance to see how she was reacting and realised that he'd obviously chosen it with her in mind in order to discomfit her. She also noticed that he was beginning to cough but was burying the sound in his handkerchief so as not to disturb the performance.

Hastings leaves the stage and Hardcastle returns and argues with Marlow over him allowing the servants to get drunk and Marlow finally discovers the house isn't an inn and Kate, still pretending to be a maid, confirms this and she acknowledges the deception, and he realises he's been fooled. He admits he'd marry her if her father would allow it but says it's unlikely because of their different stations and Kate begins to like him even more.

"I should think not indeed! A barmaid and a gentleman! *Most* unsuitable," muttered Mrs Hawkins darkly to Sally, who rolled her eyes and thought that the nursemaid had not one romantic bone in her spindly body.

Kate leaves the stage and Tony and Constance enter and discuss the safe return of the jewels and the elopement and when Mrs Hardcastle arrives, she happily believes them to be in love and promises Constance the jewellery, but then a letter arrives from Hastings about the elopement and Mrs Hardcastle discovers the truth and sends Constance away to her strict aunt's as punishment. Hastings arrives and Marlow is angry about the deception and Hastings is angry about the jewels. There seems little hope, but Tony comes up with a plan.

In Act Five, Sir Charles Marlow and Hardcastle discuss Kate and Marlow's marriage and Tony, who was supposed to take Constance to her aunt's, brings her back and she decides not to elope after all but to somehow gain her parents' permission to marry Hastings honourably and finally secure the jewellery. Marlow learns that the barmaid he loves is Kate and, after some convoluted explanations, the two couples agree to marry.

Sally clapped ecstatically and breathed a sigh of relief because she thought Marlow to be really rather sweet and she nudged Mrs Hawkins who, furtively wiping away a tear, declared the play to be a lot of immoral nonsense. Sally grinned at her and the nursemaid blushed a guilty scarlet.

Mr Owen Bray briefly returned to the stage to explain how Kate had stooped in her rank to conquer and get what she wanted because of the difficulties put upon her by society.

Thoroughly enchanted, the audience roared their enthusiastic approval, the garden staff stamped their feet and hollered and when Peggy, Jenny and Elvira stepped forward to take their final bow they received bountiful applause and Jenny, thoroughly overwhelmed by the reception, burst into tears and sobbed exultantly into her petticoat, which showed off her pretty ankles to perfection and made the footmen whistle appreciatively again.

Kirby snapped back into action and with some sharp reprimands, galvanised the maids and intoxicated footmen back to their duties and soon refreshments were being handed around to the guests as they stood in groups discussing the brilliance of the play and the actors.

Grace, after a moment to gather her thoughts, turned to the Marquis to see if he needed anything but was alarmed to find that he was slumped in his chair, a handkerchief pressed to his mouth and his eyes closed.

"Gervase? Is there anything — ?" she whispered.

He shook his head almost imperceptibly and she caught the eye of Kirby, who had come to dutifully hover nearby. He nodded and signalled to Robert and another footman and they approached their master cautiously, knowing that his temper was very likely to flare up without much warning.

But Lord Winterborne allowed them to transfer him back into the lighter carrying chair without a word of dissent and without opening his eyes and seemingly unaware that he was being manhandled; he remained unnaturally passive as he was carried from the Hall.

But Nathan, watching the proceedings, had seen the heavily bloodstained handkerchief and with a quiet word to Emery, he followed the small procession out of the Hall and up the stairs.

Emery, catching the attention of one of the passing footmen, murmured instructions to him, and the servant dashed away to fetch the doctor.

Aware that something disturbing was going on and that she should be accompanying her husband upstairs but also concerned that she had a duty to their guests, Grace was, for a moment, unable to move at all. She heard the conversations around her, the effusive compliments and the spirited dissection of the plot and reviews of the actors' performances, but it was as though they were speaking from a great distance and the words had no meaning, making an impenetrable jumble in her mind.

Her head swam and she wondered if she was going to faint.

Then, William was at her side; a strong hand under her elbow supported her and, with a confidence which belied his age, he made her excuses and resolutely guided his disorientated sister away from the curious onlookers, hoping to prevent her from breaking down in front of everyone.

Twenty-Three

Nathan was relieved the ordeal of the performance was over and that he was having to deal with something jarringly brutal. Blood and piss and pain were something that he could cope with; the army had taught him the rudiments of medical care and he'd thankfully been blessed with a strong stomach and a vigorous constitution. He was able to observe the Marquis suffer and feel sympathy for his plight but still manage to deal practically with the grim results of the disease. Mrs Hawkins came quickly and despite her sullen mutterings about the iniquities of the world of theatre, she as always proved strong and dependable when it came to nursing. He could even put up with the endless Bible quotations and praying as it helped him block out other more disturbing thoughts.

Doctor Morton arrived, having been roused from a deep slumber, and told Nathan bluntly, that Lord Winterborne was bleeding from his throat, a common consequence of the disease. He warned that it was bound to get worse, and that the Marquis was likely to become confused and irritable; he explained that the side effects of giving up alcohol were, to start with, sometimes worse than the disease itself. He listed the probable complications they might encounter and carefully spelt out to them that, even given excellent nursing, the patient was not going to recover; that this looked like the beginning of the end to him and that they must prepare themselves for the inevitable. Nathan listened to his advice, knowing full well that it was all pointless; he could see Death hovering above the cadaverous figure in the bed and even though he despised how he'd mentally tortured Grace, he wished he could spare the man the indignity and agony which were bound to follow. No one, however much they deserved it, should have to endure a protracted and painful dying. If he'd been a sick animal, they would have been able to put him out of his misery with a clear conscience.

He looked up as the door opened and Grace and William came into the bedchamber. Grace's eyes met his briefly and slid swiftly away to the patient. Nathan watched her expression alter and was astonished that she was able to regard her husband with such compassion after all he'd put her through. And yet for him, she had only a look of contempt.

Doctor Morton informed her of the state the Marquis was now in and, as gently as he could, not fully understanding the situation at Winterborne, he told her what she might expect in the next week or so and was deeply sympathetic to someone he thought was a devoted and loving wife to his patient but, at the same time, he was well aware that things were not all they seemed at Winterborne. He had heard rumours and one or two locals were keen to make assumptions and felt it their duty to tell him of their doubts and suspicions, as though he might be able do something about it. He'd seen for himself that Captain Heywood and Lady Winterborne had an unusually close relationship — at least, until this visit; he could see that something had gone awry, and they now seemed uncomfortable in each other's company. He wondered what had been going on behind the scenes. Whatever it was, he was fairly certain that it had something to do with the difficulties of caring for Lord Winterborne and the strain that would naturally put everyone under. He'd been shocked to hear that the Marquis had just attended a long theatrical performance that evening and only just managed to prevent himself from suggesting this had been extremely reckless behaviour. It wasn't his place to reprimand such people as the Winterbornes; he relied upon their valued custom and had the greatest respect for their illustrious ancestry even if he occasionally had doubts about the way they conducted themselves.

It wasn't long before the doctor had left and Mrs Hawkins asked Nathan to help her wash the patient, as his clothes were covered in blood and it would be best done while he was unconscious so as not to hurt him more than was inevitable. Nathan immediately agreed but Grace was determined to prove that she was as good as anyone when it came to nursing and that they didn't need his help.

"I will stay and help Mrs Hawkins," she said, not quite looking Nathan in the eye.

He stared at her for a moment, at her stony face and squared shoulders, and his carefully controlled temper began to fray, "Well, you can do just as you please obviously, but it seems that you're cutting off your nose to spite your face. I may not be the best nursemaid, but I can do the heavy lifting and save you and Mrs Hawkins from injury. Three are surely better than two, in *this* case," and he fixed her with a look which was both amused and exasperated at the same time, daring her to argue with him. *Anything*, even unequivocal anger, would be better than the tight-lipped silence he was being forced to endure.

Grace was incensed, but the only sign of it was that her eyes kindled briefly before the shutters came down again, masking her feelings.

"Mrs Hawkins will no doubt be grateful for an extra pair of hands," she said coldly.

And Nathan had to be content with that.

Between the three of them they managed to get Lord Winterborne out of his elegant but spoiled clothes, with Nathan lifting the Marquis so that everything else was made a little easier. Just as they'd manhandled him out of his bloodstained shirt and laid him back against the pillows, he began to cough up blood again, covering himself and the bedcovers. Mrs Hawkins just carried on as though nothing untoward had happened, mopping his face and calmly instructing Nathan to roll him onto his side so that she could change the sheet. Grace was having difficulties with the violence of the attacks, her face the colour of whey.

Nathan angrily shook his head, "For God's sake, Grace, stop being so damned stubborn. You can leave this to us. You're being absurd. Why don't you go and check on Jem?"

As she'd already been thinking that she wanted to run away from the horror of the sickroom, Grace perversely dug her heels in and bridled at his tone, "Don't you dare tell me what to do! I'll do exactly as I like. He's *my* husband — "

"Yes, and don't I know it. You remind me at *every* opportunity," retorted Nathan, goaded too far.

"And yet, it seems you've forgotten!"

"I'm unlikely to forget in the present circumstances."

"Good," said Grace curtly.

Mrs Hawkins stopped wiping blood from Lord Winterborne's chest for a moment, "I hardly think this is the time or the place for a lovers' tiff," she said in measured tones. "It would be more helpful if you were to lend a hand."

Nathan and Grace regarded her in some astonishment. She looked neither angry nor shocked. She just sounded matter of fact.

She may have smiled slightly, neither of them was quite sure, "I'm not blind, my lady. As I told you before, adultery is against the Word of God, and please forgive the presumption. If it were my daughter in the same situation — I'd hope she'd be able to find some happiness, even if it meant that her soul was in jeopardy. I've seen what you're going through and how you've dealt with it up until now — so dutiful, so dignified. You may think me strict and intolerant — I'm a Christian but also a mother. *He that is without sin among you, let him cast the first stone* — " She eyed them with a frown, "You deserve some earthly reward for how you've cared for his lordship — I've no complaints about his treatment. Now, if you could help me to remove his breeches and shoes — "

Nathan snapped into action, feeling rather like a schoolboy having been reprimanded by his headmaster. He didn't dare look at Grace.

* * *

The night passed slowly as they waited to see what would happen next. The Marquis lay still, as though already dead, barely breathing, but he had, at least, stopped coughing blood. Mrs Hawkins, in complete control, sent Grace away at two o'clock to rest and Grace obeyed without taking issue with the nursemaid's peremptory tone. She was, in fact, glad that someone was willing to take on the burden of organising the nursing; she didn't feel up to anything other than staring into space and was angry with herself for being so feeble. She just longed to be with Jem so that she could pretend things were as they used to be. Jem made her forget her woes and the world seemed a brighter place when she was with her.

Despite Grace's repeated reassurances, Sally insisted on sleeping in her dressing room so that she could keep a close eye on her mistress; she didn't like the look of her at all. She hovered like a dragonfly, watching every move Grace made, looking for cracks in the poorly constructed fortifications she was hiding behind. Normally happy to chat, Grace was subdued and uttered only the odd word here and there, as though she were talking in her sleep, but she barely slept at all and, unless persuaded, was eating very little. By standing over her and encouraging her to take each mouthful, Sally managed to make her consume a bowl of soup and some bread but otherwise she would just drift from her bedchamber to the sickroom, sit with his lordship for a few hours and then back to her room to fall asleep in the chair as though it were too much effort to even lie on the bed. One morning she dragged herself along to the nursery to see Jem and try to reassure her that everything was all right and found the little girl wide-eyed and obviously very aware that something was amiss. Grace pulled her onto her lap and hugged her tightly and then, remembering that she'd never been told anything as a child, only gleaning information from the behind-the-scenes whispering not meant for her ears, which she'd found upsetting and confusing, she decided to tell Jem very simply what was happening and hoped that it was the right thing to do.

Jem listened, her eyes wandering around the schoolroom, as though she weren't paying attention and then when Grace had finished, she burrowed her face into her mother's neck and said quietly, "Poor Papa. Just like the rabbit."

Tears sprang to Grace's eyes and she stroked her daughter's hair, "Yes, a bit like the rabbit, my love. But the rabbit is in a better place now, so it'll be happy."

"Really? Is it in Heaven?"

Not wishing to lie, Grace, who had been lectured from an early age about there being no place in Heaven for any creature without a soul, nodded, "It'll be in animal Heaven, with all the other rabbits and animals and birds."

Jem sat up looking alarmed, "With *foxes?* But, Mama, foxes eat rabbits — it'll get eaten! I don't want it to die!"

And this, thought Grace, is what happens when you try to evade the truth. "No, it'll be just fine! God will be there to look after them all and once they get to Heaven they eat — ambrosia and nectar, not each other."

"Foxes won't like that. They'll be werry cross," said Jem anxiously.

Grace smiled, knowing that she was just getting into even deeper water, "Don't worry! God will know how to sort it out. He's very clever."

"Will Papa like Heaven?"

"I should think so. It'll be peaceful and very beautiful. But he'll miss you such a lot."

Jem put her head back onto her mother's shoulder, "Will he? I make him quite cross when I'm naughty."

"You certainly do but he only pretends to be cross though. When you pull at his wig and run off with his walking cane. And that time you put a snail in his pocket!"

Jem giggled, "He said I was a — a — "

"Menace."

"Is that good?"

"Sometimes, when you love that person."

"Is the Captin a menace then?"

Oh, dear Lord, thought Grace, nervously, "What do you mean?"

Jem sat up again and looked her mother directly in the eye, "I heard Mr Talmarch say he was a menace."

"Ah, well, there you are! Mr Talmarch is very fond of Captain Heywood. They're exceedingly good friends, so I expect he meant it kindly."

Jem shrugged and made a face, "He sounded cross."

"I expect he was just funning. You know what Mr Talmarch is like. He makes a big fuss over the smallest things — like his coat getting splashed or having to walk on wet grass."

"Or Barker scratching his best boots!"

"Precisely. So, I suspect he wasn't really cross with Captain Heywood. Perhaps the Captain accidentally splashed mud on his boots or sat on one of his precious hats."

"That would make him sad. I snapped one of his feathers and I thought he was going to cry."

"He's a very sensitive man," said Grace, trying not to laugh.

"Can I ask him to play with me and Barker?"

"Of course."

"And the Captin?"

"Well, the Captain is very busy at the moment helping me look after Papa, so I don't think he'll have time, but Mr Talmarch has nothing to do but worry about his hats, so I think he'd be very glad of some company."

"I'll ask him and Uncle William to play hide and seek."

"An excellent idea, my love."

* * *

Feeling a good deal more cheerful Grace returned to her husband's bedchamber and finding Mrs Hawkins on duty, discovered that Captain Heywood had gone out for a ride with his friend, to clear his head. The nursemaid suggested that her ladyship might sit with the Marquis while she went down to the kitchens to make some fresh cordial and perhaps find something that might tempt Lady Winterborne to eat. As the very idea of food made Grace feel ill, this was not what she wanted at all, but she thanked Mrs Hawkins and was quite grateful when she was left alone with just the softly rhythmical sound of Gervase's breathing.

She picked up a book from the table beside the bed and sank into the chair to read for a while, glad for a little time to herself. She didn't read though, she just stared at the same page until it became a grey blur, her mind flitting from problem to problem like a moth ricocheting about inside a lantern.

The book belonged to Gervase: Shakespeare's *All's Well That Ends Well*. He did so love reading plays and she was glad that he'd remained well enough to see the play being performed and that it had been so well received — all the actors acquitting themselves very creditably. She tried to recall what the Shakespeare play was about, only managing to summon up Helena's enforced marriage to Bertram. She wondered if it was just the unhappy state of her mind that made her see her own situation in everything or whether her husband had deliberately set out to torment her at every step.

She flicked through the book to where the pages were wedged slightly apart and found what appeared to be two letters. One was addressed to Jem and the other to her.

She sat and looked at them for a moment, at the very recognisable spidery handwriting, at their names, at the words in the corner: *In the Event of my Death.*

Gervase was breathing but that was all. She considered for a moment opening the letter addressed to her then she carefully placed them back between the pages of the book. Whatever it was that he wanted to say it would have to wait a little longer. She was fairly certain that it couldn't be good, and she wasn't yet ready to face his vitriol, even when merely written in harmless ink. She knew that the letter for Jem would be acceptable and she need have no fear about what he might say in it.

Mrs Hawkins returned with a pitcher of cordial and breakfast on a tray. When Grace tried to avoid eating anything, the nursemaid took no notice, placing the tray on a table in front of her and handing her a plate with some bread, a cold sausage, a hard-boiled egg and some radishes.

"Some food will do you good, m'lady. Try to eat a little please."

Grace wanted to push the plate away, but Mrs Hawkins had an inflexible note to her voice, and she couldn't bear the idea of an argument when she felt so lost.

With Mrs Hawkins watching her, she nibbled her way slowly through some of the food and drank the overly sweet tea.

Mrs Hawkins nodded approvingly. She didn't like to be so domineering when Lady Winterborne was clearly suffering but knew that if she allowed her to go into a decline then she'd have two patients to care for and that poor little child would be left alone and, whatever her parents may be, Jem was an innocent and didn't deserve to be made even more wretched.

It seemed to Grace as though Time ceased to have any meaning, as it stopped functioning as it should. She kept checking to see if the clock was still working because the hands didn't seem to be moving at all.

She watched the light fade outside in the garden, the sky glowing pink and orange and then dimming to dove grey. She saw the gardeners come and go, with their scythes and wheelbarrows and saw Jem leading Emery and William and the dogs around the parterre on their way somewhere important. Jem looked happy. Grace cried silently.

She watched the dawn come up from the same spot and heard the birds begin singing. She helped Mrs Hawkins with Gervase and tried not to see his slow decline towards whatever awaited him. He remained in a coma, reminding her of a marble effigy on a tomb; his face was no longer recognisable, the skin waxy and yellow, his eyes sunken into the hollows of his skull — she could see the veins beneath the transparent skin. There was just his staccato breathing.

Doctor Morton came whenever he could but there was little he could do other than give sympathy and say it wouldn't be long. William visited once, but was so clearly distraught by what he saw, he didn't return.

A few of the actors had already left Winterborne, finding the gloomy atmosphere not at all conducive to their usual light-hearted frolics. Others, with no engagements to go back to London for, remained and seemed content to just enjoy the peace and quiet of the countryside, whilst being paid handsomely for their presence.

Grace existed in a dream world where she felt nothing, and people moved around her as though they were in some race she knew nothing about, and she seemed to move at a snail's pace.

Every so often she felt the river water close over her head and she had to fight for breath. She would surface gasping for air, only to find that she'd nodded off in a chair in the sickroom. She'd open her eyes in a panic to find Nathan looking down at her in the half-light of the candles and for just that glorious moment between sleep and awake, she'd forget everything and would be glad to see him and then the memories would come crashing in and she'd close her eyes again to block out the anguish that inevitably followed.

When she opened them again, he had gone.

* * *

At the same time as wanting to cradle Grace in his arms and tell her that he loved her, Nathan also wanted to shake her until her teeth rattled. He was so conflicted he was finding it hard to think straight. The well-trained, rational soldier side of him kept him from leaving by the back door and riding away into the night to just end the torment. But there was also the part of him that knew he must stay and not disappoint Grace again. She'd been let down too many times and that was why she couldn't forgive or forget his transgressions. Perhaps if he showed her that he could be trusted, she'd allow him back into her life.

Emery thought him ridiculous and was mostly in favour of fleeing Winterborne; he was even willing to forgo the huge reward, as long as they could go somewhere not so mired in complications and tragedy. He was missing the simple pleasures of town life: drinking, gambling and coquettish ladies who gladly flaunted their assets and wanted nothing from him he couldn't give for free.

If Nathan entered the sickroom to find Grace had fallen asleep, he was very careful not to make a sound that might wake her because he liked to stretch out in his chair and watch her without interruption. She talked a good deal in her sleep and occasionally he could make out a word or two. Sometimes he even heard her murmur his name, but as it was usually followed by what sounded like distraught mumbling, he wasn't able to take much heart from it.

He'd had a word with William, in the blandest of terms and leaving out the more distressing details, warning him about the dangers his sister and the other ladies faced if left alone with Carew, and the young man was remarkably sanguine about it, saying he would watch over them and make sure that George Carew couldn't misbehave. He remarked that while the Marquis was so indisposed, that Grace would hopefully be fairly safe, as she was closeted in the sickroom away from any harm. He went on to say he'd already formed an acute dislike for the man and suggested that if Carew *should* happen to go missing that no one would care either way. Nathan quickly assured him that there were bound to be people who would notice he'd disappeared and that it wouldn't help Grace if her brother were imprisoned or executed for murder. William had laughed, as though what he'd been saying had just been a light-hearted comment and not to be taken seriously, but Nathan had seen the pugnacious glint in his eye and knew that his sense of fraternal loyalty had been well and truly kindled. He had visions of William challenging George Carew to a duel, being fatally wounded and then any hopes of winning Grace back would be completely dashed and William, into the bargain, would be dead. With every day that passed his life just got more and more complicated.

He warned William not to make things worse and threatened him with dire consequences if he should be foolish enough to not heed his words. William, with the nonchalance of inexperience, reassured Nathan, saying that he wasn't such a blockhead that he would risk his sister's happiness for the sake of petty revenge.

Nathan wasn't entirely sure that he could believe him, so set Emery to watch over him, which, although not an ideal solution, was the best he could manage whilst so busy dealing with the Marquis and Grace. He would have to trust in William's better judgement and pray that a rush of blood to the head wouldn't lead William to do something rash and dangerous.

In the end it wasn't Grace who forced William's hand and made him forget his promise.

Twenty-Four

William was coming back from a long romp across the fields with Dancer and Thisbe; he was a little weary as the weather was still warm and muggy and not really conducive to exertion of any kind and Dancer had decided to run off after a hare, which meant he'd had to chase the infuriating dog for several fields before finally cornering him in a tangle of brambles. William's clothes were now a fearful sight and much to his horror, he'd scuffed his top boots. He was not in the best of moods. He struggled home, dragging a whining Dancer along by his ears and roundly cursing the animal for being so stupid. As the dog was muddied with twigs and goosegrass caught in his rough coat, he returned by way of the stable yard, looking for a bucket of water and a stiff brush to give the dog a bit of a clean before allowing him back into the house. There were no stable lads in sight to ask, so he found a bit of twine and tied the dogs to a rail, then went in search of what he needed in the outbuildings around the back of the yard.

He was passing one of the old disused stables when he thought he heard someone call out. It was faint and quickly muffled so he continued on his search. He'd taken only a few more steps when something made him turn back and go to investigate. He suspected it was just one of the stable kittens calling for its mother but for some reason he felt impelled to have a look. Something just didn't feel right.

He opened the battered old door and peered inside.

It was dark and smelt of compacted earth and dusty sweet hay and old leather. His eyes tried to adjust to the gloom, and he blinked blindly. A pale smudge in the far corner was the only thing that caught his eye. The windows were either blocked or shuttered and he was about to back out again when he heard a slight sound, a stifled squeal.

He took a few steps further into the darkness.

"Hallo? Anyone there?" he asked.

There were some sudden frantic movements in the corner.

"Get out and mind your own damn business," growled a man's voice.

There was then what sounded like a desperate struggle and some suffocated cries.

William moved forward rapidly and reaching down into the shadows, caught hold of a handful of the man's coat and hauled him backwards, which was easier than he'd expected as the man's breeches were around his ankles and hampered his movements. There was an angry grunt from the man and a fluttering of pale skirts and petticoats amongst the hay and he saw little Jenny Robbins desperately scrabbling to get out of his reach and pull her clothes down to cover herself.

"What the *devil* —?" roared William, and with the advantage of sudden rage, a dominant standing position and his youthful brawn, he lifted the man up and dragged him out into the yard. When he threw him down in disgust, he was not in the least surprised to see that it was George Carew glaring up at him.

"Well, I might have guessed it'd be you! You filthy *animal!*"

Carew tried to rearrange his breeches to cover his nakedness and struggle to his feet but William, filled with righteous anger, swung his massive fist, and punching hard, hit Carew square on the nose. Carew went flying, spurting blood and crashing into a water trough and William let out a bellow of triumph and nursed his bruised knuckles.

The noise of the affray brought two young lads tearing around the side of the building and William yelled at one of them to fetch Miss Weston at once and told the beefier of the two, to hold Carew down on the ground until more help arrived.

He could hear the sound of subdued sobbing coming from inside the stable and although he knew he should wait for a female to come as chaperone, he went back into the dark space to see if he could help.

"Miss Robbins? It's me, William Edgerton. Are you all right? I've sent for Miss Weston. Please don't be afraid."

There was the sound of sniffling, "I'm *not* afraid! I want to *kill* him!" declared Jenny Robbins roundly. "I'd be obliged if you'd find me a gun so that I can shoot him."

William laughed softly, "That would not be a good idea. We shall just have to be rid of him by some other more legal method. Is there anything I can do to assist you?"

More sniffing, "My gown is very torn. I cannot return to the house looking like this."

William immediately removed his coat and handed it to her. "I'm sorry, it's a little muddy. The dog chased a hare and got stuck in some brambles, but it'll cover you up for now." He looked away while she struggled into the coat. "I'm so sorry this has happened. He's a — villain and he deserves to be punished."

"Or shot," said Miss Robbins hopefully.

William, seeing her having difficulties fastening the coat, stepped forward to help but she shrank away from him.

"No, no! I was just going to help you fasten the buttons."

She smiled wanly up at him, "I'm sorry. I just — "

"Of course, you must be feeling very unsteady after your ordeal. If you'll allow, I'll just do up the buttons for you."

She put her hands down and let him help cover up her ruined gown.

"Miss Robbins? He didn't — did he, you know — ?"

She shook her head, "No, I know what you're asking, sir and you arrived just in time. He didn't. But I'd still like to shoot him."

"I fear there may be quite a queue to do that! He's not the most popular man. Would you like to come outside now and go back to the house?"

"No, thank you, I think I'll stay here until Peggy comes."

"Whatever you think is best. Would you like me to send for my sister as well? Lady Winterborne would be very comforting, I'm sure. She knows just what a terrible person Carew is."

She looked a little disconcerted, "Please don't trouble her, she has so much on her plate at the moment. This would be too much. Also, I really wouldn't like my father to find out."

"I'm sure he'd understand that it wasn't your fault and be very forgiving!"

"You clearly have never met my father, Mr Edgerton. He's not in the *least* forgiving and would think this was *entirely* my fault for running away to London in the first place."

"Oh, I *see*, you ran away from home! Well, I'm sure you had very sound reasons."

Miss Robbins blushed, "I wanted to become an actress," she admitted.

William nodded wisely, "Of course you did, and I expect he wanted you to marry some local lad and settle down?"

"He would rather I'd stayed at home and looked after him while he wrote his sermons."

"Oh, devil take it! Your father's a *parson?*"

Jenny Robbins cast her eyes down, "He is and a very pious and humourless one at that. He said it was my duty to take care of him once poor Mama died. He said a parson needed someone to run the household and listen to him practice his sermons." Her big blue eyes filled with tears, "It was so *very* dull, Mr Edgerton! I cannot even begin to tell you! I thought I might die of boredom, so I ran away. I didn't have an abigail so I couldn't take one with me. I had no choice but to go alone. Luckily when I reached London, Peggy found me, and she took me in and gave me a place to stay and taught me how to act and sing and got me a small job at the theatre. She was wonderful!"

William had turned quite pale at the thought of this tiny, angelic creature all on her own in London, "Honestly, you were so *very* lucky! You would not have understood, coming from the countryside, how very dangerous life in town can be — especially for unwary, unprotected females. You might have met up with some truly ruthless types and found yourself in a great deal of trouble. It doesn't bear thinking about. Thank God for Miss Weston! You must never do that again!" He gave her an intent look, "Miss Robbins? I hesitate to ask but how came you to be all alone with Mr Carew — in a stable?"

She frowned, "He offered to take me to see the kittens. He always seemed so gentlemanly — I never thought that he'd be just like all the rest. Peggy warned me, many times but — he was always so polite and considerate. He told me I was the best actress he'd ever seen and gave me flowers and chocolates. It was nice to have someone think I was good enough and I am *exceedingly* fond of kittens."

"'Pon my soul, Miss Robbins, you have been far too trusting. From now on you must try not to be so — *green!* This might have ended very badly indeed. You mustn't trust men! *Any* men!"

She looked up at him from her shining doe-eyes, "I trust *you*, Mr Edgerton," she said with guileless confidence.

William slapped his hand to his forehead, "Confound it! What have I just been *telling* you? I might be trying to deceive you and lead you astray! I might have nefarious intentions!"

"But you haven't though. I can tell. You're a kind man and mean me no harm at all."

William let out a groan of despair but luckily just at that moment Peggy Weston came racing into the stable and stood for a moment on the threshold to let her eyes get used to the darkness. Jenny, quite swamped by William's coat, gave a squeal of relief and threw herself into Peggy's arms and wept. Peggy wrapped her arms about her and held her tightly, murmuring tender words of support.

William, suddenly feeling very old for his age, wondered what on earth to do about the situation. He stepped outside, leaving the two girls to talk and comfort each other.

A burly groom had arrived and was holding George Carew by the collar, "What shall we do with 'im, sir?" he asked menacingly.

William cast a scornful glance over the repugnant gentleman, who was still holding up his breeches with one hand, "Toss him in the water trough if you like and then lock him up in a secure room until I can decide what's to be done with him."

With great delight the groom and the stable lad dragged Carew across the yard and pushed him into the trough. He went under the dirty water and came up spluttering.

Peggy chose this auspicious moment to escort Miss Robbins out of the stable and laughed heartily at the sight, "That'll teach 'im! Evil brute! I hope he catches 'is death! I'm takin' Jenny in now. Thank you for rescuing her, Mr Edgerton."

William, catching a glimpse of Miss Robbins's tearstained face, averted his eyes quickly, "No, indeed. Glad to be able to help. I shall make sure he gets his just desserts. I hope Miss Robbins recovers quickly. If there's anything I can do — "

"I can't thank you enough," whispered Miss Robbins as she was led away.

William watched them go and then turned his attentions to the now thoroughly sodden culprit, sitting in the trough, and still being firmly held by the rightly incensed stable hands.

George Carew glowered at William, "She was asking for it," he said rather recklessly.

William nodded at the groom and watched dispassionately as they pushed him back under the water and held him there, his limbs flailing and odd bubbling noises rising up from the churning waters.

* * *

William, having made sure that Carew was tied up securely and locked in an outhouse with barred windows and a sturdy bolt on the outside of the door, went in search of Nathan.

Captain Heywood was found in the Great Hall, with Jem and Emery and the kitten. He looked up as William, in just his shirt sleeves, strode in from the rear of the house and immediately sensing trouble sent Emery off with Jem into the garden with Barker. Emery threw him a hard-done-by look but Nathan dismissed him with a wave of his hand.

"What is it, William?"

The young man, always direct to a fault came hurtling straight to the point, "We have a bit of a problem, Nathan, with that damn George Carew. He tried to rape Miss Robbins and I have him trussed up like a hog in one of the sheds."

Nathan took a moment to digest this unwelcome news, "Is she all right? You say *tried*?"

"Thankfully he was unsuccessful. She's mostly unharmed and in fighting spirits — she's very keen to shoot him for his troubles." William shrugged, "I was in two minds about handing her a gun to be perfectly frank! He deserves no better. He got shoved into the trough instead. What do I do now though? Can't just leave him to rot in the shed, much as I'd like to."

"Good work! My instinct would normally be to straight away speak to a Justice of the Peace. In any other case, I would, without hesitation, but in a case of attempted rape, I fear that Miss Robbins would be made to go through endless hearings at the Assizes and then, if he's prosecuted, which in itself is highly unlikely, a sordid trial would follow and she'd be forced to give detailed evidence in a courtroom filled with men, who would not be, I'm sorry to say, on her side. On the evidence I've heard, the courts would eventually acquit Carew and Miss Robbins's reputation would be ruined beyond repair. It would be harrowing and, in the end, probably a pointless and damaging exercise."

"But, Nathan, we can't let him get away with this! He'll do it again to some other girl who may not be so fortunate!"

Nathan considered the young man's earnest face and came to the conclusion that the truth would come out in the end, "He's already made other attempts, I'm afraid. Having heard of his repellent exploits — from one of his victims — I was doing my best to keep him from going anywhere near — your sister again."

William blenched, "Grace? N-no! You c-cannot be serious!" he stammered, "I thought you meant he'd made *threats*!

I didn't understand that he'd — that he'd actually tried — he didn't — ?"

"I'm so sorry, William. It happened the last time Carew visited Winterborne, but Sally walked in on him and saved Grace. He's been trying to take his revenge upon her ever since. He won't stop until he has."

"Then *we* must stop him!" cried William.

"Easier said than done. I think you'd better leave it to me. I don't want Grace having any more anxieties and if you were to become embroiled in this — "

"I'm *already* embroiled!" interrupted William furiously, "I won't be pushed to one side like a child! I'm a grown man and can and *will* protect my sister. I won't let her down this time! Whatever you decide I will back you, Nathan."

Not liking William's increasing agitation, Nathan sought to soothe him, "Can Miss Robbins return to her family home so that she can recuperate in peace and quiet?"

"Good God no! Her father's a dashed *parson!* That's why she ran away in the first place! If he should find out! If she were to be put through a trial — ! Bound to get into the newspapers and everyone would talk about it. He sounds like the very devil! She *cannot* return to him. Her mother is dead. She has no one but Miss Weston for comfort. It really is too bad."

Nathan was desperately seeking solutions, "Look, we have to be careful. We cannot endanger Grace or Winterborne. Anything we may do will have serious repercussions and at the moment we have to think about the Marquis and help your sister cope with what is bound to come. It won't be easy. For now, we shall keep Carew under lock and key and not make any hasty decisions."

William looked disappointed and doubtful, "Well, I won't say I'm satisfied with that, but I expect you know best. What are we to do with Miss Robbins?"

"She's better off staying here with us for now, by the sound of it. Although, I'm not sure that she can ever be sent back to London safely. She seems to have all the wisdom of that damn kitten. I think Jem has more sense."

"She needs a guardian. She believes the best of everyone! She was perfectly happy to trust me even though I'd just that minute warned her to be vigilant. She's bound to fall into more scrapes if she goes back into the theatre. Miss Weston will have to stay here with her, of course."

"You're quite right. She needs to be protected. I have no choice but to inform Grace as she's a guest in her house — which, I have to say, will be very awkward."

"And we leave Carew in the stable for now?"

"With someone to keep watch outside. I'll organise it and we'll find a suitable punishment for him. You're not to worry, William."

"Easier said than done," replied William despondently.

* * *

An hour or so later Nathan found himself entering the sickroom just as Grace was leaving, he swiftly decided not to stand on ceremony or pander to her wounded feelings and before she could protest, he pulled her out into the corridor, away from Mrs Hawkins's keen ears.

He pulled the door closed behind him and held up a hand to quell any complaints Grace might be about to utter.

Without apology and in as few words as possible he explained what had happened, including that he had told William about her own encounter with Carew, hoping to spare her embarrassment by being brisk but, at the same time, knowing that it would be deeply upsetting to her.

She stood in silence, even paler than she was usually, her expression hostile until he mentioned George Carew and then her face crumpled, and it took her a moment to regain her composure.

"Jenny's not been — harmed?" she whispered.

He shook his head, "No, William was in time. You should be proud of him, he behaved in a manner far beyond his years and took charge of the situation like a seasoned soldier."

Grace was silent.

"Indeed, I'm sorry, Grace, to bring you such distressing news but I thought it better that you should know as it is so very serious a crime. The child has taken it better than could be expected according to William and had she had access to a weapon would, apparently, have tried to shoot her assailant."

"I truly wish she had," said Grace.

"Then Miss Robbins would be on her way to the Assizes and that would be most unfair in the circumstances."

"What will you do with him?"

"You are lady of the manor; do you have any suggestions?"

She opened her mouth to say something and then closed it and shook her head, "You decide." And she walked away along the corridor, without another word.

She went straight to Jenny Robbins's bedchamber and knocked gently upon the door.

Peggy peered out to see who it was and then, with a relieved smile, let her in.

"Oh, I *am* glad you've come, m'lady! I'm havin' the Devil's own job making her understand that Mr Edgerton won't think she's a — a fallen woman! She's got it into her silly head that he'll think 'er no better'n a doxy and she's workin' herself up into a right state!"

Jenny was sitting on the edge of the bed, her face buried in her hands, making hiccupping little sobs. Grace sat down next to her and pulled one of her hands into hers.

"Jenny, my dear, I think you're a very brave young lady and I know that my brother thinks the same. I have to tell you something and I need you to listen very carefully." She squeezed the trembling hand gently, "Mr Carew also attacked me last time he was here. He tried to rape me and if it hadn't been for Sally coming back to the room at that moment, he would have succeeded because I wasn't strong enough to resist him. You must understand that my brother would never allow such a thing to alter the way he thinks of someone. He's a very dependable young man so you should have no fear of his good opinion of you changing in any way — if anything he will champion you even more! He always played Sir Galahad in our little productions in the schoolroom and insisted upon rescuing any fair damsel in distress. He's still that chivalrous (but quite naughty) boy, I do assure you."

Jenny looked at her through wet spiky lashes, her eyes enormous and her bottom lip quivering, "Oh, thank you, m'lady! That's so kind of you. I feel such a fool for believing Mr Carew, I thought him to be an honourable man. I do *really* like kittens," she declared, smiling bravely through the tears.

"Of course you do! It was a dastardly trick to use such an irresistible temptation. He's a vile man. I want you to know that you can stay at Winterborne for as long as you like. And Miss Weston, of course. I don't think you should return to London, and Captain Heywood tells me that your father can be — a little challenging and unforgiving, so it would probably be best if you don't go back to your family home either."

Miss Robbins broke into renewed sobs and Grace gathered her into her arms and held her.

"Don't you *want* to stay here, Jenny?"

"Oh, no, I mean *yes*, my lady! I'm so *grateful!* I would love to stay. You are so kind; I simply cannot *bear* it!"

"Good Gracious! I was quite certain I must have offended you. I'm delighted to be able to offer you sanctuary. I know what it's like to have nowhere of your own and no one to take care of you. We shall deal very well together, the three of us and Sally and Jem, of course. We shall look after each other."

"Oh, my lady! You're a *saint!*"

"No, indeed, I am *not!* I am merely a very flawed human. If you only knew — "

"It wouldn't matter what you'd done! I've never met anyone like you in my whole life."

"Oh, Jenny! You really must learn to be more discerning. You cannot go around believing the best of everyone you meet; it will get you into such terrible trouble."

"Well, I certainly don't want to be like my father! He's of the opinion that everyone is destined for Hell. It was exceedingly hard to live with and when I ran away, I determined to have faith in everyone because I find that I'm very much happier that way."

Grace laughed, "You and William are much alike in that then!"

Jenny blushed rosily and looked delighted to be compared favourably with her gallant hero.

Peggy, who was leaning on the back of the armchair, and wondering if she would be able to manage without being admired every night by her adoring audiences said, "I'd be glad to stay with 'er but only so long as that evil toad ain't stayin'!"

"Captain Heywood is dealing with him, so you need have no worries. He is, at the moment, tied up in one of the old stables. He can do no harm."

"I'd like to do *'im* some harm, that's for damn sure!" avowed Peggy through clenched teeth.

Twenty-Five

It was inevitable that the news of the attack should leak out. A stable lad told a housemaid, and the housemaid told a footman and so it spread through Winterborne like a poisonous creeping mist, seeping under doors and into the ears of those who were willing to listen. A few greeted it with disbelief, believing George Carew to be the very best of fellows, but the bulk of the guests merely nodded and said they'd known all along that he was a wrong 'un. Lady Cheyne went as far as to admit that she'd seen him behaving reprehensibly on several occasions and had advised her own young abigail to avoid his company if at all possible. She added that she wished she'd now had a word with poor little Miss Robbins because she seemed to be a very good sort of girl and was clearly vulnerable, being so young and an actress, to boot.

It was unfortunate that poor Miss Robbins was prone to blushing furiously at the slightest provocation and any mention at all of the event or of her assailant, sent her into a fit of weeping or induced her to flee the room in disarray. Grace was still attached to the sickroom so was not witness to her suffering, but William observed her reactions and greatly pitied her. He tried talking to her to reassure her, but she just gazed up at him fearfully, chewing her lip and trying desperately not to cry. He was lucky if he could get even a few words of comfort out before she pressed her handkerchief to her mouth, dissolved into floods of tears and fled.

This was so in contradiction to her initial reaction to the attack, when she had wanted to shoot Mr Carew that William was left quite bewildered.

He had thought her a pretty little thing right from the first time he saw her but other than that had not given her serious consideration. Her performance in the play had made him laugh — well, not the actual acting, which he had concluded was somewhat lacking in conviction, but her splendidly high-spirited reaction to the audience. She had seemed so bright and cheerful, like a small, golden bird, set free from its gilded cage, filled with the joys of life and determined to sing prettily for everyone. If he thought of her at all, it was with a touch of amusement, but she was an actress and ladies who trod the boards were out of bounds. His mother would be outraged if she discovered he'd even *watched* a play, let alone actually knew someone who performed upon the stage. It would probably be the death of her.

For a brief wicked moment, he pictured the tragic scene: introducing Miss Robbins to his mother, she'd gasp in horror and clutch at her heart and collapse, calling him an unnatural son and accusing him of killing his own dear mother and then, with her very last breath, she would hoarsely whisper — *Catherine Wingfield!* And she'd expire in his arms.

Unfortunately, the dream then continued, with his father blaming him for her death and ruthlessly throwing him out into the snow, penniless and with a sobbing Jenny clinging to him.

It was a nightmare and he felt unequal to the task.

* * *

It was all anyone wanted to talk about of course, their eyes lighting up as they spoke in subdued voices. They wondered how any female could be so ingenuous, putting herself in such a vulnerable position which had, in the end, clearly proved too much temptation for the gentleman.

He put up with it until the next day when sitting down to breakfast, he saw Jenny across the table, her head bowed, her face pale and her eyes shut against the tears which were threatening to flow. He caught the tail end of the conversation between Mrs Leventhorpe and her husband and realised that they were discussing the appalling event right in front of the humiliated victim.

"Mrs Leventhorpe?" he said curtly, "May I ask you to please desist from talking in that manner! A lady of your superior breeding and advanced age, should know that one does not attempt to make any person uncomfortable, in *any* circumstances. It seems quite odd to me that you should wish to bring more anguish to anyone quite as lovely and innocent as Miss Robbins. To quote the Bible *it passeth all understanding.*"

Jenny peeped up at him from under her lashes, "T-that's not quite correct, Mr Edgerton. The f-full quote is: *And the peace of God, which passeth all understanding, shall keep your hearts and minds through Christ Jesus.* I suspect that you were bending it to suit your needs though."

William grinned at her, "I was indeed, Miss Robbins! But you, being the daughter of a very respectable parson, would, of course, know the actual quotation. It's lucky you are so very well versed in such matters. I'm afraid my knowledge of the Bible is limited. I suspect you could teach everyone here a thing or two about Christian charity and tolerance." He glanced deliberately at Mrs Leventhorpe, "It astonishes me how some people claim to be Christian and yet they are frequently the first to forget the Bible's teachings."

Mrs Leventhorpe lowered her eyes and concentrated upon cutting up her boiled ham into tiny, tiny pieces. There was a good deal of embarrassed shuffling and throat clearing as the guests sipped their coffee and wondered how soon they could leave the table without looking as though they were trying to escape Mr Edgerton's totally unjustified wrath.

William caught Jenny's eye and winked at her. She turned a delicate shade of pink and smiled at him gratefully.

They were interrupted by Emery sailing into the dining room, wearing a coat of violet satin, embroidered with gold thread and embellished with sparkling crystals, a magnificent Pompadour wig perched upon his head and fluttering a mother of pearl fan. He paused and raised his quizzing glass with an elegant flourish, "Gad, you look like you're all off to a funeral! Lord Winterborne is still with us by all accounts, is he not? Why the miserable faces?"

William, glad of a little light relief, let out a snort of laughter and Emery raised his eyebrows, "Was it something I said?"

Jenny giggled and looked wonderingly at William, her eyes dancing.

"No, indeed, sir! We were in dire need of some levity. You have arrived just in time!" said William cheerfully.

Emery approached the table, "Well, I am not at all sure how I should take that! But I'm delighted to have brought some joy into your dull lives. Miss Robbins, Miss Weston, you are both looking radiant this morning. I trust you're feeling more yourselves?"

"We are, Mr Talmarch, thank you kindly for askin'," responded Peggy, in her usual forthright fashion.

In a low voice to William, as he passed, he asked, "Any more news upon our fiendish villain? Is he still keeping the other rats company?"

"He is. Nathan's been to see him this morning and says Carew's still in the same belligerent mood and showing no signs of remorse. Nathan's not planning to inform the authorities because of the consequences for — all concerned."

"I understand. It would be intolerable. I'm quite sure Nate has it all in hand. We must trust in his judgement. That looks like a dashed fine ham, I shall have some of that!" he announced with relish and he sat himself down next to Miss Weston with a warm and friendly smile and applied himself to consuming a hearty breakfast.

* * *

Grace was staring out of the window, observing the jackdaws frolicking and fighting in the sky above the garden, their dark feathers gleaming as though varnished. They were a strange combination of confidence and timidity, cackling with rude mirth one minute and anxiously taking flight the next. She loved them. She felt they had similarities to her own character; she had moments when she stood her ground and then the next felt compelled to hide from sight. Sometimes she wanted to take flight and just fly away. The dreadful business with poor Jenny had brought back the rage and fear she'd felt when George Carew had attacked her. The worst thing was the feeling of helplessness; he'd had complete power over her, and she'd been unable to save herself. It had left her doubting her own strength and she'd begun to despise her weakness.

The night in the Maze with Nathan had gone some way to restoring her self-confidence, because she'd felt that she'd had the upper hand and even though she was inexperienced, he'd been so inebriated and willing to relinquish control, that she'd felt truly powerful for the first time in her life. It had been briefly liberating and even though it'd ended badly, she was still able to remember the sensation of being, for a carefree moment, seemingly invincible.

The jackdaws swooped and squabbled in their tumbling ballet against the cobalt blue sky, and she envied their careless freedom.

Mrs Hawkins returned to the sickroom with a pitcher of hot water, clean cloths and a grimly determined expression.

"I'm going to bathe Lord Winterborne now. Captain Heywood is on his way to assist. If you want to make yourself scarce, my lady — ?"

Grace went to stand by the bed, "No, I'll stay. He seems so much quieter today. His breathing seems altered, does it not?"

The nursemaid nodded briskly, "It does, you're right. He must have something important to stay for because I've never known such a reluctance to leave. He's been like this for over a week now."

"He was always uncompromisingly stubborn. He never liked to do what was expected of him. I suppose he delighted in being perverse, like a child might. He took pleasure in confounding people. Perhaps no one ever gave him guidance when he was young or stood up to him. I fear he was dreadfully indulged. We're all influenced by what we learn from an early age and I learnt to be quiet and still and obedient and to suppress my feelings which has been very useful for my life at

Winterborne. That's why I've taken pains with Jemima, making sure that she isn't afraid to speak her mind."

"She certainly does that," remarked Nathan, as he quietly entered the bedchamber.

Grace, ignoring the sudden traitorous acceleration of her heartbeat, barely glanced up, "Hopefully it will stand her in good stead in later life and she won't let herself be intimidated or deceived."

Nathan exchanged a look with Mrs Hawkins who was beginning to realise that every word spoken between them hid dangerous undercurrents.

"She'll never be afraid to speak her mind that is without doubt. You've made sure that she can be herself — brave and funny and mischievous, without fear of censure."

Grace said nothing.

"If you would be good enough to help turn his lordship, Captain?"

"Of course, Mrs Hawkins."

"And, my lady, if you could wring out the wet cloths? The sooner we get this over with the better."

They had done the same thing so many times now, it was a well-practiced routine, and they were able to wash the patient and change the bedclothes without much difficulty, and although Grace found it deeply distressing, she never allowed it to show.

Mrs Hawkins washed the patient; Grace rinsed the cloths and Nathan lifted and turned him and they removed and replaced the sodden bedclothes and his nightshirt.

It was as Mrs Hawkins was adjusting the pillows under his head that Lord Winterborne made a slight sound. They all froze. And listened.

Mrs Hawkins put her ear close to his lordship's mouth in order to hear more clearly. After a moment's silence, she looked up at them and shook her head.

"Just a sigh, a loud breath I think," she said.

Grace gulped in air and tried to still the panicked feeling in her chest.

Mrs Hawkins pulled the counterpane up and turned away to pick up a fallen cloth.

The sound came again, stronger, and was, this time, most definitely an attempt at a spoken word.

"Grace, go to him," said Nathan, as she hesitated.

She took a breath and moving nearer to her husband, lifted his hand into hers; its bony, lifeless form lay like a featherless dead bird across her fingers. He was cold to the touch. She leant forward, leaning on the bed.

"Gervase? Did you say something?"

She watched his unfamiliar face intently.

"I'm listening, Gervase."

She gasped when she saw his blue veined eyelids flicker. Glancing up at Nathan she saw he'd also seen the slight movement.

Then, "*Grace*," barely a whisper, more an exhalation of air.

She convulsively pressed his hand, "*Yes?*"

Silence.

Another desperate glance at Nathan.

A breath.

"*I'm. Sorry.*"

Grace wept, her head on his shoulder. "Please! It doesn't matter any more!"

"*You'll. See.*"

"I'll see? See *what?*" The tears were sliding down her cheeks unchecked. "I don't understand!"

"*You. Will.*"

"Gervase, we didn't — we couldn't — there is to be no heir."

The eyelids quivered but there were no more sounds.

Grace was trying to stifle her sobs so that she could hear him.

Nathan moved closer and put a gentle hand on her shoulder, "Give him permission to go, Grace. He's waiting for you to say he can leave."

She was trembling so badly she didn't think she could speak at all; she opened her mouth but only a terrible whimper emerged. She shook her head in despair, but Nathan tightened his grip.

"It's the last thing you can do for him on this earth."

Her whole body was shaking as she tried to form the words that she knew she needed to say.

"My dear — *husband* — I bear you no ill will — I forgive you for everything — you can go in peace — there's no need to worry. Jem will be safe with me, I promise, I'll look after her — and Winterborne will always survive."

She felt Nathan's arm around her shoulders, holding her steady.

The Marquis's breathing had slowed down so much, it was barely audible. The spaces between each breath were so far apart Grace was becoming dizzy, as she held her breath, waiting.

Each one, further apart.

Until no more came and there was only the aching, empty silence.

She wanted nothing more than to collapse into Nathan's arms but even though overwhelmed by unexpected anger and grief, she managed to hold fast to her disappointment in him, it gave her something solid to cling to.

He was aware that she was pulling away, so reluctantly withdrew his arm and moved across the room to the door.

Mrs Hawkins pulled the sheet up and over Lord Winterborne's face and held out her arms to Grace, who leant into them, silent sobs racking her body.

Nathan left saying that he would send for Doctor Morton and inform the guests and staff of the news.

Grace heard the door close behind him and knew that he'd see that everything was done correctly but wished he'd stayed with her. She clung onto Mrs Hawkins, who murmured prayers in a soft voice and rocked her like a baby.

Twenty-Six

It was just after noon, two days after the Marquis had died when a panic-stricken groom came running in from the stables, calling urgently for Captain Heywood. William, who had just come in from the terrace, dashed immediately to fetch Nathan from the parlour where he was patiently teaching Jem to play chess and they both listened to the very agitated young man as he tried to tell them what was distressing him so. Before he could even finish his explanation, Nathan and William were sprinting out to the stable yard.

The groom hurried after them but remained just outside the stable, unwilling to venture back in. A couple of minutes after they entered, Mr Edgerton came flying past him, retching and cast up his accounts in the corner of the yard.

The groom watched him and was glad he'd been blessed with a strong stomach. Mr Carew lying eviscerated in a darkly glistening pool of his own blood had been almost too much for him too; however, a lifetime of working with horses had inured him to the visceral sights and smells he'd just had the misfortune to encounter. But there was something about the violence of the man's death which was enough to make even his stomach churn, and he'd had to steady himself for a moment, breathing in large gulps of fresh air before running for help.

Captain Heywood came out and asked if Mr Edgerton was all right but there was only a stifled response and the Captain patted him on the back.

He turned to the groom, "Send someone at once for the nearest constable."

* * *

After the Marquis's death, Winterborne had been plunged into a strange period of muffled activity, undertaken mostly by servants with downcast eyes; overnight the house had been transformed, as if by dark magic, into a place of shadows; the mirrors were draped with black silk and an enormous hatchment, bedecked with black ribands and rosemary was fixed to the front door. The male staff all wore black armbands, and the females black ribands attached to their caps. Kirby, the butler, a huge devotee of Lord Winterborne, added black gloves and a black cravat to his uniform and assumed an expression of extreme melancholy. Someone even tied black ribands around the necks of both dogs, although Thisbe then spent the next half an hour trying frantically to remove it, ending up getting his paw caught in it and hopping about until Jem rescued him and tied the riband on the end of his tail instead, which didn't seem to bother him at all. Emery had reluctantly donned a black coat, which he said made him look sallow and murmured that as he'd hardly known the man, he should not be expected to wear deepest mourning. He regarded Nathan, who looked his best in dark colours and complained that life was vastly unfair.

The very first thing that Grace had done, straight after the death of her husband, was to go to the nursery to talk to Jem. She wanted to be the one to tell her. As it was, her mindful plans went slightly awry: she entered the room and Jem, who was studiously drawing flowers in her sketch book, looked up, carefully laid down her pencil on the desk and went directly to her mother. She took her hand and drew her to an armchair, pushed her into it and clambered onto her lap. Grace was unable to find suitable words to explain and her throat was so constricted that speech was impossible anyway.

Jem stroked her mother's face, "Is it Papa?" she asked.

Grace nodded and wished she had the little girl's ability to just accept things without falling into despair. Jem would be able to return to her drawing without becoming swamped in grief; not that she didn't feel sorrow for the loss of her father but because her attention would be readily and thankfully caught by other more trivial things and she could be easily distracted, which was a blessing. She asked questions but mainly about who now owned Dancer and Thisbe and whether Barker should wear a black riband. She had seen so very little of the Marquis in her five years that it was unlikely to have a lasting impact upon her day-to-day life.

Emery, despite his complaints, proved to be a godsend where Jem was concerned, keeping her entertained and away from any depressing formalities taking place in the house.

For Grace, her life became nothing but depressing formalities. Grave gentlemen dressed in mourning clothes asked her endless questions about what she wanted, which persistently rendered her speechless, as she had absolutely no idea what she wanted. The attorney spoke in hushed tones, using words she'd never before heard and expected her to follow what he was saying without interrupting to ask awkward or ignorant questions.

She was grateful that both William and Nathan were constantly to be found by her side and were able to intervene whenever necessary, helping her understand the complications brought to her door by her husband's death. She thought it would never end. When they had all gone and the first long evening stretched ahead of them, William sat beside her and held her hand, saying little and expecting no response. Grace found she came to rely upon his solid presence, good humour and brotherly understanding of her ever-changing moods.

Sally, grumbling about clothes moths, had unwrapped her mistress's mourning gowns and spruced them up; but she was distressed to see that the bleak colour washed out Grace's complexion and insisted upon lightening the sombre outfits of black crepe with a little white lace around their necklines. It made very little difference as the Marchioness still looked as though she might be about to faint at any moment: her skin was bloodless, and she had violet shadows under her haunted eyes. Sally thought she'd never seen her so out of looks and even suggested using a little rouge to put some colour in her cheeks, but Grace had politely declined.

Mrs Hawkins dealt with all the things which Grace couldn't face; she coped efficiently with all the requisite chores that came with a death. She had in the end banished Grace from the sickroom until all was done and Grace, although feeling guilty, had been perfectly happy to comply. Mrs Hawkins seemed entirely content to trust in Captain Heywood and the wide knowledge he'd gleaned serving as an officer in the army. He'd had to step forward when his own parents had died because his brother seemed incapable of rational thought at the time; he had reluctantly taken over the reins for a while until everything was neatly resolved and then left Alexander to reap the rewards.

The Winterborne family lawyer came and went, bringing papers and documents to be signed and counter-signed and Grace listened without hearing — she could kindle no interest in their ambitions. She felt that her life was suspended while people she barely knew made decisions on her behalf. There was dry-as-dust talk of entailments and strict settlement and trusts and pin money and, apart from how it all might affect Jem, she really didn't care at all. Nathan tried to explain but, in the end, said he'd leave it until the Reading of the Will, where it would all hopefully be explained to her satisfaction. He'd been told very little about the official side of things but the odd comment and one or two significant looks he'd intercepted from the attorney, Mr Killigrew, had begun to make him anxious for Grace.

They took the Marquis away, in a grandly theatrical coffin, to the family chapel on the far side of the estate and during a poorly attended funeral, (the local dignitaries staying away because of the persistent rumours about his lordship's peculiar way of life) he was placed in the Winterborne family crypt and his close family, senior members of his staff and the remaining houseguests were there to see him finally laid to rest. It wasn't until Grace heard the door to the crypt closing after the short ceremony that she was able to breathe a sigh of relief. It wasn't because he no longer had the power to make her suffer but just because it was nearly over, and all the talking could stop. She was so tired of the talking.

There was one more thing to get through and that was the Reading of the Will which had been arranged for the following day and again, for Grace, it would be the closing of another door.

The evening of the funeral, dinner was held in the dining room, most of the Theatricals having gradually slipped away, sharing coaches back to London and leaving only Miss Weston and Miss Robbins at Winterborne. Mr and Mrs Leventhorpe had remembered a long-standing engagement and left straight after the funeral and Lord and Lady Standon stayed for the dinner but said their farewells the next morning, leaving Grace with their praise and condolences ringing in her ears. It had all sounded rather insincere.

Marcus Delamere had proved to be rather more pleasant than some of her husband's other acquaintances and he and Lady Cheyne lingered on as though they had nowhere more important to be.

Lady Cheyne took Grace to one side and said with a tragic edge to her voice, "My dear Lady Winterborne, I must tell you, before I leave, that although I was, at first, quite disappointed that Agnes did not manage to secure the affections of your dear Gervase, I have since decided that in the end it was probably for the best. I don't think Gervase would have suited Agnes at all, even though Winterborne is a very pleasant house, and the title is a respectably ancient one."

"Hogwash!" snapped Grace, "I do hope you have a *very* pleasant journey home, Lady Cheyne. I'll bid you goodbye," and with that she walked away hoping never to see the woman again as long as she lived.

* * *

Meanwhile, constables roamed the house and gardens asking questions and poking about in dark corners hopefully expecting to find clues to the grisly murder of Mr George Carew.

Nathan watched over them as well as keeping an eye on the lawyer and the workings of the estate. He encouraged and advised the staff, oversaw the removal of the body and provided any information the officials needed for their investigations.

The chief constable, a local volunteer, was keen to get some sort of dazzling result from the murder enquiry and sucked on the end of his pencil a good deal whilst looking pensive but after several fruitless hours of questioning had all but given up hope of a satisfactory outcome.

"Captain Heywood, you say that the victim had been locked up in a disused stable because of this vicious attack on one of the housemaids?"

Nathan sighed, and repeated, for the third time, "It was one of the theatrical troupe who was attacked, the daughter of a parson, as I've already mentioned. She's merely a child. We decided to lock him up until we could decide what to do with him and so that he didn't have a chance to harm anyone else."

The constable nodded, "You didn't call a constable though, after the attempted rape?"

"As I said before, no, the victim was unprepared to go to court in case her father found out. It put us in a rather awkward position, as you can imagine."

The constable, who was finding it difficult to imagine anything other than the tasty supper of lamb stew and dumplings his wife had promised on his return, wondered how he could speed this investigation up so that he could get home before his three greedy sons ate all the stew.

"And Mr Carew was guarded at all times, whilst imprisoned in the stable?"

"He was. However, it seems that during the night whilst the guards were changing over their watch, there was a short while when he was left unattended, and no one noticed the bolt had been drawn until later when they were taking him breakfast."

"I see. And, when they returned to their post, what did they discover?"

Nathan had already answered this question several times in the last hour and was starting to grind his teeth, but knew if he was to carry this off, that he'd have to stay calm and deflect the interrogation.

"The door was unbolted, and Carew was already dead."

"We do know that whoever committed this crime made quite sure that the victim would never be able to hurt anyone ever again. I've never seen such a sickening sight in all my days as a constable. We don't really get murders around here — it's a peaceful place to live. The worst crimes are usually no more than a drunk with a broken jaw or the theft of a pocket watch or at the very worst, sheep stealing. This is something I never want to see again. It made me feel sick to my stomach."

No more than Carew deserved, thought Nathan.

"Obviously, we'll have to inform the magistrate, sir — but he's known to be reluctant to prosecute because it causes him so much additional work. Anyway, if we did manage to discover the murderer and they were convicted and taken to the Assizes, it's very likely that the prosecutor just wouldn't turn up and the accused would be released, it happens a good deal apparently," reflected the constable.

"The system sounds as though it's broken. So, what do we do now? Have you any ideas?"

"No, sir, I haven't, apart from continuing to search for the murderer. They left no clues to their identity and from what I've gleaned from my investigation so far, it could be one of any number of suspects. It seems that there are no end of people who might have had a reason to kill Mr Carew and it's unlikely that we shall be able to narrow the list down satisfactorily."

"You can discern nothing from the wounds themselves?"

The constable looked a little puzzled, "The wounds, sir?"

"In the army we were able to work out the cause of death by examining the wounds. It only took a little knowledge and common sense to tell if the soldier had been killed by a musket or a sword or some other method."

"Ah, I see what you mean! Well, I am able to tell you that the slit to his throat was probably made by someone who was right-handed and no shorter than say, five feet high and no taller than say, six feet five inches and they used a knife of some sort. I am of the belief that the stomach injuries came *post-mortem* and were made with the same weapon. It would have required a good deal of strength to inflict such deep wounds."

"So, you're saying it was definitely a man who committed the murder?"

"Or a very impassioned female! Rage can give one the power to seriously damage someone. I've seen a wife snap her husband's arm in two when given enough provocation."

"Therefore, we are no closer to a satisfactory conclusion and must continue not knowing if the murderer still lives amongst us."

"Indeed, sir. There's not much else I can do. I cannot even supply you with guards as they are scarce hereabouts — there's not much need for their services, you see. You could hire your own of course," suggested the constable with another furtive glance at the bracket clock on the mantlepiece. "I think we'd best declare it an unsolved case and I shall pass on my notes to the magistrate and if there should be any more discoveries then we can re-examine the evidence."

"I shall bow to your exemplary knowledge of the law," said Nathan, "I must say you've been exceedingly helpful, and I shall be writing to your superiors to recommend you."

They shook hands to finalise the decision and Nathan gripped his shoulder in a cordial fashion, just as though they were the very best of friends and the constable went home to his lamb stew and to regale his wife with much exaggerated tales from Winterborne, elaborating that Captain Heywood was the epitome of everything a gentleman should be, having expressed his appreciation of his efforts in solving the crime and showing a very fine understanding of the law. He added that Lady Winterborne, whom he'd had the honour to question briefly, was clearly distraught by all that was going on, and was, as he'd so often heard, a lady of unsurpassable beauty and so gracious, it was hardly to be believed. His wife, an inveterate gossip, was soon spreading the good news around the county and any dangers of the murder becoming a cause to punish the house of Winterborne were quickly quashed.

* * *

While the house was in such a state of disarray during the aftermath of Lord Winterborne's death and the discovery of George Carew's mutilated body, there had been an uneasy truce between Grace and Nathan. Without discussing it, they'd both concluded that in order to find a way through the maze of confusion and apprehension, they would have to work together or Winterborne might be tumbled like a house of cards.

Their exchanges were limited to just a very few subjects: official matters involving the estate or the murder investigation, family and guests and the animals. It made for some extremely stilted conversations, but meant that, although they couldn't avoid all awkward moments, they could at least do what was best for those depending upon them. For Grace her primary desire was to prevent Jem from becoming upset by witnessing any arguments or being anxious about her future. Grace knew that her daughter loved Nathan, in a way that she'd never loved Gervase, and it worried her that at some point she would be forced to explain why Nathan was leaving them.

Everybody was forbidden to say anything about the murder in front of Jem; there was to be no hint of the troubles within her hearing. Grace was determined to protect her come what may, but at the same time make sure she wasn't excluded just because she was a child. Grace shared with her anything she thought she'd be able to assimilate with ease.

Grace had been told about George Carew's demise by Nathan and had greeted the news with her habitual sangfroid; Nathan had spared her the grim details but had had no choice but to keep her informed on any progress in the investigation, as she was now officially head of the family. She had shown none of the conflicting emotion which churned inside her and had resisted the urge to weep with relief because the world was now rid of such a wicked human being.

"Did the constable manage to deduce anything? He seemed to be in rather a hurry to leave."

Nathan smiled, "I think he had a pressing engagement going by the number of times he glanced at the clock."

"What will happen now?"

"Very little, apparently. It seems that the law is not equipped to cope with so many unanswered questions. It's also fortunate for us that the magistrate, according to local legend, isn't keen on people making extra work for him. He prefers to hunt foxes in his spare time, not criminals, and go to the races, or watch cock fights; attending the Assizes is not really to his tastes."

"I don't understand, surely it's his duty to bring criminals to justice?" Grace didn't know why she was even questioning the magistrate's behaviour as it went decidedly in their favour.

"Magistrates are merely unpaid and unappreciated laymen according to the constable, chosen because they're rich and have very little else to occupy them. The poor constable was utterly baffled by the scores of suspects. I think he felt overwhelmed by the sheer scale of the problem and would have probably passed on his concerns to the magistrate."

"So, the murderer hasn't been found and probably never will be?"

"It certainly looks that way."

Grace was silent.

Nathan regarded her intently, "Whatever happens, Carew got what he deserved in the end, although I feel a little guilty that he was confined under my auspices at the time. However, he didn't seem to mind his victims being completely helpless so I'm not going to be too remorseful."

She nodded without looking him in the eye.

She had heard through William how Nathan had taken charge of everything and knew he was also perfectly happy to spend time with Jem whenever she demanded it and was aware that he could have left at any time and not taken on the myriad responsibilities of the Winterborne family and estate. She was finding it exceedingly hard to imagine life without him but was having to face up to the fact that one day soon he would leave them.

* * *

Mr Killigrew and his eager young associate arranged themselves at the dining table and laid out their papers, with one last speaking glance at each other and a slight shake of heads, they invited the possible beneficiaries, family and some trusted members of the staff into the room.

When everyone was seated, Mr Killigrew loudly cleared his throat and shuffled some papers to get everyone's attention. All eyes turned to him expectantly.

"Good afternoon, Lady Winterborne, ladies and gentlemen, I don't think I need to explain why we are all here today. The sad news of Lord Winterborne's passing, I'm sure, must be uppermost in all our minds. He was a much respected and colourful character, and I had the honour of serving him for some fifteen years. I have here his lordship's precise and detailed instructions, but I must remind you all that this is a mere formality — which he was very keen should take place. I understand he was fond of a bit of a spectacle! So, I think I shall just — get straight to the salient points and put you all out of your misery!" He glanced down at the document in his hand and then up at Lady Winterborne, sitting so still and expressionless at the head of the table, "My lady, it is my solemn duty to inform you that the Winterborne estate has been divided into — thirds — between you, Lady Grace Winterborne, Lady Jemima Winterborne and — Captain Nathaniel Heywood."

Grace closed her eyes. Nathan stood up suddenly and then sat down again. Mr Killigrew took a breath.

"There are, of course, some pertinent conditions. Winterborne, the house and lands and monies are to be entailed. My lady, Lord Winterborne has determined that it is to be your home for life. There are various trusts set up for Lady Jemima, for when she reaches her sixteenth year and for when she is twenty-one. There is another — important clause. Captain Heywood is to take complete charge of the running of the house and estate and is to remain on the premises for a minimum of eight months *per annum*. After a six-month mourning period, Lady Winterborne will be free to marry again and the conditions of the Will in its entirety is that you should marry — Captain Nathaniel Heywood."

There were several astonished gasps from those present and Grace buried her face in her hands. Nathan was staring at the lawyer as though he were quite deranged. Thunderstruck, Emery let out a splutter of laughter and then clapped his hand over his mouth.

"There are several other settlements to be announced," continued Mr Killigrew relentlessly, "Lord Winterborne's extremely successful shipping business — dealing with wine and brandy, tea and coffee, chocolate, sugar and spices — is bequeathed to Captain Heywood — for the benefit of Lady Winterborne and Lady Jemima."

"Groceries!" exclaimed Emery, in disgust.

" — and to be supervised by Mr Emery Talmarch, for which he will receive a substantial stipend and the Marquis's townhouse in St James's Square."

"*Oh, Good God!*" groaned Emery resting his forehead upon the table. "He was in *trade!*"

Nathan started to laugh silently, his shoulders shaking, "Well, he certainly liked to stage manage everything. He has us trussed up like chickens."

Grace rose quietly to her feet and left the room without a word. Nathan, the smile dying slowly, watched her leave.

"I think that's probably enough for now," said Mr Killigrew, "There are, of course, other beneficiaries. Mr Edgerton, you've been mentioned — he seems to have had a particular partiality for your company, I understand. Mr Kirby, Mrs

Hawkins, and other members of his loyal staff are also recipients — but I can always announce those at a later date, if you'd prefer?"

Nathan stood up, "No, it would be unfair to make them wait. Go ahead and tell them — I'm afraid I must make my excuses — "

"Of course, Captain. We can go over the details at another time." He wanted to wish him good luck but having seen Lady Winterborne's frozen face, he didn't think it would do him much good. He sent him a sympathetic look and waited until he'd left the room before divulging the rather more pleasant news to the staff.

Twenty-Seven

Nathan searched the garden for Grace, eventually finding her by the fountain. He approached her cautiously, as one might something that could explode at any moment and was quite prepared for her to scream at him or to flee, but she didn't make a sound or even the slightest movement. She was staring into the distance and seemed unaware of his presence.

"Grace? Are you all right? You must be overwhelmed by such an unforeseen announcement. I can't even begin to fathom how it must make you feel."

She kept her eyes on the distant hills, "Can't you? He's trapped us all like flies in honey. None of us can escape now without losing something. And he knew — if he tied Jem to Winterborne that I could never leave — would never *want* to leave." She laughed, "He's made sure that everyone is to lead miserable lives. God, how he must have enjoyed his scheming! He was like a puppet master and we are his puppets — even after death, he still holds the strings. Poor Emery, to believe he was safe from penury and the dreaded Newgate, only to discover the way out is through trade! What a dilemma for him! I will admit that I was relieved to hear Gervase only traded in such mundane commodities — I had begun to suspect — but am grateful that it's merely everyday items even if it is so lowering. At least I have one less concern."

"I too had the same apprehension. He's managed to confound us at every turn."

"There must be some way out of this. Can we not contest the will?"

"I'm sure we can but it might take years to resolve. These things do. You know, I believe that, given time to become accustomed to the idea, Emery will take quite well to his new supervising role and you can be confident that Jem will be safe and secure. You've been put in an untenable position but at least you and Jem have a home."

"And you?"

"I'm not unhappy with my lot. I would much rather it had not been so detrimental for you, but, if it is unacceptable to you, I would gladly give you my share of Winterborne and I could find someone who could competently manage the estate for you — "

"So, you could then leave with an easy conscience?"

"Is that what you want?"

"I? I have no say in the matter one way or another."

"That's untrue, Grace. I'll do whatever you wish. I know the Marquis has tried to bind us together for reasons of his own, but I would not have you distressed for anything in the world. I'm equally content either way as long as you're happy. I would submit to his request if that's what you want, or I will leave you everything that he's bequeathed to me and quit Winterborne. Just say the word." He was hoping to spur her into some kind of reaction that might reassure him as to her feelings, but she was determined not to give away any clue to her inner thoughts, her face impassive and her voice, colourless.

"You can do what you like. It's nothing to me. Gervase wants to control us from beyond the grave, but I won't allow it. He may have hung Winterborne around my neck, but I'm willing to tolerate all those conditions as long as it means Jem will have a home with me. But I cannot allow him to determine whom I marry. I would rather live in a ditch."

"Even though by doing as he commands and marrying me would mean you were safe from any further machinations? Everything would be neatly resolved."

Grace said nothing for a moment.

"I will never marry again," she said quietly, "Nothing could induce me."

"Not even if you were truly loved?"

Another pause.

"I will never marry. I've learnt my lesson."

"It was a very unfair lesson. You cannot judge everyone by such limited criteria. You were sold to the highest bidder and had no say in the matter. Your life was not your own because you were little more than a child and were governed by your parents and they callously gave you into the care of a husband who neither loved you nor had your best interests at heart. Perhaps it's time to do something for yourself."

Grace turned and looked him in the eye for the first time, "Oh? Would you have me run away like Miss Robbins? It didn't turn out so well for her, did it? If you're a female, wherever you go there are men who are just waiting to take advantage of you, waiting to ruin your life and destroy you. My father, George Carew, Gervase — you!"

"Damn it, Grace! You know very well that I'd no idea why the Marquis invited me here. Are you really going to throw away any chance of happiness for the sake of your pride?"

"I do not trust happiness any more. It's only fleeting and, in the end, always disappointing."

Nathan, at his wit's end, took a few steps away from her so that he wasn't tempted to shake some sense into her. He took some steadying breaths, "All right. I cannot keep fighting you, but I want you to remember that this was your doing. I don't know yet what my immediate plans are because there are obviously quite a few obstacles to overcome before an acceptable solution can be found. I'll make sure that there's someone to supervise the estate and we can contest the will. But I'll tell you now, I *cannot* stay here for eight months of the year as he's stipulated — and not be tempted by you. It's more than I can bear to be close to you — and not be allowed to touch you." He watched her face for any signs that he might be getting through to her but there was nothing.

Grace chewed the inside of her cheek.

"Are you made of nothing but ice, Grace? I thought — I *hoped* — that night in the Maze, that the ice had melted, but it seems that was just an aberration. Will you not give me a chance to prove to you that not every man is the same? God, I know I'm far from perfect but I'm damned if I'm going to just give up because you have no faith." He moved closer to her, "Just give me a sign that there might be some hope."

There came no response.

Suddenly overcome by temper, he reached out and grasped her wrist, pulling her towards him and glaring down at her in futile rage mixed with the beginnings of despair, she went to him as though she had no strength left to fight, her acquiescence pitiful and damning, she wouldn't meet his eyes and although he could see the battle going on within her, there was no weakening in her defences. The temptation to try to provoke her into some kind of reaction by dragging her into a forceful embrace was overwhelming but Carew's violations were in the back of his mind and he had no desire to be likened to such a man, or to frighten Grace with the violence he was feeling. Realising that whatever he did would be in vain, he released her and backed away, breathing hard.

"I will leave once I have done as the Marquis wished and set the house up for the future — and put in motion the contesting of the will, if that's what you wish. You will have your hard-earned freedom — I hope it brings you much happiness."

He turned and strode away along the path to the house and, dry-eyed, she listened to his footsteps recede.

* * *

William, too excited to notice her downcast expression, greeted his sister with a crushing hug, "You won't believe this Gracie, but your mad husband has bequeathed me a tidy little manor in Hampshire, a couple of thoroughbred racehorses and several hunters, a very nice place in Grafton Street and has made me godfather to Jem! Oh, and I'm to receive five thousand pounds a year apparently! I'm utterly dumbfounded! I'd absolutely no idea he might do that!"

Grace, without coherent thought, returned his embrace and held on for rather longer than she meant to, so that he knew immediately something was wrong; she had never embraced with any enthusiasm even when she was younger, and had always awkwardly pulled away first.

He tightened his arms about her, "Have you argued with Nathan again?"

She shook her head and then nodded into his chest, "Not argued, precisely. He's told me that he's going to leave Winterborne — and I told him that I didn't care."

William laughed, "You make me look positively mature! Honestly, Gracie, I don't agree with a good deal of what Gervase has done, his reasons seem a little skewed, but there's no getting away from the fact that Nathan has stayed by your side through thick and thin, even saving your life, helping you in adversity, taking on the burden of Winterborne despite having been lured here under false pretences and for some reason, which I'm unable to fathom, he seems to be rather fond of you. I mean, I know you're considered a bit of a beauty in some quarters, although I cannot see it myself, but you are without doubt the most stubborn, exasperating, impossible woman I have ever had the misfortune to know and that's including Mother and Catherine Wingfield! Any man willing to take you on must be either demented or a saint — or perhaps a demented saint! And that's coming from someone who loves you! I know you've been mistreated, and I can understand your reluctance to trust anyone but Nathan is not George Carew, or Gervase or even Father! I think you should ask yourself why he's stayed at Winterborne when it hasn't exactly been plain sailing for him. What has he done to make you shy away? Yes, he accepted the initial invitation, but he did it more for Emery than himself. And yes, he considered the ridiculous proposition for just a moment, but he didn't act upon it."

"Didn't he?" said Grace softly.

William gripped her arms and put her away from him, frowning down at her, "What on earth do you mean by *that?*"

"I'm just saying that you don't know everything and there have been developments which only I know about and if you knew, you might change your mind about your beloved Captain Heywood."

Her brother raised an eyebrow, "Ah — I *see.*"

"No, you *don't.*"

"Gracie, my love, do you think that I'm still five years old with a love of banging drums? I am nineteen years old and fully aware of what happens between a man and a woman! I'm not naive. Nor do I think that you should behave like a nun! I could see the change in you and knew it had nothing to do with Gervase or anyone else. Only Nathan could have — altered you in such a way."

Grace blushed, "He fulfilled the requirements of his contract with Gervase — however, it was, thankfully, fruitless and therefore ultimately disappointing for both of them in the end, neither getting what they wanted "

She found herself suddenly standing unsupported as William released her.

"Are you saying that you believe that Nathan — expressing his — devotion to you — in such a way — was merely the result of Gervase's schemes?"

"I know it was."

William shook his head in disbelief, "Do you know, sometimes you make me want to smash something expensively precious just to wake you up! You are beyond exasperating! God knows why he should feel such passion for you! He must have all his attics to let! He might as well have fallen in love with an icicle or a rock!"

Tears started to Grace's eyes; expecting support and receiving condemnation, she was much taken aback.

"And it's no use using those feminine wiles on me! To be perfectly frank, sister dear, I think I'm leaning towards being on Nathan's side in this skirmish."

"*William!*"

"No, I'm not sorry either — you've brought this upon yourself and I think you should fix it yourself and perhaps it'll be a valuable lesson for you."

* * *

Absolutely distraught, Grace made haste to shut herself in her bedchamber where a short while later she was joined by Sally, carrying a neatly folded pile of items which she'd been repairing with her perfect little stitches.

"Ah, there you are, m'lady! I was looking for you. I hear that the will has been read and that both Mrs Hawkins and Kirby have been given their own cottages on the estate and pensions. And, of all things, they say I was mentioned too! I am to have £100 a year! It'll make me a target for fortune hunters!" she giggled, but then, wondering why her mistress was not sharing the joke, she laid down the mending and went to sit by Grace on the bed. "Out with it! I've heard a little about the nature of the bequests, but everyone seems reluctant to discuss it. It sounds like a very good thing for you. Have you spoken with the Captain? He must be extremely happy with the outcome!"

She was somewhat alarmed when Grace flung herself backwards onto the covers, tears flowing unchecked.

"Oh, no! What have you done now?" demanded Sally.

"He's leaving! He's — *leaving!*"

"Oh," said Sally, "What have you said to him?"

"I — I wasn't happy about the way the will has been arranged! It's dreadful! He's been trapped into staying here. I would never know if he was staying because of me or because of the conditions Gervase has set out. I mean, obviously the rewards are enormous, he would have so much to gain. But the drawback is that he'd be tied to Winterborne for most of the year when I know he hates having responsibilities of any kind but particularly domestic ones. He's avoided them all his life. I would be just another burden to him."

"He's *said* this to you?"

Grace buried her face in the crook of her elbow, "Well, no, he said that he wants to stay, but if I want him to leave — he will. Don't you see? It all comes down to *me! I* have to decide. He just says he'll do whatever I want. But I don't *know* what I want! I've never had any choice before now. I can't think straight. Oh, Lord, it's all too much!"

"No, it's not. You either love him and want him to stay or you don't love him because you can't forgive him for his mistakes, and you want him to leave. It couldn't be any more simple."

Grace continued to sob for a while, her arm covering her eyes and Sally patted her shoulder absent-mindedly, trying to think of the best thing to say to comfort her.

"You should probably just let him go. Never see him again. He's brought nothing but trouble to Winterborne since he arrived. You'd be far better off without him. Can you do anything about the will? Perhaps you could get it legally altered and then he'd have no reason to stay."

The sobbing just grew louder.

"Of course, Jem would be very sorry. She loves him."

Sally thought they could probably hear the sound of weeping in the kitchens now.

Grace was beginning to feel as though the whole world was against her.

"It seems to me that you're conflicted in the worst way, but I think you know the answer already — you're just not willing to admit that your judgement has been clouded. It's hard to own up to being wrong."

Grace said nothing but the violence of her weeping lessened slightly.

Sally gave her one last pat and then picking up her pile of mending, distributed it between the linen press and blanket chest and then with a sympathetic glance towards her still prostrate mistress she left the room, leaving Grace to think things through in peace.

* * *

In the withdrawing room, Jenny was idly playing a gentle melody upon the spinet, her thoughts far away and Peggy was curled up on the window seat gazing out at the parterre. No word had been spoken for some fifteen minutes; both seemed to be in a world of their own. The melody turned into the verse of a hymn and Jenny hummed along, thinking of all the bitterly cold Sunday mornings spent singing in their village church, her breath making silvered clouds in front of her face, her fingers white and numb with cold. Being at Winterborne, despite the attack, was like being in heaven. She never wanted to leave.

The door opened and at least one of the reasons why she thought Winterborne to be heaven entered the room: Jem skipping and carrying the long-suffering kitten in her arms, followed by William, smiling cheerfully as usual.

"Good afternoon, beautiful ladies! That's a pretty tune, Miss Robbins!"

Jenny stopped playing immediately, turned a hectic shade of pink and debated what she should say to him, but as nothing occurred to her, she held out her hand to the little girl, who ran to join her on the stool. Jem put the kitten on the spinet, and it plonked its way nervously up and down the keys, making discordant notes.

"He plays far better than I do!" said Jenny, laughing.

"Oh, no! Uncle William says you play very prettily!" declared Jem.

Uncle William, making himself comfortable on the sofa, agreed, "It's true. Everything you do is remarkably pretty!"

Jenny didn't know where to look. Ever since the terrible incident she'd found it difficult to meet Mr Edgerton's rather direct gaze. She couldn't help but remember the embarrassing state she'd been in when he'd rescued her, and it made her feel dreadfully awkward. She just found herself blushing and stammering her thanks again and knew she sounded half-witted.

"Can you teach me to play a song please?" asked Jem.

William observed while Jenny taught the little girl how to play a simple tune and thought again how graceful and sweet she was. She showed no impatience with Jem's childish thumping on the keys and guided her fingers with gentleness and good humour. They giggled together as the kitten gradually became more of a nuisance and, as Jem's grasp of the notes improved, Jenny clapped her hands with delight and heaped praise upon the child. William saw again his mother's scandalised face in his mind's eye and smiled to himself.

"Jenny? Would you care to accompany me on a walk beside the river this afternoon?"

That young lady looked up in mingled delight and horror.

"I — I — " she faltered.

"She would love to," interrupted Peggy, "She's a country girl at heart and loves nothing more than being out in the open air."

Jenny looked at her friend in astonishment, "I — I would — very much like to walk by the river," she concluded and smiled bashfully at William. He, in turn, grinned back and held her gaze for a moment before she lowered her eyes in some confusion.

Peggy sighed and tried to be gratified for her dearest friend, but her heart was just a little bit sore. She was delighted that Jenny seemed to have found someone who truly liked her because she wanted her to be happy above anything. She recalled the first time she'd seen her lingering forlornly on a particularly unsavoury street corner, being pestered by lewd drunken men and obviously without a clue of the danger she was in and she'd just decided that she'd save her. It had not been a purely altruistic sentiment that had made her stick her neck out. Jenny was the prettiest creature she'd ever set eyes upon and it wasn't long before Peggy had practically adopted her, taking her into her tiny, rented room and teaching her all she knew about the theatre. She'd wanted to keep her all for herself but knew that could never be and then the offer to come to Winterborne had arrived and she'd begged for Jenny to be invited too, promising that her acting skills were improving rapidly and pointing out just how distractingly pretty she was. Consequently, she felt wholly responsible for what had happened to her friend since and therefore couldn't really blame Jenny for falling in love with her charming rescuer as he'd already captured her heart before being so heroic, with his ready smile and affable nature. Peggy knew Mr Edgerton was a nice young man with good prospects and didn't begrudge him his happiness but couldn't help feeling a little sad that it was due to her own meddling that all this had happened.

She regarded Jenny's rose-pink cheeks, her lovely bottom lip caught between her small white teeth and she sighed again. She'd never be able to explain to Jenny how she truly felt about her or tell her about the terrible thing she'd done because of her. They were secrets she'd have to take to her grave.

* * *

A little later, as the sun was gliding serenely towards the horizon and the air was filled with the humming sound of industrious bees and the gentle murmur of the river flowing by, William and Jenny walked together along the riverbank and stood for a while in silence to watch the sky reflected in the rippled water.

After a while, William turned to her and held out his hand and without hesitation, she placed hers into it.

* * *

Nathan paced and Emery regarded him from the comfort of a chair in the parlour. Emery examined his lace cuffs and wondered how he was to explain away his sudden involvement with the sordid world of groceries to his grand friends and acquaintances. He had always been so disdainful of anyone who smelt even remotely like a cit and now if he wanted to keep out of gaol, he had no choice but to become one. It was a difficult notion to take on board with so little warning. He watched Nathan thump his fist into the back of the chair again and thought that he still probably had the best of Lord Winterborne's bad deals. He was, at least, not fettered to Winterborne and frustrated by Grace's mulish conduct, with his choices narrowed by their infantile inability to just admit their feelings.

"I still say we could kidnap her," said Emery cheerfully. "It would at least be a novel and entertaining way of getting her to comply."

"Oh, I'm sure that would be bound to win her round. Perhaps you should just concentrate upon how you're going to keep track of all your hogsheads of brandy and sacks of spices. You're going to be kept busy from morning to night. There'll be no more time for gambling especially once those delightful calculating mamas find out about your new wealthy status — you'll have to beat them off with a stick."

Emery stretched out his legs and crossed his white stockinged ankles, "Ah, I hadn't considered that I shall have my pick of all the ladies — what an entrancing idea! And, for your information, I shall hire someone else to do all the tedious business stuff! I shall not mire my own fair hands with such lowly work. I plan to just reap the rewards of having fingers in every pie. Oh, maybe we could export pies! There's a thought."

"They'd rot in the hold or be eaten by the rats."

"You're merely the owner, a silent partner, not the manager! Leave all the important decisions to me. I believe I shall take to this whole being a merchant business like a fish to water!"

"The business will run aground within the first few months at this rate. You're going to have to be as clever as the Marquis at this Emery! The monies from the enterprise keep Winterborne going."

"All will be well, you mark my words, my dear friend, no need to fret," proclaimed Emery complacently.

"Well, that's all very well but what about Grace? What the hell am I going to do about her?"

Twenty-Eight

The days passed and no one saw very much of Nathan as he was either out inspecting the land, talking with the tenants or closeted in the library interviewing estate stewards, the previous one, a man with unwavering traditional ideals, having left a year or so before, after he'd decided that Lord Winterborne was just too odd to be a lifelong employer; the steward hadn't liked his attitude at all and had left in high dudgeon raining curses down upon his lordship's bewigged head. The estate affairs had, almost unnoticed, been in gradual decline ever since; the dwindling team of workers were barely able to keep up with what they already knew were their everyday jobs and lacked the foresight to understand what other matters needed attending to, without being explicitly told.

In keeping with Grace's mood, it rained all week, and she received a terse letter from the portrait painter saying that the moment the sun came out he'd be back to finish the painting; he concluded the missive with his deepest sympathies for her tragic loss and regretted that Lord Winterborne had never been well enough to see the work completed, as it was going to be his finest ever masterpiece.

The rain dripped sadly from the trees and splashed onto the terrace making puddles so large they were a strong deterrent to anyone wanting to leave the house; the gardeners huddled miserably in the stables or pestered the cook to be allowed into the kitchen to dry out in front of the fire, which was all very well, but when the excessively grubby, fragrant and foul-mouthed stable lads asked to come in, she indignantly chased them away with a broom.

The constable returned briefly to explain that although the magistrate had initially been interested in the case, he had, once he understood that no one had yet been apprehended for the murder, quickly lost interest in it and had summarily dismissed it from the list of tasks he had in hand, in favour of other more entertaining engagements. The constable asked if there had been any more developments, but when Nathan told him that there were no further revelations, he'd been quite downcast and left Winterborne feeling as though he hadn't satisfied his own curiosity or done the county proud. He knew that the inconclusive ending would haunt him.

Nathan wrote to the man's superiors and recommended him highly, saying that he'd behaved in an exemplary fashion, conducting a thorough investigation whilst being both sympathetic and courteous. The constable's wife was also delighted with him and told everyone she met that her husband was very friendly with the Winterbornes and had been promised a promotion before long.

Everyone had their own entirely incorrect suspicions about the murder culprit, but knowing exactly what George Carew had done to get himself so brutally executed, they were not looking for retribution for him; in fact, they fervently hoped that the guilty party would get away scot-free; so they kept their suspicions to themselves.

In order to make up for the house being caught in the gloom of deep mourning, the cook valiantly tried to cheer everyone up by creating dishes which were both challenging and tasty. As this didn't always work, the guests began to look forward to their meals with a mixture of trepidation and amusement, but it gave them all something benign to discuss whilst dining.

Sally had her work cut out for her trying to keep Grace's gowns in order because her mistress took to wandering aimlessly around the dustier parts of the house, where no housemaid had been in years and she'd return with cobwebs in her hair and the hem of her gown thick with grey fluff and dust which seemed to cling to and mark the black material rather more severely than her usual gowns. Sally had no idea why she felt compelled to do this and neither did Grace. When the rain eventually stopped, she took to disappearing into the more remote areas of the garden where, according to William, who had spied her several times, she was just staring into the distance, unaware of anything going on around her.

Emery tried to talk to her, but it was as though she were in some sort of trance, from which no one could wake her.

"Grace, everyone's worried about you." said Emery cautiously.

She turned away from looking at the twisted apple trees in the orchard, where he'd finally found her after searching everywhere, and stared at him as though she had no idea who he was.

"I beg your pardon?"

"We're concerned that you're — behaving a little strangely. William is afraid that you might be sickening for something. I wonder if we should fetch Doctor Morton?"

Grace blinked at him and reaching out, put a caressing hand to his face but said nothing.

He reported back to Nathan and William and there was a general consensus that she was a total mystery to them, and they had no idea how to proceed.

Jem was the only one who seemed to have the key to making her listen by the simple means of grabbing her pale, cold cheeks and turning her head towards her, forcing her mother to look in her eyes and then speaking loudly and firmly as though she were a little deaf and slow-witted to boot.

"Ma-*ma! Mama!* Are you *asleep?* I want you to tell me a story tonight. You keep forgetting. You must wake up now!"

Grace looked at her daughter and tried desperately to focus.

"I'm sorry darling — I — I am awake — I just — don't feel very well. I'll be better soon. You shall have a story tonight, I promise."

"But I'm scared, Mama! Everything is not the same. The Captin is not the same. I don't like it. Uncle William is always with Miss Robbins now. She's nice though."

Grace raised her eyebrows in surprise, "Miss Robbins? Is that so? I see. Well, that's — very — " her voice drifted away.

Jem took her by the shoulders and gave her a brisk shake, "You've fallen asleep again! It's werry annoying."

"I know, dear," said Grace vaguely.

* * *

William considered Nathan thoughtfully, "If you're sure. Don't you think it might be the last straw though?"

Nathan shrugged, "To be perfectly frank, I have no idea. I just feel as though not only have *we* lost her, but she's lost herself — it's as though she's wandering in some dark place where we cannot reach her. I've spoken at length with Doctor Morton, and he says he's seen this sort of thing in soldiers after battle — they fall into a state of shock, where they just feel numb and can't seem to understand what's going on around them."

"What is the cure?"

"There may not be one. The doctor says love and gentle care and patience. Well, she's had all of that already and it's made no difference. I'm running out of options, William."

"All right, then," said William with a sigh, "I think you're mistaken. Have you told Jem yet?"

"No, not yet. I'm dreading that. She's still got you though."

"Not quite the same thing and anyway, I shall be following close behind you in a nice comfortable carriage. And Jem seems to have developed a particular fondness for you. I suspect she senses your love for her mother, and it makes her feel secure, perhaps thinking that if you love her so much then you might be the one to stay — to be relied upon."

"What more can I do, Emery? Grace cannot hear me any more. Perhaps if I'm not here as a constant reminder of all the things which have driven her into hiding, she might allow herself to surface again." He couldn't help but think of the moment he'd pulled her from the water and breathed life back into her and a chill ran along his spine. "One last effort and then I must leave."

* * *

Grace perched on the edge of an armchair in her bedchamber watching Sally tidy the linen press. There were gowns hanging from every piece of furniture and lying across the bed; the scarlet gown was draped over the other chair having had the creases gently coaxed away by Sally's deft fingers. There were piles of petticoats and bodices and a tumble of ribbons and lace which Sally was in the process of sorting through.

"What a dreadful muddle! I don't know how it has become so tangled! Oh, there is that lace collar we were looking for — it needs some mending there on the edge and what's this? A black riband? You don't wear black ribands in your hair! How odd. Where did that come from?"

Grace cast a careless look at the riband being held up for inspection and bit her lip. It was the one which Jem had pulled from Nathan's hair and tossed to the ground — so very long ago. Grace had kept it. She had meant to give it back to him but had instead hidden it away, a secret only she knew about.

She held out her hand and Sally passed it to her with an understanding smile, "Ah, so that's it!" she murmured, "Belongs to the Captain?"

Turning the riband around and around in her fingers, Grace nodded, "I have nothing else of him."

Sally, much provoked, after many days of watching her mistress disappear before her eyes like early morning mist, snapped, "You could have had *all* of him and not just a stupid riband, had you not been so — so *childish!*"

Grace stopped fiddling with the riband, but still staring at it blankly said, "He doesn't love me. He's never told me so. Gervase made him come to Winterborne and then forced him into staying against his will. Nathan only came because of the money. He only stayed because he was to be paid a vast sum."

Sally threw down the handful of lace she was crushing between her aggravated fingers and made a derisive snorting sound, "I never thought I'd dare say this to your face, m'lady but you're a feather-brained ninny-hammer! I've heard talk that he's thinking of leaving and if he does — you'll see him no more because your stupid pride will keep you apart. He'll re-join his regiment and probably get himself killed and you'll wither away and die here in this enormous empty house and Jem will be an orphan with no one to care for her! You're so *selfish!*" As Grace made no response she continued relentlessly, "Jem deserves better. The Captain will die all alone in a filthy ditch and be eaten by rats. You'll be found all dried up amongst the dust in the east wing. We'll never know what drove Lord Winterborne to do what he did — he was a mystery to us all — " she faltered as Grace looked at her with a frown, "What is it?"

"Sally! The *letters!* I forgot all about them and haven't read them."

"Letters? What letters?"

Grace got quickly to her feet, "From Gervase. They are hidden in the book beside his bed. *All's Well That Ends Well.*"

"Wait here! I'll get them!" exclaimed Sally as she rushed out of the door, thinking that this was the first time in days she'd seen any kind of emotion from the Marchioness, and she was determined to act upon it.

She found the book and ran back and gave it to Grace.

Grace broke open the wafer on the letter addressed to Jem first and read it, "He is all amiability and filled with tenderness and good advice for her. He writes that she is the only real love he ever had in his life and he apologises for not being a better father." She stared at the thin scratchy handwriting and thought how odd that he could have such warm feelings for his daughter when he had never shown his own wife anything but lukewarm indifference. She was glad that Jem would at least have this to remember her father by; it was very little and far too late, but, in the end, better than nothing.

"Are you going to open the other one then?" demanded Sally with a touch of impatience; everything her mistress did at the moment was so sluggish that she wanted to scream with frustration.

Grace reluctantly broke the seal and read the contents.

* * *

The painter was waiting in the usual place in the topiary garden, the sun was shining down at just the right angle to finish adding the highlights to the painting. He muttered to himself about the vagaries of the wealthy and titled classes; they had no true appreciation of artistic genius and although Lady Winterborne had the excuse of being distressed by her husband's death, there really was no excuse for being so late for their appointment. The light was crucial to the completion of the painting and was changing all the time and the paints, once they were exposed to the warm air, were likely to begin drying out. He gazed at the painting gleaming richly in the sunshine, at the perfect rendering of the textures; the flesh glowed, the dogs looked alive, the house in the background was beautifully depicted and the whole was filled with the golden warmth of summer and the intense, rather mysterious atmosphere of Winterborne. He had seldom felt so pleased with himself. He had managed to capture something beyond the commonplace portrait and landscape; there was a sense of anticipation and an ominous feeling, as though a storm was looming on the horizon.

On hearing approaching footsteps and voices, he looked up to observe Lady Winterborne and her daughter hurrying towards him. He bit back a derogatory comment and welcomed them with all the courtesy he could muster.

"Ah, at last! I was beginning to fear that you had not been told I have been waiting here for an hour or more. If you could please take your places as quickly as possible — " he said, waving his hand towards the carefully arranged scene. Grace lifted up her scarlet skirts and stepped into her place; she called the dogs to heel and made sure that Jem took up the same position as before. Jem, however, was holding the kitten in her arms and after a moment, while the painter adjusted his easel and picked up his palette, he spotted the addition to his sitters with a horrified exclamation, "Oh, no, no, no! I cannot now add this animal to the painting! It is *impossible!*"

Jem looked mutinous, "Well, then I won't be in it either. Barker *needs* to be in it. He's a Winterborne!"

"I should just add the kitten if I were you," suggested Grace quietly, "You will not win this argument."

The painter looked as though he might refuse but then thought better of the impulse as it was very near the time he should be paid for his work. With a theatrical sigh he turned back to the huge canvas.

"There's something missing from the picture, Mama."

"What's that, my love?"

"The Captin," said Jem sadly. "He'd look very nice in it. Could we ask him?"

Grace looked down at her child's eager face, "Jem? You said *very*!"

"I *always* say very!" said Jem in some confusion.

Grace laughed.

"*Can* we ask him?"

"No, dear, he's exceedingly busy — he wouldn't have time."

"But when he's gone, I might forget what he looks like."

"Gone?"

"He told me he *has* to leave. He said he didn't want to, but he *had* to! He said he's not leaving *me* though. He said he'd always be with me. What does that *mean?* Why does he *have* to leave, Mama? Why can't we go with him?"

Grace, finding herself under a severe and seemingly endless bombardment of unanswerable questions, was beginning to feel slightly giddy and like a city under siege.

"I don't know, Jem, I really don't know."

"He said he loves me like I was his very own daughter! That makes him like my — father, doesn't it, Mama?"

"Oh, Jem! You must stay still for the painter or he'll get cross!"

"I really don't care because nothing will matter once the Captin is gone away."

Grace was silent.

The painter dashed in a few orange highlights across the vibrant red of the gown. He was feeling steadily more on edge as his sitters conversed. He carefully added pinpoints of light to the dog's eyes and some glints of blue into Lady Winterborne's long dark hair. He felt the need to work rather more quickly than usual — he didn't like the turn the conversation was taking.

"Barker will miss him as well," mused Jem. "Will Mr Talmarch have to leave too?"

"I don't know. Perhaps, as they are such great friends."

"Uncle William said *he'll* stay because he has to look after you, Mama."

"Did he?"

"I saw him kissing Miss Robbins. She was very pleased and kissed him too! Do you think they'll get married?"

"It certainly looks that way," sighed Grace.

"Will you ever get married again or will you always be a — widow?"

"Widow?"

"I heard Bridie call you that. A widow. What does it mean?"

"It means that your husband has died."

"Oh. It's a funny word. I thought she said you were a *window*! Do you *like* being a widow?"

"No, not really."

"Does it make you feel sad?"

"Of course. Oh, Jem, *please!*"

The kitten, being clutched rather too tightly, began to struggle, splaying its star-shaped paws and curling its needle-sharp claws into Jem's arm, "Ow! Barker! Don't *do* that! Keep still! You're going to be in a painting for ever so people can see how sweet you are!"

"If you could *both* keep still — " said the painter wearily.

Dancer and Thisbe, having had enough of posing, suddenly became distracted by a tantalising glimpse of a squirrel lolloping across the grass just behind the painter's easel and, without warning, shot off at great speed after it. Jem let out a shriek of laughter as Dancer knocked the artist's table over, scattering paints and brushes and jars all over the lawn. The painter swore fluently and threw the brush in his hand to the ground with extreme violence and tore at his lustrous locks in anguish. Jem handed her mother the kitten and raced off after the runaway dogs.

Grace collapsed onto the grass, in clouds of scarlet silk, which billowed and settled around her.

It was at this moment that Nathan stalked into view, his expression grim, followed by Emery and William, both looking anxious. They all came to a standstill as their eyes fell upon the shambles before them.

Jem giggling, as she chased after the capering dogs, who had cornered the squirrel up a tree, the painter madly cursing amongst the debris and looking as though he was about to have seizure or burst into tears, and Grace sitting in the midst of it all holding the kitten and laughing.

Emery was the first to come to his senses, "I think we've arrived just in the nick of time gentlemen! William, why don't you endeavour to capture the dogs and save the squirrel and I will try to talk to the painter and stop him from ripping the canvas to shreds. Nathan, Grace is all yours! I wish you luck, good friend!"

* * *

Nathan eyed Grace with some misgiving; he hadn't expected to find her helpless with laughter and it had caught him completely off guard. The dogs were still barking frantically, despite William's best efforts to calm them and the squirrel was bounding from branch to branch as though taunting them. Jem was hopping up and down and clapping her hands in glee and squeaking excited instructions to her beleaguered uncle.

He turned back to Grace who had her face buried in her hands and was convulsed with uncontrollable giggles.

"This is probably not the ideal moment to speak with you Grace, but I'm afraid I must and will have my say."

She uncovered her face and looked up at him, her face quite pink from laughing, "*Must* you? Right here and now, in the middle of all this chaos? How like you to pick such a ridiculous moment!"

As these were more words than he'd heard from her beautiful lips in weeks, he was taken aback and for a moment could think of nothing to say at all, entirely forgetting the reason he'd come to see her, mesmerised by the sight of her so filled with life and responsive.

Behind him, William suddenly lunged and caught hold of Thisbe by the leg and let out a triumphant shout.

Emery was patting the weeping painter's shoulder and telling him that he had no choice but to continue because the painting was a work of divine brilliance and the world would be bereft without such a talent as his.

'Yes, I must, I'm afraid," continued Nathan, "I must leave Winterborne, Grace. I'm leaving today. I've resolved all the problems with the estate and hired a fine young man as steward — he comes with some excellent testimonials from his last place of work, and I've made sure that the investigation into Carew's murder goes no further — the constable seems quite content with the result — or lack of results. It appears that nearly everyone here had some grievance with Carew and therefore there were too many suspects to even begin to consider. Also, the magistrate is a feckless scoundrel — fortunately for us. I've already talked to Jem and explained as best I can, and William is quite happy to stay and see you through the next few months, to make sure that any problems there may be are rectified. I've spoken to Mr Killigrew about my third of the estate and we've come to an agreement about the shipping side of things. He seems to think that we can contest the will and once it has been acknowledged and gone through all the correct channels, it should be passed without any impediment.

So, you'll be able to continue as before and Winterborne will survive, just as you told the Marquis it would. Emery will be able to run the business from London and I suspect will find it quite enthralling once he gets his teeth into it — he's much brighter than he looks."

Grace smiled as she watched Emery help the painter pick up his brushes whilst continuing to heap praise upon the much-mistreated artist.

"Thank you," she said quietly, "For — everything."

Nathan closed his eyes for a brief moment to fix this image of her into his mind forever. Surrounded by scarlet silk, her dark hair tumbling about her shoulders, her cheeks flushed and her eyes still sparking from the laughter. She looked unbelievably tired and far too thin, with dark shadows under her eyes but still so intoxicatingly beautiful that his heart lurched in his chest.

"I don't regret coming to Winterborne, you know? It was the best thing I ever did," he admitted, "I fell in love with you the first moment I saw you — you were wearing that gown."

She looked up at him in surprise.

"You and Jem were running across the garden as I was riding down the approach to the house. You were the first thing I saw. Just a flash of red and then later when we were officially introduced, you were so different, so restrained and cold, so — suppressed — you enchanted me, and I wanted to set you free. It was my mistake not understanding that you'd no real desire to be released. What happened between us, on my side, at least, had nothing whatsoever to do with Lord Winterborne and what he asked of me. I swear I only fleetingly considered it, but, of course, you would never be able to believe me because you have known only lies and deceit your whole life."

He stood looking down at her and tried to imagine a lifetime without her and wondered if he could really just ride away from her.

"You see, I cannot go on like this any longer, Grace. I can't live here at Winterborne with you so close and not go quite mad. I would have to touch you eventually and that would drive you even further away from me. So, you see, the best thing I can do is to leave and hope and pray that you find some other fortunate man to take the Marquis's place and maybe he'll be able to melt all that ice and win your heart."

Grace could find no words which might help her express how she felt, she seemed to be caught in a trap of her own making and every time she struggled against it, she became ever more entangled.

Nathan shook his head in disbelief and turned to Jem who was tugging a struggling Dancer across the lawn by the black riband around his neck.

"Jem, it's time. I must go now," and he held out his arms to her.

The child let go of the dog and ran helter-skelter to him and threw herself up into his embrace. He swung her round and round and she kicked out her legs and squealed with joy, but when he finally brought her back to earth she clung onto his legs and wouldn't let go.

"Please, Captin! Please don't leave us! Nobody spins me round like you do! I don't want you to leave!"

Nathan kissed the top of her curly head and then squatted down on his haunches beside her and took her sad little face in his hands, "Just remember what I told you. When you're old enough you can come and look for me. Emery will know where to find me. I may be very old by then, but I'll still be overjoyed to see you. Your mama will take good care of you until then and so will your Uncle William and you'll probably forget all about me after a while."

"I'll *never* forget you! Not *ever!* I *will* come and find you — I promise!"

"Good! I shall hold you to that. Now, one more hug and promise me you'll take care of your mama for me."

Jem nodded furiously as she flung her arms about his neck.

Nathan, gritting his teeth so hard it hurt his jaw, put her away from him and stood up. He glanced back at Grace and saw that she was watching him with a slight frown marring her forehead. He raised his hand in farewell to William and Emery, one last, lingering look at Grace, and he turned and strode away to where he had tied his horse.

He'd gone about ten paces when he suddenly stopped in his tracks. He span around and swiftly returned to where Grace was still sitting on the ground.

He reached down and roughly hauled her up into his arms, looked angrily into her astonished face and then pulling her hard against him, kissed her so fiercely that she thought she might faint. He then pushed her away as though her touch burned him, so that her legs gave way and she slumped back to the ground in a heap.

"I love you, Grace," he said, "Even though you're such a damned fool. And, stupidly, I will always love you, which makes me equally foolish."

And he walked away.

* * *

Damnation! He'd lost. He'd done his best to win her round — to bring her to her senses, but he'd failed. He'd had a forlorn hope that her defences might have finally been weakened, but it was too late, nothing could change her mind. If she could resist Jem's entreaties and if her heart hadn't melted when she'd heard what he'd had to say, then all was indeed lost.

He untied his horse, thanked the groom who had stayed to make sure everything was all right and swung himself up into the saddle. Emery had promised to bring all his baggage later when he returned to London in the carriage, so he was travelling light.

He rode along the drive and into the open fields beyond the formal garden and didn't look back.

Jemima watched him go and then looked down at her mother who was not moving. She glanced at Mr Talmarch, who looked very sad indeed and then at Uncle William who was looking rather cross. The kitten was pouncing on the folds of the scarlet gown, its striped tail swishing angrily.

Jem really did wonder about grown-ups, they confused her.

She went to her mother, walking carelessly across the lovely bright silk skirts and knelt down beside her, "Mama! *Mama!* You have to wake up now or it'll be too late!" and she grabbed Grace's shoulders and shook her as hard as she could.

Grace opened her eyes wide and saw her child's frightened face so close to hers; she saw her bewilderment and heard the desperation in her voice. She suddenly couldn't catch her breath and she felt the river water closing over her head. She gasped and clutched her chest which was aching just like when she'd woken up from the near-drowning.

"*Jem!* He's leaving! We must stop him!" She struggled to her feet, grabbing the kitten and holding it out to Emery, who took it rather gingerly and held it at arm's length, well away from his coat.

"Come, my darling, we must run like the wind!" cried Grace and snatching Jem's hand, she darted away across the garden towards the orchard, with Jem racing along beside her.

Nathan allowed his horse to canter up the field to the gently rolling hill that rose in front of Winterborne; a formal, wide swathe of grass cut through the woodland, providing a good gallop for any approaching riders or an elegant walk for those wishing to view the house from its best aspect.

As he neared the top, he felt the warm breeze coming over the slope and knew it came from another county altogether, another place, somewhere filled with strangers and adventure and all the things he had once craved. Now, all he desired was to be tied down to one place, to one woman, to one life —

He kicked his horse gently and they reached the crest of the hill.

Grace and Jem burst out from beneath the cover of the apple trees and ran across the meadow at the foot of the hill. Ignoring the pain to her bare feet, Grace kept her eyes on the distant rider, now a small speck on the horizon. She knew they were being followed by William and the two cavorting, baying dogs and further back by Emery holding the kitten in one hand and his wig in the other.

Jem was shouting, "Faster! Faster! He's nearly gone!"

Then suddenly she couldn't see him any more, he'd vanished from view.

Grace didn't stop.

She thought she'd never stop. She'd keep running until she found him. Even if it took the rest of her life. She wasn't running away, for the first time in her life — she was running *to*.

Nathan reined the horse in, and looked across the countryside ahead of him, it looked unfamiliar and somehow inhospitable.

He thought he heard a sound, far off and faint. The sound of madly barking dogs. Then a cry. And another.

He wheeled the horse around and galloped back up the hill. Looking down the slope towards Winterborne, he saw a flash of scarlet.

Grace called his name, but could hardly make a sound, she was so out of breath. Jem, screamed at the top of her lungs, the sound quite high and piercing, like a screech owl.

Dancer and Thisbe, having the time of their lives, hallooed as though they were on a wild hunt and chasing down their quarry.

Emery had given up and was sitting in the long grass, heedless of his elegant coat, the kitten cradled in his lap.

William, seeing the rider reappear on the horizon, staggered to a halt and watched as his sister, a blur of fiery colour, dashed up that hill, her long dark hair flying, his little niece gamely running beside her.

Nathan spurred his horse into a reckless downhill gallop and when he neared his heart's desire, he leapt from the beast and stood watching them struggle the last part of the way with an exultant smile.

Grace, with tears streaming down her face, caught her foot in a tangle of weeds and fell to her knees but Jem pulled at her arm and she managed to get to her feet again and stumbled the last few steps, falling into Nathan's outstretched arms, slamming him backwards onto the grass and landing on top of him, knocking the breath out of him.

She was panting so hard, and sobbing so noisily, she couldn't make herself understood at first, but as she was covering his face with salty kisses, and babbling his name over and over, he felt fairly confident that she had finally come to her senses.

He rolled her over into the grass and pinned her so that she couldn't escape and gazed down into her beautiful, tear-soaked, flushed face, "You'd better be damned sure this time my lady, because I'm never letting go of you again."

Still breathing hard, Grace smiled up at him, "If — you don't kiss me very soon — Captain Heywood — I *shall* change my mind!"

Nathan groaned and did as he was bid, eagerly covering her mouth with his and making sure that she had no further reason for complaint. He tasted her tears and kissed them away, he traced the line of her rather hot cheek with a wondering finger.

"God, I love you so much, you infuriating woman! I was just about to turn back when I heard those wonderful dogs — I'd decided I'd just have to kidnap you, like Emery suggested, and *make* you love me."

"Oh, Nathan, I'd have gone so willingly! I've loved you from that shocking kiss in the linen cupboard! I was angry with myself for being so weak and then I found out — about Gervase's plan and I convinced myself that I was justified, and I allowed my fear of being trapped and deceived again to get the better of me. I'm sorry, my love! I am indeed a very foolish creature and I fear you will be sorely tested if you stay! Perhaps you should escape while you still can."

"Astonishingly, despite knowing you are bound to lead me a merry dance, I've no desire to escape at all. I'm going to stay here and make sure that you know that I love you and Jem more than anything in the world."

"Well, in that case, I shall have to make an honest man of you because I'm heartily sick of being a widow! Please will you marry me as soon as we possibly can without scandalising the whole county?"

"God, *yes!*" said Nathan, laughing and kissing her at the same time.

They were finally forced to cease their passionate embrace when a persistent child insisted upon joining in by hugging them both rapturously.

Grace pulled Nathan to her and whispered in his ear, "I shall be in the Maze at ten o'clock tonight, waiting impatiently for you!"

"You won't have to wait, my love, because I shall already be there!"

"Can I come too please?" implored Jem happily.

"No!" responded Grace and Nathan in perfect unison.

The End

The Letter

My Dear Grace,

The fact that you are reading this letter means that you are free from my tyranny at last. It also means that I am dead, which is a strange thought! Frankly, it'll be a relief for all concerned. I am not foolish enough to believe that I am easy to live with or that anyone will mourn my passing. As you sow, so shall you reap. I am fully prepared for what is bound to come.

My nature was formed early and refused to change. At the beginning I chose you for my wife because I knew every day would be torment for you and I believed it might be entertaining to observe and might hopefully distract me from the boredom of living. However, I quickly grew weary even of that and as Jemima gradually became the child she is, I watched you become the mother you should always have been. It was a lesson. I learnt to love her as best I could. Rest assured I see very little of me in her, perhaps only her strength of mind. I have watched you grow and change, even though you tried to hide from me, and I suppose I was proud that I had been clever enough to choose the right bride.

My capacity for affection is small and I had to find some kind of solace in places you will never know about, places good people shun. Of course, I drank to find salvation, but found none — I merely hastened my own timely end. When I became sick and was told that time was limited, I came to the conclusion that I couldn't leave things as they were — I had to make reparation of some kind, so I decided to find the ideal father for Jem and the perfect husband for you. I found the process oddly cathartic.

It took longer than I thought and at several points I feared I would fail in my quest, but in the end, I believe I achieved the impossible. Over the last two years we had many guests to stay and *amongst them were selected candidates for the job, but never once did you take any notice of them — until Captain Heywood arrived. And then I knew for certain that I had finally found the right man. It was then just a case of leaving it to Nature and with a little prompting from the wings — my work was done. It's very clear to me that you love each other — so don't try to spoil it Grace with your misplaced pride and unreasonable fears.*

I would like to apologise for any grief I may have caused you — I'd like to say I didn't mean any of it, but I think you'll know the truth.

I won't tell you to take care of Jemima because I know that you always will.

I've left you all amply provided for and am fairly certain that I've covered every eventuality.

I think perhaps the thought of dying has clouded my judgement — I find myself becoming maudlin, so I will just conclude by saying that you will have to learn to trust Captain Heywood and stop thinking that he's like all the other men in your life. He stood up to me and refused my commission and he stayed at Winterborne with nothing to gain — but you. Don't be a fool, Grace.

It won't be long now, thankfully.
All's Well That Ends Well.

Gervase

Historical Romance
by Caroline Elkington

Set in the years shown

A Very Civil War (1645)
Dark Lantern (1755)
The House on the Hill (1765)
Three Sisters (1772)
The Widow (1782)
Out of the Shadows (1792)

A VERY CIVIL WAR
1645

Con's life in the small Cotswold village, where she spent an idyllic childhood, is nothing out of the ordinary, which is good because she likes ordinary. She likes safe.

Her three boisterous nephews have come to stay for the summer holidays, and she's determined to show them that life in the countryside can be fun — she has no idea just how exciting it's about to get.

Whilst out exploring with them in the fields near the village, they find themselves face to face with a Roundhead colonel from the English Civil Wars and, due to some glitching twenty-first century technology, Con is transported back to 1645 and into a world she only recognises from books and historical dramas on television and finds hard to understand. She reluctantly falls for the gruff officer, who is recovering from injuries sustained in recent hostilities with Royalists but must battle archaic attitudes and unexpected violence in order to survive.

With no way of getting back to her family and her nice secure real life and unable to reveal who she really is, for fear of being thought a witch, she struggles to acclimatise to her new life and must fight her growing feelings for Colonel Sir Lucas Deverell and deal with the daily problems of life in the seventeenth century and the encroaching war. When she intervenes to save a dying man, suspicions are raised and she begins to fear for her life, with enemies on all sides.

Constance Harcourt discovers a love that crosses centuries and all barriers, but which could potentially end in heartbreak. Can the power of True Love overcome the power of the Universe?

This is a time-slip story filled with passionate romance, the very real threat of persecution and war, the charm of the Cotswolds and touches of Beauty and the Beast.

Dark Lantern
1755

An unexpected funeral, a new life with unwelcoming relations and a mysterious stranger who is destined to change her life forever. Martha Pentreath has been thrust into a bewildering and perilous adventure.

Set in 1755, on the wild coast between Cornwall and Devon, this swashbuckling tale of high society and secretive seafarers follows Martha as she valiantly juggles her conflicting roles, one moment hard at work in the kitchens of Polgrey Hall and the next elbow to elbow with the local gentry.

Then as dragoons scour the coast for smugglers, she finds herself beholden to the captain of a lugger tellingly built for speed. Unsure whom to trust, Martha soon realises that everything she thought she knew was a lie and people are not what they seem.

With undercurrents of The Scarlet Pimpernel, Cinderella and Jamaica Inn, this is a story of windswept cliffs, wreckers, betrayal, secrets, murder and passionate romance.

Martha fights back against those who would relish her downfall and discovers the shocking truth about her own family. But she will find loyalty and friendship and a love that will surprise her but also bring her heartache.

THE HOUSE on the HILL
1765

After falling on hard times due to a family scandal, Henrietta Swift lives with her grandfather in a dilapidated farmhouse and is quite content to live without luxury or even basic comforts.

However, she's being watched.

Someone has plans for her and despite suffering misgivings she has no real choice but to accept their surprising proposition in order to give her beloved grandfather a better life.

It leads her to Galdre Knap, a darkly mysterious house, where her enigmatic employer, Torquhil Guivre, requires a companion for his seriously ill sister, Eirwen, who is being brought home to convalesce.

With her habitual optimism, Henrietta believes all will be well — until the other-worldly Eirwen arrives in a snowstorm. The house then begins to reveal its long-buried secrets and Henrietta must battle to save those she loves from the sinister forces that threaten their safety and her happiness.

In the process, she unexpectedly finds true love and discovers that the world is filled with real magic and that she is capable of far more than she ever thought possible.

Here be Dragons and Enchantment and Happy Ever Afters.

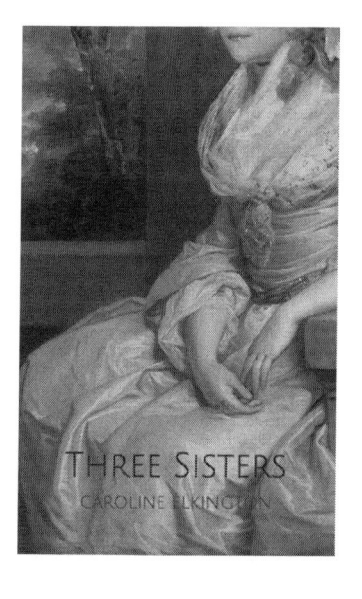

THREE SISTERS
1772

The prim and proper Augusta Pennington has taken over the management of a failing Ladies' Seminary with her two sisters, grumpy Flora and wild Pandora. Their elderly aunts, Ida and Euphemia Beauchamp, can no longer run the school and have been forced to hand over the reins. They are losing pupils, as they lag the fashions in female education, and are struggling financially.

Their scandalous and irascible neighbour, Sir Marcus Denby, is reluctantly drawn into their ventures by the younger sister, Pandora, who tumbles from one scrape into another, without any concern for her safety or her family's reputation.

With the help of Quince, a delinquent hound, Pandora befriends Sir Marcus's estranged daughter, Imogen, who has been much neglected by her beautiful but venomous mother.

Augusta, initially repelled by Sir Marcus's notoriety, tries desperately to resist the growing attraction between them. It takes a series of mishaps and the arrival of some unwanted guests to finally make Augusta understand that not everything is as it seems and love really can conquer all.

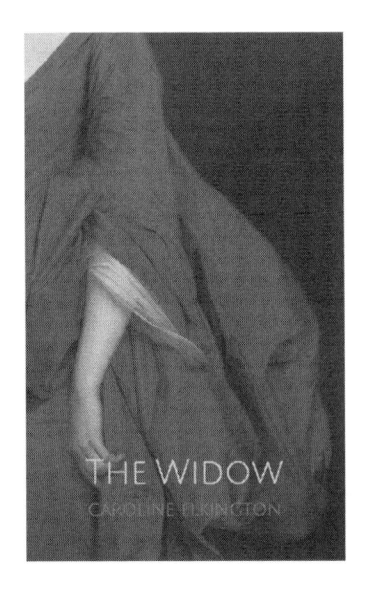

THE WIDOW
1782

Nathaniel Heywood arrived at Winterborne Place with no intention of remaining there for longer than it took to conclude a business proposition on behalf of his impulsive friend Emery Talmarch.

Impecunious, cynical and world-weary, he is reluctant to shoulder any kind of responsibility. Nathaniel was just looking for an easy way to make some money to save Emery from debtor's prison and possibly worse. He had no idea that he would be offered such an outrageous proposal by his host, Lord Winterborne, and find himself swiftly drawn into a web of intrigue and danger. He wants nothing more than to escape and be trouble-free again.

Above anything else he wanted his freedom.

And then he meets Grace.

OUT of the SHADOWS
1792

In this deeply romantic thriller, an inebriated and perhaps foolhardy visit to London's Bartholomew Fair begins with an eye to some lighthearted entertainment and ends with a tragic accident.

Theo Rokewode and his close friends find themselves unexpectedly encumbered with two young girls in desperate need of rescue. As a result, their usually ordered lives are turned upside down as danger stalks the girls into the hallowed halls of refined Georgian London and beyond to Rokewode Abbey in Gloucestershire.

Sephie and Biddy are hugely relieved to be rescued from the brutal life they had been forced to endure but know that they are still not truly safe. Only they know what could be coming and as Sephie loses her heart to Theo, she dreads the truth about her past being revealed and determines to somehow repay her new-found friends for their gallantry and unquestioning hospitality, but vows to leave before the man she loves so desperately sees her for what she really is.

Her carefully laid plans bring both delight and disaster as her past finally catches up with her and mayhem ensues, as Theo, his eccentric friends and family valiantly attempt to put the lid back on the Pandora's Box they'd unwittingly opened that fateful night at the fair.

ABOUT CAROLINE ELKINGTON

When not writing novels, Caroline's reading them - every few days a knock on the door brings more. She has always preferred the feel — and smell — of a real book.

She began reading out of boredom as she was tucked up in bed by her mother, herself an avid reader, at a ridiculously early hour.

In the winter months she read by moving her book sideways back and forth to catch a slither of light that shone through the crack between the hinges of her bedroom door.

Fast forward sixty years and she's someone who knows what she wants from a book: to be immersed in history (preferably Georgian), to be captivated by a romantic hero, to be thrilled by the story, and to feel uplifted at the end.

After a long career that began with fashion design and morphed into painting ornately costumed portraits and teaching art, she has a strong eye for the kind of detail that draws the reader into a scene.

Review This Novel and See More by Caroline

Point your phone's camera at the code.
A banner will appear on your screen.
Tap it to see Caroline's novels on Amazon.

Printed in Great Britain
by Amazon